Praise for George Pelecanos's

SHAME THE DEVIL

Named one of the "Year's Best Crime Novels" (2000) by *Booklist*

"*Shame the Devil* is one of those books that's easy to admire.... It's tough and skillful, with an intense, contrapuntal rhythm that keeps moving among a range of story lines set on a collision course of violence and destruction, tempered by a hint of redemption to salve the conscience.... Along the way, there are action scenes as fierce as any you will read and street talk that hits the ear as smart and accurate.... George Pelecanos's tale is a masterpiece of fictional construction."
— Paul Skenazy, *San Francisco Chronicle*

"Set against a backdrop of greasy-spoon diners, church basements, dive bars, and sparsely furnished apartments, the narrative is unsettlingly harsh yet captivatingly tender, the gritty back-and-forth of everyday urban life vividly etched."
— *Publishers Weekly*

"Bringing together threads from all his previous work, Pelecanos delivers a sort of summarizing chapter to what has become a magnificent serial novel depicting life on Washington's inner-city streets in the postwar era."   — Bill Ott, *Booklist*

"Gritty is the word to describe George Pelecanos's *Shame the Devil*. The tale is full of atmosphere and suspense as broken souls haunt seedy bars and run-down joints in the Washington, D.C., area."   — Paul Kaplan, *Library Journal*

"For some time George Pelecanos has been the best-kept secret in crime fiction — maybe all fiction.... The word among writers and those in the know has long been 'Read Pelecanos.'"
— Michael Connelly

"One of the best crime novelists alive, George Pelecanos is an American original."
— Dennis Lehane

"*Shame the Devil* is Pelecanos's finest effort yet, and the hardest to pin down; while the need for revenge and closure is its keystone, the book's strength is in the way in which it explores grief and loss. Pelecanos's touch is compassionate and sure. *Shame the Devil* is a thriller that transcends genres and establishes Pelecanos as not just a great crime writer but a great writer, period."
— *Times* (London)

"Having written about violence for close to a decade, Pelecanos goes deeper here, using his most immediately grab-you-by-the-head action setup to frame a drama about a support group for survivors. Climax tries to have revenge both ways, as both necessary and no good, but villain is so queasily and memorably creepy you just want him gone."
— Peter S. Scholtes, *Minneapolis City Pages*

"Pelecanos is a powerful writer...He deserves to be listed among the best."
— *Observer* (London)

"You would be hard-pressed to read a better crime novel this year."
— *Glasgow Herald*

"Pelecanos is a fresh, new, utterly hard-boiled voice."
— *Washington Post*

SHAME
THE
DEVIL

SHAME THE DEVIL

A Novel

GEORGE PELECANOS

BACK BAY BOOKS
Little, Brown and Company
New York   Boston   London

Back Bay Books / Little, Brown and Company
Hachette Book Group
237 Park Avenue, New York, NY 10017
www.hachettebookgroup.com

Originally published in hardcover by Little, Brown and Company, January 2000
First Back Bay paperback edition, July 2011

Back Bay Books is an imprint of Little, Brown and Company. The Back Bay Books
name and logo are trademarks of Hachette Book Group, Inc.

The characters and events in this book are fictitious. Any similarity to real persons,
living or dead, is coincidental and not intended by the author.

The publisher is not responsible for websites (or their content) that are
not owned by the publisher.

Library of Congress Cataloging-in-Publication Data
Pelecanos, George P.
Shame the devil: a novel / by George P. Pelecanos. — 1st ed.
   p. cm.
   ISBN 978-0-316-69523-7 (hc) / 978-0-316-13340-1 (pb)
   I. Title.
   PS3566.E354S53 2000
   813'.54 — dc21   99-29854

               10 9 8 7 6 5 4 3 2 1

                            RRD-C

              Printed in the United States of America

For Emily

WASHINGTON, D.C.
JULY 1995

ONE

THE CAR was a boxy late-model Ford sedan, white over black, innocuous bordering on invisible, and very fast. It had been a sheriff's vehicle originally, bought at auction in Tennessee, and further modified for speed.

The car rolled north on Wisconsin beneath a blazing white sun. The men inside wore long-sleeved shirts, tails out. Their shirtfronts were spotted with sweat and their backs were slick with it. The black vinyl on which they sat was hot to the touch. From the passenger seat, Frank Farrow studied the street. The sidewalks were empty. Foreign-made automobiles moved along quietly, their occupants cool and cocooned. Heat mirage shimmered up off asphalt. The city was narcotized — it was that kind of summer day.

"Quebec," said Richard Farrow, his gloved hands clutching the wheel. He pushed his aviator shades back up over the bridge of his nose, and as they neared the next cross street he said, "Upton."

"You've got Thirty-ninth up ahead," said Frank. "You want to take that shoot-off, just past Van Ness."

"I know it," said Richard. "You don't have to tell me again because I know."

"Take it easy, Richard."

"All right."

In the backseat, Roman Otis softly sang the first verse to "One in a Million You," raising his voice just a little to put the full Larry Graham inflection into the chorus. He had heard the single on WHUR earlier that morning, and the tune would not leave his head.

The Ford passed through the intersection at Upton.

Otis looked down at his lap, where the weight of his shotgun had begun to etch a deep wrinkle in his linen slacks. Well, he should have known it. All you had to do was *look* at linen to make it wrinkle, that was a plain fact. Still, a man needed to have a certain kind of style to him when he left the house for work. Otis placed the sawed-off on the floor, resting its stock across the toes of his lizard-skin monk straps. He glanced at the street-bought Rolex strapped to his left wrist: five minutes past ten A.M.

Richard cut the Ford up 39th.

"There," said Frank. "That Chevy's pulling out."

"I see it," said Richard.

They waited for the Chevy. Then Frank said, "Put it in."

Richard swung the Ford into the space and killed the engine. They were at the back of a low-rise commercial strip that fronted Wisconsin Avenue. The door leading to the kitchen of the pizza parlor, May's was situated in the center of the block. Frank wiped moisture from his brush mustache and ran a hand through his closely cropped gray hair.

"There's the Caddy," said Otis, noticing the black DeVille parked three spaces ahead.

Frank nodded. "Mr. Carl's making the pickup. He's inside."

"Let's do this thing," said Otis.

"Wait for our boy to open the door," said Frank. He drew two latex examination gloves from a tissue-sized box and slipped them over the pair he already had on his hands. He tossed the box over his shoulder to the backseat. "Here. Double up."

Roman Otis raised his right hand, where a silver ID bracelet bearing the inscription "Back to Oakland" hung on his wrist. He let the bracelet slip down inside the French cuff of his shirt. He put the gloves on carefully, then reflexively touched the butt of the .45 fitted beneath his shirt. He caught a glimpse of his shoulder-length hair, recently treated with relaxer, in the rearview mirror. Shoot, thought Otis, Nick Ashford couldn't claim to have a finer head of hair on him. Otis smiled at his reflection, his one gold tooth catching the light. He gave himself a wink.

"Frank," said Richard.

"We'll be out in a few minutes," said Frank. "Don't turn the engine over until you see us coming back out."

"I won't," said Richard, a catch in his voice.

The back kitchen door to May's opened. A thin black man wearing a full apron stepped out with a bag of trash. He carried the trash to a Dumpster and swung it in, bouncing it off the upraised lid. On his way back to the kitchen he eye-swept the men in the Ford. He stepped back inside, leaving the door ajar behind him.

"That him?" asked Otis.

"Charles Greene," said Frank.

"Good boy."

Frank checked the .22 Woodsman and the .38 Bulldog holstered beneath his oxford shirt. The guns were snug against his guinea-T. He looked across the bench at his kid brother, sweating like a hard-run horse, breathing through his mouth, glassy eyed, scared stupid.

"Remember, Richard. Wait till you see us come out."

Richard Farrow nodded one time.

Roman Otis lifted the shotgun, slipped it barrel down into his open shirt, fitting it in a custom-made leather holster hung over his left side. It would show; there wasn't any way to get around it. But they would be going straight in, and they would move fast.

"Let's go, Roman," said Frank.

Otis said, "Right." He opened the car door and touched his foot to the street.

"C'MON," SAID Lisa Karras, "put your arms up, Jimmy."

Lisa's son raised his hands and then dropped them as she tried to fit the maroon-and-gold shirt over his head. He wiggle-wormed out of the shirt, giggled as he backed up against a scarred playroom wall. Looking at him, Lisa laughed too.

There were mornings when she would be trying to get him off to school or get herself to an appointment and Jimmy would keep pushing her buttons until she'd lose her temper in a big way. But this was not one of those mornings. Jimmy had been out of kindergarten since June, and Lisa had not picked up any freelance design work in the last month. This was just a slow morning on a hot summer day. The two of them had nothing but time.

"Hey, kiddo, I thought you said you wanted some ice cream."

Jimmy Karras zoomed over and raised his arms. Lisa got the short-sleeved Redskins jersey on him before he had a chance to squirm out of it, then sat him down and fitted a pair of miniature Vans sneakers on his feet.

"Double knots, Mom."

"You got it."

Jimmy stood up and raced off. He skipped once, something he did without thought when he was happy, on the way to the door.

Ice cream at ten A.M. Lisa almost laughed, thinking of what her peers would have to say about that. Most of the other mothers in the neighborhood were content to sit their kids down in front of the television set on hot days like this. But Lisa couldn't stand to be in the house all day, no matter the weather. And she knew that Jimmy liked to get out too. A trip to the ice cream store would be just fine.

Jimmy stood on his toes at the front door, trying to turn the lock. A rabbit's foot hung from a key chain fixed to a belt loop of his navy blue shorts. The rabbit's foot was white and gray, with toenails curling out of the fur. Lisa had given her husband, Dimitri, a few sharp words when he had brought it home from the surplus store, but she had let the matter drop when she saw her son's eyes widen at the sight of it. The rabbit's foot was one of those strange items—pocketknives, lighters, firecrackers—that held a mutual fascination for fathers and sons. She had long since given up on trying to understand.

"Help me, Mom."

"You got it."

She rested the flat of her palm on his short, curly brown hair as she turned the lock. His scalp was warm to the touch.

"Mom, can we go for a Metro ride today?"

"One thing at a time, okay, honey?"

"Could we take the Metro to the zoo?"

"I don't think so. Anyway, it's too hot. The animals will all be inside."

"Aw," said Jimmy, flipping his hand at the wrist. "Gimme a break!"

Jimmy ran down the concrete steps as she locked the front door of the colonial. She watched him bolt across the sidewalk and head toward the street.

"Jimmy!" she yelled.

Jimmy stopped short of the street at the sound of her voice. He turned, pointing at her and laughing, his eyes closed, his dimples deeply etched in a smooth oval face.

Mrs. Lincoln, the old woman next door, called from her porch, "You better watch that boy!"

Lisa smiled and said cheerfully, "He's a *handful*, all right." And under her breath she added, "You dried-up old crow."

As Lisa got down to the sidewalk of Alton Place, Jimmy said, "What'd you say, Mom?"

"Just saying hello to Mrs. Lincoln."

"You mean Mrs. Stinkin'?"

"Now, don't you ever say that except in our house, honey. Daddy was just kidding when he made up that name for her. It's not nice."

"But she does smell funny, though."

"Old people have a different smell to them, that's all."

"She smells."

"Jimmy!"

"Okay."

They walked a bit. They stopped at the corner of 38th Street, and Jimmy said, "Where we goin' for ice cream, Mom?"

"That store next to the pizza parlor."

"Which pizza parlor?" said Jimmy.

"You know," said Lisa Karras. "May's."

ROMAN OTIS went in first, putting a hard shoulder to the door. Frank Farrow stepped in next, cross-drawing the .22 and the

.38 revolver at once. He kicked the door shut behind him as Otis drew the sawed-off and pumped a shell into the breech.

"All right," said Otis. "Don't none a y'all move."

Charles Greene, the pizza chef, stood still behind the kitchen's stainless steel prep table and raised his hands. Mr. Carl, a short man with a stub of unlit cigar wedged in the side of his liver-lipped mouth, stood to the side of the table. On the tiled floor beside him sat an olive green medium-size duffel bag, zipped shut.

"What is this?" said Mr. Carl, direct and calm, looking at the armed white man with the gray hair.

Frank up-jerked the .38. "Raise your hands and shut your mouth."

Carl Lewin raised his arms very slowly, careful not to let his sport jacket spread open and reveal the .32 Davis he carried wedged against his right hip on pickup day.

"Against the wall," said Frank.

Greene and Mr. Carl moved back. Frank holstered the .22, stepped over to the duffel bag, and opened it. He had a quick look inside at the stacks of green: tens, twenties, and hundreds, loosely banded. He ran the zipper back up its neck and nodded at Otis.

"Okay, pizza man," said Otis. "Who we got in the front of the house?"

Charles Greene licked his dry lips. "The bartender. And the day waiter's out in the dining room, setting up."

"Go out there and bring the waiter back with you," said Otis. "Don't be funny, neither." Greene hesitated, and Otis said, "Go on, boy. Let's get this over with so we can all be on our way."

Greene had a look at Mr. Carl before hurrying from the kitchen. Mr. Carl stared at the gray-haired white man without speaking. Then they heard footsteps returning to the kitchen and a chiding young voice saying, "What could be so important, Charlie? I've got side work."

The waiter, who was named Vance Walters, entered the kitchen with Greene behind him. At the sight of the men and their guns, Walters nearly turned to run, then swallowed and breathed out slowly. The moment had passed, and now it was too late. He wondered, as he always did, what his father would have done in a situation such as this one. He raised his hands without a prompt. If he'd just cooperate, they wouldn't hurt him, whoever they were.

"What's your name?" said Frank.

"Vance," said the waiter.

"Over there against the wall with your boss," said Frank.

Otis watched the waiter with the perfect springy haircut hurry around the prep table. One of those light-steppin' mugs. Vance with the tight-ass pants. Otis knew the look straight-away. Marys like Vance got snatched up on the cell block right quick.

"I'll get the bartender," said Frank to Otis.

Frank Farrow left the kitchen. Otis pointed the shotgun at each of the three men against the wall in turn. He began to sing "One in a Million You" under his breath. As he sang, he smiled at Mr. Carl.

DETECTIVE WILLIAM Jonas cruised up Wisconsin in his unmarked and made the turn up 39th. The cold air felt good blowing against his torso, and for a change he was fairly relaxed. It wasn't often that he rolled on the clean, white-bread streets of upper Northwest's Ward 3. Most of his action was in neighborhoods like Trinidad, Petworth, LeDroit Park, and Columbia Heights. But this morning he had an interview with a teenage kid who worked at the chain video store over near Wilson High. The kid lived in Shaw, and he had grown up with a couple of young citizens charged with beating a pipe-head to death outside a plywood-door house east of 14th and Irving. Jonas hated to roust the kid at work, but the young man had been uncooperative on his home turf. Jonas figured that the kid would talk, and talk quick, at his place of employment.

William Jonas had two sons at Wilson himself. They took the bus across town from Jonas's house on Hamlin Street, over in Brookland.

It wouldn't be too long before he had his boys in college and could retire his shield. The money was already put away for their schooling. He'd been saving on an automatic-withdrawal plan since they were boys. Thank the good Lord for blue chips. With his pension and the house damn near 75 percent paid off, he and Dee could enjoy themselves for real. He'd be in his middle fifties by then—retired and still a relatively young man. But it was a little early to be dreaming on it. He had a few years left to go.

As he went slowly up 39th, Jonas noticed a parked car on his right, looked almost like an old cop car, with a man behind the wheel, sitting there with all four windows rolled down. The man was pockmarked and sweating something awful; his sunglasses slipped down to the end of his nose as he bent forward, trying to put a match to a cigarette. Looked like his hand was shaking, too, and…damn if he wasn't wearing some kind of rubber gloves. As Jonas passed, the man glanced out the window and quickly averted his eyes. In the rearview Jonas saw Virginia plates on the front of the car—a Merc, maybe. No, he could see the familiar blue oval on the grillwork: a Ford.

Veazy Street, Warren, Windom…Now that had to be the only car he'd seen all morning with the windows down on a hotter-than-the-devil day like today. Everyone else had their air-conditioning on full, and what car didn't have air-conditioning these days? And the man behind the wheel, white like everyone in this neighborhood but still *not* like them, had seemed kind of nervous. Like he didn't belong there. Wearing those gloves, too. Twenty-five years on the force and Bill Jonas *knew*.

He had a few minutes before his interview with the video-store kid. Maybe he'd cruise around the block, give that Ford another pass.

RICHARD FARROW hotboxed his smoke while watching the black car hang a left a few blocks up 39th. Any high school kid with an ounce of weed in his glove box would have spotted the unmarked car. And the driver, some kind of cop, had given him the fish-eye as he passed.

The question was, Was the black cop in the black car going to come around the block and check him out again?

Richard touched the grip of the nine millimeter tucked between his legs. The way he had it, snug up against his rocks and pressing on his blue jeans, it had felt good. But now the sensation faded. He grabbed the Beretta and tapped the barrel against his thigh. He dragged hard on his cigarette and flicked the butt out to the street.

God, it was hot.

What the fuck was he doing here, anyway? Sure, he'd done his share of small-time boosts — car thefts, smash-and-grabs, like that — with his older brother when they were in their teens. Back between Frank's reform school years and his first four-year jolt. Then Frank got sent up for another eight, and during that time Richard went from one useless job to the next, fighting his various addictions — alcohol, crystal meth, coke, and married women—along the way. The funny thing was, when Frank got out of the joint the last time, he was smarter, tougher, and more cc nected than Richard would ever be. Yeah, crime and prison had been good to Frank. So when Frank had phoned and asked his little brother if he would be interested in a quick and easy score that he and Otis were about to pull off, Richard had said yes. He saw it as a last chance to turn his life around. And to be on a level playing field—to be a success, for once—with Frank.

Richard looked in the rearview. The black car had circled and was coming up behind him on 39th.

Richard turned the key in the ignition. A natural reaction, that's all. He realized Frank had told him not to, but...*fuck* it, it wouldn't do any good to get himself down about it now. He'd done it.

The cop car was slowing down. It was crawling.

"Come on, Frank," said Richard. He heard the high pitch of his own voice and was ashamed.

Richard stared straight ahead as the cop car accelerated and passed. Richard exhaled, removed his glasses, wiped at the sweat that stung his eyes.

The cop car stopped at the next corner, pulled over, and idled beside a fire hydrant.

Richard steadied the Beretta, pulled back on the receiver, eased a round into the chamber. What was he doing? What was he going to do now, shoot a cop? This was crazy. He'd never shot anything, not even an animal in the woods. Frank had told him to carry the gun. *Frank* had made him bring the gun.

Richard Farrow looked at himself in the rearview mirror. He saw a pale, wet mask of fear.

* * *

FRANK FARROW pressed the flat of his palm against the bartender's shoulder. He pushed him firmly through the open door into the kitchen. The bartender, heavy and broad of back with a friendly pie-plate face, stared at the three men against the wall. A long-haired, sharply dressed black guy was holding a shotgun and singing to himself on the other side of the prep table. He stopped singing as Frank entered the room.

Frank said to the bartender, "What's your name?"

"Steve Maroulis."

"All right, Steve. You're going to be smart, right?"

Maroulis nodded and said, "Yes."

"Is there any rope here?"

Maroulis looked at the pizza chef, tried to make a casual gesture that played clumsy. "I don't know."

"*Who* knows?" said Frank.

"Got some clothesline rope over in that utility closet," said Charles Greene. "That there's the onlyest rope we got."

"Get it, Steve," said Frank.

"Gonna have to tie you gentlemen up," said Otis. "Give us time to, uh, *effect* our getaway."

Maroulis went to the closet on the opposite wall and opened its hinged gate.

Mr. Carl watched the black guy with the funny hair. The joker was holding the shotgun loosely, barrel-down against his thigh. How long would it take to raise a sawed-off and pull the trigger? Two seconds? He could draw the .32 quicker than that. He did have that element of surprise. Hell, not even his own employees knew he carried a piece. He could wait until the gray-haired one got distracted. Shoot the spade first, the gray-haired sonofabitch next. Then, after it was over, find the one who tipped these two to the pickup.

Mr. Carl hitched up his slacks, kept his hands on his belt line.

Go ahead, Maroulis, Mr. Carl thought. *Just keep ratfucking through that closet.*

Frank turned around. "How's it coming, Steve?"

"I don't see the rope."

"It's on the bottom shelf, man," offered Greene.

Vance Walters felt his knees weaken. He willed himself to stand straight.

Now, thought Mr. Carl.

I'll do it now, while gray-hair's got his back turned. These two are nothing. Lettuce-pickers. I'll shoot the spade first and then the gray-haired bastard. Someone will pin a fucking medal on me —

"Let's go, Steve," said Frank. He looked up at the wall: A stainless steel paper-towel dispenser hung there, shiny and clean. He could see the reflection of the men behind him in its surface.

Otis glanced at his wristwatch, turned his head to the side. "C'mon with that rope!"

Carl Lewin's hand inched inside his jacket.

Now. Nigger, you are going to die now.

In the towel dispenser's reflection Frank Farrow watched Mr. Carl reach into his jacket. He saw Mr. Carl's hand on the grip of a gun.

Frank spun around and leveled his gun at Mr. Carl. Their eyes met and locked. Mr. Carl's finger jerked in spasm. Frank squeezed the trigger of the .38 three times.

Mr. Carl took two rounds in the chest. The third blew tiling off the wall behind him. Mr. Carl winced, spit the cigar and a spray of blood onto the prep table. His hands flopped comically at the wrists as he dropped to the floor.

Frank went to Mr. Carl. He stood over him and kicked him in the stomach. He stepped back and shot him again. The corpse jumped and came to rest.

A sliver of tile had cut into Vance Walters's cheek. His hand flew to the spot as tears welled in his eyes. But he didn't let the tears go. He swore to himself then that he wouldn't cry.

Charles Greene was silent, stunned, openmouthed. Steve Maroulis stood still, the clothesline slack in his shaking hands.

A look passed between Frank and Otis. Otis took the clothesline from Maroulis's hand and tossed it over the prep table to Charles Greene.

"Okay, bartender," said Otis. "You and the waiter: Lie down on your bellies."

"You," said Frank, pointing the .38 at Greene. "Tie them up. Feet to hands."

DETECTIVE WILLIAM Jonas thought he heard something. Muffled, like. Couldn't be gunshots, not in this neighborhood. Kids lighting off a string of firecrackers or ladyfingers, most likely — it *was* July. Or a car or Metrobus backfiring on Wisconsin. Hard to tell with the air blower on full and the crackle coming from the mic.

He had called in the plate numbers of the Ford, and now he was waiting to see if the car was on the hot sheet. He'd have word on that momentarily, and then he'd be gone. He didn't know why he was wasting his time messing with this one, anyway. He was Homicide, not a beat cop. He had done his beat time, and he had worked hard to get his shield. Still, there was definitely something wrong about that sweaty white man wearing those gloves back in the white car.

Jonas got the negative response. He ordered in a cruiser anyway to check out the suspicious vehicle and its driver, and thanked the dispatcher. He replaced the mic in its cradle and pulled away from the curb.

He drove up toward Nebraska Avenue, took Albemarle Street over to Wisconsin, and parked his car in front of the big video store. He looked at his watch: a little early to take the kid off his shift. He had, what, ten, fifteen minutes to kill? Maybe he'd go on back and see what was up with that guy on 39th. By now the uniforms would have arrived. By *now* they'd be talking to the guy, checking him out. He was awful curious to hear what the guy had to say.

William Jonas pulled out of his spot and swung his vehicle around on the main drag. He headed south on Wisconsin.

"PUT YOUR heads down," said Frank to the three men lying bound on the floor behind the prep table. The pizza chef, Greene, had tied Maroulis and Walters. Otis had tied Greene. Frank Farrow had dragged Mr. Carl's body next to a drain set in the center of the room. His blood ran slowly down a slight grade in the floor and dripped through the grates of the drain.

Greene and Walters had lowered their heads. Maroulis had kept his head up; the carotid artery swelled in his neck.

"Please," said Maroulis. "We haven't seen anything. None of us will remember you. I'm speaking for all of us—"

"Put your forehead on the tiles."

"Please." Maroulis's eyes were pleading, wild and red. He looked at Frank. "Don't make me put my head down. Please."

"Do what I say and you won't get hurt."

Maroulis put his head down slowly. In a low voice he began to pray: *"Pateri mon..."*

Otis listened to the bartender, chanting some kind of bullshit in a tongue he had never heard. Well, the bartender was the smart one of the bunch. He knew his bossman had gone and done them all by making that play.

Frank looked at Otis. Frank holstered the .38 and drew the

.22 Woodsman with his right hand. He stepped quickly to Maroulis and shot him in the back of the head.

Greene began to scream. Frank waved gun smoke out of his face as he walked over to Vance Walters.

Walters felt the cool touch of metal behind his ear. Frank shielded his face from the blow-back and put his finger to the trigger.

"Dad," said Walters. He yelled, "Daddy!"

His last moment felt like fire and confusion.

"Naw, man," said Greene, tears rolling one after the other down his cheeks. "Not me, man, I hooked you up!" He sobbed and begged and screamed as he writhed violently against the rope. A line of saliva dripped from his mouth to the floor.

Frank stepped around Vance Walters's corpse. He put the muzzle of the Woodsman to Greene's head.

RICHARD FARROW had heard the gunshots come from inside the pizza parlor, but apparently the black cop had not. He had pulled away and been gone ten minutes. Richard was relieved at first, but growing shaky again as the time ticked off. He smoked another cigarette, tapped his hand on the wheel, spun the automatic on the hot vinyl seat beside him.

Richard figured the cop had called in the Ford's plates. But the plates had been lifted just that morning from Union Station's long-term lot. Those Spanish guys in that garage had done them a solid there. Yeah, they'd done good —

Another gunshot sounded from inside the pizza parlor. Then another, and another behind it.

No, brother. God, no . . .

"PHEW," SAID Roman Otis. "One of 'em done fouled his britches."

"Put another round in each one and let's go."

"What, you think they gonna walk away?"

"Do it, Roman. Do it and let's go."

Yeah, thought Otis, Frank is one smart man. He's going to tie us together now, forever and for real.

Otis shrugged. He holstered the shotgun and drew the .45.

RICHARD FARROW left the motor running and got out of the car. He paced back and forth in the street. The heat of the asphalt came through the thin leather soles of his shoes. He looked down his arm and saw the nine millimeter in his hand. He looked toward a low-rise apartment building on his left and saw a curtain drop shut.

He heard four more shots.

"We are fucked," said Richard. He glanced back at the car. No—he *couldn't* go back to that hot car. Richard began to stumble-walk across the street toward the rear entrance of May's.

He turned at the sound of a big engine. The black unmarked cop car was blowing toward him on 39th.

WILLIAM JONAS accelerated when he saw the sweaty white man with the aviator shades standing in the middle of the street, holding a gun.

"Aw, shit," said Jonas. The cruiser he had called for hadn't arrived. No time to think about that now.

He hit the brakes fifty yards from the man, turned the wheel, skidded his car to a stop so that it blocked the street. He keyed the mic, screamed into it for backup. He dropped the mic to the floor, pulled his weapon, chambered a round, opened the door, and rolled out of the car onto the street. He got up into a crouch and positioned himself behind the hood of the car. He straightened his gun arm and rested it on the hood, his head and shoulders clear.

"I'm a police officer!" he yelled. "Throw the weapon to the side! Get down on your stomach and cradle your hands behind your head, now!"

The man paced a few steps, dizzy with confusion. He looked over at the back of the commercial strip, made a move toward it, changed his mind and walked back toward the Ford.

"Drop the weapon!" screamed Jonas.

The man looked in the direction of Jonas like he was hearing him for the first time. He opened the door of the Ford.

"I said drop it!" Jonas could hear a siren now. The backup would be here in a hot minute, maybe less. If the guy by the Ford could only hold onto his shit, then maybe everything could turn out all right.

FRANK FARROW looked through the partially opened door as Roman Otis checked his gun and listened to the screech of tires.

"Okay, Richard's got company."

"How many?" said Otis.

"One for now."

"One's better than two."

"Richard's just standing there, out in the street. Goddamn-it, I told him... All right, gimme the bag." Otis tossed the duffel over to Frank. "How many you got left in that forty-five?"

"Four."

"I've got two in the thirty-eight." He holstered the .22 — useless at this range — and grasped the handles of the duffel bag.

"You know what we gotta do," said Frank.

Otis shrugged. "Can't *do* nothin' else." He hand-brushed his hair back behind his ears.

Otis went to the door, yanked it open, and charged out into the sunlight. Frank went out behind him, calling his brother's name.

WILLIAM JONAS watched the man reach for the door handle of the Ford. Someone yelled, "Richard!" The man looked back at the center of the commercial strip. Two men carrying guns and a duffel bag bolted from a door. Jonas speed-scanned: One of them was white with gray hair and a gray mustache, the other a tall, dark-skinned man with Las Vegas–looking hair. The image of them registered as Jonas returned his sight to the man by the Ford. The man by the Ford pointed his gun at Jonas.

He's scared. He won't shoot....

The man by the Ford steadied his gun with both hands.

Jonas thought of his wife and sons. He closed one eye, aimed, and fired his weapon.

Jonas's first round penetrated the door of the Ford. His second round found its target. The pale white man's sunglasses went funny on his face as he crumpled and swung down, his arm hooked around the window frame. Jonas could see a black line running like a worm down the front of the man's face.

A round sparked off the hood in front of Jonas. He blinked, moved his gun arm, fired at the two men who were standing still and firing at him. He squinted, saw smoke coming from their guns, heard his windshield spider, kept firing even as a bullet tore into his bicep and another hit his shoulder as he was jerked up and back. He took another bullet high in the chest. It was like a hot needle going in. He screamed as he fell, firing his weapon into the front quarter panel of his own vehicle, feeling the shock of his back hitting the hard, hot pavement and the wind blow from his lungs. He stared up at the blazing sun and listened to the siren grow louder. He fought for breath and got it. He turned his head to vomit. He dropped his Glock and heard the dull sound it made on the street.

Goddamn plastic gun. Oh, sweet Jesus, I am hit.

LISA KARRAS couldn't believe the heat. She had called the weather service, but the temperature given on the recording didn't begin to describe the feeling of actually being outdoors. Not that Jimmy seemed to notice. He was ahead of her, walking faster even as she slowed her pace.

"Jimmy, honey, c'mon. We've got all day. The ice cream store's not going anywhere."

He turned around and jogged backward, pointing to his mother with that evil, beautiful smile of his that couldn't help but break her down.

"I'm not biting for that," said Lisa. "I'm telling you, sweetheart, I can't go any faster than this."

Jimmy turned frontward and broke into a run. She called out to him weakly, but by now he was out of earshot, charging down Alton, halfway to 39th. Fireworks sounded from far away.

"WHERE YOU goin', man?"

"I'm going to finish that cop."

"You hear them sirens? The two of us ain't gonna make it if we stay. And I ain't leavin' you here, you know that."

"He killed my brother," said Frank.

"Then we'll just have to come back at a better time," said Otis. "Do him the same way."

Jonas's unmarked blocked the road. A patrol car skidded into the Wisconsin Avenue turnoff, rolled up 39th, and came to a stop behind the unmarked. The driver radioed for backup while his uniformed partner crawled out of the car.

Frank and Otis moved quickly to the Ford. Frank picked up Richard and threw him across the backseat of the Ford. He tossed the duffel bag on top of Richard, ignoring the uniform's shouted commands, and got under the wheel. Otis was already on the passenger side of the bench.

Frank yanked down on the tree and fishtailed coming out of the space. Sirens wailed from several directions. They heard the pop of gunshots behind them, and neither ducked his head.

Otis wiped sweat from his forehead, glanced at the speed-ometer: fifty, sixty...okay, shit, it would be all right. Frank always did know how to handle a ride.

"Gonna be a trick to get us out of here," said Otis. He hol-stered the .45.

Frank saw a flash of cop car moving toward them on the street called Windom to his right.

"Punch this motherfucker," said Otis.

Frank pinned the accelerator. The car lifted, and both of them were pushed back against the seat. The Ford blew through the four-way and caught air coming over a rise.

"Watch it," said Otis, as something small ran backward into the street ahead. "Hey, Frank, man, slow down...."

SOMETHING WAS wrong. There were ambulance or police sirens all over now, and Lisa Karras knew something was wrong. She broke into a run.

"Jimmy!" she yelled, frantic because he was still going toward the intersection of 39th and he was too many steps ahead and it was too hot. "Jimmy!"

He turned and ran backward. She saw his crooked smile and the flush of his cheeks as he tripped back off the curb. She saw surprise on his face, but only for a moment. A blur of white car lifted him and pinwheeled him over its roof. He was hinged at an awful angle as he tumbled over the car.

That is not my little Jimmy, thought Lisa Karras.

That's just a broken doll.

FRANK FARROW gave the cracked windshield a spray of fluid and hit the wipers. Blood swept away and gathered at the edges in two pink vertical lines.

Roman Otis turned his head, looked through the rear glass. A woman was in the street, her hands tight in her hair. Her mouth was frozen open, and she was standing over a small crumpled thing.

Frank gave it a hard right onto Nebraska Avenue, downshifted the automatic to low coming out of the skid, and then brought it back up to drive. He passed a Jetta on the right and crossed the double line passing a ragtop Saab.

"There's Connecticut Avenue," said Otis. "I remember it from the map."

"I see it."

"You ain't gonna make that yellow, partner."

"I know."

Frank shot the red; a car three-sixtied as they went through the intersection and down a steep grade, Frank's hand hard on the horn. Vehicles ahead pulled over to the right lane.

Otis breathed out slowly, checked the backseat, looked across the bench.

"Look—about your brother."

"Forget it."

"Your brother did good, man. Remember it. He kept that cop busy and he did *good.*"

Frank was expressionless.

"Frank."

"I said forget it. Where's the switch?"

"Tennyson at Oregon. About a mile up ahead."

Otis closed his eyes. Frank's brother was dead, stretched out under a bag of money. Otis and Frank had just killed five — four whites and a black — including a kid. Maybe even killed a black cop, too. Be hard to find a jury of any racial mix that wouldn't give the two of them that last long walk. And here was Frank, colder than the legs on Teddy Pendergrass, barely breaking a sweat.

Well, no one would ever accuse Frank of being too human. One thing was certain, though: There wasn't anyone else you'd want to be riding with when the death house was calling your name.

TWO

FRANK FARROW parked behind an LTD on a residential street named Tennyson, near Oregon Avenue at the edge of Rock Creek Park. To their right a long stand of trees bordered a huge old folks' home, and across the street to their left stood a row of identical split-level houses.

Farrow got out of the Ford, eye-scoping the houses on his left as he went quickly to the LTD and found its key under the driver's-side mat. He popped the LTD's trunk, went back to the Ford, and leaned into the open window.

"I'll get Richard and put him in the trunk. Clean the interior out and follow with the bag. Dump your guns in the trunk, too, and we'll split."

"Any curtain action from those houses?"

"None that I could see. Come on."

They drove through the park, cruised by upper-class houses with Jags and Mercedeses parked in their driveways, and passed over the Maryland line into Silver Spring. Otis found HUR, the station he had discovered in his motel room, on the dial.

"You are," sang Otis, "my starship; come take me out tonight...."

Farrow took East–West Highway across Georgia Avenue and made a sharp left down a street of cinder-block garages set beside the railroad tracks. They parked in front of an unmarked bay between Rossi Automotive and a place called Hanagan's Auto Body. Farrow gave the horn two sharp blasts; the bay door rose, and Frank drove the LTD through.

The garage was cool, clean, and dimly lit. A Hispanic in a blue workshirt with the name "Manuel" stitched above the breast pocket dropped a hose to the smooth concrete and walked over to the LTD. Another Spanish, Jaime, rubbed his hands on a ruby shop rag and eyed the men inside the car.

"Where's our gear?" said Farrow to Manuel.

"In the offi."

"You said 'offi,'" said Otis. "But you *meant* 'office,' right?"

Manuel nodded and smiled thinly, careful to mask any displeasure at the remark. He had straight black hair and slanted eyes, making him look like a brown-skinned Asian. The other one, Jaime, had bony, unmemorable features, except for a line of tattooed teardrops dripping from his right eye.

Farrow said, "Bring our stuff here."

Manuel returned with two large packs and dropped them at the feet of Farrow and Otis, who had gotten out of the car. Farrow and Otis removed their gloves and tossed them on the concrete. Farrow had retrieved the duffel bag from the trunk, leaving the lid open.

"You listen to the news, amigo?" said Farrow.

"Is on the radio already," said Manuel. "You have trouble, eh?"

"My brother's dead," said Farrow, noticing a nerve twitch in Jaime's cheek. "He's in the trunk of the LTD."

"What you goin' to do about that?" said Manuel.

"I'm not going to do anything," said Farrow. "You are." Farrow picked up his pack and the duffel bag and went into the office. Otis hoisted his pack and did the same.

Farrow changed his clothes quickly—plain work pants, a lightweight short-sleeved shirt, and oilskin shoes. While Otis changed, Farrow took his shaving gear to the office bathroom, placed his Swiss Army knife, his Norelco electric, and a glass tub of black Meltonian Shoe Cream on a steel shelf welded below the mirror. He used the knife's scissors to cut off the bulk of his mustache, then shaved his upper lip clean with the razor. He dipped his fingers in the shoe cream and massaged it into his hair until his hair was no longer gray. He looked five years younger—at least. He found a pair of nonprescription black-rimmed glasses in his shaving kit, put them on, and looked in the mirror: Now he was a different man.

Back in the office, Otis had changed into a brown-on-beige monochromatic shirt-and-slacks arrangement with matching brown weave shoes. He had tied his hair back tightly in a ponytail and wore wire-rimmed shades that darkened in the light.

Otis smiled when Farrow walked back into the room. "Lookin' all Clark Kent on me now."

"You take your share?"

"I took it." Otis picked up his pack. "Too bad about that pizza boy. I know he would have talked when it got hot. Shame, though, we had to do him like we did."

"We *did* have to. Come on."

"**OKAY, AMIGO,**" said Farrow as he and Otis reentered the garage. "Come on over here."

Jaime ground a live butt under his boot and followed Manuel to where the hard men stood. Farrow chin-nodded in the direction of two cars parked in the back of the garage.

"That us?" said Farrow.

"Yes," said Manuel. "The Taurus is yours."

"I ask for a shitwagon?" said Farrow.

"You asked for something that would not attract attention," said Manuel. "The body is rough, I admit. I did not touch the metal."

"Does it run?"

"It will run, yes. It's a SHO. I took the identifying bumper off. It looks quiet, like an old man's car. But it is very quick. Redline it if you wish."

"How about mine?" said Otis, looking at the two-tone brown-and-beige '79 Mark V parked beside the Taurus.

"The Bill Blass model," said Manuel, a glint in his eye. "What you asked for. Under the hood is—"

"I ain't never gonna look under the hood, Man-you-el, you know that. Will it take me across country?"

"Were it not for the ocean, it would take you around the world."

"What about the sounds? You put that unit in I was tellin' you about?"

"Yes. You load the disks in the trunk."

Otis said, "Always wanted me a box like that, too."

Farrow reached into the duffel bag and tossed a thick stack of bills to Manuel. "Count it with your fingers," said Farrow. "Go ahead."

Manuel went through the money.

Farrow looked at Jaime and said, "Now you."

Jaime shrugged, took the money from Manuel, licked his thumb and forefinger elaborately, and counted the bills.

Farrow said, "It's what we agreed upon, no?"

Manuel regarded Farrow and nodded slowly.

"Give it here," said Farrow, and when Jaime handed him the money he said, "I'll just keep this stack as a souvenir. It's got your fingerprints on it—in case there's any question of who was involved in what."

"We'll keep it on file," said Otis, "just like the FBI."

"But let me make this clear," said Farrow, "in case you get the feeling you want to unburden your conscience."

"You don' haf to worry," said Manuel.

"Let him make it clear," said Otis.

"Well, we all know the code. I mean, we all came up the same way. But to remind you . . . You and Jaime, you ever feel the need to talk, I want you to remember something—"

"Let me tell this part, Frank," said Otis.

"Go ahead."

"You talk," said Otis, "we're just gonna have to go ahead and fuck up your families. *Comprende?*"

"Is no problem," said Manuel, shaking his head, his eyes closed solemnly.

"Didn't think it would be," said Otis.

Farrow tossed a new stack of money to Manuel. "That's yours to keep. Count it."

"I trust you," said Manuel, and Otis laughed.

"The keys under the mats?" said Farrow.

Manuel nodded. Farrow and Otis began to walk away.

"What would you have us do with the man in the trunk?" Manuel asked.

Farrow turned. "You keep old car batteries here, right?"

"Yes."

"Do this: Drop a battery on his mouth until his teeth are busted out."

"Now wait—"

"Pour battery acid on his face and fingers. Cut his head and his limbs off, and bury his pieces in different spots. Bury the guns and the gloves as well."

"But...he is your *brother*."

Farrow did not reply. He and Otis walked to the cars.

"That fingerprints-on-the-money thing," said Otis. "That was pretty slick."

"They're scared enough to believe it."

"I think you put the fear into 'em for real," said Otis. "So where you gonna be?"

"Remember Lee Toomey?"

"Sure. He settled in this state, didn't he? Down on the Eastern Shore?"

"Right. He hooked me up with a straight gig."

"Straight, huh."

"For a while. You?"

"You need me, you can get me through my sister Cissy, out in Cali."

"She still in the L.A. phone book?"

"You know it."

Otis clapped Farrow on the arm, shook his hand as he would another black man's.

"All right, Frank."

Farrow said, "All right."

Manuel had opened the bay door and was waving them on. Farrow drove the SHO out first, and Otis followed in the Mark V.

Manuel Ruiz closed the door and walked toward Jaime, who stood by the LTD's open trunk. Jaime Gutierrez was staring into the trunk while trying to put fire to a cigarette.

His hand shook, and it was difficult to touch the flame to the tip.

Manuel put his thumb to his fingers and crossed himself. He went to the far corner of the garage, where a couple of old batteries were resting on wooden pallets. He lifted one of the batteries and carried it back to the LTD.

WASHINGTON, D.C.
JANUARY 1998

THREE

NICK STEFANOS tucked a black denim shirt into jeans and had a seat on the edge of his bed. He leaned forward to tie his shoes and felt a rush of dizziness. Cool sweat broke upon his forehead. He sat up and waited for the feeling to pass. In an hour or so he'd be fine.

Stefanos shaved with a cup of coffee in front of him and the last Jawbox booming from his Polk speakers back in the bedroom. "Iodine," the CD's soul-tinged rocker, had just kicked in. He rubbed his cheek, downed a last swig of coffee, and gargled a capful of breath wash. In his bedroom he grabbed an envelope and a shrink-wrapped CD off his dresser.

Stefanos snagged his brown leather jacket off a peg by the door, turned up his collar, locked the apartment, and left the house. He picked up the morning *Post* from his landlord's front lawn and got under the wheel of his white-over-red Coronet 500, parked at the curb. He turned over the engine and drove a couple of miles out of Shepherd Park to the Takoma Metro station, where he caught a downtown train.

He found a seat on the right side of the car. Seasoned Red

Line riders knew to go there, as the morning sun blew blinding rays through the left windows of the southbound cars, causing a sickening, furnace brand of heat. "Doors closing," said a recorded female voice, and Stefanos couldn't help but smile. It always sounded like "George Clinton" to him.

The train got rolling as Stefanos pulled the Metro section from the *Post* and scanned its front page. One of the section's rotating columnists had written yet another piece on the ongoing dismantlement of Home Rule.

Quietly, and with surprisingly little resistance, the Feds had taken over the nation's capital. Congress had appointed a control board and a city manager, a white female Texan who would oversee a town whose black residents made up more than 80 percent of the population. A former military general had been put in charge of the public school system, with little positive effect. Under his "leadership," public schools had opened seven weeks late the previous fall due to long-neglected repairs. D.C. residents continued to pay taxes but had no meaningful voting representation in the House or the Senate, and the elected city council had been stripped of its power. The mayor was now in charge of little more than parades.

Meanwhile, fat-cat politicians from Virginia and North Carolina, and suburbanites who made their living in town but paid no commuter taxes, ridiculed the District of Columbia relentlessly. Stefanos, a lifelong Washingtonian, was fully aware of the problems. Like most residents, though, he didn't care to hear about them from leeches, tourists, and self-serving Southerners.

Stefanos read an article below the fold that detailed the state of the Metropolitan Police Department. The former chief of police had resigned under allegations of mismanagement and corruption; his roommate, a lieutenant on the force, had been accused of shaking down closeted homosexuals outside Southeast's bathhouse strip. The Homicide division, with more than sixteen hundred unsolved cases and a less than 40 percent closure rate, was under particular fire. Some Homicide detectives had recently been caught overinflating the hours on their time cards. Murders occurring in the city's poorest neighborhoods were lazily investigated at best. An apparent serial killer was loose in the Park View section of town. And the most emblematic, high-profile case of the decade remained unsolved: the slaughter at the pizza parlor called May's, dating back to the summer of 1995.

The mention of May's triggered a pulse in Stefano's blood. In the 1980s, when Stefanos was still taking cocaine with his whiskey in after-hours establishments, he had spent many late nights being served by Steve Maroulis, the house bartender at May's. And he had crossed paths with Dimitri Karras, the father of the child killed by the speeding getaway car, on several occasions over the past twenty-two years. That Stefanos knew two victims of the same crime was not surprising. Stefanos, Maroulis, and Karras were all of Greek descent, and though spread out now, the Greek community in D.C. had a shared history.

Stefanos looked out the window at a trash-strewn field bordering the old Woodie's warehouse off North Capitol. Graffiti outlaw Cool "Disco" Dan, a D.C. legend, had tagged the loading dock. Below the moniker, someone had spray-painted a tombstone, on which was written, "Larry Willis, RIP," and below that, his eulogy: "Heaven for a G."

The Red Line train entered a tunnel. Stefanos folded the newspaper, preparing for his stop.

STEFANOS STEPPED off the Judiciary Square station escalator and walked over to the Superior Court building at 5th and Indiana.

He passed through a metal detector, navigated halls crowded with youths, their parents, uniformed cops, sheriffs, and private and court-appointed attorneys, and went down to the large cafeteria on the bottom floor.

He bought a cup of coffee, sugared and creamed it to cut the taste, and walked across a red carpet to a table close to the front entrance, where he had a seat in a chair upholstered in red vinyl.

A voice from a loudspeaker mounted on the wall announced, "Herbert Deuterman, please report with your client at this time to courtroom two-thirteen...."

Nearby, a middle-aged white attorney wearing rumpled, mismatched clothes talked his idea of black to a few of his bored black coworkers seated at the same table. He described a defendant who had accused him of being a racist, and then said, "If this homey knew me the way y'all know me, he'd've known that the only color that matters to me is *green*. I put it to this boy point-blank straight."

As the attorney laughed, a woman seated at the table said, "So, you gonna cut a deal with his lawyer?"

"I'm gonna cut one every which way but loose. You can believe that."

"Long as you don't have to break a sweat, right Mr. Watkins?"

"Sugar, I'm gonna do as little as possible, and a little bit less than that."

A kid sitting at the table to the right of Stefanos listened as his lawyer described the plea-out he was about to make "upstairs" on his client's behalf, and how "Judge Levy definitely does not want to send another young man into an already overcrowded system, and she won't, if she sees that your heart is in the right place."

Stefanos looked at the kid, still in his teens: skinny, sloppily dressed, and slumped in his chair. Today was his court date, and no one had even instructed him to tuck in his shirt. "And try to get that scowl off your face," said the tired young attorney, "when you go before the judge. You can do that for a minute, can't you? Speak clearly and show remorse, understand?"

"I hear you," said the kid. "Can I go get me one of them sodas now?"

"Go ahead."

The young man glanced over at Stefanos and gave him a hard look before rising out of his seat to walk, deep-dip style, toward the cafeteria line.

Stefanos had choked down half his coffee by the time Elaine Clay entered the cafeteria. Clay was a Fifth Streeter, one of the court-appointed attorneys available to defendants under the Criminal Justice Act. In her middle years, with the legs to wear the skirt she wore today, she was tall and big boned, with a handsome, smooth chocolate face. Even before she had begun throwing work his way, Stefanos had heard of her rep from the cops who frequented the Spot, the bar where he worked part-time. Most cops derided the CJA attorneys — they were the enemy who undid police arrests. But over the years the strength and consistency of Elaine Clay's performance had elicited a kind of muttered-under-the-breath respect from the cops. It had been one of the Spot's regulars, in fact, homicide detective Dan Boyle, who had put Clay and Stefanos together the first time.

Stefanos stood as Elaine approached the table.

"Nick," she said.

"Counselor."

They shook hands. Elaine had a seat, dropping a worn leather bag at her side.

"Well?" she said.

"Here you go." Stefanos placed an envelope into her hand. "I think I got what you were looking for."

She studied the photographs from the envelope. "You got a night and a day shot."

"Yeah. The day shot shows that the bulb of the street lamp's been broken out. The night shot shows what you can see on that corner without the light—nothing. Newton Place dead-ends at the western border of the Old Soldiers' Home property there, and there isn't any light over that fence, either. There's no way that cop saw your client dealing weed out of that car."

"The arrest was six months ago. You took these pictures, what, last week?"

"Eight days ago. I know, it doesn't prove the light was out the night those cops arrested him last summer. It doesn't disprove it, either."

"The prosecutor will argue relevance—that a busted street lamp from a week ago has no relevance to a crime that occurred six months ago. And the judge will sustain it."

"Yeah, but I figure it'll put, whaddaya call it, the seed of doubt into the jury's mind."

"Seed of doubt? You're getting fancy on me now, Nick."

"Sorry. But if the prosecutor can't prove without a doubt that someone saw the kid dealing—"

"They caught him with a Baggie of herb in the Maxima."

"Where was the buyer?"

"By then the alleged buyer had beat it on foot."

"That's possession, not possession with intent to distribute."

"That's my case. Which is why I'm going to use these photos—they're the only thing I've got. I get this reduced to a simple possession charge, they throw the jury trial out. Under the new District law, crimes carrying penalties of less than six months go before the judge without a jury."

"The kid'll walk, then."

"It depends on who I draw behind the bench and what their temperature's like that day. But most likely my client will get a tongue-lashing and community service."

Stefanos lit a smoke, side-exhaled, and tossed the match into the Styrofoam cup. In accepting these assignments from Elaine Clay, he'd known all along what his role would be. Still, it was hard to feel clean about his part in this daily cycle. He wondered how Elaine did this, every single day.

She pulled a manila folder from her bag and dropped it on the table. "I've got something else for you, Nick, if you want it."

"What is it?"

"I'm defending a kid named Randy Weston on a murder charge. The trial's coming up in a couple of weeks."

"So?"

"Weston's a known low-level dealer with priors. On the day of the murder, he was seen arguing with another dealer, Donnel Lawton, who'd been encroaching on Weston's turf. Lawton was shot to death that night at First and Kennedy with a Beretta ninety-two. An anonymous informant made Weston as the triggerman. And when the police searched his place they found a Beretta nine. The markings from the slug that killed Lawton matched the gun."

"An anonymous informant?"

"A woman. It was enough to get a warrant."

Stefanos tapped ash off his smoke. "Sounds open-and-shut to me."

"Weston's got an alibi. He was with his girlfriend that night. She's not cooperating, but I believe him. He doesn't look like a killer. It's his eyes — and after a while, you just know."

"Does it make a difference to you if he's guilty or innocent?"

"No. I defend them all the same way, Nick. I thought it might make a difference to you."

Stefanos hit his smoke. "What else makes you think Weston's telling the truth? Besides, you know, his eyes."

"Around the time of the murder, a kid who works in one of those neighborhood Chinese grease pits, place called Hunan Delite, says he was closing up his parents' shop, heard shots and tires screeching on the road, then saw an old vehicle speeding past on Kennedy."

"What kind of an old vehicle?"

Elaine peered inside the folder. "A red Tempo, I think. No, here it is...a red Ford Torino."

"What's Weston drive?"

"A Legend."

"Color?"

"Red."

"Even if you find the driver of the Torino, and even if he has something to do with the crime, the prosecutors will bring up the sameness of color in court."

"You're talking about two cars with over twenty years' difference in terms of style."

"Maybe." Stefanos looked around the cafeteria. "But I'm not interested."

"You're interested. I can see it—"

"In my eyes?"

"Thought you might want to pick this one up, see what you can do with it."

"I told you the first time you hired me—"

"I know. You no longer get involved in, how did you put it, 'murder gigs or other kinds of violent shit.'"

"I said that?"

"Something like it."

Stefanos dragged on the filter of his Camel. "Get that big Indian you use. Nobody fucks with that guy."

"He's busy on another case."

"What about Joey A.?"

"Joe A.'s tied up, too." Elaine pushed the folder across the table until it touched Stefanos's hand. "Look, I need your help, Nick. I've got another one of these files in my office. Take this one with you, okay?"

"I don't think so." Stefanos moved his hand and dropped his cigarette into the half inch of coffee left in the cup.

"Right. Let's put that aside for now, then, and shift gears."

"What, you've got something else?"

"Well, yes."

"Go ahead."

"I mentioned that I was working with you to my husband last night. Marcus said he thought you might know his friend Dimitri Karras. You remember Dimitri, don't you?"

"Sure. I haven't seen him for over ten years. But I was just thinking about him on the way over here. The *Post* ran their quarterly Pizza Parlor Murders piece in this morning's paper."

"Dimitri's been in a real bad way."

Stefanos nodded, drew a fresh cigarette from the pack, tamped it on the table. He rolled the cigarette between his fingers.

"There can't be anything worse than to lose a child, Nick."

"Wasn't he with your husband in those record stores?"

"Yes. Marcus cashed out ten years ago, went back to school and got his M.B.A. In the meantime, Dimitri met his future wife, Lisa, in rehab. Dimitri and Lisa got married and had a child straightaway. Marcus and a friend named Clarence Tate created a retail consulting business designed to help African American startups and brought Dimitri in as a partner, despite the fact that Dimitri's—"

"Greek Like Me?"

"Dimitri was always good with people, so that didn't seem to matter all that much when all was said and done." Elaine spread her hands out on the table. "But when Jimmy was killed, he pretty much fell apart. After a year or so, Marcus and Clarence couldn't carry him anymore. And Dimitri didn't want them to. It just didn't work out."

"What about Karras and his wife?"

"They didn't make it. She's still at their old house, pretty much a shut-in. He's living in an apartment on U at Fifteenth, still making do on what's left of his inheritance."

"Marcus feels guilty."

"Yes. He feels like, if Dimitri can get himself into a work environment—get around people again, every day—he can start that healing process he needs. It would be like, you know, placing him with some kind of family."

Stefanos cleared his throat and slid the unlit cigarette back in its pack. "I'll ask around. If I hear of any job openings around town I'll let you know."

"I was thinking of that place you work."

"The Spot? Elaine, you ever seen the place? It's just a shitty little bar in Southeast."

"They serve food, don't they?"

"Yeah, we serve food. In fact, we just hired a couple more people for the kitchen. The owner expanded the menu. He's trying to beef up the lunch business."

"Well, there you go. Dimitri could do kitchen work part-time. Wash dishes, anything. With you there, he wouldn't be walking into a nest of strangers. Marcus was thinking—"

"Marcus?"

"Okay, it would be a personal favor for me, too. Look, I didn't think you'd mind if I asked."

"I don't mind." Stefanos stood. "Like I said, I'll ask around, Elaine. How's that?"

"Thanks, Nicky." She wrote down a phone number, tore off a piece of paper, and handed it to Stefanos.

Stefanos reached into the side pocket of his leather, pulled out a CD, and put it in front of Elaine. "Here you go."

Elaine's face brightened. "What's this?"

"*Live Evil.* It just got reissued on domestic disc. I knew you were an electric Miles freak, so..."

"You know, I'd always see the Japanese pressing of this in the stores, but I never wanted to spring for it."

"I heard a couple of tracks at the listening station. Some of the pieces were recorded right here at the old Cellar Door in 1970. Johnny McLaughlin on guitar, Michael Henderson on bass—it's a boss band. It doesn't cut *Agharta*, but it's pretty hot."

"Nick, that was so sweet."

Stefanos winced. "A woman shouldn't ever call a guy sweet, Counselor. It's like calling him dickless or something."

"But it *was* sweet."

"Yeah, okay, it was sweet." Stefanos shuffled his feet.

"You all right? You're looking a little run-down."

"I'm fine. Listen, I'll talk to you later, hear?"

"Soon."

They smiled at each other, and Stefanos turned to go. She watched him walk from the cafeteria and disappear into the crowd gathered at the entrance.

"Who was that?" said the young attorney at the table to her left.

Elaine turned to face the man who'd been a CJA attorney for less than a year. "Nick Stefanos. An investigator I use."

"From his appearance, I'd say that guy's been around the block a few times."

"I suspect he has."

"He looks like some kind of ghost."

More like a street angel, she thought, as the voice from the loudspeaker called the young attorney's name.

"That's me," he said. "Show time."

"Don't forget your client," said Elaine.

"There he is. He's coming now."

Elaine looked at the kid, thought immediately of her own son, Marcus Jr., now sixteen years old. The kid's shirt was out and his boots were unlaced. M.J. had begged her to buy him that same brand of boots this Christmas past.

"You might want to tell him to tuck in his shirt," said Elaine. "Lace up those Timbies, too. He's liable to trip on his way up to the bench."

"Timbies?"

"His boots."

The attorney stood from his chair and collected his papers. "That Stefanos guy," he said. "You mind if I borrow him sometime?"

Elaine shook her head. "Sorry."

"He does good work, doesn't he?"

"Yes, he does good work. But he's mine."

FOUR

THE GROUP gathered once a week in the basement of a Presbyterian church at 23rd and P. A social worker with the police department had set up the support sessions originally and assigned the group a freelance shrink, who, after three weeks, was politely asked to leave. Two and a half years had passed, and the group continued to meet.

Ernst, the church's live-in custodian, stood near the group, seated in a disjointed circle in the middle of the common room. "Please," said Ernst. "Pull the plug on that coffee urn when you're done."

"We'll take care of it, Ernst," said Bernie Walters.

"Ya, sure," said Ernst, giving them a fangy smile. Clumps of gray hair grew from several large moles on his face. He was older than dirt, and it seemed an effort for him to lift his hand to wave before he walked from the room.

When he left, Thomas Wilson said, "Where's Ernst from, with that accent of his? Anybody ever figure that out?"

"Latvia," said Dimitri Karras.

"Where the hell is that?"

"He's a good old bird," said Walters, who at fifty was the senior member of the group and its unofficial leader. "Anyway...where were we?"

They started, as they always did, by getting reacquainted. They talked about the things that had happened at their jobs, what they'd done on the weekend, the trades the Skins needed to make to win next season, celebrity deaths, favorite television shows, the latest high-profile trial.

After a while they refreshed their coffee cups and came back and took their seats. Bernie Walters lit a cigarette.

"Funny how you're the only one of us that smokes," said Stephanie Maroulis.

"You know us veterans," said Walters, snapping shut the hinged lid of his lighter. "Marlboro reds and Zippos. We never go anywhere without 'em."

"*Vanity Fair* did a piece on the Zippo lighter," offered Karras, "and its place in American society relative to Vietnam."

"Here it comes," said Thomas Wilson. "'Relative to Vietnam.' Now the professor's gonna explain to us unwashed types what it all means."

Karras had been, among other things, an American lit instructor in his past life. He had mistakenly mentioned it to Wilson and Walters one night over beers at the Brew Hause.

"Give it a rest, guys," said Stephanie, trying to head off the inevitable.

But Karras said, "I could bring in the magazine for you, Thomas. If you didn't want to take the time to read it you could just, I don't know, look at all the pretty models and dream."

"Look at 'em and yawn, you mean. I've seen those gray girls you're talking about. Clothes look like they been draped over a wire hanger and shit. Naw, you can keep your Caucasian junkies, Dimitri. And anyway, you know I prefer women with a little back on 'em."

"Yeah, but what do they think of you?"

Karras smirked at the glimmer in Wilson's eyes. Wilson liked to try and shock the group—play their idea of the street spade if he could get away with it. Karras didn't let him get away with it.

Walters pushed up the bill on his faded Orioles cap—just the bird, no script—and scratched his graying beard. He was barrel-chested gone heavy, but he carried the weight on a broad back.

"So what'd the article say, Dimitri?" said Walters.

"It talked about how the soldiers used to have all these sayings engraved on their lighters. 'Born to Die,' like that. How the GIs were very attached to those lighters."

"I used mine," said Walters, "to burn villages. I must have torched at least a dozen like that. You could set a really good fire to those straw roofs they had. That article say anything about that?"

"It did say something, now that you mention it."

"Course they do know a lot about Vietnam—in New York."

"I mentioned your smoking," said Stephanie, "because, I don't know, usually in these kinds of groups it seems like everybody smokes. Right, Dimitri? It's unusual that it's only you who lights up, Bernie."

"Yeah, that's true." Karras thought of his old rehab group, where he had met Lisa. "I was never a smoker myself. But I used to come out of my old group wanting to just throw my stinking clothes away."

"The reason I thought of it," said Stephanie, "was that my husband was in GA for a while. You know, Gamblers Anonymous. I ever tell you guys that? Steve used to come home and say that everyone there smoked but him."

Karras shifted in his seat. This part—the first mention of the spouse, or the best friend, or the son—invariably made him uncomfortable. And Stephanie seemed to be the one who always kicked it off.

"What'd Steve like?" said Walters. "The ponies?"

"He liked any kind of action," said Stephanie, "and May's was a place where you could always place a bet. Numbers, the over-under, horses...Steve liked it all."

"So what sent him into GA?" said Wilson. "Must have been one special time where he hit the bottom, right? Always is."

Stephanie pushed a strand of her shoulder-length chestnut hair behind her ear. Karras liked to watch her do that; she was not a small woman, but her movements were graceful. And she had nice hands.

"It was this one weekend over the holidays. Must have been the Christmas of ninety-three. Steve had lost a bundle on the weekend NFL play-off games, and then a couple hundred more on some college basketball game that same day. We had a family get-together that night, Steve's mother was there—this was the year before she passed away—and Steve got a little looped on whiskey. Steve did like his Crown Royal."

Wilson chuckled. "Charlie used to tell me, 'We got this bartender, every night after he closes down the place, he dims the lights and pours himself a drink—only one—out of this pretty-ass bottle he keeps up on the top shelf.'"

"That was his routine." Stephanie smiled. "Anyway, that night, it must have been midnight or so, Steve was really loaded. He got on the kitchen phone with his bookie and tried to place a bet, letting him know that he was good for the losses he had taken that afternoon. Well, this bookie wasn't having any of it. Steve blew his cool, started screaming at the guy over the phone. Then Steve glanced over and saw his mother sitting at the kitchen table, looking at him with something close to disgust in her eyes. And Steve did look like hell that night—sweaty and red faced from the drink. I guess his mother shamed him with that look of hers. On Monday morning he made a phone call and got himself into GA. And he never gambled again. He was stronger than I thought he would be. He surprised me."

"Those programs work," said Walters, keeping it going. "Surrendering your will to a higher power. I'm telling you, it does the trick."

Thomas Wilson looked over at Karras, who wore a frown of agitation. Wilson believed in God himself. And he had real affection for Bernie Walters. But Bernie never had the good sense to give that bullshit a rest.

"Ah, come on," said Karras. "God didn't help me kick cocaine. It was the love of a woman. It was living, breathing flesh. I fell for Lisa and decided that I wanted to sleep next to her for the rest of my life. That to do that, I needed to live. And then, when Jimmy was born, there wasn't any question. I never even thought about coke again. But God? Gimme a break."

"Where were we?" said Walters.

Stephanie tried to catch Karras's eye, but he was staring ahead. Picturing his son alive, Stephanie knew. She'd come to recognize that empty gaze of Karras's face. Wilson looked at a spot on the floor between his feet and patted the shaved sides of his face.

"Smoking," said Karras. "Tonight's theme."

"Right," said Wilson. "All right, here's something. I can remember the first time me and my boy Charles bought a pack of cigarettes. At the Geranium Market, up on the corner of Georgia and Geranium Avenue?"

"That place is still there," said Karras.

Wilson nodded. "I don't know who runs it now. But back then this Jewish guy had it. Man by the name of Schweitz. Yeah, kind old guy. I told Mr. Schweitz the smokes were for my moms. He was friendly with my mother and he knew my mother didn't smoke. He sold them to us anyway, though. Probably knew we'd get turned off by it right quick. And did we ever. We took that pack of Kools—*had* to be double O's 'cause we *knew* that all the bad brothers smoked those—over to Fort Stevens Park, and don't you know we smoked them right after the other. I can still picture Charles, taking a pull off that stick, trying to blow rings, checking it out, lookin' all cross-eyed and shit....Damn, what was that, almost twenty-five years ago? Anyway, right about then, both of us got sick. You should've seen Charlie, huggin' one of those Civil War cannons they have over at the fort."

"Bet you never smoked again," said Walters.

"Charles never did. But I did. See, I was never as smart as Charles. When I came back to D.C. after being away for a few years and Charles saw me lightin' up, he wouldn't let up on me, calling me a fool and everything else he could think of in front of the ladies. I stopped smoking soon after." Wilson cleared his throat. "Charles always did look out for me like that."

"It's good to remember it," said Walters. "That your friend loved you, I mean."

"Yeah, we were like kin." Wilson sat up straight. "Bernie?"

"Let me think." Bernie Walters tapped ash off his cigarette. "Right. The first time I caught Vance smoking was at this dance he was in charge of when he was in junior high. I don't know what he had to do with it, exactly. He liked to put that kind of stuff on—do the promotion, decorate the gym, all that. I went to pick him up, and I saw him standing outside with a couple of his friends. They were passing a butt back and forth. I got pissed off, not because he was smoking but because of the way he looked with that cigarette. He was holding it up, pitchfork style, the way some women do. I guess he was trying to be... what do you call that, Professor?"

"Cosmopolitan," said Karras.

"Right, like that magazine. So when I came up on the group, he knew he was busted. He took me aside and asked me not to yell at him right there in front of his friends. Well, I gave him that much. But on the way home I really let him have it. Told him he looked like a damn girl, smoking that cigarette." Walters regarded the Marlboro between his fingers. "It was dark in that car, but I could see the tears come into his eyes. It hurt him so much for me to call him a girl. Not that he was confused. He knew who he was, even then. No, that wasn't the problem; the problem was *me*. If I could have shown just a little understanding, it wouldn't have been so rough on him, growing up the way he did. Hell, he didn't even like cigarettes. The only reason he tried smoking at all was because I smoked. He thought... I mean, can you imagine what was going on in his head to do something like that? To smoke a cigarette to try and please your dad? You all ever hear of such a thing?"

"The two of you got a lot of things straight before he died," said Stephanie. "Don't forget that."

"We got some things straight," said Walters.

For a while no one said a thing. Then Wilson said, "Dimitri?"

"Yeah."

"Your turn, man."

"My son was just five years old when he was murdered," said Karras. "So forgive me if I don't have any smoking stories for you tonight. But if I think of any, I'll let you know."

FIVE

FRANK FARROW took the last dinner plate from a gray bus tray and used an icing wand to scrape what was left of a rich man's lunch into the garbage receptacle by his side. He fitted the plate onto a stack of them and set the load down into the steaming hot water of the soak sink in front of him. He used the overhead hose to rinse off the bus tray and dropped the empty tray onto the floor, where the boy would come and pick it up.

Farrow had dumped silverware into a plastic container called a third. He dripped liquid detergent into the third, filled the container with hot water, and capped it tightly with a plastic lid. He shook the third vigorously for about a minute, then drained the container of suds and rinsed it out. The silverware was clean.

Farrow grabbed the bottle of Sam Adams he had placed on the ledge over the sink. Grace, the waitress with the howitzers, had brought the beer in to him after lunch, told him it was on her for the good job he had done "turning those dishes" during the rush. He watched her wiggle her ass as she walked out of the dishwasher's room, and he whistled under his breath, because that was what she wanted him to do.

He looked into the brownish water of the sink. The plates could soak for a while. He decided to go out back and have himself a smoke.

He snatched his cigarettes off a high shelf, took his beer, and went to the doorway leading to the kitchen. Bobby, the faggoty young chef who called himself an artist, was boning a salmon on a wooden cutting block. He was gesturing broadly with his hands, describing the process to an apprentice, a kid from the local college who was struggling to stay interested. The other kitchen help, black guys from the north side of town, were walking around behind Jamie the Artist, their hands on their hips, their white hats cool-cocked on their heads, elaborately mouthing his words in mimicry, passing each other, giving each other skin.

Farrow stood in the doorway watching them with amusement. When Bobby looked up, Farrow said, "Dishes are soaking. I'll be out back, catching a weed."

"Okay, Larry," said Bobby with a wave of his hand.

Larry. That's what they called Farrow in this town.

THERE WAS a small alleyway off the back of the kitchen. The owners of the hotel had erected latticework along the edge of the alley's red bricks. A piece of lattice above, thin with grapevine, completed the camouflage and hid the alleyway from the guests of the hotel who liked to stroll in the adjacent courtyard.

Farrow stood out here on his breaks, smoking, peering through the gaps in the lattice, watching the guests walk in the courtyard, silently laughing at them, thoroughly hating them. Well-to-do white people. There wasn't anything more pathetic. Khaki pants, Bass Weejuns, outdoor gear, sweaters tied around the neck for those days when the weather was on the warm side but "unpredictable." They had come down here with their spouses for an overnight at the "quaint" bed-and-breakfast. They'd go "antiquing" around the town, have a nice dinner, wrestle for a couple of minutes in the four-poster bed, go home the next day just as sad and unsatisfied as when they arrived. The point was, they could tell their friends they had spent a quiet weekend on the Eastern Shore. Farrow guessed it was all about making some kind of statement.

He'd look at the husbands, stepping out of the elevator of the Royal Hotel on their way to the dining room, their hands just touching the round backs of their shapeless, overweight wives, and he'd see boredom in their eyes, and something like contained desperation. For them, it had come down to this: They had to spend two, three hundred a night, and drive two hours from the city, just to fuck a woman they no longer desired to fuck. When all the time they'd rather be getting their dick yanked by some stocky Korean woman in a massage parlor for forty bucks.

Then there were the husbands with their trophy wives. These men thought that people looked at them with envy. But the truth was, people looked at them and imagined wrinkled, bony old men struggling to stay hard inside of luscious young women.

Well, that was their problem, not his. But it was funny just the same.

He took a swig of his beer. The day was cold but not bitter. It felt good to be away from the heat of the sink.

Here in Edwardtown he was known as slow-witted Larry. Larry with the black-framed glasses who never met their eyes. Who had gotten the job on the recommendation of Mr. Toomey, the electrician who serviced the Royal Hotel. Larry had never even filled out an employment form.

"I'll work for half pay if you give me cash money under the table," said Larry to his boss, Harraway. Larry looked down at his own shoes, chuckled in a humble, homespun way, and said, "Had a little trouble once with the IRS, you understand, and they're aimin' to take most everything I earn for the rest of my life."

"We can do that," said Harraway. "I'm no fan of the government myself."

Farrow had been down here in Edwardtown, a small Maryland city thirty miles south of Delaware on the Edward River, for two and a half years. A liberal arts college sat on the northeast corner of the city limits. Outside of town, farmers rotated soybean and corn while their wives worked at the local Wal-Mart, and crabmen made a modest living on the river.

The north end of town housed blacks and poor whites. The south end—nineteenth-century clapboard row houses on narrow cobblestone streets—meant old white money clamped in rigor-mortised fists. The Royal Hotel was on High Street, one block away from the river. As in every small town in the country, High Street was the area where the landed gentry had always resided.

This was the kind of people Farrow hated most. Strange that he would be down here now, washing their dishes.

This was only temporary, though, and when he thought about it rationally, Edwardtown had been the perfect place for him to lie low. But now, he felt, it was time to make a move.

He hotboxed his smoke and dropped it on the bricks. He crushed the butt beneath his boot.

FARROW DROVE the hopped-up Taurus up High Street, took Kent Boulevard over along the campus, where that famous 1960s novelist had tenure. Farrow spent much of his free time in the campus library, which stocked a good deal of worthy fiction. He had read one of the famous writer's early novels and had once seen him, a small bald man with tortoiseshell eyeglasses, crossing the library floor. He had enjoyed the man's book but felt in the end that the writer had been holding back, had not gone far enough into that black rotted place that surely would have existed in his lead character's mind.

In the end, the writer had been afraid. In general, thought Farrow, that was the flaw in most people, a timidity that separated them from those who were strong. They used their idea of Goodness and Love as an excuse for living a life of weakness. People were afraid to go to that black place and use it when the time came, or even admit that it was there. To be powerful and free while on this earth, and to stay alive as long as possible, these were Farrow's goals. In death there was only the equality of failure.

Farrow hit the interstate, open country on either side. He passed farmland with flocks of gulls resting in the icy pockets of plow lines. Ahead, the straightaway lay clear and stretched for a quarter mile. He downshifted the Ford to second, red-lined it, caught air at the peak of a grade, slammed the shifter into third as the wheels touched asphalt. Manuel had been right about the Ford: It could really fly.

SIX

ROMAN OTIS stepped up onstage. There were just a few people in the late-afternoon crowd, sitting at the bar. The joint was down on the east end of Sunset, just past Fountain, one of those places that served Tex-Mex as an afterthought. The sign said El Rancho, but in his mind Otis called the place El Roacho because he had seen plenty of them crawling the brick walls. No, he'd never eat the food at El Roacho, but they did have a nice karaoke machine set up with a premium sound system, and that was why he came. Otis had slipped the owner a few bucks to buy the tapes of some of those old ballads and midtempo tunes he loved so much.

Past the stage lights that shone in his eyes, Otis could make out silhouettes at the bar, a couple of Chicanos and a woman named Darcia, nice-lookin' woman with a fat onion on her, who had come in to hear him sing. At the end of the bar sat Gus Lavonicus, top-heavy and kind of leaning to the side, with that cinder-block-of-flesh-looking head of his. Otis would be done in a few minutes, and Gus could have waited outside in the Lincoln. But Gus was a thoughtful kind of guy who liked to support Otis whenever he performed. Otis felt it was a damn shame that his sister and Gus weren't getting along.

The music track began. Otis closed his eyes as his cue for the first verse neared, and then he jumped in. He kept time with his hand against his thigh, kept his other hand free to gesture along with the music. He thought of it as a kind of punctuation, what he liked to call his "hand expressions." This would have been his signature as a performer had his life gone the other way. But it hadn't gone the other way, and to get negative about that now went against his principles of positivity. He was fulfilled, in his own small way, just singing in places like this when he got the chance.

"So very hard to go," sang Otis, " 'cause I love you sooooo…"

Yeah, this was a good one. He sounded right, stretching out and bending those vowels against the Tower of Power horn section. This here was one of his favorites, had inspired him to get the custom-made "Back to Oakland" ID bracelet he wore.

"Thanks, y'all," said Otis as the music ended, Gus and Darcia's applause filling the dead air. "I appreciate it. I truly do."

Otis stepped down off the stage and went to the bar. He put his car keys down in front of Lavonicus.

"Go ahead and get the Mark warmed up, Gus," said Otis. "I'm right behind you, man."

"You sounded good, bro," said Lavonicus.

Lavonicus got off his stool, uncoiling to his full seven feet. He ducked his head to avoid a Budweiser mobile suspended from the ceiling as he turned. One of the Mexicans nudged the other as Lavonicus passed.

Otis pushed his long hair back off his shoulders, rubberbanded it in a tail. He said to Darcia, "Get up, baby. Let me have a look at what you got."

Darcia stood up, smiled shyly, struck a pose. She wore cinnamon slacks with a matching top.

"Now turn around," said Otis, and as she did, Otis nodded his head and said, "Yeah," and "Uh-huh."

"You like the way I look, Roman?"

"Baby, you know I do."

"We gonna see each other tonight?"

"Wished I could, but I can't. Gonna be out of town for a few weeks, I expect. But when I get back we're gonna hook up, hear? Maybe I let you cook me a nice meal. Afterwards..." He leaned forward and whispered in her ear. She giggled as he brushed a hand across her hip.

"For real?" she said.

"I'm gonna get a nut in you *real* good, baby. I wouldn't lie."

Otis signaled the bartender with a finger-wave over Darcia's glass. The drinks were cheap here, cheaper still this time of day. He left dollars on the bar, kissed Darcia on the neck, and walked across the wooden floor. Wasn't no kind of trick to gettin' pussy when you got down to it. You just needed to know how to talk to a woman, that was all.

"SAY, MAN," said Otis as he scanned to 100.3, L.A.'s slow-jam station, on the radio dial.

"What," said Lavonicus.

"You get to keep one of those red, white, and blue balls when you came out of the league?"

Lavonicus breathed through his mouth as he thought it over. He had thick red clown lips and large gapped teeth. Otis found him to be an ugly man—like that Jaws-lookin' sucker from that bad run of Bond movies—but he understood why his sister Cissy loved him. The man was as loyal as a spinster to her vibrator.

"Naw, I didn't keep one," Lavonicus said, his voice monotonous and deep.

"'Cause I'd pay good money to have me one of those with some of your old teammates' autographs on it. Especially Marvin Barnes and Fly Williams. Listen, I was incarcerated when y'all were playin', and they didn't even televise those ABA games back then. But even so, Barnes and Williams were legends in the joint. Those were two black men who took shit from no one."

"Barnes and Williams both ended up doing time."

"That's what I know."

"Barnes." Lavonicus shook his head. "He could party all night and still play. Fly gave himself that nickname, but nobody was more fly than Marvin Barnes. The man drove a Rolls-Royce, wore a full-length mink, platform shoes...shit."

"Y'all had Maurice Lucas, right?"

"Uh-huh. Freddie Lewis, too. Caldwell Jones..."

"And Moses Malone?"

"For a while."

"Shoot, man, why didn't you win the championship?"

"We beat the Nets and Dr. J. in the first round of the playoffs."

"Yeah, I remember that."

"But the Kentucky Colonels took us to school after that. Hell, Roman, we were just out there having fun." Lavonicus smiled. His knees touched the dash. He lowered his head to look through the windshield. They were heading west on Little Santa Monica. "Where we going, bro?"

"Frank's supposed to call me any minute on my cell. Gotta pull over when he calls, 'cause we need to have a serious talk."

"What about after that?" said Lavonicus.

Otis said, "Gonna pick us up a couple of guns."

Otis turned up the volume on the radio. The O'Jays were doing "Brandy." Now that was one pretty song.

"Sippin' on a cherry soda pop," sang Otis, "building houses made of sand..."

He looked out the driver's window as he sang, let his hand dangle in the wind. Palm trees in the middle of the city. Who would want to live anywhere else?

Now he'd have to make some money to keep this lifestyle going. Because it couldn't get much better than this. Cruising through Los Angeles in a Mark V, the sun shining every day, listening to the O'Jays...free.

SEVEN

"I'LL GET this," said Bernie Walters as the waitress laid the check on the table.

Thomas Wilson put his hand over the check and slid it in front of him. "I got it, man."

"C'mon, Thomas, you always buy."

"That way, y'all can't never say that a man who hauls trash for a living didn't hold up his end."

Walters and Wilson sat at a four-top in the Brew Hause, a glorified beer garden on 22nd, one block east of the church. The waitresses here were forced to wear ridiculous outfits, a combination of Heidi and Pippi Longstocking, and it showed on their embarrassed, overworked faces. Karras and Stephanie Maroulis had done a round and left a half hour earlier.

"So you and Charles used to hang at Fort Stevens when you were kids," said Walters.

"Yeah. We played army, cowboys-and-indians and shit over at that fort all the time."

"Vance always wanted to go there when he was a boy, but I

never got around to taking him. Might as well add it to the list: another thing I never did with Vance."

"You were a good father, Bern."

"Yeah, sure." Walters swigged beer. "Hey. I just thought of something. A company motto for your uncle's business. Okay, you ready? 'We don't just talk trash. We *haul* trash.' What do you think?"

"It's good. But one of our competitors in the District uses a phrase damn near like it already. Even has it painted on the side of his pickup."

"Maybe that's why I thought it up. Maybe I've seen his truck and I didn't remember. Like one of those subconscious things."

"You don't get into the city enough to have seen it."

"The city? You can have it. I come downtown once a week for the meeting, and believe me, that's enough. When I retire from the U.S. Postal Service, which is gonna be damn soon, I'm gonna move down to my property in St. Mary's County and never look back."

"What you got, some kind of *Gone with the Wind* thing goin' on down there?"

"What I got *temporarily* is a pop-up trailer-tent with a Jiffy John beside it. Five acres of woods and a little clearing by a deep creek. You oughtta come down."

"I love you like a brother, Bernie. To tell you the truth, though, it doesn't sound like my thing."

Walters stabbed his cigarette into the ashtray and patted his breast pocket, where he kept his pack.

Wilson dropped money on the table. "Hey, Bern. Dimitri and Stephanie left together again tonight. You notice that?"

"She doesn't drive. He gives her a lift home. So what?"

"Dimitri lives down below Malcolm X Park, and she lives

uptown, on Connecticut. *You* live out in the suburbs. If it's just a question of a ride, make more sense for you to drop her off on your way."

"She didn't ask me. And besides, the two of them being Greeks and all that, they probably have a lot to talk about."

"And Karras is a booty monger from way back."

"Cut it out."

"I'm tellin' you, man, 'cause I know. One can spot another from a mile away."

"You're major league in that department, huh? So why is it that I never see you with a woman, Thomas?"

"Shoot, none of the fräuleins in this joint are to my taste, that's all. What you gotta do, you gotta come up around *my* way if you want to see me operate. 'Cause you know I like to play in the nappy dugout."

"What the hell is that?"

"Forget it."

"Yeah, forget it. And forget about Dimitri and Stephanie, too. Everybody's got to grieve in their own way. You've got your own private way, whatever that is. Stephanie gets by on her positive attitude. I tend to lean on the good Lord. And Dimitri—"

"Likes pussy. Matter of fact, I got ten dollars right here says that Dimitri is hittin' it right now."

"Leave it alone, Thomas."

"I'm just makin' conversation."

"Yeah, okay." Walters drained his beer. "You ready?"

"Sure, Bernie. Let's go."

"SO," SAID Karras. "Would you like to be undressed from in front or behind tonight?"

Stephanie smiled. "Oh, I don't know...in front, I guess."

Moonlight and streetlight illuminated her deep brown eyes in the darkened room. Karras unbuttoned her blouse. He peeled it off her shoulders, and she slipped her arms free. He unfastened her bra and dropped it to the floor.

Karras cupped her heavy breasts, leaned in and licked a mole centered between them. His tongue flicked at her right nipple. She stroked his gray hair, and he came up and kissed her deeply on the mouth.

They moved to the bed and undressed completely. Then they were naked atop the sheets. Karras put a pillow beneath her. She was ready for him, quick of pulse and wet. Her smell was strong in the room.

"*Ella*, Thimitri."

"Not yet."

"No, now."

"So you're giving the orders around here, eh?"

"C'mon."

He penetrated her, pulled out, rubbed the head of his cock along the inside of her muscled thigh.

"Quit playin' around." She reached down. "Whaddya, need a map or something?"

"Careful, you'll tear it off."

"It feels sturdy enough."

"Okay…okay."

Stephanie arched her back as he walked her rib cage with his fingers. She took his hands and put them on her breasts. He buried himself inside her until there seemed no more of her. Then she adjusted her hips and he slid farther into her gloved warmth.

"There we go," she said.

"*Opa*," said Karras.

*   *   *

KARRAS WASHED himself, phoned his apartment, came back into the bedroom, and had a seat on the edge of the mattress.

Stephanie got up on one elbow. "What's wrong?"

"Nothing. I just got a message from a guy, called my place. I haven't seen him in years. Greek guy named Nick Stefanos. My old man used to work for his grandfather a long time ago."

"What'd he want?"

"He wants to give me a part-time job in a bar he works in, down in Southeast. Kitchen help." Karras rubbed his cheek. "Things do come around."

"Why's he calling you now?"

"My friend Marcus's wife, Elaine? She hooked it up. Elaine uses Stefanos as an investigator on some of her cases."

"Are you going to talk to him?"

"I don't know."

"It would do you good to get out in the world a few hours a day."

"I know it."

"I'm serious."

"Stephanie, I know."

She pulled him down on the bed, her hair falling and touching his face. She smiled, looking into his eyes. "You were really ornery tonight, Dimitri."

"Sometimes I don't feel like talking."

"You still come to the meetings, though."

"I like being with you guys," he said. "Aside from the pleasure of that, it doesn't do much good. Look, don't try to make me your project, Stephanie."

"You're not. We need each other, though. All of us, I mean. Can't you see it?"

He kissed her cool lips and pushed back her hair.

"I need *this*," he said.

"Make no mistake," said Stephanie. "So do I."

BERNIE WALTERS cracked open a can of Bud and took it downstairs to the rec room of his three-bedroom house in Wheaton, off Randolph Road. He had a seat in a leather recliner and hit the remote, which he had Velcroed to the chair.

When Vance was a teenager he was always misplacing the television's remote. After carrying mailbags all day through Bethesda's business district, Walters would come home with no more ambition than to put his feet up and watch a little tube. The remote always seemed to be missing when he got downstairs, and that drove him nuts.

"What's the big deal with the remote, Dad?"

"I been on my dogs all day. The big deal is, once I get settled in my chair at night, I don't want to get back up."

Both Vance and Bernie got tired of that exchange. Bernie rigged up a kind of sheath for the remote and Velcroed it to the right arm of the chair.

Vance's friends got a big charge out of it. Vance's dad, the Vietnam vet and mail carrier—with that combo, he had to be some kind of wack job, right?—had gone and rigged a permanent remote control to his chair. Remote on the right arm, ashtray on the left. He even heard one of those friends call the recliner "the captain's chair," then hum a few bars of the *Star Trek* theme when he thought Walters wasn't listening.

Yeah, Vance's friends got a big laugh out of Bernie Walters. The captain's chair, the ten-point buck's head mounted on the wall of the rec room, the glass-doored gun case with the beautiful oiled shotguns aligned in a row, the bumper sticker on his truck that read, "Know Jesus, Know Peace; No Jesus, No Peace," the prayers and psalms framed and hung throughout the house. It was okay by Walters for those kids to think what-ever they wanted. And for the members of the group as well. He knew it made them uncomfortable to hear him talk about the Lord at the meetings. Well, they had their own way of getting through this and he had his. Because they had become his closest friends, he felt he owed it to them to talk about God's plan. He knew that everything happened for a reason, even the bad.

As for Vance, he had never seemed to be embarrassed by his old man. Bernie had heard Vance describe him one time as a "blue-collar eccentric." Whatever it meant, it didn't sound bad, not the way Vance said it; by the tone of his voice, you'd almost get the impression that Vance was proud.

Vance's friends stopped coming around when his mother, Walters's wife, Lynne, got the cancer in both of her breasts. She'd found the lumps fairly early, but fear had made her wait too long to get herself checked. After the diagnosis she opted for the radical mastectomy, but it couldn't save her and she went six months later, heavily doped on morphine, at home in their marriage bed.

Bernie Walters's father died that same year, in a nursing home on East–West Highway.

So it ended up just Bernie and Vance. By then Vance had entered Montgomery College, hoping to do a couple of years on the Takoma Park campus before heading for New York to attend one of the design schools in the city. At home he spent most of his time in his room, listening to CDs, studying, and talking on the phone with his friends. He worked three or four shifts a week waitering at the pizza parlor on Wisconsin, sav-ing for his move to New York.

When Bernie wasn't working, he liked to hang out in the rec room or the laundry room, where he had a workbench set up.

During warm-weather months he would drive his pickup down to Southern Maryland and spend each weekend on his property, hunting, casting for perch and catfish, walking the woods, and drinking beer.

Walters hit the up-channel button on the remote and landed on a late-night talk show. The host with the gap-toothed grin said something, then stared unsmiling into the camera as the audience laughed. Walters shook a cigarette out of his pack and gave it a light.

Those last couple of years Vance and Bernie had pretty much led separate lives. Now he wished they'd talked more — he wished he'd said those things to Vance that he'd never said.

Vance talked to *him* now. In his early-morning dream time, Bernie could hear Vance's voice as a child sometimes, calling his name. Often Vance would be shouting, and this would scare Bernie, and sadden him. But he couldn't stop it. He knew it was Vance's spirit that was talking to him in his dreams. He knew.

He *would* tell Vance those things that he had not told him before. These would be the very first things he'd tell him when they were reunited. If he was certain of anything, it was that he and Vance and Lynne would all be together again, someday soon, in the hands of the Lord.

STEPHANIE MAROULIS draped an arm over the shoulder of Dimitri Karras and laid the flat of her palm on his chest. She'd go to sleep now, drawing on the warmth of his body, spooned against him in the bed.

Over the gray-haired head of Karras she could see the framed photograph of Steve set on the nightstand beside the bed. Steve was at the Preakness with his oldest friends grouped around, all of them on an afternoon beer drunk, happy, high in the sun and secure in the knowledge that it could not end. In the photo, Stephanie, smiling and smashed as the rest of them, stood behind Steve, her hand on his shoulder, her fingers brushing the base of his thick neck.

The photograph had been on the nightstand for seven years. It was Steve's favorite snapshot of the two of them and his friends, and as long as she lived in this place, the one-bedroom condo they'd bought soon after they were married, she'd leave the picture where it had always been. Leaving it there after Steve's death was an act of neither superstition nor sentiment. The photograph *belonged* there. She saw no reason to move it now.

"Doesn't it make you sad?" asked Karras the week before. "I mean, to have to look at it every night before you go to sleep."

"It makes me happy to know that Steve and I had one day as good as that one. Most people never even get that."

"I couldn't," said Karras, his voice trailing off, and she'd hugged him then, the way she was hugging him now.

She stroked his chest. Karras had a decent build for a man in his late forties. Not like Steve, who'd always been on the heavy side. She used to call Steve "the Bear," because he felt as big as one, sleeping next to her. She liked to be with a man who had some weight on him. Karras had a handsome face, a straight back, and a flat stomach. Even at his age, he was the kind women noticed, and wondered about, on the street. But Karras was always sad. He didn't have Steve's smile, the kind that said he appreciated the moment and the people he was sharing it with. No, Karras wasn't Steve. But she was getting used to having him around.

Stephanie closed her eyes.

She enjoyed going to bed with Karras after the meetings and sleeping with him once a week. She needed the companionship, and she needed the sex. Their being together, it helped Dimitri, if only for the night, and she knew it helped her.

If she could have talked to Steve right then, she'd explain their relationship to him like that. And she believed he'd be happy for her, pleased that she was slowly finding her way out of the dark places she'd visited after his death.

She fell to sleep, knowing Steve would understand.

THOMAS WILSON had a slow drink at the Hummingbird on Georgia Avenue and got into his Dodge Intrepid, parked out front. He turned the ignition, hit the preset button, brought up WHUR. Quiet Storm: Every city in the country with a sizable black population had the format now, but the original had been created on HUR. And here was Gladys Knight, singing "Where Peaceful Waters Flow." You couldn't get much more beautiful than that.

Wilson headed over to Underwood, where he lived alone in the small brick he'd grown up in. Momma had died suddenly when he was away, back in the '80s. His uncle Lindo, who owned the hauling business, claimed it was from a broken heart.

None of the women in the bar had looked at him tonight. Seemed they never did. He wasn't yet forty, but he looked ten years older, and he felt far away from what was hip and new. He favored the music that he had come up with. He dressed like 1989. He still wore his hair in that same tired fade.

The truth was, he didn't have the spirit to mack the women anymore. With Bernie, it was easy to claim all that bullshit about how he, Wilson, "operated" up around the way, loved to "play in the nappy dugout" and every other tired thing you could think of. Boasting aside, after Charles had been killed there wasn't much fun in it anymore for real. He shared with many men the secret opinion that half the fun in hitting pussy was in talking about it afterward with your boys. Charles was his main boy going back forever. So it wasn't no surprise that Wilson's urge to slay the freaks had died with Charles.

The glow from the dash threw greenish light on the gray leather seats of the immaculate car. He cleaned the Dodge and had it detailed regularly at the brushless place near the Maryland line.

It was a beautiful car. He was always unhappy.

The meetings were good. The meetings helped. As the session day neared he looked forward to seeing these people who had become his friends. He liked hearing their stories, and going back and forth with Karras, and the idea that his personality—always up and funny in front of them—drove the group toward some kind of better place. That his being there with them made a positive difference in their ruined lives.

But after the sessions, he couldn't help feeling down. For various reasons, real or imagined, they all shared feelings of guilt. Wilson took solace in the belief that God and Father Time would take care of the rest of them. But he knew he'd never be healed himself. No, this sickness of his would never go away.

DIMITRI KARRAS stared straight ahead at the items on the nightstand: the photograph of Steve and Stephanie, an old Panasonic clock radio, his Swiss Army watch, a small stack of pocket change, Stephanie's hoop earrings. The red LED numerals changed to 2:31 on the clock. He'd been lying there, not at all tired, for the last two hours. Stephanie had fallen asleep long ago, the sound of her deep breathing filling the room. There was that other sound, too, always there at night in Karras's head.

When Karras was a boy, he was playing by himself one summer day in the alley behind his mother's house on Davenport. It was a still, hot day, quiet but for the drone of Mr. Scordato's window unit next door and the occasional call of cicadas passing through the trees.

Karras had been bouncing a basketball in the alley, distracted all afternoon by a vaguely putrid smell, the source of which he could not find. And then he saw the robin, lying beneath the apple tree that grew in the small square of backyard by the alley's edge. He found a small fallen branch, stripped it of its leaves, and went to the bird.

The smell got stronger as he approached. It was the awful smell of spoiled things, and he choked down a gag. As he reached the fallen bird and got down on his haunches, he could hear a sound, like the faraway crunch of soldiers marching on gravel, rhythmic, continuous, relentless. He leaned forward, slid the stick under the robin, and turned it on its side. Hundreds of writhing maggots were devouring the decaying bird. The sound he had heard was the sound of their feast.

Karras opened his eyes. For the past two and a half years, he had been paralyzed and haunted by grief. Staring at the photograph of a smiling Steve Maroulis, Karras wondered if Stephanie was haunted, too. If she ever pictured Steve in his coffin the way he pictured his son, lying in the dark beneath the ground in that small wooden box.

At night, when he could not sleep, Karras would see Jimmy in his coffin, rotted away and covered in maggots. And Karras would hear that steady marching sound coming from every corner of the room. He could shake the pictures from his head but not the sound. Never the sound.

"God, stop," whispered Karras, blinking tears from his eyes. It was strange, hearing his own voice speak those words in a pleading way. Invoking the name of God, this was a ridiculous thing for him to do, nothing more than a reaction, really, a habit unbroken from a churchgoing youth. Because he didn't believe in God, any kind of God, anymore.

Bernie Walters claimed that to live without God was to live without hope. And why, said Bernie, would anyone want to live in a world without hope?

Well, God was Bernie's crutch, not his. Karras had his own reason for staying alive. Since Jimmy's death, the feeling had never weakened. In fact, it grew stronger every day.

EIGHT

NICK STEFANOS caught an uptown Red Line car and picked up his Dodge in Takoma Park. He slipped Lungfish's *Pass and Stow* into the tape deck and headed back south via North Capitol. The band locked into a killer groove on "Terminal Crush" as Stefanos drove the Coronet 500 alongside the black iron fence of Rock Creek Cemetery.

At a stoplight just below Florida Avenue, he saw a woman pull a butcher's knife from the trunk of her parked car and wave it wildly at a laughing man. A dozen ugly people in varying stages of decay stood outside a corner liquor store, huffing smokes and drinking from brown paper bags. Behind them, taped to the store windows, colorful posters depicted beautiful black models promoting malt liquor and menthol cigarettes. A guy with matted dreads walked toward Stefanos's driver's-side window, one hand slipped into a bulged jacket pocket. Stefanos locked his door.

The Capitol loomed dead ahead, crowning the street. On this particular winter day, the press and public were fixated on the alleged extramarital affairs of the sitting president and giving odds on his possible impeachment. It was the media event of the decade, the subject of sarcastic lunch conversations all across town. But few talked about the real crime of this city, not anymore: American children were undernourished, criminally undereducated, and living in a viper's nest of drugs, violence, and despair within a mile of the Capitol dome. It should have been a national disgrace. But hunger and poverty had never been tabloid sexy. Beyond the occasional obligatory lip service, the truth was that no one in a position of power cared.

The man with the matted hair tapped on Stefanos's window just as the light turned green. Stefanos gave the Dodge gas.

NICK STEFANOS drove into Southeast and found a space on 8th Street. He walked toward the marine barracks, passing a real estate office, a women's bar named Athena's, an alley, and an athletic-shoe store fronted by a riot gate. He came to the Spot, a windowless, low-slung cinder-block structure in the middle of the strip. He pushed on the scarred green door and walked inside.

Hanging conical lamps and the light from a blue neon Schlitz logo colored the room. Stefanos hung his leather on a coat tree by the door and stepped off the landing into the bar area.

Ramon, the long-time busboy, was coming up from the cellar with two cases of beer cradled in his arms. Wisps of reefer smoke swirled behind him, the smell of it deep in his clothing. He was a little leering guy who wore a red bandanna on his head and scarred suede cowboy boots on his size-seven feet. Ramon stayed high throughout his shifts.

"Hey, amigo," said Stefanos, flicking Ramon's ear as he motored by.

"Ow. Chit, man."

"Did that hurt?"

"*Maricón*," said Ramon, showing capped teeth with his smile. "You lucky I got my hands full."

"Yeah, sure. Better get those Buds in the cooler, though. *Before* you kick my ass, I mean."

"I already got it all done. This beer is the last of it. The mixers, the liquor, the bev naps...everything's all set up."

"Thanks. I'll get you later."

Stefanos went toward the kitchen, passing the reach-through at the side of the bar. He could hear the radio, set on WPGC and playing the new Puff Daddy single, and the raised voices of Phil, James, and Darnell. Maria would be in there, too, making the salad special, quietly working on the presentation of the plates. Stefanos walked in under the bright fluorescents, stepping onto the thick rubber mats that covered the tile floor.

It was a small kitchen to begin with, way too small for what it had become. A stainless-steel prep table stood at the entrance, topped by dual steel shelves. The top shelf was lipped; live tickets were fitted into the lip in the order in which they came in. Beyond the prep table were two workstations, each capped by a steel refrigerator. The dish-washing station was located along the back wall of the room. On the shelf over the grill sat an Amana commercial microwave with a door that never closed on the first attempt. Over the sandwich bar sat the most important and most fought over component of any restaurant kitchen: the house boom box. Beside it, a Rudy Ray Moore poster, now gray with grease, had been taped to the wall.

Maria Juarez worked the cold end of the menu and James Posten, the grill man, worked hots. Their stations were on opposite walls, so that Maria and James's backs were to each other while they worked lunch.

Darnell, the bar's career dishwasher, had previously handled the lunch business himself, preparing the one daily special and placing orders on the reach-through, from which the day tender or the waitress would retrieve and serve them. In those couple of hours, Ramon would bus the trays in and wash dishes when he was able. But when the owner of the place, a smallish bespectacled man named Phil Saylor, had decided to expand the menu, he had hired Maria and James and made Darnell the expediter — the person who called out the orders, garnished the plates, and moved the lunches onto the reach-through. Since Ramon would be occupied out in the dining room with the extra table turnover, Phil had suggested they hire a new dishwasher, but Darnell, who had been washing dishes at the Spot since serving out an armed-robbery sentence at Lorton years earlier, wouldn't hear of it. He took a small raise and told Phil he'd get to the dishes after the lunch rush was through. The popularity of the new menu had surprised everyone, though — it was previously assumed that the Spot's regulars would not care to consume any substance that required chewing — and the three-hat arrangement with Darnell wasn't exactly working out as planned. Since the new system had been put in place, there was often high confusion in the kitchen during the rush, and the dining room had run out of plates and silver more than once.

"A little late, aren't you?" said Phil Saylor with halfhearted force, noticing Stefanos by the door. It was about as tough as the mellow Saylor got with his employees.

"I had an appointment," said Stefanos, his eyes staying on Saylor's, letting him know with his overly serious look that the appointment had to do with his "other" life. Saylor was an ex-cop, which explained the high percentage of plainclothesmen and uniforms among the Spot's clientele. Phil was retired, but the profession had never entirely left his blood. Invoking his investigative gigs was a cheap way for Stefanos to reach Saylor, but it worked.

"Try to make it on time," mumbled Saylor.

"I will."

"Nick," said James Posten, who sported a fox-head fur stole draped over his uniform shirt. "How you doin', man?"

James wore eye shadow and carried a walking stick with an amber stone glued in its head. He went six-four, two eighty, and most of it was hard.

"James."

"Ni," said Maria Juarez. Her reddish lipstick clashed with the rinse in her shoulder-length hair. She was on the short and curvy side, with the worn, aging-before-her-time look of many working-class immigrant women across the city. When she smiled her lovely smile, the hard life and age lines on her face seemed to fall away.

"Hey, baby."

"Check this out," she said, pulling a locket away from her chest and opening it up for Stefanos to see. He went to her, looked at the photograph of her gorgeous five-year-old daughter, Rosita, cut to fit the locket's oval shape.

"She's beautiful," said Stefanos, noticing the patch of discoloration on Maria's temple.

"She doing good in school," said Maria. "The teacher say she smart."

"How could she not be," said Stefanos, "with a mother like you?"

"Ah, Ni!" she said, making a wave of her hand, then wiping her hands dry on her apron as she returned, blushing, to her salads.

Darnell removed his leather kufi and wiped sweat from his forehead. The knife scar running across his neck was pink against his deep brown skin. "You got business in here, Nick? 'Cause we're trying to prepare for lunch."

"Just, you know, stopped in to brighten everyone's day."

"Yeah, well we gotta get this place set up, man."

"What're the specials?"

"Chef's salad," said Maria.

"Got a nice grilled chicken breast today," said James, raising his spatula in the air, affecting the manner of a school-taught chef. "Marinated it overnight in teriyaki, some herbs and shit. I'm not lyin', man, that bird is so tender you could fuck it— *excuse* me, Maria."

"Is okay," said Maria.

"Wouldn't want to lie about that," said Stefanos.

"Tell the truth," said James, "and shame the devil."

"Thought you were gone," said Darnell, trying to get around Stefanos.

"I'm goin'," said Stefanos, shaking Darnell's hand as he passed, then putting pressure on the fleshy, tender spot between Darnell's thumb and forefinger.

Darnell smiled, caught a grip on Stefanos's other hand, pushed down so that it bent unnaturally forward at the wrist. They stood toe-to-toe, grunting, until Stefanos yanked his hand free.

"All right, man," said Darnell, clapping Stefanos on the shoulder.

Stefanos said, "All right."

"You guys through playing?" said Saylor.

"Yeah," said Stefanos.

"So what are you still standing here for?"

"I was wondering, Phil," said Stefanos. "Could I have a word with you, out in the bar?"

"SO HOW well do you know this guy?" said Saylor.

Stefanos folded a dry bar rag into a neat rectangle, tucked it behind the belt line of his jeans so it rested against his hip. "Old family friend."

"How old?"

"His old man worked for my grandfather in the forties, when my grandfather had his grill over on Fourteenth and S."

"Okay, but how well do you know him?"

"I've run into him a couple of times in the last twenty years."

"Uh-huh." Saylor scratched his chin. "If his father worked for your granddaddy, then he must be pretty old."

"I'd say he's cruising up on fifty."

"He must be a real go-getter. Fifty years old and he wants to work in the kitchen of a joint like this."

"I don't even know if he does want to work here. A mutual friend of ours suggested it. You remember the Pizza Parlor Murders a couple of years back?"

"I remember it. So what?"

"Dimitri Karras's son was the kid who got run down by the getaway car."

"Christ."

"Yeah. This guy's no loser. The bottom fell out on him, is what it is. He's trying to put it together, and I thought we could help." Stefanos locked eyes with Saylor. "Look, Phil, the setup we got right now isn't exactly working out. Darnell hasn't caught a grip on the expediter position, and Ramon can't bus tables and wash the load of dishes we got with the business we're doing. Put Darnell back at the sink and bring Karras in to expedite for two hours a day. He's not desperate for money, so it's not a case of how much you pay him. It would do the guy good to just go somewhere every day. Get into the flow of normal life again, you know?"

Saylor pushed his glasses up on his nose. "You think he can do it? I mean, I feel sorry for the guy about his kid and all that, but I don't want to bring someone with emotional problems in here who's gonna screw up my business."

"Karras was some kind of college instructor if I remember right. And he used to run a multistore retail operation. So I gotta think he can handle this."

"Yeah, but does he have any restaurant experience?"

"He's a Greek, Phil."

"Good point. Okay, talk to him. See for yourself if you think he'll work out. I'm gonna leave it up to you. But I'm only gonna pay ten bucks an hour for two hours a day's worth of work. A free lunch goes with it, and a beer if he'd like. That's it, you hear me?"

"Thanks. You'll talk to Darnell?"

"Yeah, I'll do that. In the meantime, let me outta here before we open. You know I get too nervous when this place heats up."

Phil Saylor patted the John Riggins poster hung over the bar, then stopped to look at the framed Declaration of Independence print hanging by the service station. He smirked, reading the signatures of the Spot's regulars scrawled in childlike, drunken script alongside the signatures of America's forefathers.

"Hey, here's yours," said Saylor. "'Nicholas J. Stefanos.' I like that curlicue thing you did after your last name. And Boyle's name, you can barely read it. Jesus, you guys must have been drunk that night."

"I don't remember, to tell you the truth. But at least we had the sense to use the same color pen."

"Comedians," said Saylor. He was shaking his head as he headed for the door.

MELVIN JEFFERS raised his up-glass and said, "Another one of these, Nick. And give that Barry a little volume, will you? 'Cause you know this here is my favorite cut."

Stefanos kicked the house stereo up a notch. He poured rail

gin and a hair of dry vermouth into a shaker filled with ice, and strained the mixture into a clean glass. He walked the drink down to the last stool, where Melvin was in place, seated by the service bar. He set Melvin's martini on a bev nap.

"Here you go, Mel."

Melvin was the Spot's singer; every dive like this had one. He was the musical director during lunch—he arrived daily at noon and left promptly at two P.M.—and in this two-hour period he continuously sang along softly to the tapes, many of which he brought in himself. Melvin Jeffers was a small, neat man with an erect bearing. He wore clean traditional clothing and kept a close-cut Afro. He wrapped his hand around the stem of the up-glass, closed his eyes, and went into his best Barry White.

"'I don't want to see no panties,'" chanted Melvin solemnly. "'And take off that brassiere, my dear.'"

Stefanos hash-marked Melvin's check.

"Another Manhattan," said the man everyone called Happy, seated in the middle of the bar, staring straight ahead. A filterless cigarette, its untapped ash hanging like a wrinkled gray dick, burned down close to his yellowed fingers.

Happy's suit was aqua blue. His shirt and tie were kelp green. Happy wore clothes refused by the Salvation Army.

Stefanos made Happy his drink, which was not, strictly speaking, a Manhattan. Happy liked the sophisticated sound of the name but not the sweet vermouth which crowded the bourbon. Stefanos dropped a maraschino cherry in the glass, served the drink, and said, "Here you go, Happy."

"You put any liquor in it this time?" said Happy, talking from one side of his mouth.

"No. We're trying to cut back on our overhead."

Happy didn't laugh. No one had ever seen him even crack a smile.

Stefanos marked Happy's check.

"Ordering," said Anna Wang, the lunch waitress who had come on as a college student and stayed three years past graduation.

Stefanos went down to the service station, where Anna was taking a hit off his cigarette. She pulled the Camel from her mouth, smoke curling up into her nostrils. She wedged the cigarette back in the V of the ashtray.

Stefanos said, "That's called a French inhale, what you did just there."

"When in Paris," said Anna, making a quick gesture down the bar at Happy.

"What's your pleasure?"

"Three Bud drafts, a Light bottle, a sea breeze, and a frozen marg, no salt."

"Who's the frozen drink for?"

"Linda, that woman with the hair, from the Treasury? She's at table three."

"Tell Linda I don't do frozen drinks. She wants a Slurpee she's gotta go to Seven-Eleven."

"How about I tell her the blender's on the fritz?"

"Okay. Tell her that."

Ramon went by with a bus tray, brushing Anna's leg as he passed.

"I need silver," said Anna to Ramon.

"Okay, *chica*," said Ramon, giving Anna a quick wink for good measure.

Anna rolled her eyes and said, "If he'd spend more time getting the dishes and silverware turned over and less time trying to get in my pants, things would run smoother around here."

"I'm working on that," said Stefanos. "But I can't guarantee the little guy will leave you alone. He's like Jordan in the lane: not to be denied."

"Can I have that frozen marg—please?"

"No."

Stefanos got Anna her drinks: the beers, the sea breeze, and a frozen margarita, no salt. Anna dressed them and jockeyed them out to the dining room. Stefanos drew a third pitcher for two Department of Labor drunks, turned the tape over for Melvin, and refilled the coffee cup of a recovering alcoholic named Dave, who was reading a Howard Browne paperback at the bar. Stefanos made another Manhattan for Happy, served it, and emptied his ashtray.

"What's the special today?" asked Happy.

"Grilled chicken breast," said Stefanos.

"Any good?"

"Chef says you could fuck it."

"Gimme one of those," said Happy.

Stefanos said, "Right."

NINE

DAN BOYLE, a thick man with dirty-blond hair and pale eyes, ambled into the Spot at half past two. He sported a lined raincoat that looked as if it had been trampled by a horse, a worn Harris tweed jacket underneath, and a Colt Python holstered beneath the jacket. Dan Boyle had a seat across from the ice chest at the empty bar.

"Nick, how's it goin'?"

"Going good."

"Gimme the combo."

Boyle dropped his deck of Marlboro reds onto the mahogany bar while Stefanos poured three inches of Jack Daniel's into a beveled shot glass. He served Boyle the shot and uncapped a bottle of Bud that he had buried in ice. He pulled another bottle from the same place and put one foot up on the edge of the chest.

Boyle put down half his shot. His fingers were like white fish sticks, and they covered the glass. He picked up his beer bottle and tapped Stefanos's. Both of them drank. It was Stefanos's first sip of the day, and the beer was good.

Boyle made a head motion in the direction of the house speakers. "What're we listening to?"

"Gaunt."

"Cunt?"

"Gaunt."

"Y'know something? When Melvin takes off at two, the musical selection goes to shit around here. Does Phil know you play this stuff?"

"Phil doesn't care as long as the reading on the register tape matches what's in the cash box."

"I should complain."

"You are complaining. Anyway, Boyle, I don't see you running screaming toward the exit."

"You know I'd never do that." Boyle winked clumsily over the lip of his glass. "'Cause this here is my oasis in the asphalt desert."

Stefanos wiped his hands dry on his bar rag. "I read in the *Post* how you got a new boss."

"Yeah. The *acting* chief of police promoted a guy who's never worked Homicide."

"Nice picture of him in the paper."

"He's got a sweet smile, doesn't he? Like I'm gonna march into hell behind that guy."

"It won't make a difference. Guys like you don't really have bosses, Boyle. You're one of those rogue cops you hear about. Like the ones you see on TV shows. The guys who are always quitting, tossing their gun and shield on their lieutenant's desk before storming out of the office."

"Except I don't quit." Boyle waved his index finger around the top of the glass. "Hit me."

Stefanos took the Jack off the middle shelf and poured. "What do you hear about a kid named Randy Weston? He's up on murder charges for doing a dealer named Donnel Lawton. Up around First and Kennedy?"

"I'm not familiar with the case." Boyle lit a smoke. "Elaine Clay got you running on that one?"

"She mentioned something about it, that's all."

"You watch yourself if you're going to be hanging around Kennedy. People think, it's just off North Capitol and New Hampshire, it's residential, nothing's going to happen, right? I've seen some really bad shit go down on that strip. Remember the First and Kennedy Crew? The kid who shot up the police station a few years back, he was a member. Our guys were investigating a multiple homicide in that neighborhood the first time they brought him in. Things happen down there, brother. So you just watch yourself, hear?"

"Thanks, Dad." Stefanos put fire to a Camel. "So how're the kids?"

"Great. I walked into my daughter's room last night—she's all of thirteen—and I see this poster of a rapper hung on her wall. Wearing one of those slingshot swimsuits, too; the guy's got a crank on him that would scare a mule. He's one of those former drug dealers who make records now, raps about busting a cap in someone's head, fucking women in the ass, all that. The same kind of boofer I see on the street every day, lookin' at me like he wants to cut my throat. A dude bragging about being a cop killer and getting paid for it—that's my daughter's hero. And then, the same night, some guy calls for her on the phone; I can tell by the sound of his voice he's a common little street—"

"Boofer?"

"I was gonna say 'punk.'"

"I should have waited to read your lips instead of your mind."

"So I give the phone to my daughter, and I gotta watch her face light up for *him*. I tell my wife we ought to move, but where are we gonna go, huh? We already live in the suburbs."

"You could try Utah."

"Ah, I hear they got 'em out there, too."

"What do you want, Boyle? You think she ought to have a poster of *you* up on her wall?"

"Look, I don't expect you to relate."

"You're right; I can't relate. But I do understand you, Boyle. I got you pegged for just about the most enlightened guy I know."

Boyle smiled. "Good thing you and me have got an understanding, Nick. Nothing like spilled blood to hold a couple of guys like us together, right?"

Stefanos dragged on his cigarette, watched Boyle crush his dead in the ashtray. Boyle got up, drained his shot, upended his bottle, finished his beer. He dropped a five and some ones on the mahogany and walked out of the bar.

MAI, THE Spot's second-string tender, came in around four and ate her dinner at the bar. Mai was wide of hip, with round shoulders and a plain, kind face featuring rosy Raggedy Ann cheeks. At work she wore her blond hair pinned back in pretzels. She was a German with a green card and a weakness for marines. Conveniently, the barracks were right down the block.

"Where you off to tonight, Nicky?" said Mai. "Gonna see your girl?"

"What?" said Stefanos. "Do I ask you personal questions about Sergeant Slaughter?"

"His name's Sergeant DeLaughter."

"Go ahead and answer her," said Anna Wang, sitting beside

Mai with one of Stefanos's Camels hanging from her pouty mouth. "You don't need to be embarrassed. We're practically like your sisters."

"Does that mean we can take showers together?"

Mai laughed as Anna blew a smoke ring in his direction.

"How *is* she, Nick?" said Anna. "C'mon."

"Alicia's fine."

"That's all you're gonna say?"

"She's fine."

Roberto Juarez, Maria's husband, entered the Spot and stayed up on the landing. He was a humorless man with a thin mustache, hard forearms, and thick, heavily veined hands. It made Stefanos angry to look at Juarez's hands.

Stefanos put his head in the reach-through. "Maria! Your husband's out here!"

"I'll be right there!"

"So long, *señorita*," said James Posten in a musical way.

James came out of the kitchen, fully dressed for the weather, swinging his walking stick by his side. James cooked round-trip on the D.C.-to-New York Metroliner three nights a week, and he was off to work.

"What's this?" he said, making a gesture toward one of the house speakers.

"Beastie Boys," said Stefanos. "*The In Sound from Way Out.*"

"That's some beautiful shit," said James. "I thought they only shouted."

"They *play* on this one," said Stefanos. "Say hello to the Big Apple for all us provincial types down here."

"Closest I'll get to that apple is beneath Penn Station. But I'll make sure and soak up some of the vibe."

He waved good-bye to Mai and Anna, and walked toward the front door. Juarez did not step aside to let him pass. As

James went around him, Juarez smiled thinly and gave James a small air-kiss. James ignored him and left the Spot.

Maria emerged from the kitchen, a cheap nylon coat over her uniform. Her smile faded as she reached her husband. The two of them went quietly out the door.

"Phil said he wanted to talk to me," said Darnell, stepping off the rubber mats and coming out into the bar area, his full apron wet from the sink. "You know what it's about?"

"He's gonna get you some help for lunch, I think," said Stefanos.

"I told him I didn't need no dishwasher."

"It's for the expediter's position."

"Oh. Y'all don't think I can handle it, is that it?"

"We can all use help from time to time, Darnell."

"Uh-huh. Well, I'll listen to what the man has to say," said Darnell. "He *is* the boss."

Stefanos looked at Mai. "You about ready to jump in here?"

"Let me just finish the rest of this chicken. It's really tender."

"Nick's gonna take some home with him tonight, on account of it's so tender." Anna grinned as she stubbed out her smoke. "Just in case he doesn't hook up with Alicia."

STEFANOS LEFT a little rubber on the street as he gave the Coronet 500 gas on the green.

From the shotgun bucket, Anna Wang side-glanced Stefanos. "Nick, don't you think this car is a little noisy?"

"I put custom pipes on it. You know, dual exhaust. It runs more efficiently now, and it's faster."

"And noisier."

"I didn't notice."

"Everybody at that stoplight did."

"They were just checking out the boss lines on the car. You know what they used to call the shape of this model? 'Coke bottle,' on account of the way the metal cuts in on the rear quarter panels."

"You remind me of why I never dated Chinese guys. Those dudes, all they want to talk about is their cars and the next car they're going to buy. They're all gearheads, like you."

"I'm no gearhead."

"Yes, you are."

"You know, good thing you're cute. You remind me of this really pretty four-barrel carb I saw the other day."

"You think I'm cute?"

"Sure. If I wasn't—"

"Fifteen years older than me?"

"I was gonna say 'attached.'"

"You're attached, all right. But thanks for the compliment, Nick."

Stefanos pulled over on 7th Street, just south of the Mount Vernon Square Metro stop. Anna's apartment building, a beat-to-shit white building with white columns and forest green doors, was across the street. A guy wearing an army jacket and socks without shoes stood outside the door, insulting people who were walking by. A young man a half block south was leaning into an open car window, selling crack in the middle of the day.

"Now, go straight inside," said Stefanos.

"I thought I'd ask that guy up for a drink first."

"There's an idea. And then he could, I don't know, hack you up into little pieces while he cries for his mommy?"

"Thanks for the ride, Nick."

"My pleasure."

Stefanos watched Anna cross the street, one hand gripping

the strap of her backpack. She lived on the subway line, but he drove her home whenever he was able. Anna was his friend, and he couldn't stand to think of anyone hurting her. It wasn't just Anna; lately, he couldn't stand to think of anyone getting hurt at all.

LOU REED was singing "Perfect Day" from the juke as Nick Stefanos navigated the crowd at Rio Loco's on U at 16th. He found Alicia Weisman at the bar and kissed her on her mouth.

"How's it goin', sweetheart?"

"It's going good. How about for you?"

"Great, now."

Stefanos smiled. She had small, light brown eyes, great blossoming laugh lines, and a crooked nose. Her lipstick always overshot her lips. Her hair was in some kind of irregular-length cut, and the color of it changed every few weeks. No one would ever mistake her for double-take pretty on the street, but she was pretty to Stefanos, and looking at her made him smile.

"Mind if I sit down?" said Stefanos.

"I was saving the stool for you."

"I bet it wasn't easy."

"You don't know the half of it. I've been beating them off."

"That must have made them happy."

"Not like that, silly."

Stefanos had a seat, lit a cigarette for himself, lit Alicia's. The bartender placed a bottle of Bud in front of him. Stefanos chin-motioned the call rack, and the bartender returned with a shot of Old Grand-Dad.

"Ah," said Stefanos, sipping the bourbon and lifting his bottle. He tapped Alicia's and drank.

She said, "Hey."

He rubbed her back and gave her another kiss.

"What's up tonight?" he said.

"I was gonna go over to Arlington. Kevin Johnson's at Iota, and Dana Cerick's new band is the opening act. Plus, we just put out the seven-inch on this band that's playing a couple of sets at Galaxy Hut. I should drop by and see how they're doing. Wanna go?"

"Johnson's cool. But I think I'll pass on the Wilson Boulevard crawl."

"Afraid to go into Virginia?"

"Yes."

Stefanos had another round while Alicia nursed her beer. The booze was working, and he liked the feel of her next to him. He didn't want her to go. But Alicia and a partner ran a small record label in town, and much of her work was done at night.

"I gotta run," she said.

"Meet me at my place later?"

"Want me to?"

"Damn straight."

She kissed him and said, "Bye."

He watched her go toward the door. She had a spring in her step, and strangers were smiling at her as she passed. Stefanos felt lucky as hell.

STEFANOS DOWNED his third shot and took his beer bottle with him to the pay phone in the back of the house. Robert Plant was coming back in after the glorious Page solo on "Ten Years Gone," and Stefanos sang along. Some college guys playing a drinking game at a table smirked at him—an old-school guy with a load on, singing a seventies number—as he passed. He found the note Elaine Clay had handed him, dropped thirty cents in the slot, and punched some numbers into the grid.

He got an answering machine that simply said, "Leave a message."

After the tone Stefanos said, "Hey, Dimitri. Dimitri Karras. I hope I've got the right number. This is Nick Stefanos. I don't know if you remember me. Your father used to work for my *papou* down on Fourteenth Street back in the forties. You and me met a couple of times. My *papou* had you talk to me once when he thought I was getting off the track. Back in, like, seventy-six. Like I said, you might not remember. Anyway, I was talking to Elaine Clay today, and she said you might be interested in some part-time work. Well, it happens we've got an opening down at this little bar I work in, down in Southeast? Place called the Spot. On Eighth Street, about a block from the marine barracks. I was thinkin', I'm working a shift tomorrow, why don't you stop by after lunch and we could talk. I'll show you around, introduce you to the crew, like that....If you're interested, I mean. If not, no sweat. I mean, it's up to you. Well, here's my phone number, too, if you want to talk..."

Stefanos left his number and hung up the phone.

"Shit," he said, realizing then that he was half lit, wondering what kind of cockeyed message he had just left on the machine.

He went back to the stick and settled his tab. He bought a go-beer from the tender, slipped the bottle in the inside pocket of his leather, and left the bar.

STEFANOS IGNITIONED his car and turned on the radio while he looked in the ashtray for the tail end of a joint he had placed there a few nights back. There was a news brief on the radio: A local middleweight contender who had been in and out of trouble with the law over the years had been gunned down in the lobby of the cancer institute of the Washington Hospital Center, where he had been receiving treatment for a malignant tumor. The assassin had stood over him and emptied his gun into him after he had fallen. Five bystanders were injured by wild shots. The boxer was dead.

Stefanos had seen Simon Brown fight the boxer at the Pikesville Armory in Baltimore County when the boxer was coming up through the ranks. The boxer had taken himself out in the fifth round with an alleged broken hand. Even with that loss, the middleweight had been talked about then as a fighter with a future.

"A murder in a hospital, where people be goin' to get well," said the announcer. "Look, I'll say it again for y'all who haven't been listening. Black-on-black violence is wrong. We are killing our own people. This madness has got to stop. Don't smoke the brothers. Peace."

Stefanos found the joint, fired it up. He took in what was left of it and dropped the roach out the window. He opened his beer, took a swig, and placed the bottle between his legs. He pushed a Steve Wynn into the tape deck and pulled out of his spot.

Stefanos drove east on U, cut up 15th to Irving, and took that east, passing the hospital where the boxer had been killed. He liked to drive the city at night when he had a buzz, and he had one now. He found himself on North Capitol, and he took it north for a couple of miles, cutting a left onto Kennedy Street before the New Hampshire Avenue turnoff.

He knew all along he'd come here tonight. He turned the volume down on the deck and cruised slowly down the dark street.

He passed boxy apartment buildings, barber shops, braid parlors, hair and nail salons, a variety store, a Laundromat, a CVS chain pharmacy, two bars, a barbecue joint, and several houses of worship, including a storefront *iglesia* and the Faith Mission Temple, whose parking lot was fenced and topped by concertina wire. He passed the Brightwood Market, which seemed to be the center of the neighborhood; several young and not-so-young men stood outside, their shoulders hunched, their hands deep in their parkas and Starter coats. A couple of men were boxing playfully, feinting and dodging under a dim street lamp.

One of the men outside the market yelled something at Stefanos as he drove by. Stefanos went along.

He pulled over past the 1st Street intersection, in front of the Hunan Delite, a place that advertised "Fried Chicken, Fried Fish, Chinese, Steak and Cheese." The carryout was the last of several businesses on that particular hundred-block of Kennedy. A Lexus with custom wheels and spoiler sat parked in the six-space side lot.

Through the plate glass window Stefanos could see a kind of lobby and a wall-to-wall Plexiglas shield that separated, and protected, the employees from the clientele. A revolving Plexiglas tray, like a commercial lazy Susan, had been screwed into the middle of the shield. The tray took money in and was large enough to put food orders out. There was a printed menu posted above the shield that was normally lit but had been turned off. A young Asian guy, clean-cut in a turtleneck and slacks, swept the lobby behind a locked front door.

In his rearview, Stefanos saw a couple of the men from outside the Brightwood Market walking down the sidewalk toward his car.

Stefanos no longer worked at night. He wouldn't even think of getting out of his car here after dark. It wasn't paranoia. It was real.

He drove west.

*   *   *

NICK STEFANOS parked on Colorado at 14th and walked around the corner to Slim's, a small jazz club run by Ethiopians. Live music hit him as he went through the door into the nearly packed house. He wove around tables of middle-class, middle-aged blacks and one interracial couple. There was one empty deuce, and he took it, his back to the wall. He shook out a cigarette from his deck of Camels and put fire to tobacco. He dragged deeply as the waitress set a shot of Beam Black and a cold bottle of beer down in front of him.

"Thanks, Cissy."

She was tall and lovely, with clear reddish-brown skin. "You want to run a tab tonight, Nick?"

"I better."

Applause filled the room. The leader of the quartet, Marlon Jordon, took a small bow, his trumpet in both hands. The band had a hot rhythm section, and Jordon could blow. They launched into "Two Bass Hit" as Stefanos downed his shot. Heads were bobbing. Some of the patrons were keeping time with their feet, their palms slapping at the tabletops. Stefanos dragged on his cigarette and closed his eyes.

Beautiful. When it's this good it's fucking beautiful. I'll never stop drinking. It just feels too fucking good.

HE WAS drunk by the time he made it home. It was only a couple of blocks from Slim's, but he had driven it with a hand over one eye.

He walked around the back of the house to his apartment. Inside the door, on a small cherry-wood table, he saw the day's mail. Atop the stack sat an unstamped manila envelope, labeled with his name and address. He opened the envelope and examined its contents: the folder on the Randy Weston case. Elaine Clay had messengered it over earlier in the day.

Stefanos dropped the folder on the table and went into his bedroom. He could see Alicia's form beneath the blankets of the bed.

"Hey," said Stefanos.

"Hi," she said.

He got out of his shirt, removed his wristwatch, and dropped it shy of the dresser top. He bent down, picked up the watch, and put it in place. He unzipped his jeans and stumbled getting out of them.

"You all right?" said Alicia.

"Yeah. I, uh, had a few. I didn't realize..."

"Come to bed. Come on."

He got under the sheets. She was naked and warm. He turned on his side, and she pressed herself against him, kissing him behind his ear. He could feel her sex and her hard nipples against his back.

"Alicia?"

"Ssh."

She rubbed his back, and after a while he fell to sleep.

TEN

L**EE TOOMEY** lived on eight acres of woodland ten miles south of Edwardtown, on Old Church Road off the interstate. The old church, hugged by a stand of oak, had been gutted and rebuilt and now carried a new facade of white aluminum siding. Farrow passed the New Rock Church and a half mile later made the turnoff onto Toomey's gravel drive.

Toomey's utility truck, boldly lettered with the company name of Toomey Electric, was parked before his house alongside Toomey's black El Camino. Farrow parked the SHO on the other side of the truck, walked around a bicycle carelessly dropped in the yard, and knocked on the front door of Toomey's brick rambler.

Viola, Toomey's wife, answered the door. She had mousy brown hair, a nothing chest, a flat ass, and a buckshot of acne on her chin. Farrow didn't know how Toomey could stand to fuck her. Viola carried Ashley—a white-trash name for a kid if Farrow had ever heard one—their two-year-old daughter, in her arms.

"Hi...Larry."

"Viola. Lee asked me to come on out."

"He's back in the den."

She stepped aside, bumping her back on the wall. Viola was afraid of Farrow, and that was good.

Farrow went through a hall to an open kitchen, which led to a den with sliding glass doors giving to a view of thick, gnarled woods. Toomey, short gone dumpy with long hair and a full, red-tinged beard, sat in a recliner, staring through the glass. His chubby, featureless son, Martin, sat in front of the television set, his hand furiously manipulating a joystick as two armor-clad men fought onscreen.

Toomey had been a bad motherfucker up at Lewisburg when Farrow first met him, one of the Aryan Brotherhood who took shit from no one. He was the enemy of Roman Otis then, as well as Manuel and Jaime and T.W., but since he had found Jesus, his racial outlook, and general demeanor, had changed. He had not forgotten the con's code, though, and when Farrow had first called, he reluctantly told him to come down to the Eastern Shore, where he would introduce Farrow to a straight job and, it was implied, put him on the path to righteousness.

Toomey knew Farrow had been coming off some sort of heist. It was only later, when Farrow told him, that he learned about the extreme brand of heat that Farrow and the others had drawn. Farrow wasn't much worried that Toomey would rat him out; there was the code, and the penalty for breaking it would always be in the back of Toomey's mind. Toomey had a family now. Surely Toomey understood.

Jesus was the wild card. Religion was an irrational concept and it bred irrational acts. Toomey had been trying to get Farrow to join the New Rock Church for months now, and Farrow suspected that this was the reason Toomey had summoned him, once again, today. Toomey had gone all the way over for that full-of-shit new Reverend Bob, who had taken over the reins of the church one year back.

"Lee," said Farrow.

Toomey turned his head. "Larry."

Farrow stood over him, watched Toomey's fingers drum the arm of the recliner. "You wanted to see me?"

Toomey looked at his son. "Martin, why don't you go on out and ride your bike some, give Larry and me a little privacy."

Martin's eyes did not move from the television screen. "Chain slipped on my bike, Dad. Can't ride it."

"Just give us a few minutes here, son."

"I'm in the middle of my game."

Farrow went to the electronic box that sat atop the set and ripped the wires out of its back. Martin stood up, his hands wiggling at his side, and looked at his father.

"Go on, Martin," said Toomey.

Martin left the room. Farrow had a seat on the couch across from Toomey.

Toomey sighed and forced a smile. "Thanks for coming out, Larry."

"You can quit all that Larry bullshit, Lee. Call me by my given name. It's just you and me."

"Okay."

"What do you want?"

Toomey clapped his hands together. "Well, the Reverend Bob would like to see you. He's been asking after you for some time."

Farrow reached inside his jacket for a cigarette, lit it, shook out the match, tossed the spent match on a glass table set before the couch. The match made a yellow-black mark on the glass.

"What's he want with me?"

"Wants to bring you into the flock, Frank."

"He's a man of the cloth. That means he wants something."
Farrow dragged on his cigarette. "What's he *want?*"

Toomey looked away. "He knows."

Farrow flicked ash to the carpet. "Knows what?"

"He's a smart man, Frank. Got all sorts of degrees. He worked at Rikers for a while when he was younger, as some sort of counselor. He picked me out of the crowd the first week he came to town."

"You telling me he's blackmailing you?"

"*No*, sir. I donate my labor to the church because I want to. I rewired that entire structure, and I'm proud to say it didn't cost the church a penny. I'd do more if I could."

"That's nice. But how did he connect you to me?"

"He's seen us together this past year, once or twice in town. Seen you goin' in and out of the liquor store, too, the one on the interstate stocks those fancy wines?"

"So?"

"Like I say, he picked me out as an ex-con. I figure he picked you out, too."

"I'm gonna ask you again. What's he want?"

"I told you already, he wants to bring you in—"

"He wants money."

"A donation would be a part of you joining the congregation, yes."

"I'm just a dishwasher in town. Where would he get the idea that I've got money, Lee?"

"Now, Frank, you know...you know I haven't told him a thing."

Farrow stared at Toomey while he smoked his cigarette down to the filter. Toomey slid a glass of ginger ale across the table, and Farrow dropped the cigarette into the drink.

"I guess I better go see him," said Farrow. "He in today?"

"He drives a pretty Buick."

"There was a platinum-colored Park Avenue parked outside the church when I drove in."

"That would be his."

"I'll drop in on him right now, then, since he's being so persistent. Small town like this, can't really avoid it any longer, I guess." Farrow got up from the couch. "Say, Lee, you know that pistol you gave me when I first came down here?"

"Sure . . . sure, I remember. I was wanting to get rid of it for a long time, 'specially with kids in the house—"

"I took it up to that wildlife refuge they got, fifteen miles north of Edwardtown. You know, in the winter there's nobody on that land. Never even seen a ranger. Anyway, I tried that little gun out. Shot one of those white birds with the long legs that lives there. One of those birds they claim is protected. Anyway, that's a real fine weapon you sold me. Yeah, that pistol shoots real straight."

Toomey picked at his beard and stared at the carpet. "I ain't proud of the life I had before. And I am not goin' back to it, I can tell you that. Look, I don't want to have nothin' to do with guns anymore, Frank."

"I know it, Lee. Just wanted to thank you is all."

Farrow went to the front door; Viola stood in the foyer, holding her little girl. She reached for the knob, turned it, held the door open for Farrow.

"Good-bye, Larry."

"Viola. Ashley."

Farrow left the house. Martin was standing by the tree line, looking Farrow's way. Martin grabbed a branch to steady himself when Farrow stared back. Farrow smiled at Martin and walked to the Ford.

*   *   *

FARROW PARKED next to the platinum Park Avenue outside the church. He went to the church's varnished front door and knocked, and soon the door swung open. A large thin-lipped man with a gray pompadour stood in the frame.

"Reverend Bob?"

"That would be me."

"My name is Larry. I'm an acquaintance of Lee Toomey. Lee said you've been wanting to see me."

"Yes, Larry, thanks for stopping by. Please come in."

Farrow followed the reverend through a kind of lobby into the body of the church, which was done entirely in stained wood: wooden beams, wooden pews, paneled walls, a parquet-floored altar with a slatted wooden podium in its center. A wooden cross hung from the ceiling, suspended over the podium. A bible with an ornate gold-leaf cover lay open on the podium's face.

"Nothing fancy, as you can see," said the reverend, turning left at the center aisle, signaling with a wave of his hand for Farrow to keep moving. "I don't believe in marble and icons. Everything we collect in the form of donations goes back out in some form to the community."

"Nice carpentry work," said Farrow.

The reverend pushed on a side door, holding it open for Farrow.

"Local craftsmen did it for us on the weekends. Nearly everything in this building's been donated by the members of the congregation. Your friend Lee did the electrical work, free of charge."

"He mentioned it. You got a Buick dealer who's part of the flock, too?"

The reverend turned his head briefly as he walked down the stark hall. "How's that?"

"That's a pretty car you got out front there."

The reverend chuckled. "My one indulgence. Come along."

He led Farrow into an office and closed the door behind them. There were framed degrees and awards on the walls, no photographs indicating family. The reverend had a seat behind a cherry-wood desk and laced his fingers together, resting them on a green blotter before him. Farrow sat across from him in a leather chair with nail heads along its scrolled arms.

The reverend's hands were pink and soft. He wore a fine cotton, starched white shirt, onyx cuff links, and a black-faced watch with a small diamond set in the face. When Farrow was a young man, his father had worn a Movado watch just like it. The sight of it on the reverend's wrist tightened Farrow's stomach.

Farrow kept his eyes lowered in the hat-in-hands position. "What can I do for you, Reverend Bob?"

"I've seen you around town, Larry. With Lee and at other times, too. I'm curious—are you a practicing member of any particular denomination?"

"You're gonna have to cut down on the size of those words."

"I apologize. Do you belong to any church?"

Farrow shifted in his seat, trying to appear uncomfortable. "I did once. I'm afraid I've lapsed."

"It's never too late to come back to the fold."

"With all due respect, Reverend Bob, I'm not interested." Farrow tried a sheepish, down-home smile. "Besides, I make it a practice to have a few beers on Saturday nights. Sometimes I have more than a few, and on Sundays I sleep in."

"We have drinkers in our congregation, Larry. Drinkers

and womanizers and tax cheaters, and maybe worse. The service works for those folks, too. *Especially* for those folks. Our church is about atonement and forgiveness."

Farrow looked directly into the reverend's brown olive-pit eyes.

"I'm not interested," said Farrow.

The reverend looked away for a moment, then returned his gaze to Farrow and leaned forward over the desk.

"This isn't about just going to church, Larry. It's about how this church reaches out to greater Edwardtown. Why, just this morning I was making my rounds out at the retirement community on the edge of town, speaking to some of our senior citizens who are in the nursing ward. I sometimes bring them candy, cards, flowers...all of that costs money."

"Tell me, reverend. What do you tell those people, exactly? The ones who are going to die."

"Why, I tell them to have no fear. That the journey is just beginning. That they're going to a better place."

"And you believe that."

"Yes."

"I envy you, then. A man who doesn't fear death."

The reverend leaned back in his chair. "How do you know Lee Toomey, Larry?"

Farrow shrugged, pausing to re-create the story he had told others in the kitchen many times before. "I got family up in Wilmington. I was heading up to Delaware to see them a couple of years back, working my way north from Richmond, where I was living at the time. I took a ride into Edwardtown on a chicken truck, decided to spend the night.

"Well, I had a beer that night at this bar in town, and the bar owner had put this bulletin board up in the head. Lee had posted a card that said he was looking for help on this one job.

It was straight labor, really. I didn't want to go home and see my people with empty pockets, so I called him up and we met and he took me on.

"Anyway, I got to liking the town in those two weeks I worked for him. When the job was done, Lee, being the kind of man he is, got me an interview with the Royal Hotel's restaurant. Lee's in with those people; he's got their account. I took a dishwasher's job in their kitchen, and I been with them ever since."

"That's a nice operation they got there."

"They do real well."

"I had an outstanding dinner there one night, not too long ago: twin fillets with a peppercorn sauce, and some very good red wine. Their house red was outstanding. You know something about wines, don't you, Larry?"

Farrow said, "Why do you ask how I know Lee?"

"I was wondering if you knew him before he came to Edwardtown. From his past."

"I don't know anything about Lee Toomey's past, Reverend."

The Reverend's thin lips turned up in a gaseous grin. "So you like Edwardtown."

"Yes. How about you?"

"Well, I'll tell you. I've lived in New York and some other glamorous places, too. But it was always my dream to come to a small town like Edwardtown to build a congregation from the ground up."

And to fleece the local hayseeds for everything they have.

"I moved around a lot," said the reverend, "searching for I didn't know what until I came here."

Failure.

"And because I never had a wife or children of my own—"

Faggot.

"—this congregation has become my family. I'd like very much for you to become a part of that family."

Salesman.

"You mentioned donations," said Farrow. "What could I contribute? I'm unskilled labor. I don't see a kitchen here, so you surely don't need me to wash dishes. As far as dollars go, I have next to zero."

"We don't ask for much. Whatever you could afford would be appreciated. Most people think they have nothing, but if they cut here and there…Take you, for instance. You must have a little extra something, Larry. Maybe something tucked away beyond your dishwasher's salary?"

"What makes you think that?"

"Oh, I don't know. I just happened to be talking to my friend Harry, the gentleman who owns the Wine Shoppe out on the interstate. He tells me you come by a couple of times a week to buy, what did he tell me it was, some reserve California cabernet he stocks. What does that go for, Larry, thirty dollars a bottle? Now just think if you cut out one bottle a week, what it could mean to the people we reach out to in this town."

"That's not very Christian, is it?" Farrow said genially. "I mean, asking around about my private life like that?"

"I didn't have to ask," said Reverend Bob, his tone thoughtful and sincere. "Tell me, Larry. Where were you incarcerated, exactly?"

Lewisburg. San Quentin. Whittier and Preston reformatories before that…

"You're wrong about me, Reverend. I've never been incarcerated in my life."

Reverend Bob's voice went velvet. "I have no interest in your private affairs, Larry. If you have money, where you got it…I don't care. What you're doing here in Edwardtown is no business of mine. Neither is your past. Remember what I said: atonement and forgiveness. Now, I admit I tend to be overzealous at times. It's just that I'm so committed to building this church. I could use your help."

"I understand." Farrow forced a smile. "Give me a few days to think things over. We'll talk about this again, though. That's a promise."

"Take as long as you wish."

Farrow stood. "Take care, Reverend."

The reverend spread his hands and said, "Praise the Lord."

Farrow opened the door, closed it softly behind him, and walked from the church.

FARROW SAT at the bar of Linda's, a long, deep tavern on High Street that catered primarily to tourists and the town's lesbian population, sipping a Snow Goose Winter Ale. Farrow liked to come here early in the evening, before the live folk and jazz bands took the stage, when there were very few patrons. In this hour he could drink quietly and without conversation. He was careful not to overtip the bartender, a prematurely bald graduate student, as this would only encourage the young man to talk.

Farrow took his beer and walked past the billiards tables and shuffleboards to the rest-room enclave in the back of the house, where a pay phone was mounted on the wall. He dialed a two-one-three exchange and got Roman Otis on the line.

"How we doin', man?" said Otis.

"A situation came up here that I have to take care of. After that I'm ready to roll."

"Then I'm ready, too."

"You flush?"

"I'm about busted flat in Baton Rouge and waitin' on a train.

Supposed to see a man about that this afternoon. Man *owes* me some money. Gonna do that thing and then I'm clear. Could use a temporary change of scenery and some new prospects. How about you?"

"I've been living like a monk," said Farrow. "I'm doing all right, but it's time to leave."

"Where you want to meet, man?"

"You still got that cousin of yours likes to talk too much, did that Lorton jolt?"

"Yeah, Booker's out and livin' up there in southern Maryland, outside D.C."

"We'll meet at his place."

"Ain't we still hot up that way?"

"No. I read the D.C. paper every day. They've never had a thing. We've got unfinished business there, Roman."

"If you say we do, Frank, then we do."

"You mail off that photograph I sent you?"

"Did it. Listen, Frank…"

"What?"

"Remember my sister's husband, Gus? Tall guy on the white side?"

"Tall, hell. He's a giant. Polish guy, right?"

"Some shit like that. He played professional, Frank, long time ago. ABA ball. Was the backup center for the Spirits of St. Louis."

"What about him?"

"When I came out here, I was lookin' to invest some of my hard-earned cash. Gus had the idea we should loan out some of my money to those unfortunate citizens got themselves burdened with bad credit ratings."

"You got in the vig business. What did I tell you about that?"

"You were right. Didn't work out the way Gus planned. Gus feels real bad about it, Frank. Plus he and my sister Cissy need to put a little country between 'em for a while. So Gus is riding with me right now."

"He's all right?"

"Gus is solid. See, he couldn't play ball for shit, Frank. Oh, he could grab a rebound or two if the ball bounced right into his hands. But they used him for something else. The coach would tell him that a certain player had been ridiculing him before the game. Basically, they'd put him in the game just to fuck motherfuckers up. This is the man who made Artis Gilmore have bad dreams. Gus sent some starters to the hospital for real, ended a couple of careers. He's tough."

"Bring him along."

"Right."

"When can you be at your cousin's?"

"Gonna take me about a week to make it across country in my short."

Farrow said, "I'll see you then."

FARROW WALKED back into the bar. Grace, the waitress from the Royal Hotel, was sitting on the stool beside his and working on a vodka tonic. He slid onto his seat and lit a cigarette.

Grace smiled. "Thought I'd find you here."

"How'd you know it was me?"

"You left your Kools on the bar. Not many white men I know smoke Kools, and in the five years I've lived in this town I have never seen a black in this place."

"They've got their own bars on the north side of town."

"Yeah, it's great, isn't it? That's why I moved to the Eastern Shore from Baltimore. People stay with their own down here in Edwardtown. It's the way things ought to be."

"Your idea of paradise, right?"

"Well, it's not perfect." She lowered her voice. "A perfect world would be no niggers at all."

Grace laughed shortly while Farrow finished his beer and thought of his friend Roman. He noticed Grace studying her thumbnail. He said, "You all right?"

"I did this today at the restaurant. Sliced the nail halfway down to the cuticle. I haven't had a chance to cut it down or put a Band-Aid on it."

"You oughtta take care of that."

"I will."

"So, you about ready?"

"Where we going?"

"My place."

Grace swallowed the rest of her vodka, placed the glass down on the bar. "I was watching you this afternoon, Larry, standing over that hot sink. I like to see a man sweat. I like the way it smells."

"That a fact."

She leaned in to him so that her cheek touched his. She had a cheap permanent with damaged ends, and her hair smelled of chemicals.

Grace whispered, "Looking at you made me all wet."

Farrow stabbed out his cigarette. He signaled the bartender and said, "Let's go."

FARROW LIVED in a stone house fronting the Edward River. His efficiency was on the third floor at the rear of the house and held a double bed, bathroom, and porcelain kitchenette. The room's one window gave to a view of a cobblestone alley.

Grace sat naked on Farrow's bed, drinking red wine from a goblet. Her breasts were huge and heavy, with pink nipples as large as English muffins. She sucked in her stomach, watching him walk toward her in his underwear.

"You stay in shape," she said.

"Sit-ups and push-ups," said Farrow. "Every day."

"How long you been doin' that?"

"Long time."

"I gotta start doing something to break a sweat."

"Start right now."

She giggled and licked her lips clumsily. "This wine is yummy."

"You like it, huh?"

"I don't know good from bad, to tell you the truth."

He stood before her and said, "Really."

"I hope it's not expensive wine," she said. "'Cause I'm gettin' ready to waste a little. Hope you don't mind."

Grace got up off the bed. She took a long sip of wine and spit it out onto Farrow's chest. She put the goblet on the nightstand. She got down and licked the dripping wine from his stomach up to his chest. She licked his nipples and pulled down his underwear and played with his balls. He had an erection now, and he pushed her down on the bed.

Grace's head bounced on the mattress one time, and her eyes grew wide. "You like to play rough? I like it rough, too, Larry."

He pulled her to the edge of the bed so that her legs hung off the side. He fucked her like that, watching himself slide in and out of her, keeping his eyes there, imagining he was banging one of the many trophy wives he had seen walking through the lobby of the hotel. Thinking of doing those rich women the way he was doing Grace made him go even harder. He flashed on the reverend's pale face and got short of breath. He took Grace's hand in his own and worked his thumbnail under hers. His thrusts lifted her back off the bed.

"*Shit*, yeah," she said, spittle forming around the edges of her mouth.

When she came she sounded like a woman giving birth, and in the middle of her spasms Farrow ripped her thumbnail clean off. As she screamed, Farrow shot off inside her with a violent shudder.

He withdrew and stood over the bed. Grace was crying, thrashing her head from side to side. Blood snaked down her meaty forearm.

"I'm sorry," he said. "Grace, I'm so sorry. I didn't realize what I was doing, I was so excited..."

"Aaaah, God," said Grace. "God, God, God..."

"I've got some medical tape and disinfectant in the bathroom," said Farrow. "I'll be right back, and we'll fix you up."

In the bathroom, Farrow could hear Grace muttering the word "fuck" over and over again. He looked in the vanity mirror. Tears had formed in his eyes. His lips were twitching, and he put his hand over his mouth.

Farrow turned the bath spigot on full so that Grace could not hear him laugh.

ELEVEN

ROMAN OTIS drove south on Sepulveda, past gas stations, pager shops, drive-throughs, and big box retailers. The people weren't beautiful here, not like the blondes and moussed boys of Beverly Hills and West Hollywood, and trash littered the gutters and the small squares of worn grass fronting the boxy apartment units and Spanish ramblers along the boulevard. Otis passed beneath the freeway and drove into the lot of a garden apartment complex situated beside a dry drainage ditch with old tires and discarded toys lying in its bed.

"Be right back," said Otis, smiling, checking his gold tooth out in the rearview.

Gus Lavonicus watched Otis step along the walkway toward the apartments, not too fast, and not like he didn't have somewhere to go, either. He wore reverse pleated slacks, a lightweight sport jacket, a nice black polo shirt underneath, soft Italian loafers, those shades of his that adjusted their tint to the light, that ID bracelet with the funny inscription, and a previously owned Rolex watch. Otis had style.

Lavonicus looked down at his plain blue pants and the black

size-eighteen work boots he ordered special from the Real Man Big and Tall catalog. It wasn't like a guy his size had many choices.

Maybe Cissy would look at him with a fresh set of eyes if he dressed sharp like her brother Roman. Probably not. It seemed lately that nothing about him could make Cissy happy. She was having a change of life. Her periods seemed longer, and when she was having them she was meaner than any woman he'd ever known. He had asked her to look into some of that period medicine he'd seen at the drugstore, and at the suggestion she threw a fit. She screamed at him like his mother used to scream at him back in the mountains of Eastern Europe. Ah, his mother was a real screamer, too—he'd sworn he'd never marry a woman like that.

When Lavonicus played for the Spirits of St. Louis, Cissy would wait for him outside the locker room with all the other basketball whores. But Cissy was different—she had love in her eyes for him then. He guessed he was never happier, playing ball and getting paid for it and falling in love with Cissy back in 1975.

Those were a nice bunch of guys on that team, crazy but nice. They knew how to get him pumped up for the game. The coach would tell him that a player on the opposite team had laughed at him, called him Retard Man or something like that. A hard feeling would develop in his stomach, and he'd tell the coach he was ready to go into the game. He'd find the player who'd laughed at him and submarine that player as he went up for a rebound, step on his knee, maybe, when he was down on the court. Sometimes he'd just go ahead and drive a hard elbow into the player's Adam's apple if he could get away with it, or knock the player into the scorer's table when he was trying to save a ball from going out of bounds. After those things happened he would often be sat down, and upon his return to the bench his teammates would slap him five, laugh about it, pat him on the back. By then he'd feel a whole lot better. He'd look for Cissy in the stands—the Spirits were only drawing three thousand fans a game then, so it wasn't hard to spot her—and she'd give him a broad wink. Those were really good times.

He smiled and felt his eyes grow heavy. When he opened his eyes it was to the sound of the car door opening and closing, and Otis was beside him in the driver's seat.

"Got 'em," he said, tossing a small gym bag over his shoulder.

"Where to now?"

"Back across town to Silver Lake," he said. "Lonnie Newton's crib."

LONNIE NEWTON was a small-change coke dealer who had experienced a run of good luck in the past six months. Roman Otis had staked the original thousand that had put Newton in business, but as yet Newton had not repaid the debt.

Newton lived in a two-bedroom rental house set on a hill in Silver Lake, at the top of Cumberland Avenue. Otis drove the Lincoln over the crest of Cumberland, took it down where the road snaked along and narrowed for the next fifty yards, parked behind an old import with Jersey plates. A dark-haired woman got out of the import and gave Otis the fish-eye as she walked to her house.

"Whatever, baby," said Otis, taking a .45 from the gym bag, checking the load, and slipping the gun inside his jacket. He waited for the woman to enter her house. He waited for "Ladies Night" to end on the radio. He said to Lavonicus, "Come on."

They walked back up Cumberland.

"Here it is," said Otis, nodding at a narrow set of concrete steps that pitched radically up the hill and ended at a small house.

"I can only do this one time," said Lavonicus. "My knees, bro."

"Only gonna do it once," said Otis. "I promise you that."

They went up the steps, passing hibiscus and pine and a huge avocado tree whose top rose twenty feet above the roof-line of the house. As they stepped onto a wooden deck they could hear the thump of bass coming from behind the side door.

Otis knocked on the door. He waited and knocked again. The door opened, and a tall, lean young man stood in its frame. The young man frowned first, then smiled.

"Lonnie Newton," said Otis.

"Roman. Heard you were lookin' for me."

"Guess that pager of yours don't work so good."

"Aw, I left that old pager in a club, man, with some freak I was doin' at the time. Got a new pager now. Got a new freak, too." Newton looked Lavonicus up and down and said, "This your partner I been hearing about?"

"Gus."

"Aha, ha, ha," laughed Newton, stamping one foot on the floor. "Ssh, ssh, ssh..."

"You gonna ask us in, Lonnie?" said Otis.

"Better not. I got company."

"We won't be but a minute."

"Look here, man, I ain't got what you're lookin' for. Not here."

"Go ahead and ask us in."

Lonnie Newton shrugged and stepped aside. Otis went in, and Lavonicus followed, ducking his head to avoid the top of the door frame.

A small shapely woman in a short black skirt sat on the living-room couch, bobbing her head to the music coming from the stereo. The track featured a vocalist rapping languidly over an easy, scratchy wah-wah guitar with some popping bass behind it. The woman was hitting a blunt and did not look up as the men entered the room.

The living room fronted an open kitchen. A bedroom was set off to the right, and a stairway before it led down to a second bedroom. A bay window ran the length of the living room and offered a panoramic view of the city and mountains beyond.

"Turn that music down, will you, Lonnie?" asked Otis.

"What'samatter, man, ain't you down with it? Or would you rather be listenin' to the Commodores and shit?"

"Turn it down. Can't hear myself think."

"Thought you was Cali," said Newton, counterclockwising the volume. He looked at the woman, smiled, then looked at Lavonicus. "How about you, Frankenstein? You into the West Coast sound?"

Lavonicus's ears pinkened and his mouth dropped open as Newton laughed. Otis shook his head. The Newton boy was making a mistake. It was because the woman was in the room. Newton wouldn't show fear in front of his woman; that was understandable. But he was pushing it too far the other way. Some men were stupid like that. Newton was one of those men.

Violence didn't bother Otis, but it was usually messy and often costly, and he preferred to avoid it when he could. He thought he'd give the Newton boy a chance.

"Excuse me, young lady," said Otis to the girl. "Give us a few minutes alone, will you?"

"Go on, girl," said Newton.

She snatched the blunt up out of an ashtray and headed toward the stairs.

"Not there," said Newton. "Get in the bedroom."

She went into the bedroom, closing the door behind her.

"Nice-lookin' lady," said Otis, knowing then that the money was in the bedroom.

"Compton freak," said Newton.

Otis went to the bay window and scanned the view. "Beautiful up here, man."

"Yeah, the neighborhood's red hot. Madonna just bought a house out this way. Maybe I'll stop by and give her one of those personal housewarming presents you hear about."

"Think she'd like that, huh?"

"Pretty as I am?"

Still acting cocky, thought Otis. And the woman wasn't even in the room.

"You know, Lonnie, to live in a place like this you must be doin' all right."

"It's a rental. But, yeah, I'm doin' fine." Newton picked a rolled number out of his bag of dope. He lit the fatty and drew on it deeply. "You want some of this?"

"Maybe later."

"Your loss. 'Cause this here is some chronic motherfuckin' shit."

Otis turned from the window to face Newton. "Let's talk business, Lonnie."

"You mean that thousand dollars again? Told you I didn't have it here."

"Where you got it, man, a bank? You got no bank account, Lonnie, so don't be frontin' behind that shit."

"Look here, man," said Newton, gesturing with the joint in his hand. "Word is you're out of the loan business, Roman. Most of your clients done, what's that word, *reneged* on their contracts. It's like any business, you know what I'm sayin'? You make the rules, you got to enforce them. Otherwise, people just won't take you serious."

"Now you're gonna tell me how to run my business."

"I'm a man. Maybe I'm the only man you been dealing with lately. And, man to man, I'm here to tell you that your business is through. My debt is erased, hear? Not that I plan to forget what you did for me. We'll work out something away from the money side."

"That a fact."

"Look, man, you want my advice, you ought to just go ahead and concentrate on that singin' career of yours. I hear from a couple boys I know down on Sunset that you're not half bad. Your song selection's about twenty years too late, but there's money in that old-school bullshit now, you can believe it."

Keep talking, young man. Just keep talking.

Newton gave Otis the once-over with pink, sleepy eyes.

Newton smiled and said, "I like you, Roman. Tell you what. I got an OZ of cola in the back room. How about I lay a gram on you and your personal tree here, you two can do a little clubbin' tonight, have a good time."

"I don't want it."

"How about this, then?" Newton placed the joint in the ashtray, picked up a watch off the table, and lobbed it to Otis. "Nice Hamilton I bought off the street. It's yours if you want it."

"I look like I need a Hamilton? I'm *wearin'* a Rolex."

"Take it as a backup. Go ahead."

Otis studied the face of the watch and tossed the watch across the room.

"Silly-ass boy," said Otis sadly. "That ain't even a Hamilton. It's a gotdamn *Hormilton*, man."

"The money, Lonnie," said Lavonicus.

"The money, Lonnie," said Newton, mimicking the big

man's monotonous drawl. Newton clapped his hands together and laughed. "Aha, ha, ha...." He stamped one foot on the floor and went, "Ssh, ssh, ssh...."

Otis reached into his jacket, found the grip of the .45.

"The money," said Lavonicus.

"Damn, Gus," said Newton, "why you so serious? Someone forget to put the bolts in your neck this morning?"

Newton was laughing as he went and stood before a framed mirror nailed to a wooden beam that ran from the floor to the ceiling. He looked in the mirror with admiration, patted his nearly shaved head, smoothed it where the barber had cut a faint part on the side.

"I look good, too," said Newton. "Bitches be formin' a line outside my door, know what I'm sayin'?"

Lavonicus grabbed Newton by the back of the neck and slammed his face into the mirror. The frame flew apart and the glass seemed to disintegrate. Lavonicus released his grip and Newton fell back in a heap on the floor.

Otis pulled his hand from his jacket and looked at the wooden beam where the mirror had hung. The beam was splintered and dented at the point of impact.

"I kill him?" asked Gus.

"I don't think so. Go in the bedroom and find the money."

Lavonicus went into the bedroom. The woman sat on the edge of the bed, staring at the floor, her fingers wound tightly together.

"I'm not going to hurt you," said Lavonicus. She reminded him of a young Cissy.

He tossed the bedroom and found a rubber-banded roll of hundreds under a stack of sweaters on the closet shelf. Lavonicus took the money out to the living room, held it up for Otis to see.

Otis ran a glass of water in the kitchen, kneeled over Lonnie Newton, and poured the water over Newton's face. His face was slick with blood, and beneath the blood was hamburger. For a moment, as the water washed the blood away, Otis and Lavonicus could make out a riot of small cuts and one deep gash running from Newton's eye to the corner of his mouth. The cheek was filleted there, hanging away from the face.

Newton's eyes opened. He moved his head, and pink saliva slid down from his mouth to the floor.

Otis took Newton's chin and straightened his face so that he could see Lavonicus standing over him.

"Take a look, Lonnie. Just wanted you to remember it. That's a face you're gonna be seein' in your sleep."

"He'p me," said Newton sloppily. "Pleee."

"Gonna have to get your girl to help you, man. That is, if she still plans on hangin' around." Otis stood up. "By the way. You approve of how we, uh, *enforce* our rules?"

Otis rolled the Baggie of herb into a tight tube, sealed it with his tongue, and placed the tube in his jacket. Might be wantin' some herb on that cross-country ride. He turned up the volume on the stereo before he and Lavonicus left the house.

THEY TOOK the steps down to the street.

"Say, Gus—when you get mad, you ever do my sister the way you did Lonnie back there?"

"I'd never touch Cissy, bro. I swear to God."

" 'Cause you sure do got a temper on you, Gus."

"I pushed him too hard. I didn't judge his weight too good. He was way lighter than me, I guess."

"They're all lighter than you, man."

Otis and Lavonicus went to the car. Otis drove slowly down Cumberland.

Lavonicus said, "We got two thousand."

"Ought to be plenty enough to get us to D.C."

"What are we gonna do there, Roman?"

Otis adjusted his shades. "Frank'll get us into some kind of drama. You can *believe* that."

TWELVE

DIMITRI KARRAS entered the Spot a little after two the day after Stefanos called him and had a seat two stools down from a gray-complected guy in a baby-shit brown sport jacket. Karras rested his forearms on the bar, waited for the tender to finish marking one of several bar tab checks wedged between the bottles on the call rack. The bartender turned around and dropped a cocktail napkin in front of Karras.

He made eye contact with Karras and said, "Dimitri?"

"Nick."

They shook hands.

Karras saw a guy who kept late nights. A scar ran down one of his cheeks. There was silver flecked in the temples of his close-cropped cut. He remembered the boy with the curly shoulder-length hair, the skinny kid wearing the jeans and Sears work boots, standing in the warehouse of Nutty Nathan's, thumb-flicking the ash off a cigarette. Cocky, with everything in front of him. That boy was gone.

Stefanos saw a guy with gray hair and tired, dying eyes. He looked to be in shape, but the shell was hard and empty. No trace of the handsome, brown-haired ladies' man with the desperado mustache. Karras was only halfway through the race, but there was nothing left.

"You look good," said Stefanos.

"You too," said Karras.

"Yeah?" said Stefanos. "How about this? How about we say that's the last time the two of us will ever lie to each other?"

Karras chuckled. "Sounds good to me."

"Can I get you something?"

"No, I'm all right."

Stefanos leaned on the bar. "How long's it been, man?"

"Oh, I don't know. I was trying to think this morning. The last time I saw you was in eighty-six."

"The morning Lenny Bias died."

"Yeah. Every Washingtonian remembers what they were doing that morning, right?"

Stefanos nodded. "And before that, back around the Bicentennial weekend. My grandfather had sent you over to give me a talking to."

"I wasn't one to be giving you any lectures. But, hey, I tried."

"I didn't listen."

"You weren't supposed to listen. Hell, you were, what, nineteen years old? Which puts you at—"

"Forty. You?"

"Forty-eight."

The preliminaries were done. Stefanos struck a match, kept his eyes on Karras's as he lit a cigarette. "I heard about your son. My sympathies."

Karras nodded.

Stefanos exhaled a stream of smoke. Karras said nothing, and Stefanos took another slow drag.

Stefanos said, "So you got my message."

"Yes."

"You workin' now?"

"No."

"You interested?"

Karras had a look around the bar. Posters of John Riggins, Larry Brown, Phil Chenier, and Earl Monroe. A neon Globe poster advertising a concert by the Back Yard Band. A signed Chuck Brown glossy. An old Captain Beefheart, *The Spotlight Kid*, playing on the stereo. Some quiet patrons, a couple who looked like cops, none who looked like lawyers. No green plants.

Karras said, "Maybe."

A young Asian waitress with nice wheels bellied up to the service bar and said, "Ordering."

"Excuse me a second," said Stefanos. He went down to her, retrieved some bottles from the cooler, and set them on a bar tray.

When he returned, Karras said, "Elaine tells me you're a private investigator."

"Well, not exactly private. I do work for the public defender's office down there. I work for Elaine exclusively."

"Nothing else, huh?"

"Not anymore." Stefanos crushed out his cigarette. "You wanna meet the folks in the kitchen?"

"Sure." Karras slid off his stool and walked along the bar. "Who's the guy in the brown suit?" he asked, jerking his thumb over his shoulder.

"His name's Happy."

"He doesn't look too happy to me."

"He's pacing himself," said Stefanos.

Maria Juarez and James Posten were dancing to the salsa

music coming from the boom box when Karras and Stefanos entered the kitchen. Maria had the flat of her palm on her stomach and was moving two steps forward, two steps back, smiling at James, who was counting out his steps, twirling, holding a spatula up at head level.

"Cha-cha-cha, *señorita*," said James. "We havin' us one of those carnivals now."

"Watch my feet, Jame," said Maria.

Darnell stood over the sink, the hose in his hand, his back to the door, one foot tapping time to the beat.

"Hey, everybody," said Stefanos as the song ended. "Meet Dimitri Karras, the guy I was telling you about."

Stefanos had briefed them earlier, told them that Karras might be dropping by. Darnell turned and appraised him; Maria did the same.

James turned the volume down on the box, crossed the room, and shook Karras's hand. "How you doin', man? James."

"Dimitri. Good to meet you."

"James is the grill man," said Stefanos. "And this is Maria — colds and salads."

"My pleasure, Mitri."

"My hands are kinda wet," said Darnell. "So you'll understand if I don't come on over there."

"It's all right," said Karras, but Darnell had already turned back to the sink.

Ramon came in, deliberately bumped Stefanos as he passed.

"Ramon's our busboy," said Stefanos. "And the bar-back. And the all-purpose resupplier. Anything that's stored down in the basement, you let Ramon get it."

"We got some serious rats in that basement," said James. "You wouldn't catch me down in that motherfucker on a bet. Excuse me, Maria."

"Is okay."

"Ramon brings in the lunch tickets along with the bus trays," said Stefanos.

"'Cause we don't want no waitresses comin' around here," said James, "pressuring us to get their food out."

"The waitress always in a horry," said Maria.

"A beeg horry," said James. "You got that right, *señorita*."

"Ramon will set the ticket down in front of you. You'll slip the ticket in the lip of the top shelf, right here, in the order it came in. Then you call out the order. The time on specials varies. Salads are premade, so they're always ready to go. Burgers take longer to cook, obviously, so you'll want to call those out first, then call out the cold sandwiches from the same ticket later on."

"Don't want to have my burger up there, gettin' cold," said James, "while you're waiting on Maria to put up a chicken salad on toast."

"Right," said Stefanos. "It can get complicated sometimes. The object is to have the hots and the colds from the same ticket come to you at the same time. Maria and James talk to you, let you know where they are in the process. You check the order against the ticket, garnish it, put it out on the reach-through when it's ready to go."

"Ain't all that big a deal, Dimitri," said James, who went to the box and scanned off the Spanish AM station, finding an R&B/disco station on the FM dial.

"My music time up already?" said Maria.

"Yeah," said James. "We back to my joint now."

James closed his eyes and began to sing soulfully to the Seal cut coming from the box, Karras noticing the purple eye shadow on his lids. Past James, Darnell had his arms raised above his head. Ramon was punching Darnell in the stomach with short, alternating jabs.

Darnell smiled. "C'mon *with* it, little buddy. That all you got?"

"Any questions?" said Stefanos to Karras.

"I guess not. Not right now." Karras said to the others, "Nice meeting you all."

"Nice to meet you, man," said James, and Maria gave him a smile.

Stefanos and Karras left the kitchen and stood by the service bar.

"I got the impression Darnell wasn't too happy to see me," said Karras.

"Darnell's a man," said Stefanos. "You're taking away some of his responsibilities. He's a little hurt, maybe, but he'll get over it. And we do need the help. Think you can handle it?"

"Yeah, but—"

"The pay's twenty dollars a shift, cash. That's a hundred a week. Including a lunch and a beer, if you want it. It isn't much, I know. Walking-around money, basically."

"I don't have a problem with the money—"

"Good." Stefanos handed Karras a paper menu. "Here. Have a look at this tonight. Course, you won't learn a thing until you jump in. But familiarize yourself with it anyway. Be here about eleven-thirty tomorrow. Okay?"

Karras said, "Okay."

"See you then." Stefanos lifted the hinged gate and stepped behind the bar.

Karras neared the Asian waitress as he headed for the door.

"Dimitri Karras," he said, stopping in front of her and extending his hand.

"Hey," she said, shaking it. "Anna Wang."

Karras was out on the sidewalk, buttoning his coat, when he realized he had taken a job.

THIRTEEN

"ALL RIGHT, James," said Dimitri Karras. He squinted at the ticket hanging in front of him. "I've got a cheddar, medium. A bacon cheddar, medium rare. A provolone, medium. And—"

"Stop there, Dimitri," said James Posten. He dropped three burgers on the grill. "Cheddar medium, provolone medium, bacon cheddar, medium rare."

"That's right."

"Go ahead, man."

"A chicken steak, no cheese, everything."

"Got it. Here comes your hot pastrami, buddy."

Maria Juarez was humming as she halved an egg-salad sandwich on white and put it on a plate. She slid it onto the shelf just as James delivered his pastrami. Karras garnished both sandwiches with chips and pickle spears, pulled the corresponding ticket from the lipped shelf, and placed the two plates on the reach-through. He rang the hotel desk-style bell there with a strike of his palm and said, "Order up!" into the space.

Mai put her head in the space, slapped a ticket on the wood, picked up her order, and carried it away. Karras took the ticket and put it in the back of the line on the lipped shelf.

"Another special," said Karras, reading the ticket. "Darnell, your meat loaf's really moving today. Looks good, too. I know what I'm having for lunch."

"Don't get your heart set on it for lunch." Darnell stood over the soak sink, his back turned to the rest of the kitchen. "How many you think we served?"

Karras checked the hash marks on a pad he kept by his side. "Fifteen by my count."

"I only cut sixteen out of that piece."

Ramon came through the door with a bus tray. As he went by, Karras said, "Ramon, when you go back out to the floor, tell Mai and Anna: eighty-five on the meat loaf."

"One mo?"

"Right."

"Dimitri," said James. "These burgers gonna be up in a minute. You can call out your colds."

"Thanks, James. All right, Maria. I need a cold cut, everything, no onions. A tuna on rye, plain. And a Maria's salad."

Maria laughed. "Jame, the salad moving!"

"I know it, *señorita*. Good thing you put your name on that one, because it *is* your masterpiece."

Anna Wang walked in, put a ticket in front of Karras. "Food's coming out great, everybody."

"Thanks, baby," said James. "But I know you didn't come in here to shower us with compliments."

"Well, I *was* wondering about the order for my eight-top."

"You can just get your hot little self back on out there, too."

"All right, I'm gone." Anna buzzed out of the kitchen.

"Hit me, Dimitri," said James. "I'm all caught up."

Karras gave James the new hots, repeated the order, studied

his tickets, rearranged them according to cooking times. James crowded the grill with meat, then went to the radio and turned it up.

"Luther Vandross," said James. "Sing it, my brother." James sang the chorus of the song in baritone. Maria looked at him and cracked up. The two of them laughed, hugged each other briefly, then split apart and went back to their stations.

"Jame likes Luther," explained Maria to Karras with a smile. There was a blue mark under her right eye.

"Luther is *serious*," said James, transferring the burger order onto plates. "I remember listenin' to him when he sang for that group Change, didn't even have his name on the cover of the album, and I can remember thinkin', who the fuck is *this?*"

"You ready, Maria?" said Karras.

"Go ahe, Mitri."

He recited her colds. He didn't repeat the order because by now he knew that you never had to tell Maria twice.

Darnell turned his head halfway around, watched Karras work. Karras was doing a good job, and for a moment Darnell thought he'd tell him. But the moment passed, and Darnell went back to his dishes and the sink.

KARRAS SAT at the bar, eating the last of the meat loaf with a side mound of garlic mashed potatoes with gravy pooled in its center. Darnell made a nice meat loaf, not too dry, with just enough onion in it to give it taste.

Karras liked this time of the afternoon. He had done a good job at lunch today, and that was something in itself. He'd prepared his own food after the rush while Maria listened to her half hour on the Spanish station, wrapping her salads away for the night. Then he'd brought his food out to the bar and eaten it quietly, his personal reward. This had been a good day.

A beefy guy in a tweed jacket sat two stools down to Karras's right, nursing a shot of something along with a beer. Karras only knew him as the Irish homicide cop who frequented the Spot. Down the bar sat Happy, staring straight ahead, and beyond Happy sat a couple of GS-10s, arguing over sports trivia while splitting their second pitcher of draft. Mai was behind the stick, her arms folded, a cigarette in one of her thick hands, listening intently to the Carpenters mix she had going on the box.

Karras considered today's lunch. It had gone well. His first few days on the job had been pretty rough; there were a couple of times, when he was in way over his head and the tickets were flowing into the kitchen in bunches, that he thought of just bolting. He'd heard restaurant people talk about being "in the weeds," and that's how it felt. You couldn't see your way out, and the next step was panic.

But it had worked out. And every day he grew more confident and got better at his job. He had begun to figure it out: the rhythm, the personalities, the way James and Maria interacted, knowing when James could take a hot call, watching his body language signal overload and knowing when to pull back and wait. Working the kitchen was a kind of challenge, and he was beginning to beat it. And there was the other thing, too. During the lunch rush he could only think of the task at hand. For two hours every day, he could forget.

"You mind?" said the Irish cop.

Karras looked over. The cop was putting a match to a cigarette.

"No, go ahead."

Darnell came from the kitchen and had a seat next to Karras at the bar. He removed his leather kufi and wiped his face with a bar napkin. Mai drifted over and Darnell said, "Mix me up one of your specials, Mai."

"You got it," said Mai.

"So, Dimitri," said Darnell, "how's that meat loaf?"

"Beautiful," said Karras. "I was afraid I wasn't gonna get it, the way it was moving."

"The heel's the best part anyway, you ask me."

Mai served Darnell a mixture of pineapple and orange juice. He thanked her and had a long sip.

"How long have you been cooking?" said Karras.

"I started back when I was doin' this little stretch at Lorton. I guess Nick's already told you about that. I got a job in the kitchen as a dishwasher. This guy that had been cooking for years there kind of took me under his wing."

"You're good at it."

"Yeah, I can put a meal together, I guess. Thing is, Phil doesn't let me stretch out too much here. Wants to keep this a meat-and-potatoes, middle-of-the-road, bar-food kind of place. I'd like to do a whole lot more."

Karras pushed his empty plate to the side. "Listen, Darnell..."

"You don't have to say nothin', man. You're doin' a good job. Things have been running smoother since you got here, and I'm happy about that. I just wasn't suited for that position, that's all."

"You were trying to do too much, is what it was. I can't take too much credit, either. I've had a lot of help. James and Maria have been great."

"Yes, those two sure can do it. 'Specially Maria. She can sense when that food's coming off the grill, like she's seein' behind her back."

Karras drummed his fingers on the bar. "Let me ask you something about Maria."

"Go ahead."

"I've noticed marks on her face—"

"Her husband. He drinks at night and sometimes he drinks too much. When he does, he beats her."

"Can't we do anything?"

"Nick asked her if she wanted us to report the guy. She said no. I think she's afraid. Afraid for herself but mainly for that beautiful girl of hers. So there it is. Everybody's got their own little world of problems they got to deal with, man. We're all out here just doin' the best we can."

Darnell swallowed the rest of his juice and got up off the stool.

"Thanks, Darnell."

"Let me get on out of here and back to those dishes."

Darnell headed toward the kitchen.

"What's up, Darnell?" said the cop.

"Officer Boyle." Darnell didn't stop or turn his head.

When Darnell had entered the kitchen, the cop leaned over, extended his hand, and said, "Dan Boyle."

"Dimitri Karras."

They shook hands.

"Yeah, Nick told me your name. I said to him, Now we got two Greeks in this joint."

"Uh-huh."

Karras hoped that would end the conversation. There were certain kinds of drinkers who had a sleepy kind of cruelty in their eyes. Boyle had that look—and he was a detective in the bad bargain. Along with everything else, Karras had lost his faith in cops.

Boyle said, "You know, when I asked Nick who the new guy was and he told me your name, it rang a bell. It wasn't just that your name had been in the papers a few times these last couple of years."

"Yeah?" So this Boyle character knew about the murder of his son.

"Yeah, it was something else."

"What was it?" asked Karras tiredly. "You figure it out?"

"Well, it turns out it was your last name I was picking up on. I have this uncle, Jimmy Boyle, was a beat cop in this town and then a homicide detective later on. I'm going back to the forties, understand? Anyway, I can remember, even as a kid, my uncle talking about this friend of his he grew up with, back when the poor immigrants lived in Chinatown. I don't know the story, but my uncle claims this guy had something to do with him getting his gold shield. Pete Karras was his name. He died before I was born, so I never met him or anything like that. But around my uncle it was always Pete Karras this and Pete Karras that."

"Pete Karras was my father."

"Christ," said Boyle, "wait till I tell my uncle."

"He's alive, huh?"

"Yeah, he's alive. Boy, I had a feeling, too."

Boyle finished his shot with a quick toss. Karras noticed the butt of Boyle's revolver beneath his jacket as he threw his head back to drain his beer. Boyle took a last drag off his smoke, crushed the cherry in the ashtray, stood up, and left a heap of ones on the bar.

Boyle went over to Karras and squeezed his shoulder. He leaned in close. Karras could smell the whiskey and nicotine on his breath.

"Nice meeting you," said Boyle. "My sympathy for the loss of your son."

Karras nodded but said nothing. Boyle left the bar.

FOURTEEN

NICK STEFANOS parked his Dodge between the customized Lexus and a black Maxima in the Kennedy Street lot beside Hunan Delite, where Jerry Sun, the partial witness in the Donnel Lawton case, was employed.

Today Stefanos wore his version of a uniform: blue Dickies pants, a blue shirt, and a charcoal waistcoat. He carried a cell phone that he had rigged to an oversize case.

The blue shirt and pants, the phone that looked like a pack set—he wasn't impersonating a cop, exactly. But he looked enough like the species to give pause to the people he was hoping to talk to on the street.

Stefanos pushed open the door of Hunan Delite. Lunch was over, and there was only one customer, an obese woman in tights and a sweatshirt, in the lobby. She leaned her back on a red eat-in counter and avoided eye contact with Stefanos.

The place smelled of fried food and grease. A speaker mounted in the lobby was set on PGC. Callers to the station were giving their shout-outs to friends, family, and lovers.

Stefanos went to the lazy Susan contraption set in the

Plexiglas wall. An old Asian woman came forward and stood before him, spoke through several teardrop cutouts in the glass.

"What you have?" she asked.

Stefanos opened his billfold. Inside was his investigator's license, a photo ID that simply said "Investigator," white letters against a red background, barred across the top. He placed the open billfold flat against the glass and spoke into the cutout teardrops.

"I want to speak to Jerry Sun. Could you get him, please?"

The woman left without a word. Stefanos heard a foreign tongue in a raised voice. He waited. A clean-cut young man in a black turtleneck came to the glass. It looked like the same young man Stefanos had seen the night he had driven by.

"Yes?"

"Jerry Sun?"

"That's right."

"I'm an investigator working on the Donnel Lawton case."

"I've already talked to the detectives, two times."

"I have a few more questions, if you don't mind."

Jerry Sun looked over his shoulder, then back at Stefanos. "Go around the store and meet me behind."

"See you there."

The obese woman studied Stefanos as he walked out the door.

Jerry Sun stood against the brick wall beside the rear entrance to the kitchen. As Stefanos approached, he noticed the tail of a rat disappear beneath a nearby Dumpster.

"Nick Stefanos."

Stefanos offered his hand. Sun took it tentatively.

"Make it quick, okay? I've got to get back inside."

"You run this place?"

"With my mother."

A couple of young men passed by on the sidewalk. One of them yelled, "Hey, Jerry-San, whassup?" His friend laughed.

Jerry smiled tightly and half-waved back.

Stefanos said, "You get that much?"

"Sure, all the time. Customers ordering in a Chinese accent. People who make fun of my mother."

"But you stay."

Sun shrugged. "I'm the oldest son of six children. It was my responsibility to stay. This place has put three of my siblings through college."

"Not you?"

"The birth order decided my fate. It was just an accident. But I accept it." Sun lost his frown. "Don't get me wrong; it's not so bad. There are people who mock us, but there are plenty of nice people down here. I grew up in Montgomery County. But in some ways I've grown up with a lot of these neighborhood people, too."

"Known many who've died?"

"Yes."

"Donnel Lawton?"

Sun touched the right stem of his rimless glasses. "I knew him by sight, yes."

"How about the guy who was accused of killing him?"

"Randy Weston? I knew him as well."

"Better than Lawton?"

"We played together, right where we are standing, a couple of times when we were children. He showed me how to put a spiral on a football, something my father would not have known. But that was a long time ago. We didn't speak as adults except when he was giving me a food order or I was taking it. He showed me respect, nothing more."

"Was Weston in the life?"

"I've heard that both Weston and Donnel Lawton sold drugs. But if they did, it was minor. Neither of them was the kingpin down here, this much I know. Listen, I've already told this to the police."

"I'm not the police. I'm working for the lawyer defending Randy Weston."

"I don't mind cooperating, but I've told the police everything I know."

"All right, I'll try not to drag this out. A couple of quick questions here..." Stefanos opened the loose-leaf pad on which he kept his notes. "You told the police you heard gunshots the night of the Lawton murder. That was at what time?"

"Just after nine-thirty at night."

"How do you know it was nine-thirty?"

"Just *after* nine-thirty. Because we close then, and I had just locked the door."

"You recognized the sounds as gunshots?"

"Two gunshots, yes. And I know what that popping sound is."

"When you heard the shots, were you in the lobby or behind the Plexiglas?"

"In the lobby, sweeping up."

"So you could see clearly through the front window."

"Yes."

"Let's see....After the gunshots, you say you heard rubber laid on the street, then saw a red Ford Torino blow by."

"That's right."

"The boxy version from the sixties or the more rounded version from the early seventies?"

"Rounded."

"Color?"

"Red." Stefanos saw a light in Sun's eyes. "Like I already told the real cops."

"What about tags?"

"No tags."

"You mean you couldn't make out the state?"

"I mean the car had no tags on it. That much I could see."

"Okay. I'm not gonna keep you, Jerry." Stefanos handed Sun his card. "Mind if I call you if I think of something I missed?"

"Sure." Sun's eyes lit with amusement once again. "Just call information and ask for Hunan Delite."

Stefanos grinned. "This city's probably only got, what, a hundred or so of those in the phone book?"

"Yeah, it took a long time for my family to come up with the name."

"You spelled 'Delight' wrong. You aware of that?"

"You're very funny."

"I'm trying."

"The thing is, we barely sell any Chinese food. Some fried fish, and then the rest is steak and cheese. 'Steak and cheese everything,' that's what I hear all day."

"Thanks for your help," said Stefanos.

"That your Dodge parked next to my Lexus?" said Sun.

"Yeah."

"Those pipes. You put them on yourself?"

"They're Borlas. I bought 'em through *Hot Rod* and had them installed."

"Nice."

"Take care, Jerry."

Sun waved and walked away.

STEFANOS WALKED across the street to the Brightwood Market and stopped the least threatening looking young man he could find. He identified himself as an investigator and asked the man if he had been acquainted with either Donnel Lawton or

Randy Weston. The young man shook his head. He asked him if he had heard anything on the street or had any knowledge at all about the murder. The man walked off without a word.

Stefanos had spoken loudly in hopes of getting a blind response to the names from the other men who stood around outside the market. He heard an obscenity muttered and looked around: A couple of the men stared at him with smirking eyes. He asked them as a group if any of them had known Donnel Lawton or Randy Weston. They ignored him completely.

In the year he had worked for Elaine Clay as an investigator, he had been threatened several times in a benign way, slapped across the face by a woman on the doorstep of her row house, and chased down the street by a clubfooted drunk wielding a butcher knife. There had been no serious incidents. This was as much due to luck as it was to the precautions he had taken in his manner and dress.

And there was something else, too. A black man could seriously injure or kill another black man in town and get a tepid response from the police and the press. When a black attacked a white, though, the cops and the media came down hard on both the perpetrator and the neighborhood. It had always been that way. As a white investigator in a predominantly black city, Stefanos had an edge.

There was nothing here for him today. He hadn't expected there to be. He glanced at the market's windows and down along the concrete landscape as if he were looking for something in particular, and then he walked back to his car.

RONALD WESTON lived with his mother and younger sister in an apartment on 9th, between Missouri and Peabody, about a mile northwest of 1st and Kennedy. The radio towers of the Fourth District Police Headquarters rose behind the roofline of the complex, a half dozen boxy units with screened porches in the rear.

Stefanos parked on 9th. He had phoned Ronald Weston early that morning, and Weston had told him to come on by.

Weston opened the door to the apartment. He was a thin boy, not past his mid-teens, wearing an oversize T-shirt, extrawides, and unlaced Timberland boots. His ears were too long for his face. He had large brown eyes and crooked teeth. He gave Stefanos a casual nod, reaching for hard.

"Nick Stefanos. I called."

"Come on in."

Stefanos followed him back through a hall. Go-go music grew louder as they entered a living room. A Nintendo 64 was hooked up to a large-screen television in a cheap hutch set against the wall. Fast-food wrappers littered a glass-top table, and a Big Gulp soda sat half full amid the wrappers.

A phone rang. Ronald Weston found the cordless beneath a Taco Bell bag. He activated the phone, said something to the caller, said to Stefanos, "Hold up," and walked away. Stefanos could see him in the kitchen, hand gesturing as he spoke. From Weston's shy smile Stefanos guessed that he was talking to a girl.

Stefanos went to a portable stereo, saw a Northeast Groovers CD atop a nearby stack. He turned the volume down to conversation level as Weston came back in the room.

"All right, man. Had to talk to this jazzy girl I know. I'm all done with that."

Stefanos had a seat on the couch and pulled out his pad and a pen. Weston chose a hard-armed chair beside the glass table. He kept the phone held loosely in his hand.

"So Ronald—"

"Yeah."

"Like I told you on the phone, your brother Randy's trial is coming up. We're still working on his defense, and I need to ask you some questions."

"They gonna put me up there on the stand?"

"I don't think so."

" 'Cause whatever I said, *they'd* say I would lie for my brother, right?"

"Would you?"

"To keep him out of jail? Goddamn right I would."

"Okay, but do me a favor. Just don't lie to me today."

Weston looked Stefanos over. "You get paid, right?"

"Yes."

"They pay you good?"

Stefanos looked down at his pad. "Your brother—did he deal drugs?"

Weston laughed and shook his head. "Damn, you go right to it, don't you?"

"Did he?"

"Why you think I'm gonna tell you that?"

"Look, I'm not going to pass on any information that would hurt your brother. Like I told you, I'm working for the woman that's defending him. I'm just trying to find out what happened, okay? So let me ask you again: Did Randy deal drugs?"

Weston licked his lips. "He had a little thing goin' on, yeah."

"Rock?"

"Uh-uh. Powder. He didn't fuck with no rock."

"How big was his operation?"

"Wasn't no operation, man. He just had a little somethin' personal goin', like I said. Little extra on the side to put next to his other money."

"What other money? He had a job?"

"No. Not since last year."

"But he did have his own apartment down the street from here, and a nice car. And a girlfriend, too. So his business must have been bigger than what you're describing."

Weston looked past Stefanos. "He had a couple of younguns runnin' for him, that's all. No gunslingers, no kind of drama like that."

"Down around First and Kennedy?"

"Yeah. But it wasn't no thing. Boy name of Forjay runnin' the shit down there, and Randy always made sure to step out of Forjay's way. Randy, he just gettin' a little bit of it for his own self."

"Okay. What about Donnel Lawton?"

"I didn't know him personal."

"Lawton was a known dealer down in that neighborhood. Did Randy ever talk about him?"

"Not that I know."

"Witnesses saw your brother and Lawton arguing the day of the murder."

"Look, Randy was doin' business down there. Maybe Lawton was lookin' to shake out on Randy's strip. Man tries to do you like that, you got to step *to* him, know what I'm sayin'?"

Stefanos said, "Your brother own a gun?"

"No."

"Never owned a Beretta ninety-two?"

"He never did own any kind of gun."

"The cops found a ninety-two in your brother's apartment. The markings on the slugs taken from Lawton's corpse matched that gun."

"Maybe they did, I ain't gonna argue it. But if they found the murder gun there then somebody *put* it there and framed my brother up good. My brother was hard when he had to be, but he wasn't down with no guns."

"Let's go on to something else. Your brother's girlfriend."

"What about her?" said Weston distastefully.

"I'm talking about Erika Mitchell."

"I know who you mean. And *fuck* that bitch."

"You don't like her."

"Bitch was with Randy the night Lawton got doomed. Randy told me they went to some movie together down at Union Station."

"Which show?"

"That Bruce Willis joint, out in space? Randy said it was the nine-forty-five."

"If that's true, then Erika could testify that the two of them were there."

"She could. But now she won't alibi my brother. She be changin' her story now, say she wasn't with him that night."

"Why would she do that?"

"You need to be askin' her."

"I will."

"And while you're at it, maybe you ought to be talkin' to her pops. She live with him out there in Chillum. Randy always had to pick her up there, get the treatment from her father, like where you be takin' my little girl and shit. So I know her father saw the two of them go out together the night Lawton was killed."

Stefanos made a notation. "One more thing. What kind of car does your brother drive?"

"Late model Legend. Cherry red with limo tints."

"He ever drive a red Ford Torino?"

"One of those old-time cars?"

"Yes."

Weston shook his head and pursed his lips. "Naw, man."

"He know anyone who owns one?"

"Even if he did, Randy wouldn't be drivin' no hooptie and shit."

The phone rang, and Ronald answered it. He said, "See you then, girl," and cut the connection.

"Your girlfriend?" asked Stefanos, trying to get through Weston's shell.

"Just some girl I know. She on her way over here now." Ronald smiled. "Gonna hit it like a girl like it to be hit, too."

Stefanos rubbed his eyes. He wanted to tell the kid that he didn't have to prove anything. He wanted to tell him that he was tired of it, that he just didn't care.

"What're you, Ronald? Fifteen?"

"I'm sixteen. Why?"

"No school today, I guess."

"Half day."

"Teachers' meetings or something?"

Ronald grinned. "You caught me, Mr. Investigator. Gonna take me in?"

Stefanos closed his pad. He stood and zipped up his jacket. "Thanks for talking with me. If I have any more questions, I'll give you a call."

Stefanos went down the hall. Weston followed and put a hand around Stefanos's arm. Stefanos stopped and turned.

"You gonna help my brother? 'Cause my brother can't do no hard time."

"I'm gonna try."

"Look here," said Weston. "I *know* Randy. My brother didn't kill nobody, man, for real."

"I believe you," said Stefanos.

Outside the apartment building, Stefanos lit a cigarette and crossed the street to his Dodge.

FIFTEEN

DETECTIVE **DAN** Boyle fired up a cigarette off the dash lighter, cracking his window as he drove his unmarked into Northeast. He dragged hard on his Marlboro and kept the smoke down in his lungs.

Talking to the Karras guy at the bar had naturally made him think of his own kids. How rough he was on them sometimes, and how much he loved them. Christ, if anything ever happened to them...How could Karras just sit there quietly like that, eating his lunch? He guessed that Karras had just learned to live with it and was keeping it buried someplace deep inside. But Boyle would be crazy if it were him. Maybe this Karras *was* crazy, and no one knew.

Talking with Karras, it had also reminded Boyle that his friend Bill Jonas had called a couple of days earlier and asked that he drop by. Boyle had a witness to interview out in the Langdon Park area, and Jonas lived in Brookland, not far off the route. This would be a good day for Boyle to visit Jonas.

Boyle figured that Jonas wanted to talk about the case. That was what they usually discussed during Boyle's visits. But Boyle had no new information since his last visit. The Pizza Parlor Murders had been transferred over to a newly formed cold-case squad, a unit created in part due to citizen outrage at published reports of the department's extreme number of unsolved homicides. Now the Feds were involved, too, in an "advisory capacity." From what Boyle heard, no additional progress had been made.

Boyle went down the commercial strip of 12th and found Hamlin, a block of well-kept middle-class homes aligned on a gently graded street. He parked in front of Jonas's house, a brick split-level with forest green shutters, and popped a breath mint in his mouth to cover the smell of booze. He got out of his car, noticing a curtain part in the front window of Jonas's home. Probably one of Bill's boys, checking him out.

Boyle looked around as he approached the house. The relative quiet of the street was deceptive. You could be lulled into thinking you were safe here, but there was plenty of crime on these blocks, some of it of the more violent kind. Anytime you have a black neighborhood, reasoned Boyle, you're gonna have crime.

"HEY, DAD," said Christopher Jonas. "Here comes your redneck friend."

"Boyle?" said William Jonas, looking up as his son peered through the parted curtains of the living-room window. "Yeah, I'm expecting him."

"Looks like he slept in that raincoat of his, too."

"Probably was just sitting on it on some bar stool. Listen, Boyle's rough around the edges, but he's all right."

"All cops are all right to you."

"He's just a little ignorant is all it is."

"That's all, huh? Well I'll bet you a Hamilton he asks about my game, like he always does."

"Ten dollars? You're on." Bill Jonas grinned. "How *is* your game, by the way?"

"Mr. Magoo could play basketball better than me. I'm a scientist, not an athlete. Proud of it, too. But your buddy there, when he looks at me, he sees a young black man and all he can think of after that is basketball."

"All right, Chris, all right. Remember, I asked him out here, so be polite."

Boyle knocked on the front door.

"You need a push, Dad?"

"No, Chris, I got it." William Jonas wheeled himself across the living-room floor. "You show Mr. Boyle inside."

"CHRIS, RIGHT?"

"That's right. Come on in."

As Boyle passed him in the foyer, Christopher Jonas caught the stale stench of nicotine and whiskey. Boyle went up a small flight of stairs to the living room, where William Jonas sat in his wheelchair beside a flowery couch. Boyle shook his hand.

"Bill."

"Dan."

Boyle removed his raincoat and draped it over the arm of the couch. He had a look at Bill Jonas: gray hair, a gut that rested on his lap, thin, atrophied legs. Jonas had aged ten years in the last two.

"I'm out, Dad," said Christopher Jonas, getting into a coat and slinging a leather book bag over his shoulder. "You need anything before I go?"

"No, I'm all right. Your mother will be home soon. Take care, son."

Bill Jonas made a face at his boy, rubbed two fingers together to indicate he had won the bet. Christopher rolled his eyes and left the house.

Jonas said, "Would you like a cup of coffee, Danny? A beer, maybe?"

"I could stand a beer."

"Help yourself to one in the kitchen."

"Anything for you?"

"I don't drink the stuff." Jonas looked down at his ample belly. "Last thing I need now is to fall in love with alcohol."

Boyle left the room and returned with a can of beer. He noticed that Jonas now held an envelope in his hand. Boyle popped the can, had a swig, and sat down on the couch.

"So how's it going?" said Boyle.

"Not bad. Rehab's taken me a mile." Jonas pointed to an aluminum tripod cane leaning against the wall. "I can take steps with that. From my bedroom to the bathroom, that sort of thing, which is a big load off my wife. And with the walker I can go even farther."

"You gonna improve much more, you think?"

"Doctors didn't think I'd come this far. The slug that nicked my spine did a lot of damage. But I just have to keep working at it, Dan. I mean, what else can I do?"

"You'll get it. How you fixed for money?"

"Between my disability pay and my pension, I'm fine. College is all taken care of; I'd already saved that. Christopher's in school, and Ted is on his way next fall. So me and Dee are out of the woods as far as that goes. Lookin' forward to enjoying some good years together now."

"Good. I'm happy everything's working out."

Jonas watched Boyle take a slow sip of beer. He'd never be able to explain to his son Christopher how he could sit here with a guy like Boyle. Jonas knew all about Boyle, his problems and instabilities, his bigotries and hatreds. All of it. He knew, but right now he didn't care.

"Anything going on?" asked Jonas.

"Not that I know of," said Boyle. "The cold-casers are focusing on it again, I know that. And they won't stop. A quadruple homicide, five if you count the kid, it never goes away in the public's mind. So far not a thing, but, hey, you never know. I mean, they just now caught that guy who was killing all those women in Park View."

"I heard that, yeah. Tell me again what they know about *my* case."

"Christ, Bill. Again?"

Jonas nodded. "Start with the guns."

"Okay." Boyle squinted as he thought. "The weapons used in the kitchen: a twenty-two Woodsman and a forty-five."

"A Woodsman's an assassin's weapon."

"Maybe, or the guy who was using it had just been around enough to know that it works real good close in. Anyhow, they never found the guns."

"What about motive?"

"Money, but not from the registers. Gambling money. May's was a known bookie joint. Hell, the federal boys were surveilling it for months, from a beauty salon across Wisconsin Avenue. They had infrared cameras pointed into the bar area at night, for Christ's sake. Our people think the shooters were knocking off the place for book money. A couple of old employees came forward and told us as much. May's was the last stop on a weekly bag run, and apparently the shooters knew it."

"How would they know it?"

"Somebody tipped them off would be the obvious answer. Carl Lewin, the guy they called Mr. Carl, he had served federal time for gaming. Lewin was the bag man—and from what we got at the crime scene, it looks like he was armed. He made a play on the shooters, and they got the draw on him first. The other vics probably would have lived if Lewin hadn't of made that play. It made them all witnesses to a murder. They got tied up and shot with their heads down on the tiles."

"Should have been plenty of blood."

"There was. And footprints tracking out of it. It'll help to convict if we catch the guys."

"How about fingerprints, hair samples, like that?"

"No prints. No hair that didn't belong to the victims. Traces of powder, the kind they have on those examination gloves doctors put on when they jam their fingers up your ass."

"Okay, they wore latex gloves." Jonas nodded. "Now let's take it outside. I killed the driver of the Ford in the street."

"We don't know that for sure."

"I killed him."

"But we can't confirm that without a corpse."

"The shooters, then," said Jonas. "I got a pretty good look at them."

"Right. And the witness from the apartment window pretty much duplicated your description. The likenesses have been out on the national networks for two years now. They've been cross-checked against wanted lists, lists of guys who have broken parole. Nothing."

"What about the Ford?"

"The Ford was abandoned on Tennyson. Blood on the backseat, most likely the blood of the man you shot. Again, no prints. The tags were stolen locally. The vehicle was traced to an auction down South, bought under a phony name. The Ford was a sheriff's car before it went to auction."

"Funny joke."

"Yeah. There must have been a drop car waiting on Tennyson,

but it was a workday so there weren't many people around. The ones who were around were seniors. And they didn't see a thing."

"The one I killed," said Jonas. "The white shooter called him Richard."

"That's right."

"Why would he use his name? These guys were older. Pros from the looks of it. They wouldn't be likely to make that mistake."

"We been over all this a hundred times."

"Maybe we missed something, Dan."

"Okay. Maybe the white shooter had an emotional attachment to the one you shot, and in the heat of things he made a mistake. So you shot his best friend, or lover, or his brother, maybe."

"Or his son. The white shooter was all gray."

"The point is, knowing his name hasn't gotten us anywhere so far. His name might not even have been Richard. You know that." Boyle leaned forward. "Here's what I think, Bill. The leads we got on this case aren't gonna break it. It's like most of the investigations we've handled. Somebody's gotta come forward. An old employee, someone who has something to deal by ratting out the shooters...like that."

"You guys have hit all the ex-employees pretty hard, haven't you?"

"Goddamn right we did. We went back two years into the May's files, talked to all of them, then brought them back in and talked to them again. Carl Lewin's partner, the skinny man, he's serving time right now on racketeering. He could have avoided a Leavenworth jolt if he knew anything, but in the end all he knew is that he got took for a lot of money that day."

"I just can't believe it. In broad daylight, these bastards do what they did. We have nothing, and they just get away."

"Listen, the reality is that there probably aren't going to be any new leads. Even the pizza parlor is gone. Nothing's left of the old place but that plaque you dedicated last year."

Jonas handed his envelope to Boyle. "Which brings me to this."

Boyle opened the envelope and examined its contents. It was a photograph that had run in the *Washington Post* over a story about the "healing process" begun the day the Sub Place opened at the old May's site. There had been a ceremony arranged by the chain's public-relations people, and William Jonas had been tapped to dedicate a bronze plaque that served to memorialize the victims. In the original photograph, Jonas was in his wheelchair and flanked by his son Christopher. In the photograph Boyle held in his hand, Christopher's face had been punched through and torn out. A strip of paper had been glued across Christopher's body. It was cut from a typical bill received in the mail. It read, "Your account is past due."

"When did you get this?" asked Boyle.

"Couple of days ago. It was sent to the station house and forwarded here."

"And you think—"

"Yeah. I think it might have come from the shooters."

Boyle forced a reassuring smile. "Could have come from anybody, Bill. What we do for a living, we're gonna accumulate a lot of enemies."

"I know it. But the man I killed that day was the *only* man I've ever killed. I've been threatened plenty in my career, mostly by the families of men I put away. But the majority of that was talk. This here has a different kind of tone to it, wouldn't you say?"

"It is pretty direct."

"And it comes straight out of the local paper, which means the one who sent it could be right here in town. It worries me, man."

"You can get the *Post* anywhere in the country."

"It worries me just the same."

Boyle looked down at the blank envelope Jonas had handed him. "This the way it came?"

"No, it was mailed. I have the original right here." Jonas wheeled himself to an end table, opened a drawer, wheeled himself back, and dropped the envelope in Boyle's lap.

"Can I touch it?"

"My prints are already all over it. Go ahead."

Boyle studied the envelope. "Typed address...mailed from Los Angeles. I'm gonna take this with me, Bill. And the photograph, all right?"

"That's why I asked you to come by."

"Don't worry. It's nothing, most likely."

"That's my boy whose face is cut out there."

"I know."

They sat without speaking for a minute or so. Boyle closed his eyes and drank beer while Jonas stared down at the afternoon sunlight spreading across the floor.

"The families of those people," said Jonas, his eyes still on the floor.

Boyle nodded. "I met one of them, just before I came over here. Dimitri Karras, the father of the boy got hit by the car. Karras is working in the kitchen of a bar I drink in from time to time."

"The department still sponsoring that support group for those people?"

"Yeah. What I heard is that the group asked the shrink we

put in there to leave. But they still meet on Tuesday nights, and we still pay for the space. As much as they were in the news, it's hard to forget them: Karras and the bartender's wife. The waiter's father. The pizza chef's best friend. Bet that's one happy group, right?"

"I ought to stop by one night and sit in with them. For a long time I thought I'd be intruding. And there was that other thing, too—I dreaded seeing those folks. I had the idea that they'd think maybe I could have done more that day—"

"You did plenty."

"I know, but that's what was goin' through my mind. How did Karras seem to you?"

"Quiet," said Boyle.

"Those people won't be right until we find the shooters." Jonas rubbed his cheek. "Maybe they'll never be right."

Boyle stood up and got into his raincoat. He slipped the envelope and photograph into the inside pocket. "You want me to get a watch put on your house for a while?"

"No, that's okay."

"Bill, you're still listed in the phone book, for Christ's sake. Better let me do that, just for grins."

"It's okay. Like you said, it's probably nothing. Didn't mean to overreact. But someone threatens your kid—"

"No problem. How's Christopher doin', by the way?"

"Real good. Studying to be a biologist."

"That's great. He's one tall kid, too. Bet he can jam a basketball without even thinking about it."

Jonas chuckled and shook his head.

"What's so funny?" asked Boyle.

"Nothin'. You just cost me ten bucks, is all."

"How's that?"

"Never mind. Listen, Dan...keep on it, hear?"

"Bet it," said Boyle.

The two of them shook hands. Boyle killed his beer, crushed the can, and set it on the living-room table.

Jonas got himself over to the window and watched Boyle amble down the sidewalk toward his car. Two teenage boys approached him, and Boyle opened his raincoat enough so that the butt of his Python showed. The boys stepped off the sidewalk and let Boyle pass.

Stupid bastard, thought Jonas. Stupid, crazy bastard.

He needed a cop like Boyle now.

SIXTEEN

DIMITRI KARRAS opened his eyes. He stared up at the bedroom ceiling and unballed his fists. He'd been trying to nap, but he'd flashed on Jimmy and knew then that he'd never get to sleep. Other people were startled into insomnia by thoughts of their own mortality. With Karras it was always the image of his little boy.

He got out of bed and went to get something to drink.

His apartment on U Street, near 15th, was sparsely furnished with his old Trauma Arms living-room furniture, moved from the rec room of his house in upper Northwest. From that house he'd also taken his clothing, his books and records, and his stereo. Nothing else. He'd left Lisa with everything the two of them had accumulated in the course of their marriage and found himself this apartment a year after Jimmy's death.

That he and Lisa wouldn't make it was almost predictable. He'd sworn to himself that he wouldn't blame her for what happened, though he couldn't stop thinking that if she'd kept up with Jimmy that day, stayed by his side.... That was the problem; he couldn't *stop* himself from thinking. And vocalizing those thoughts in the many horrible, unreasonable arguments that followed.

Blame and guilt, said Lisa's shrink, the one who always seemed to take Lisa's side. Blame and guilt would kill their marriage if they let it. They let it, almost from the start. It wasn't long before the two of them were done.

When he moved to the apartment he thought it would be better, being away from Lisa, and especially being away from their house, where memories laughed at him in every room. But it wasn't much better in the apartment. It was only more quiet. So quiet sometimes that he'd catch himself speaking out loud. He'd check himself then because he knew that this kind of quiet could drive him mad.

Karras stood at the sink drinking water. He watched a roach crawl over the backsplash of the countertop and disappear. Jimmy would have called it a "woach." Just about everything he'd see or hear reminded him of Jimmy when he let it. Jimmy in death was a scream that was always in Karras's head.

Karras paced the apartment. He found himself sitting on the edge of his bed.

Sometimes he'd be sitting in his bedroom like this in the old house, and he'd hear Jimmy fall, and he'd hear him begin to sob. Jimmy would call, "Daddy!" and Karras would say, "I'm in the bedroom, son," and Jimmy would come in and run into his arms. Karras would hold him, rub his back, and kiss his head. Karras could still smell Jimmy's scalp, the peculiar mix of sweat and Johnson's shampoo.

Karras looked at the open entrance to his bedroom. He stared at the space, but there was nothing, no one, there. After a while he looked away and saw his reflection in the dresser mirror. He noticed that he had been crying, and he wiped the tears from his face.

The meeting was tonight. He'd be with his friends. He'd lie down with Stephanie later on. Things would be much better tonight.

But that was a few hours away. He decided to take a shower and change his clothes. Maybe he'd go down to the Spot, sit at the bar, find someone to talk to. Kill some time.

NICK STEFANOS was sitting at the bar of the Spot, having a bottle of beer when Karras stepped down off the landing. Karras slid onto the stool to Stefanos's right.

"Hey, Dimitri."

"Nick. What, you're hanging out here on your night off?"

"I'm never off. I worked this afternoon, something I'm doing for Elaine. I'm meeting my friend Alicia tonight, but I had a few hours to kill first. What about you?"

"I've got my group later on. I had some time to kill as well."

"Dimitri," said Mai, stepping up behind the bar in her Marine Corps T-shirt.

"Mai. Give me a ginger ale, please. From the bottle, not the gun."

Mai had an Abba CD playing on the house system. It bothered Stefanos that groups like Abba and the Carpenters were considered hip now. Stefanos figured that anything that blew the first time around still blew, period. Retro appreciation was nothing more than blind nostalgia.

"Hey, Mai," said Stefanos, "give us a break with this 'Dancing Queen' bullshit, huh?"

Mai set a glass of ginger ale on a bev nap in front of Karras. "My shift, Nicky, my music."

She drifted away as Karras looked down the bar. A couple of neighborhood guys were arguing about what the Wizards "needed," and a plainclothes cop from the Prostitution and Perversions division sat alone, sipping a red cocktail.

"She's right, Nick. She ought to be able to play what she wants when she's behind the bar. Besides, none of the customers seem to mind."

"Helen Keller would notice more than those guys," said Stefanos.

"In the kitchen it's the same way. Everybody arguing over what's coming out of the boom box. What they did back there was, each person got their own time slot to listen to whatever they want."

"Yeah, I know. Maria gets her half hour right after the rush."

"The thing is, what I noticed, the Spanish station she likes plays one song during that period and the rest is news. So she gets ripped off."

"Sounds like you been thinking about work a lot, Dimitri."

"I just noticed it, is all."

Stefanos signaled Mai for another beer. She served it, and he lit a cigarette.

"Phil tells me you're catching on," said Stefanos. "I know from the shifts you and I have pulled together, the food's coming out pretty fast."

"Thanks," said Karras. "And thanks for hooking me up. It's been good for me, man."

"Yeah, this place gets under your skin."

Karras looked through the reach-through at the end of the bar. Ramon was in the kitchen, trying out a spin-kick on Darnell. Darnell stepped away from it and laughed.

"Me and Darnell," said Karras, "we had a talk. It wasn't any big thing. I get the feeling we're going to get along all right."

"You're doing a good job. He's not the type to hold a grudge. It's like I told you, he's a man."

"That guy could do more if someone took him under their wing. He could open his own little place if someone showed him how."

"No one's ever taken that much interest in him, I guess."

Karras watched Stefanos close his eyes lovingly as he took a long swallow of beer.

"I met Dan Boyle today," said Karras.

"Uh-huh. He was curious about you. You know, twenty-four and seven a cop and all that."

"He says his uncle was boyhood friends with my father."

"Yeah. He claims his uncle used to drink coffee in my grandfather's lunch counter, too, when his uncle was walking a beat. My *papou* never mentioned him, but it makes sense, I guess."

"Strange guy, Boyle."

"Not really. He's not too hard to figure out."

"You know him pretty well?"

Stefanos hit his cigarette. "Me and Boyle have a history together."

Karras looked into his glass. "He knew about my son."

"Not surprising. He's Homicide."

"Maybe he knows what's happening. The progress, I mean, with the investigation."

"Don't think about it. Getting on the wrong side of Boyle can hurt you. But so can being his friend. My advice is to keep your distance." Stefanos crushed out his cigarette. "Just stay away."

"Maybe you can ask him what's going on for me."

"Sure. I'll ask him."

Karras thought of the passage of time, looking Stefanos over. "I remember the first time I met you. You were a kid. A stock boy at that place on Connecticut."

"Nutty Nathan's."

"How'd you get from there to here?"

"You want the condensed version of twenty-two years?" Stefanos flicked ash off his smoke. "I got married, moved up through the ranks at Nathan's, and became a 'retail executive.' Then I got divorced and blew up my career when I stumbled into investigative work. I walked into this bar one day, and here I am."

"You're just working for the Fifth Streeters now?"

"Not anyone but Elaine. The private cop business wasn't for me. Too many things happened." Stefanos rubbed his nose. "What about you? You were some unemployed, post-hippie pot dealer when I met you. And I seem to remember you turning me on to some high-octane flake in the bathroom at a Scream concert one night back in, hell, when was it?"

"Eighty-six. That's right. I was all of those things. Directionless, I guess, is the best word to describe who I was. Then I met Lisa while I was cleaning myself up. We had Jimmy.... Shit, man, everything was different after that. I never even had the slightest desire to get fucked up ever again, from the day he came to us. It's like, he was born and I was *re*born, that make sense? Everything changed." A tightness entered Karras's face.

"Don't talk about it, Dimitri," said Stefanos. "You don't have to, okay?"

Karras nodded. "Okay. I know where that goes, and it's never good. Thanks."

They sat there for another hour. Stefanos had another beer and a shot of Grand-Dad to keep the beer company. Karras, who knew too well the rituals involved in getting high, had been noticing Stefanos romance the alcohol. He watched him kill his beer and knew he would automatically signal Mai for another.

"Hold up," said Karras, putting a hand on Stefanos's bicep. "Don't order another beer."

"What are you talking about, man? I've got another hour and a half before I meet Alicia."

"Another hour and a half, you're gonna have a load on. You want to meet her like that?"

Stefanos thought of the last night he'd been with Alicia. How he'd been too drunk to talk to her. How he'd been too drunk to get an erection, even with her next to him, naked in the bed.

"You got a better suggestion?"

"I've got my group; it's getting ready to start." The group had always been hermetic by agreement, and for a moment he wondered how the others would take to the idea of a stranger's joining them. He said, "Why don't you come with me?"

"You're not trying to get me into one of those ten-step things, are you? Because, listen, I *like* to drink. I know who I am, and I'm not looking to make any changes."

"No, it's not that. I just want you to meet my friends. Anyway, what're you, gonna sit on that stool and listen to Lobo for the next hour and a half?"

"I believe this is Bread."

"Whatever. Come with me, man."

"All right." Stefanos reached for his wallet. "Let's go."

BY THE time Karras and Stefanos walked into the common room of the church at 23rd and P, the group had already convened in the center of the room. Tonight there were two additional men in the circle: an older man in a wheelchair and a young man with similar features seated in a folding chair beside him.

"Hey, everybody," said Karras, his voice echoing in the hall.

"Dimitri," said Stephanie Maroulis, her eyes flashing on his. "We've got company tonight."

"I see," said Karras, and as he approached the group and got a closer look at the man in the wheelchair, he knew.

"Bill Jonas." Jonas extended his hand and Karras shook it. "And this is my son Christopher."

"Dimitri Karras." He nodded at the young man.

"Nice to finally meet you," said William Jonas.

"And you," said Karras. "Well, good, I'm glad you broke the ice by coming here, because I brought someone tonight, too. Meet my friend Nick Stefanos."

Stefanos went around the group, shaking hands. Jonas, the homicide cop crippled by the May's shooters, told Stefanos his friend Dan Boyle had mentioned his name before, and Stefanos nodded politely.

"You're a private cop," said Jonas, "right?"

"That's right," said Stefanos, who immediately went to the urn to draw himself a cup of coffee. He felt eyes on his back, or maybe it was his imagination.

"Hey, Ernst," said Bernie Walters, the father of the slain waiter, as an old guy with gray hair-clumps growing from his face entered the room from a side door.

"Everything all right?" said Ernst.

"Yeah," said Thomas Wilson, the pizza chef's friend, "we're okay, Ernie. You can go ahead and stand guard next to the collection box upstairs, or whatever it is you do. Us straights gonna be all right tonight down here. Got us a couple of lawmen sitting in."

Stefanos had a seat, studied Wilson as he spoke.

"We'll let ourselves out, Ernst," said Walters.

"Unplug the coffee urn before you go," said Ernst.

"Make a deal with you," said Wilson. "We'll unplug it if you clean it for a change."

"Yeah, sure," said Ernst, shaking his head. "You guys."

"Maybe I better get going," said Stefanos to Karras.

"It's okay," said Karras. "Stay."

They watched Ernst leave. Then there was a silence as they looked to Jonas, expecting him to start things off. But it was his son who spoke first.

"I came home late this afternoon," said Christopher Jonas, "and found my father sitting in the living room, thinking. He told me he'd like to drop in on this meeting tonight, but he wasn't sure if you'd want him here. I know from talking to my father these last couple of years how all of you have been in his thoughts. I hope you welcome him tonight."

"We're all happy to see you," said Stephanie Maroulis without hesitation. "We all appreciate your sacrifice, and everything you did."

"That's a fact," said Bernie Walters.

Thomas Wilson nodded his head, looking at the floor.

"Thank you," said William Jonas. "I was thinkin', if you all don't have any objection . . . I was thinking we'd start off tonight with a prayer."

"I'd sure like that," said Walters, his eyes going to Karras. "Any objections?"

Karras didn't mind, any more than he'd mind using a Ouija board for grins or having his palm read at a party. If it made the rest of them happy, it was okay by him.

Stephanie mouthed the words "thank you," and Karras smiled.

They joined hands, all of them, in the circle, and bowed their heads. William Jonas began to pray: "Father in heaven, thank you for the gift of friendship we are receiving here tonight. And for our many blessings...."

Karras closed his eyes, gripping the hands of the ones to the right and left of him. It was crazy; for a moment, he thought he felt his son's touch.

SEVENTEEN

NICK STEFANOS screwed a cigarette between his lips and dropped thirty-five cents into a pay phone. He turned up the collar of his leather. Outside the Mobil station at 22nd and P the wind blew cold across the open lot. He dialed Elaine Clay's home number, struck a match, cupped it until the flame touched tobacco, and took in a deep draw of smoke.

"Elaine, it's Nick. Bad time?"

"I'm sitting down to dinner. What's up?"

"Working the Randy Weston case. I met with Jerry Sun today, the Chinese guy who saw the red Torino. And I talked with Randy's brother Ronald."

"And?"

"Ronald told me that Erika Mitchell could alibi Randy for that night, but now she's got a sudden loss of memory."

"What she said was, they did go to a picture together, but she can't remember for sure what night it was."

"I checked the movie schedule in the morgue materials at the MLK library. The late shows at Union Station started at around nine-thirty that night. Jerry Sun said he heard gunshots just after nine-thirty. The girl could get Randy off if she'd say they were together at one of those shows. Why won't she?"

"I don't know."

"What about her father? Supposedly he keeps her on a short leash."

"He's a former D.C. beat cop, and he doesn't remember anything, either. Funny, a cop who doesn't remember details. Right?"

"I'm going to try and interview both of them."

"Good."

"Ronald Weston is certain his brother didn't kill Donnel Lawton. Weston says his brother's no killer, that he wouldn't own a gun to begin with. You gonna put Ronald up on the stand?"

"You saw him. He might be a sweet kid for all I know, but he refuses to come off that way. And he's got juvenile priors. Besides, he only knows what his brother told him, and that won't hold water. The prosecutor will take him apart up there. He'd just be another ineffective character witness with nothing concrete to say."

"Okay. Let me keep working on it."

"Great. And Nick, thanks for hooking Dimitri up with that job. He's talked to Marcus and he thinks it's done him good."

"I think so, too. I just left him, as a matter of fact."

"You two Greek boys are bonding, huh?"

"Yeah, we just slaughtered a lamb in the alley. It's really good when it's fresh, you know? Hold on a second while I wipe this blood off my chin."

"Nick, I just wanted you to know, Marcus and I appreciate it."

"Glad to help. Listen, I gotta bolt."

"My family's waiting as well. Take care, Nick."

"You too."

Stefanos met Alicia Weisman at a gallery on the south end of 7th Street. She was standing in front of a large piece, one of a series of Fred Folsom paintings depicting the characters inhabiting the old Shepherd Park strip club on a typical night. Alicia wore a black corduroy zippered shirt over black tights and utilitarian black boots. A black leather jacket was draped over her arm.

"Hey, baby," said Stefanos, kissing her neck. "Sorry I'm late."

"Where you been?"

"I'll tell you later." He looked the painting over and chuckled. "Well, he captured it, all right."

"You used to go to that place?"

"All the time." Stefanos tugged at the triangle of T-shirt showing beneath Alicia's corduroy. "Hey, I don't want to be the one to point this out, but—"

"I know. I wore a little white by mistake."

They went downstairs to another gallery and took in the Jim Saah photographs on display. Stefanos studied Saah's portrait of three very Greek women sitting on a Kárpathos stoop. He smiled and marked the number of the photograph on a sheet he had picked up by the door.

"Hungry?" said Stefanos.

Alicia said, "I'm starved."

They had dinner at a restaurant without signage at 5th and H in Chinatown. Except for Stefanos and Alicia, the patrons were all Chinese. This was the most inconspicuous restaurant on the strip and, for Stefanos's money, the best. Stefanos ordered shrimp dumpling–noodle soup and Alicia asked for plain roast duck over rice.

"So what do you think of the art on this one right here?" asked Alicia, pushing a CD booklet across the table.

"Looks like one of those numbered Prestige jazz jackets. An Eddie Lockjaw Davis record, something like that."

"You're right. How'd you *know* that?"

"My grandfather used to buy hot records from his customers down on Fourteenth. We had crates of them down in our basement on Irving Street. He didn't listen to jazz, but he thought I'd get something out of it. He was right."

"Well, what do you think of this? The group's going for that fifties bop look."

"Are they jazz?"

"They're more on the soul-punk side."

"Whatever they are, I think the cover art looks hot." Stefanos sipped his tea. "You're doing a good job, you know it?"

"I'm having fun." Alicia had a swig of Tsing Tao. "Feel like seeing some music tonight?"

"Sure."

"The Black Cat's got a good bill."

"You comped?"

"You got it, Daddy-O."

"Let's check it out."

The Black Cat was on 14th Street, spartan like the old 9:30 but without the new 9:30's frat-boy crowd. The club had an all-ages policy and good sight lines, helped by a couple of rows of stadium seats against the wall, so that every kid in the place, even the short ones, could check out the band.

There was a genial guy who always stood outside the club politely asking for donations, and Stefanos gave him a buck. The opening band, an excellent local outfit called Last Train Home, was in midset, covering Manifesto's "Sugar," as Stefanos and Alicia entered the club. Stefanos went to the bar, bought a couple bottles of Bud, and brought them over to Alicia, who had situated herself in the center of the crowd. The Brace brothers were in harmony onstage against a tight rhythm section as Stefanos tapped Alicia's bottle. Stefanos was glad he had stopped drinking earlier; taking a sip, it was like hitting his first of the night and it tasted damn good.

The Silos, the night's headliners, came out a half hour later. Walter Salas-Humara took center stage and ripped through a set from *Heater*, his group's latest album, as Stefanos downed two more beers. He was sweating beneath his leather by the time Alicia got close to his ear and suggested they go.

They made love next to an open window in Alicia's Mount Pleasant apartment. She was narrow shouldered, with small, red-nippled breasts and full, round hips. Stefanos loved her hips. He tasted the salt of her sweat and kissed the insides of her thighs as he slowly made his way to her sex. Burying his mouth in her, he took her there like that.

Afterward, Stefanos looked at the curtains hanging still on either side of the open window.

"Aren't those curtains supposed to be billowing?" he said.

"There's no wind, silly."

"'Cause I saw that in a movie once. One of those erotic thrillers on cable."

"Come up here and kiss me."

"Maybe I ought to brush my teeth first. As a courtesy, I mean."

"Come here."

BERNIE WALTERS signaled the waitress for another beer.

"Me, too, Helga," said Thomas Wilson as she arrived.

Walters pointed at Stephanie Maroulis. She put her hand over her glass and shook her head.

"So what's up with your friend?" said Wilson.

"Nick?" said Dimitri Karras.

"Yeah."

"What do you mean, what's up with him?"

"When we were all walking over here, before we split up, that Nick character was really checkin' out my car on the street there."

"You drive a Dodge, right?"

"That's right."

"Nick's a Dodge freak, man. He's got an old Mopar from the sixties that he babies."

"Gearhead, huh?"

"I liked having him there," said Walters, shaking a cigarette from his deck. "With another smoker in the room, I didn't feel like a leper and all that."

"Well," said Wilson, "it was a different night for us, I'll say that much."

They were all avoiding looking at Stephanie. She had broken down in the meeting, talking about her husband, Steve. It wasn't like her to do that. Her role was the Cheerful One, and it had taken them by surprise. She still had the tracks from the tears that had fallen down her face.

There was an uncomfortable silence. Then the waitress returned and served Walters and Wilson their beers.

"Thanks, Helga," said Wilson.

"It's Helen," said the waitress tiredly, pointing to her name tag.

"Why they go to all the trouble makin' you dress up like Oktoberfest gals," said Wilson, "then go and let you use your American names?"

"I don't know. I'll bring it up at the next board meeting." The waitress rolled her eyes and walked away.

"Just tryin' to make the girl smile, is all," explained Wilson.

"They're probably not allowed to laugh on duty," said Karras, "seein' as how they're supposed to be Germans and all that."

Wilson laughed, reached across the round-top and gave Karras finger-skin.

Stephanie cleared her throat. "It was different tonight, Thomas, you were right. And better, I think."

Walters pushed his Orioles cap back on his head. "That Bill Jonas is a good guy."

"There was something about him," said Stephanie. "It just felt easy, talking around him. Look, I'm sorry if I lost it back there—"

"That's all right," said Karras, reaching for her hand, taking it and stroking it, not caring that the others were there.

Wilson looked away. Walters pretended to study his burning cigarette.

"We better get going," said Karras.

Stephanie opened her wallet and left money on the table.

"We on this weekend, Dimitri?" said Walters. "Gonna be a little cold down there on the property, but the weather should be clear."

"Sure, Bernie. Saturday's good for me."

"We got to take two cars, buddy. It's my vacation, and I'm staying down for the week."

"Okay. I'll follow you down."

Stephanie and Karras said good-bye and left the bar.

Wilson cleared his throat. "Guess I was right about those two, eh, Bern?"

"Oh, I always knew the two of them were together," said Walters with a wink. "I was just letting you go on."

"Whatever makes them happy," said Wilson softly.

"The Lord's brought them together, Thomas. I been watching

the way they look at each other. They don't know it yet, but to me it's plain."

"What is?"

"You ask me, it looks like those two are falling in love."

NICK STEFANOS pulled the blankets up over his shoulder. "We gonna leave that window open all night?"

"I like to hear the city sounds," said Alicia Weisman.

"Well, it's warm enough under these blankets. And there's you."

His arm was beneath her. She shifted so that her chest was pressed against his.

"I had a good time with you tonight," said Stefanos.

"And me with you."

"I wasn't my usual sloppy self, right?"

"I wouldn't ever call you on that. You told me who you were when we hooked up. I'm not looking to be your mother. I just want to hang out with you, Nick. I like being your friend, and I like making love to you. Let's enjoy it and not get too far ahead of ourselves."

"Well, it was Dimitri Karras who said that you and me'd have a better time if I showed up sober. He dragged me out of the bar and to that meeting."

"Who was there?"

"The cop who was crippled at the crime scene. Family members of the victims and one of the victim's friends. I've been through that before. I had to deal with this woman whose son was murdered down by the Anacostia River a few years back. It's one of the reasons I cut back on picking up those kinds of jobs."

"I can't imagine how awful it must be for those people."

"The woman who was married to the bartender, she kind of

broke down tonight. I felt like walking out when she was telling her story. But I stayed. It would have been disrespectful to leave, you know?"

Alicia stroked Stefanos's hair. "You're not going to go back there, are you? I mean, there's nothing you can do for them, Nick."

"That's right," he said. "There's nothing anyone can do for them now."

THOMAS WILSON drove his Dodge across town and parked it on Georgia. He entered a supper club down near Kenyon. Neighborhood folks, a couple of guys in suits who looked like they had been there since coming off their nine-to-fives, a few workingmen with just enough for a draft high, and a skinny, pipehead-lookin' sucker sat at the bar. Wilson had a seat on the end, all by himself.

He ordered a Courvoisier up with a side of Coke, and had a look around the bar.

There were some round-the-way girls in the place, but they appeared to be taken. The ones who weren't didn't have that look he liked. Shit, who was he kidding? Those women hadn't so much as turned their heads in his direction when he'd walked into the joint.

He could smell a sweet hint of reefer coming from the bathrooms down along the supper club's back hall. Rick James was doing "Mary Jane" on the house system. He found this funny, but there was no one there to share the joke.

He looked at his reflection in the bar mirror. He saw a tired man with tired threads and a third-rate Arsenio Hall fade. The eyes in his face stared back at a stone dead end.

He had another drink. He was angry enough to get into a fight tonight, but he knew he'd lose. He never was all that good with his hands, anyway. Charles always used to crack on him about that.

"Charlie," said Wilson, staring into his drink.

Wilson flashed on the detective in the wheelchair, his son by his side. Thomas Wilson closed his eyes tight and brought the cognac to his lips.

BERNIE WALTERS pressed down on the scan button on the remote that was Velcroed to his recliner. He sipped his beer, watched the channels flash by: the Spanish soap opera station, the cowboys and their girls doing some fancy line dance, the black-and-white movie station, the show about the cops in Brooklyn with all the actors who looked too pretty to be cops... nothing on. He killed his beer and lit a cigarette.

He put the empty in the carrier at the side of the chair and pulled a fresh one. He had gone through three already. Those fancy triple-bocks he'd tried down at the Brew Hause had really messed up his head.

Nothing to do this week except work. He had switched to a sorter's position since his feet had gone bad on him. Now that friendly guy Mike Hancock, the one who looked like Magnum P.I., had taken his Bethesda route. He was happy for Hancock, who had a nice wife and a couple of kids.

Walters remembered when it was all in front of him like that. He drank some more beer.

Yeah, there wasn't much to look forward to this week.

There's nothing to look forward to ever again.

Well, there was his vacation. On Saturday he'd go down to the property with Dimitri, hang out, show him around, drink some beer. Do some shooting in the woods, because that's what Dimitri had asked to do. Spend the rest of the week down there by himself.

As for tonight...he'd just get drunk tonight.

He'd get good and drunk, because when he was drunk he slept solid. He didn't remember his dreams when he slept drunk. He did hear Vance's voice as a child, though, saying his name. He could never get drunk enough to stop that.

I love you, Vance. I was always proud of you, son.

He wanted to be with Lynne, his wife, and he wanted to be with Vance. He was ready now. He knew that he could live on for a good many years, and he knew that however long he lived, it was God's decision, not his. Still, he was ready. Sometimes he prayed to be taken.

Yes, he had thought of suicide, many times. He had thought of it but never once considered it beyond the thought.

The Lord said that it was a sin to take one's life. Bernie Walters would just have to wait.

DIMITRI KARRAS propped himself up on one elbow and kissed Stephanie Maroulis on the mouth. He looked at her lush figure on the bed and ran his hand down her arm.

"I guess I'm not much good tonight," she said.

"It's okay. *This* is good. We can just do this."

"You sure?" Stephanie smiled weakly as she reached down and brushed her fingers down the shaft of his hardening cock. "Because you're mouth is saying one thing and your body's telling me something else."

Karras grinned crookedly.

Stephanie turned and looked at the photograph of Steve Maroulis on the nightstand. "You know, it wasn't like me to get that way in the meeting. I've been doing pretty well up to now, don't you think?"

"Yes."

"But there was something about Bill Jonas being there that

made me want to talk about it. About how it was for Steve, at the end."

"I know."

Stephanie had told the group how her husband had been robbed many years before at an after-hours, high-stakes card game down off New York Avenue, near the Henley Park Hotel. The gunmen had made the gamblers put their heads down on the carpet. Steve had been the last to comply; he thought that if he were to put his head down, they'd kill him. His fear was so great that he'd fouled himself that night. He had told Stephanie that putting his head down was the hardest thing he'd ever done.

"I didn't mean to cry," said Stephanie. "It's just, when I was telling it, I could imagine seeing him there in that kitchen, how afraid he must have been....I couldn't help myself, Dimitri."

"I know," repeated Karras. Her hair had fallen across her cheek, and he brushed it away. "I've been thinking of you these last few days, Stephanie. What I mean to say is, you've been in my head. I know this is supposed to be a once-a-week thing, us being together. But I was looking forward to seeing you tonight. I was hoping this night would come sooner, understand? I'm not certain that I know what it means."

"I've been thinking of you, too."

DIMITRI KARRAS awoke in the middle of the night, confused and oddly ashamed. He felt a strange sense of having committed a betrayal. It was as if he were considering breaking a promise he'd made never to be happy again.

He walked barefoot down a hall to the darkened kitchen and found Stephanie's wall-mounted phone. He dialed the number of his old house and let it ring several times.

Lisa's tired, fragile voice came through from the other side. "Hello."

Karras did not answer.

"Hello? Is anybody there?"

He listened to Lisa breathing, and then there was a soft, final click.

Karras stood in the kitchen with the receiver pressed against his cheek. After a while he hung the phone in its cradle and returned to Stephanie's bed.

EIGHTEEN

THE MORNING after he had spoken with Roman Otis, Frank Farrow phoned his boss and told him that he was going home to Wilmington to bury his father, who had died in his sleep the previous night.

"You comin' back, Larry? You were the best dishwasher we ever had."

"I don't think so. I've got to look after my mother now. You understand."

Farrow packed his personal belongings into a small duffel bag and threw the bedsheets stained with Grace's blood in the alley Dumpster. He paid off his landlord, telling her the same story he had told his boss.

Farrow drove the Taurus SHO southwest toward the Chesapeake Bay Bridge and rented a room in a motel on Kent Island. He registered under the name of Louie Pino and paid cash in advance for a five-day stay.

The first day he kept to his room and read a paperback novel. That night he ate dinner at the bar of the Angler's Restaurant, a small locals' spot in Grasonville that served delicious vegetable crab soup and soft-shell sandwiches. After dinner he drank beer slowly until closing time and went back to his motel room with a Dundalk woman named Rita whom he had picked up at the bar.

In the next four days he read two paperback novels written by Edward Anderson and A. I. Bezzerides, and at night he ate and drank at the Angler's with Rita and took her back to his room, where he made Rita's eyes roll back in her head with his workmanlike, rhythmic thrusts. Rita said nothing to anger him, and he did not hurt her.

On the fifth day he drove the SHO down the road, parked it behind a restaurant, removed its plates, and walked back to the motel with his duffel bag in his hand. He had noticed that every morning a blue-collar man left his Ranger truck on the edge of the motel parking lot, out of sight of the manager's office, and was picked up by another blue-collar man. The two of them would then go off together to their jobs. Farrow removed the Ranger's plates, replaced them with the SHO's plates, broke into the pickup easily using a bar tool he owned, hot-wired the ignition, and drove northeast. A bumper sticker on the Ranger read, "There Is No Life West of the Chesapeake Bay."

HE THOUGHT of his brother as he made open road.

Richard had always been somewhat of a follower. Frank had easily turned him against their father, a Beverly Hills lawyer, at a very young age. But Richard could never go all the way like Frank. So as Frank began to seek perfection in his chosen career of crime, Richard continued to stumble through the subworld of amateur criminals inhabited by the true lowlifes: meth-heads and dope fiends, runaways and their pimps, street grifters, fences, and the like.

In the meantime, Frank did his reform school stretches and then two major jolts as an adult, where he fell in love with the books in the prison libraries and made the contacts within the walls that would enable him to graduate to an ever higher level of success outside. Some believed that incarceration was a mark of failure, but Frank disagreed. Prison was an essential element of any career criminal's education.

When he had been released from his last sentence and done his parole, Frank was ready, and Richard, of course, was not. But he had brought Richard along on that final job because that was what a brother was obligated to do.

Frank cracked the window and lit a Kool.

The Farrow brothers' birth mother had died very young — Frank remembered her vaguely and Richard not at all — and their father remarried quickly. To Frank's mind, the father loved only money and its accoutrements. Frank hated him and his friends, and he would always despise everyone like them. By the time his father married for the third time, there was no familial connection that remained. Their father no longer considered Frank and Richard, who had been in serious trouble since their teens, to be his sons. Frank and Richard had not had any kind of contact with him for years. For all Frank knew or cared, their father was dead.

Now Richard was dead, too. Frank didn't dwell on it. He had loved Richard, he supposed, but he had no illusions of the afterlife, and he was free of sentiment. He knew there was no spiritual world where the two of them would meet again. Richard was now what all men were in the end: food for worms. Sentiment aside, though, Frank would have to kill the man who had killed his brother; retaliation was a part of the personal code he had adopted long ago.

Frank was fascinated by the murder trials he had seen on

TV. He'd watch the victims' families, how they sat quietly in court, their soft hands resting in their laps, waiting for a justice that would never fully come. He was sure that they thought of themselves as good people. He only thought of them as weak.

Weakness. It separated him from the straights. This separation would keep him alive.

FRANK PARKED the Ranger alongside the platinum Park Avenue in the lot of the New Rock Church. He checked the load on the .38 that Toomey had given him and holstered the gun against the small of his back. He reached into his duffel bag, retrieved a pair of latex examination gloves, and fitted them onto his hands. He looked around the empty lot and down Old Church Road. The road was clear. He stepped out of the truck.

Frank knocked on the door of the church and put his hands deep in the pockets of his coat. The door opened, and the Reverend Bob stood in the frame.

"Larry?" he said, donning his salesman's smile. "Why, I heard you had left town."

"I'm back. Can I come in?"

"Certainly."

The reverend stepped aside to let Farrow pass through, and shut the door behind them. Farrow walked slowly down the center aisle of the church, allowing the Reverend Bob to get in front of him.

"Shall we go to my office?"

"Here is good," said Farrow, stepping up onto the altar floor. He stood in a bar of light that entered narrowly from a glass panel on the roof and widened as it fell.

"Well . . . okay," said the reverend.

Farrow heard a catch in the reverend's voice.

The reverend stepped up onto the altar and stood beside him. Frank looked at him, immaculate in his starched white shirt.

"That's a Movado, isn't it?" said Farrow, nodding at the reverend's wrist.

"Yes." The reverend smiled. "I bought it secondhand. Of course, a new Movado is a little dear for a man in my profession."

"My father owned one of those. He was so proud of it, too. Always shot his cuffs around his friends, made sure they got a good look at it. My brother and I stole it off his dresser one night. I gave it to some street kid outside the Whiskey, over on the Strip."

The reverend looked at him quizzically. "Why do you mention this, Larry?"

"My father fired our maid the next morning. A Chicano woman with four children. He was paying her twenty-five dollars a day."

"Larry?"

"My name's Frank Farrow."

Farrow took his hands from his coat and dropped them at his sides.

The reverend looked at Farrow's gloved hands and backed up a step. "What...what do you want?"

"I told you I'd be back. When I make a promise like that, I keep it."

The color drained from the reverend's face. He looked desperately around the empty church and back at Farrow. He tried to smile and use a tone of sincerity, but his voice shook as it came forth.

"Listen...Frank, is it?"

"Frank Farrow."

"Frank, I never meant to offend you or infringe on your privacy. I was only looking to bring another person into our congregation. If you were ever incarcerated, it makes no difference to me."

"You were right on the money, Reverend Bob. I've been in one kind of prison or another for the better part of my life."

"Frank—atonement is everything in the eyes of the Lord. Whatever you did, you served your time."

"You have no idea what I've done. And you shouldn't have pried." Farrow reached into his coat and drew the .38 from where it was holstered in his belt line. "Get on your knees."

Tears dropped instantly from the reverend's eyes. He raised his hands as in prayer. His lip trembled violently, but he couldn't speak.

"On your knees," said Farrow.

The reverend dropped to his knees on the altar. Urine spread across his crotch and darkened the thighs of his slacks. The stench of it grew heavy in the church.

"Are you afraid?" asked Farrow.

The reverend nodded.

"It's funny," said Farrow, looking down at him. "I find that those the most afraid are those who believe in God. The same ones who hide their eyes at horror movies are the ones who bow their heads in a place like this. And for what? Something that does not, cannot, exist."

"Please," said the reverend.

"Your journey is just beginning," said Farrow with a smile. "You're going to a better place. Isn't that what you've been telling those old people out at the home, the ones who are about to die?"

"Yes, but—"

"But, what?"

The reverend looked up at Farrow with bloodshot eyes. "What if I was wrong?"

Farrow laughed. His laughter echoed in the church and then it was erased by the deafening explosion of the .38. The reverend's hair lifted briefly from his scalp and fragments of his brain sprayed out across the altar. He fell back; his head made a flat, hollow sound as it hit the wooden floor. A widening pool of blood spread behind it.

Farrow stood over the reverend and shot him again in the side of the face. He walked from the church.

FARROW DROVE a half mile down Old Church Road in the opposite direction of the interstate until he reached Lee Toomey's house at the edge of the woods. Toomey was loading some cable wire into his utility truck as Farrow pulled the Ranger into the yard. Toomey's eyes clouded when he saw that it was Farrow behind the wheel. He noticed the light yellow gloves on Farrow's hands as Farrow stepped out of the truck and crossed the yard.

"Lee."

"Frank. Thought you left town."

"I didn't. Where's that family of yours?"

"Martin's playin' that TV game of his. My wife and daughter are in the kitchen, I'd expect."

"Let's walk into those woods a bit."

Toomey spit tobacco juice to the side. "Why would we need to do that?"

"We won't be but a minute. C'mon."

They went in through a trail and then off the trail until they were out of the house's sight line. Toomey leaned against the trunk of a pine and regarded Farrow as he lit a cigarette.

Farrow let the Kool dangle from his mouth. He pulled the

.38 and tossed it to Toomey. Toomey caught it and stared back at Farrow.

"I just used that on the Reverend Bob, back in the church. Blew the top of his head off, right up there on the altar. That's a real efficient weapon you gave me, Lee."

"Thought I heard a shot," said Toomey slowly, not taking his eyes off Farrow's.

"What you need to do now," said Farrow, "is get over there with some cleaning supplies. I wouldn't wait for the blood to get too dried in. Scrub that altar down real good and drive the reverend out to that nature preserve we talked about. I was you, I'd bury him up there. Ground'll be hard, but not too hard. You can thank this mild winter for that. Then I'd throw your gun in the bay, seeing as how it's got your prints all over it."

"You," said Toomey.

Farrow chuckled. "You know, for a moment there I saw the old Toomey in your eyes. Now, that was one bad-ass boy. Getting the Jesus into you, though, it really tripped you up. You and I both know how soft you are now. You'd never make any kind of play on me."

"That's right, Frank. I never would."

Farrow dragged on his smoke. "But just to make sure, I ought to let you know that I'm not going to be far away. I've got a little business to take care of up in Washington, D.C., probably keep me in this part of the country for the next couple of weeks. If I even get an idea that you've been talking to the law about me, Lee, I want you to remember that I'm just an hour and a half away. I can easily get down here and make a visit to that beautiful family of yours. Or I could pay someone else to do the same. And I'd never forget. Do you understand?"

Toomey felt his blood ticking and his head grow hot. He hadn't had this feeling for a long while, but it was a familiar feeling, nonetheless. He wanted to kill Farrow right now. He *could* kill him right now.

Toomey said, "I understand, Frank."

"Good. You'll be okay if you move fast and leave nothing behind. The reverend leaving town, well, it happens. Folks'll just figure he was throwing it to one of the parishioner's wives. Anyway, you bury him deep enough and they'll never find him."

"I'll do it."

Farrow looked at Toomey. "See you around, Lee."

Farrow dragged on his cigarette, dropped it on a bed of pine needles, and crushed it beneath his boot. He walked out of the woods and straight to the truck. Toomey stayed behind, the gun in one hand, the other picking at his beard.

LATER THAT night, when Toomey had finished his task, he phoned Manuel Ruiz at the garage outside D.C.

"Manny?"

"Yes."

"It's Toomey, bro."

"Lee, what's up?"

"Frank Farrow's heading back to D.C.," said Toomey. "We need to talk."

NINETEEN

TWO O'CLO," said Maria Juarez. "My time, right, Mitri?"

"Yeah, Maria," said Dimitri Karras, checking his watch. "Go ahead and let it roll."

Maria slipped the tape that Karras had bought her into the boom box and turned up the volume. Karras had picked it up at an international record store near the old Kilimanjaro Club the night before. He had asked for something danceable and Latin, and the clerk had assured him that this one moved.

A Spanish female vocal with Tito Puente's band behind it came from the box. Maria met James Posten in the middle of the kitchen, and the two of them began to dance, James doing his idea of a cha-cha. Darnell, from where he stood over the sink, turned his head and smiled. He looked over at Karras, leaning on the expediter's station, and nodded one time.

"Olé, baby!" said James. His eye shadow was on the maroon side of the rainbow this afternoon.

"Like this, Jame," said Maria, taking two steps in, retreating two steps, and twisting her hips on the dip.

"That's what *I'm* talkin' about," said James, following her lead, twirling the spatula like a baton.

"You doin' it, Jame," said Maria.

"Tell the truth," said James, "and shame the devil."

Karras studied Maria's face. She had shown up that morning with her right eye blood gorged and swollen close to shut. She had a truly beautiful spirit; anger had welled up in him immediately when he had walked in that morning and seen her face. He was glad he had picked this day to give her a gift.

Anna Wang entered the kitchen, a cigarette dangling from her lips, a tray of butter patties in her hands. She joined Maria and James momentarily on her way to the refrigerator, where she stowed the covered butter in the rear.

"Nice work today, Karras," said Anna on her way out the door.

"She wants somethin'," said James, still dancing. "You could bet it."

"Just giving the man a compliment, J. P.," said Anna.

Karras said, "Thanks."

A half hour later they had begun to shut down the kitchen. James switched the radio to R&B as Maria covered the components of the cold station with plastic wrap. Ramon hurried in with a bus tray and dropped it off on the edge of Darnell's sink. He stepped on Darnell's foot deliberately, and Darnell grabbed his hand, pressing his thumb down on the crook of Ramon's thumb. Ramon pulled his hand away and stood there rubbing it, a crooked smile on his face.

"Ah, here we go, y'all," said James as the Army Reserve commercial came on the radio at its usual time. James turned it up as the announcer's voice rose with the build of the music.

Karras, Darnell, Maria, James, and Ramon stopped working. At the same moment they all raucously sang, "Be...all that you can be!"

James and Maria doubled over in laughter, their hands on each other's shoulders. Darnell gave Ramon skin.

Karras smiled ear to ear. His face felt odd, and then he knew why. He had forgotten what it felt like to smile with that kind of abandon. It had been a long time.

"HOW'S THAT flounder?" said Darnell, sliding onto a stool next to Karras at the bar.

"Good—what'd you, brush it with butter?"

"Yeah, and squeezed some lemon on it, too. Wrapped it up in foil and baked it in the oven. That's the way you need to be cookin' fish. Simple like that. Course, I would have spiced it some. Phil doesn't want anybody thinkin' we're turnin' this place into a soul-food joint, nothin' like that."

"It's good just like this," said Karras.

"Thanks, baby," said Darnell to Mai, who had placed a glass of juice in front of him. "What're we listenin' to, anyway?"

"The Bee Gees," said Mai, shooting a finger to the ceiling and cocking her hip, her breasts jiggling beneath her Semper Fi T.

"Sounds like someone's pullin' hard on that singer's berries."

"My shift," said Mai, stepping away.

"Say, Dimitri," said Darnell, "I been lookin' at your tickets as I was walking by. You get a medium burger on the ticket, I noticed you call it out medium rare to James."

"That's right. I figured out early, James always overcooks his burgers by one level, no matter what. So I adjust on the call rather than waste time arguing with him."

"You trickin' him, huh? I should of thought of that my own self. Me and him used to have some serious fights when I was doin' the expediting. The man was just thick that way."

"I used to manage all the employees in my friend's record

stores," said Karras. "Over the years I picked up some experience with diplomacy."

"So much to learn about runnin' a business."

"You could do it, Darnell. You're smart. And you've got a work ethic like I've never seen."

"That's for other people, man."

"It's for anybody who's got what you've got, and a will. Look, my friend I told you about, the record store guy? He makes a living now setting people like you up."

"Dishwashers?"

"African Americans looking to open up small businesses in the city. I'm meeting him tonight at the Wizards game. I'm gonna talk to him about you."

"Look here, Dimitri, square business: I know my limits. It's just not for me."

"All right, Darnell. But you know I'm gonna talk to you about it again."

Darnell drank down his juice and used the napkin to wipe sweat off his face. The bell over the front door jingled, and Roberto Juarez entered the bar. He stayed up on the landing as always and waited. Karras nudged Darnell.

"I see him," said Darnell under his breath.

Karras looked through the reach-through at the end of the stick. James had his hands on Maria's shoulders, and he was close to her face, giving her a serious talk. She nodded her head and kissed James on the cheek.

James emerged from the kitchen, his fox-head stole worn over a clean outfit, his amber-stone walking stick in his hand. He stepped around Maria's husband on the landing, who smiled and said something to James in Spanish. Karras couldn't understand the words, but he knew from the tone that Maria's husband had called James some variety of faggot. James kept walking and left the bar.

Ramon stood by the stairwell to the basement, leaning against the frame, picking at his cuticle with a penknife, watching.

"Hard life," said Darnell as Maria came from the kitchen in her cheap coat, meeting her husband with her head down and following him out the door.

"Yes it is," said Karras.

"That was real kind of you, buying her that tape."

"It made her happy for a little while, I guess."

Darnell got off the stool and stood, stretching his long frame. "Well, let me get back to my dishes."

"Nick coming in today?"

"He's working one of his cases. I expect I'll see him tonight."

NICK STEFANOS sat in the living room of Terrence Mitchell's house, off Sargent Road in the Chillum district of Prince George's County. Mitchell lived on a treeless street of clean ramblers near power lines strung between steel towers set on rolling hills of brown grass. Many of the homes around Mitchell's had barred storm doors, but Mitchell's was along the lines of a fortress: It featured a high chain-link fence crowned by double-rowed barbed wire, a padlocked gate protecting the driveway, and a No Trespassing notice as big as a stop sign on the fence. In the driveway sat an immaculate late-model blue Volvo sedan.

The interior of Mitchell's house was no less cold. Certificates from the Metropolitan Police Department and the U.S. Army hung on the walls. A photograph of a young Mitchell in his blues and a photograph of a younger Mitchell in army fatigues, surrounded by his buddies in Vietnam, showed him with the same stoic, humorless face.

Soon after the interview began, Stefanos's first impression at seeing the home's security setup was confirmed. Mitchell, the ex-soldier, ex-cop, was some sort of paranoid. He never smiled once during their meeting. It couldn't have been any kind of fun for his daughter, Erika Mitchell, to live under his roof.

"So let me get this straight," said Stefanos. "You don't remember if your daughter went out with Randy Weston on the night of the murder."

"That's right."

"Randy tells his attorney that you gave him a lecture the night he picked her up for the movies. Randy had gotten her home past her curfew the last two times he'd taken her out. Randy says you went into one of those 'three strikes you're out' things with him."

"I could've, yes. But I don't remember what night it was."

"You being a cop and all, I thought you'd remember the exact night."

Terrence Mitchell was a broad-chested man with a thick mustache, dark skin, and a full head of hair, not yet gray. He might even have been a handsome man when he smiled. He almost smiled at Stefanos then — but didn't.

"I don't remember what night it was."

Stefanos swallowed spit. He was thirsty, but Mitchell had not even offered him a glass of water when he'd entered the house.

"You like television, isn't that right, Mr. Mitchell?"

"What's that?"

Stefanos nodded at the large-screen television set in a bookshelf across the room. "Randy Weston says you watch a lot of television. Loud."

Mitchell blinked his eyes slowly to indicate that he was bored. "I lost some of my hearing on the job, Stefanose."

"It's Stefanos. The reason I mentioned the loud part is, Randy couldn't help but remember that you were watching *Home Improvement* while you were giving him that lecture. I mean, the laugh track was blaring in his ear. *Home Improvement* runs on Tuesday night; Donnel Lawton was murdered on a Tuesday night."

"That show runs every Tuesday night. It doesn't prove I was watching it, or lecturing Weston, on that particular Tuesday night."

Stefanos made a nonsense note on his pad. Of course it didn't prove that Mitchell talked to him that Tuesday night. It didn't prove shit. He was trying anything now. If Mitchell or his daughter weren't going to cooperate, then Elaine Clay had no case.

"Let me ask you something." Stefanos looked up and held Mitchell's eyes. "If Randy Weston were not a drug dealer who was dating your daughter, would your memory improve?"

"He is a drug dealer, Stefanos. I was a street cop in D.C. for many years." Mitchell looked Stefanos over. "A *real* cop. I saw firsthand what people like that do, to individuals, mothers, fathers... to families. When my wife left me, I made a solemn promise to protect my little girl. The truth is, I don't really care if that boy goes to jail."

"Even if he's innocent?"

"He's not innocent."

"But if you knew he was with your daughter at the time of the murder—"

"I'd deny it. And I'd deny this conversation. Cops lie all the time on the stand to get a conviction, you know that. I've done it before. If it means getting that boy away from Erika, I'd lie again."

Stefanos shut his notebook. "So what makes you different than the ones out there, breaking the law?"

Mitchell's eyes narrowed. "Say that again?"

Stefanos didn't repeat it. He stood from his chair. "Do you know where your daughter is so I can contact her?"

"I always know where she is. I drop her at the Fort Totten station at seven-forty-five sharp every morning, and then she goes off to work. And I pick her up at five-forty-five, the same time, same place, every evening. She's a stylist at a shop over in Greenbelt."

"What shop?"

"You're gonna have to find that out for yourself."

"I'm going to talk to her, Mr. Mitchell."

"Go ahead. She'll tell you the same thing I have. She doesn't exactly remember."

"Right." Stefanos walked for the door, turned. "By the way. You talked about families. Randy Weston's got a kid brother, not a bad kid but on the edge. And Weston's got a mother, too, works a government job downtown. She's trying real hard to keep it together, I'd expect. There's all sorts of families trying to make it out here. I just thought you'd like to know."

"You see yourself out?"

"I got it. Thanks for your time."

DRIVING SOUTH on New Hampshire, Stefanos remembered something Anna Wang had said about the Chinese guys she'd known. He crossed the District Line and took the Kennedy Street cutoff heading west.

TWENTY

S TEFANOS WALKED into the order area of Hunan Delite and went to the lazy Susan below the teardrop holes cut into the Plexiglas. He listened to the new Usher single coming from the tinny speakers mounted in the lobby while he waited to catch Jerry Sun's eye. Sun came forward, and Stefanos placed his license against the glass.

"Stefanos," said Sun. "I remember. What can I do for you?"

"Do you sell steak and cheese?"

"Very funny. C'mon, man, I got things to do."

"I need to talk to you. I'll make it fast."

Sun made a head motion. Stefanos walked back out the door and around the building. By the time he got there, Sun was leaning against the Dumpster, cleaning his eyeglasses on his shirt.

"Jerry."

"Nick!"

"Okay, okay. Listen, here's the thing: I know this Chinese girl, friend of mine named Anna, waitresses in this place I bartend for."

"She sounds real nice. But I've got a girlfriend, Stefanos."

"I don't think she'd dig you anyway. She doesn't date Chinese guys. Says they're more interested in their cars than their women."

Sun smiled a little and shrugged.

"So I was thinking," said Stefanos, "about how you noticed the pipes on my sled."

"So what?"

"What about that red Torino you saw speeding away from the murder scene? You notice anything more than what you gave me the first time?"

"Need help, huh?"

"I'm a Mopar man. I don't know a thing about Fords. You know what they say: You drive a Dodge, you drive in style; drive a Ford, you'll walk a mile."

Sun rolled his eyes. "What you want to know?"

"Anything."

"Okay," said Sun. "It was called the Twister Special when it came out. The factory put a decal on the side so you knew; it was supposed to look like a tornado or something, ran from the front to the rear quarter panels. It was a very fast car. The stock engine was a four twenty-nine, SCJ."

Stefanos smiled like David Janssen and scribbled in his notebook. "Goddamn, Jerry. Anything else?"

"Ford only made ninety of that particular car. I'd call that a very limited edition. A car like that, it shouldn't be so hard to find."

"Keep going."

"I only saw it go by quick, but from what I saw the car was in perfect condition. Like it had been garaged. Or restored."

Stefanos looked at Sun with admiration. "Why didn't you tell me the first time around?"

"You didn't ask. Smart guy like you, I was wondering when you were going to get around to it."

"That car you saw. You know whose car that was, Jerry?"

"No idea. I'm serious about that, too."

"Tags?"

"Like I told you before. No tags."

"I guess Anna was right about you guys."

"Yeah, I been jacking off to *Motor Trend* since I was nine years old."

"Doin' your own viscosity tests, huh?"

"I gotta run, Stefanos."

"Okay. Say, I'm kinda hungry. How *is* the steak and cheese here, Jerry?"

"I wouldn't recommend it. Tastes like dog shit, you want to know the truth."

Sun turned and walked back toward the rear kitchen entrance.

"Hey, thanks," said Stefanos. Sun waved over his shoulder and went through the door.

ON KENNEDY, Stefanos dropped a quarter and a dime into the pay phone slot. He lit a cigarette, got Elaine's assistant, waited for Elaine to get on the line.

"Nick, what's going on?"

"I talked to Terrence Mitchell. It's not that he doesn't remember if Randy and his daughter went out the night of the murder. He does remember, but he won't testify to it. He'd rather get that drug dealer out of his daughter's life than get him off. He told me straight up that he'd lie."

"Nice. That means we're—"

"Fucked. It also means Randy Weston's innocent. I know that now. And the car thing? The Torino's real. I got a line on it from Jerry Sun, the guy who runs the Chinese joint down here in the neighborhood. The car's a special model, Elaine. We should be able to track it down, despite the fact that it was out there without tags that night."

"Give me the details. I'll get our people to run it through the system."

Stefanos read off the information Sun had given him.

"This could be what breaks this," said Elaine. "Nice work."

"Thanks. In the meantime, I can check with some mechanics. Ford restorationists, specialists. Car like that, they'd remember it."

"Hold on a second, Nick."

Stefanos dragged on his Camel. He double-dragged and watched his smoke dissipate in the wind.

"All right," said Elaine, "I'm back. Was looking for my address book.... Here it is. Marcus has this friend, Dimitri knows him, too, works on old Continentals exclusively. Genuine tough guy, a Truck Turner type, has a garage over in the Brookland area. I've got his number right here."

"What's his name?"

"Al Adamson," said Elaine. "Say Marcus hooked you up."

"THERE GOES Strickland," said Marcus Clay. "Gonna go right in on Shaq, challenge his wide ass."

"Man is fearless," said Dimitri Karras.

The crowd at the MCI Center cheered as Rod Strickland sunk the layup. Karras and Clay slapped each other five.

"Rod," said Karras with admiration. "Best point guard in the East."

"Might be the best guard in the NBA, you ask me. The man sees the entire floor. He can dish without telegraphing, and he can take it to the hole at will. And what I really like is, he's got the fire. The rest of the Wizards had that fire, we'd hear the fat lady sing again, you can believe that."

"Webber can do it."

"When he wants to," said Clay, "C. Webb can do it all. That young man's got more natural ability than I've seen on anyone in a long while. But look right there."

Webber had dropped away from the rest of the defense and was walking backward, slowly, toward the half-court line.

"He's always lookin' to leak out for that fast break," said Clay, "when he should be crashing those boards."

"You can't blame that on Webber entirely. That's a coaching thing right there."

Karras clapped at a Calbert Cheaney jumper that made the nylon dance. His elbow knocked Clay's, causing him to spill beer on his chin.

"Hey, watch it, man."

"Sorry."

"You just spilled about two dollars' worth of my five-dollar beer."

"Yeah, good thing you and I never did drink too much. We'd go broke in this place."

Clay looked around. "It's beautiful, though, isn't it? Finally got us our own venue in the city."

"Like the Garden. And these are good seats."

"The business pays for them, man. Midcourt, club level. You can't beat it, and I write it off. If you were to come back to the company, you'd get a third of the games."

Karras ignored that and said, "Only thing I miss now is the Washington Bullets."

"You gonna go on that nostalgia trip again?"

"You wanna tell me why they had to change the name of the

team? Because it encouraged violence? Shit, Marcus, basketball jerseys don't kill people—"

"They changed the name to *sell* basketball jerseys, man."

"It's like go-go music, Marcus."

"Now you're gonna get on that."

"I'm serious. Every time someone gets shot within a hundred yards of a go-go concert, the *Post* dredges up their old warhorse about how the music is related to the violence. Getting the public all paranoid about go-go, it's ridiculous. For what? So they can make a case for taking away the one thing the young people of this city can still call their own?"

"I hear you, man. And so does that family in front of us."

"Nobody tried to stop rock and roll because of Altamont. Or after the stampede when the Who played Cincinnati."

"*The Kids Are All Dead* tour?"

"*The Kids Are All Right.*"

"Gotta excuse me, I been out of the music business for a while. You want a hot dog or something?"

"Yeah, okay. Can I borrow twenty dollars?"

They watched another five minutes of game. Tracy Murray hit two free throws to further the Wizards' lead.

"The shots at the line are gonna win this game," said Clay. "The Lakers have made half of theirs. We made damn near all of ours. It's like I'm always telling Marcus Jr.: fundamentals."

"How's M. J. doin', man?"

"Good. Made the honor roll at Wilson. You'll see him at my birthday thing. You are coming, right?"

"I'll be there."

"Course, M. J. would have liked to have made the game tonight. Wanted to check out Kobe."

"He'll see him—the kid's got a long career ahead of him."

"He's got, what, four points this evening? The way he's playin' tonight, I'd say the young emperor has no clothes."

"The Lakers are a year away in every department. Look at their talent. Van Exel, Horry. Eddie Jones is *bad*. And Kobe Bryant is only gonna get better."

"Anyway, I told M. J. that I had to save the Lakers game for my boy Dimitri. 'Cause I know how much you like the Lakers." Clay side-glanced Karras. "Goin' all the way back to Gail Goodrich, when you modeled your game after his."

"Aw, shit, now you're gonna start that again. I told you a hundred times, my game was always closer to Walt Frazier's."

"Well, you used to wear those Clydes of his, anyway."

"And I could drive the paint like him, too."

Clay and Karras laughed and shook hands. Clay squeezed Karras's shoulder.

"It's good to see you, man," said Clay.

"Good to see you, too."

"You look different. Happier or something. Am I wrong?"

"No, you're right. My new job has helped. And so has time."

"You still seeing the bartender's wife?"

"Once a week for now. That's helped as well."

"What about Lisa?"

"I called her late the other night. . . . I don't know why. It was a mistake. Nothing's changed. Nothing's *going* to change." Karras finished his warm beer and put the plastic cup down on the concrete. "I know now that there's two kinds of people in this world: those who've lost a child and those who haven't. I'll never be whole again, Marcus. I've accepted that."

"But you got to keep trying."

"I am." Karras wiped his mouth dry with a napkin. "Speaking of work, I've got this friend down at the Spot, dishwasher named Darnell. Smart guy, a good cook, and a really good worker. I think he's a good candidate to open his own small business. He's not looking for a bar, just the food side of things."

"I'll talk to him, that's what you want."

"He lacks confidence, I think."

"When the time's right, then. Maybe you could come in with him, make it less painful for him. Be a good way for you to ease back on into the company, too. Clarence was just sayin' the other day how we could use your people skills again."

"Like I said, Marcus. I need a little time."

O'Neal fought three defenders under the bucket and came up for a monster dunk. The hometown crowd had to applaud his effort.

"Now there's a guy whose game has come around," said Karras.

"You're not lyin'. Shaq is the real Raging Bull."

Karras looked over at his friend. Marcus had put on a few pounds, but it was natural weight gain and he kept it hard. His closely cropped Afro was salted with gray, and there were gray flecks in his thick black mustache.

"You still playin'?" said Karras.

"Still got that once-a-week thing over at the Alice Deal gym. My knees are gonna betray me one of these days, I know. And I can't run the court with those young boys anymore. But I'm doin' all right for an old man, I guess."

"You'll never give it up. You're the original ball freak, man."

Clay pointed his finger at Karras. "What about you? God-damn, Dimitri! Was a time when you would not leave the blacktop. You even used to drag me to those ABA games back when D.C. had a team in the seventies."

Karras smiled. "The Capitols."

"Yeah, we'd have to go down to the old Washington Coliseum to see 'em play, too. What a dump that was."

"Hey, we saw some good ball. They had Rick Barry for a while, right? And we got to see the Doctor when he was young and playin' for the Squires, don't forget that."

"What was that team had all those crazy boys on it? The Spirits of St. Louis, right?"

"Marvin Bad Boy Barnes."

"Hey, Mitri," said Clay, "remember that backup center the Spirits had, big, Lurch-lookin' mug, had a clown's face, like? They used to put him into the game just to inflict pain."

"I don't remember his name. But yeah, it's hard to forget a man that ugly." Karras squinted. "Hey, check out that cheerleader, Marcus. The Asian girl, back row center."

"Yeah, she is fine. But look at you, all gray and shit, staring at some twenty-year-old girl."

"I was just commenting on her beauty, is all."

"I know what you was doin'," said Clay. "Booty monger like you."

TWENTY-ONE

NICK STEFANOS stood on the platform of the Fort Totten Metro station at seven-forty-five in the morning, blowing into his hands to warm them against the cold. He looked out into the parking lot at the blue Volvo pulling into the Kiss and Ride lane. He knew Terrence Mitchell would be right on time—he was that kind of man. Erika Mitchell stepped out of the passenger side, shut the door behind her, and walked across the lot.

Stefanos leaned against the side of a wind shelter as Erika emerged onto the platform. Her skin was dark, and she wore bright red lipstick on her ample mouth. She was a big-legged girl with big, straightened hair.

The lights at the edge of the platform blinked as the Green Line train approached. Erika boarded the train, and Stefanos took his time walking into the same car. She took the first seat by the doors; he had a seat three rows behind her.

"George Clinton," said the recorded voice as the doors closed.

Stefanos settled in for the ride. Greenbelt was four stops

away, and the trip would take a little while. But Erika got out of her seat two stops shy of Greenbelt and exited the car at the Prince George's Plaza station. Stefanos followed her down to the parking lot and hung back at the newspaper racks as a chromed-up, ice-green Acura pulled alongside her.

The driver stopped the car so that it blocked traffic. He got out, walked over to Erika, and put his hands gently on her shoulders. He was tall and lean, midtwenties, wearing wide-leg jeans and a Nautica shirt with an unbuttoned thigh-length leather over the shirt. He wore his hair in a blown-out, seventies-style Afro. Erika and the tall man kissed, and then she got into the shotgun seat of his ride. The driver pulled away.

In the time that Randy Weston had been held on the murder charge, Erika Mitchell had found a new man. Or maybe he had been there all along. Even a control freak like Terrence Mitchell, thought Stefanos, couldn't stop a young man and woman from getting together. He wondered if Erika Mitchell even had a job.

Stefanos checked his watch. He returned to the station and caught a train back to Fort Totten.

STEFANOS FIRED up his Dodge and drove east, down Michigan Avenue and along the north-south railroad tracks of Brookland. He parked on the street, found the bay with the green door that he was looking for, and rang the bell. The door opened. A man stood in the frame, wiping his hands on a pink shop rag.

"Al Adamson?"

"That's right."

"Nick Stefanos. I phoned yesterday, remember? Marcus Clay sent me."

Adamson's biceps filled out the sleeves of his coveralls, and his upper body strained the fabric at his chest. He was shaved bald with a full beard and wore small rimless glasses. His face was deeply lined. Stefanos put him in his early fifties.

"Come on in," said Adamson.

Stefanos followed him into the bay. A drop light hung over the open hood of a triple-black Mark III. Adamson went right to the car, grabbed a wrench off a cloth laid out across the top of the front quarter panel, and got to work.

"You can talk to me while I do this," said Adamson. "I got to get this water pump out and replaced by noon."

"Like I said, Marcus put me onto you. Well, Elaine, really. I do investigative work for her, down at the courthouse."

"I called Marcus after you called me. He said you were all right. Said you gave Dimitri Karras a job."

"Yeah, he's doing well."

"Damn shame about his son." Adamson stopped working for a moment. "I lost my kid brother to violence back in nineteen seventy-six. You never forget, not really." Adamson loosened a bolt. "Karras still wearin' those Hawaiian shirts?"

"Not that I know of."

Adamson chuckled to himself.

Stefanos said, "I'm looking for the name of a specialty Ford mechanic. Someone who might work on a Torino from the early seventies. One of those Twisters they had, limited edition."

Adamson looked up. Light flashed off the lenses of his glasses. "I don't recall that car."

"Like I say, limited. Real limited. Fast car, but stock. Maybe a restoration job."

"Restoration, huh? There's a few guys I can turn you on to. Guys I've run into over the years. You're lookin' for D.C. boys, right?"

"Inside the Beltway ought to do it."

Adamson backed up and stood. "Be right back."

Stefanos smoked a cigarette, waiting for Adamson to return. He crushed the smoke under his shoe as Adamson came back into the bay. Adamson stared at the butt flattened on the concrete.

"I tell you you could do that in here?"

"No."

Adamson glared at Stefanos. Stefanos picked up the butt and dropped it in the pocket of his work shirt.

"Here you go, man," said Adamson. He handed a slip of note-paper to Stefanos. "Had to transpose that out of my Rolodex."

Stefanos read off the names. Adamson's handwriting was like a doctor's — nearly illegible. "Clewis?" he said.

"Supposed to be C. Lewis. As in Charlie. Has a shop over in Hyattsville."

"Okay. And what's this? Manul Rulz and—"

"Manuel Ruiz and Jaime Gutierrez. Two mechanics up in Silver Spring, right over the District line. They specialize in Ford restorations."

"Okay. I think I can figure this out."

Stefanos uncovered a stick of gum from its foil wrapper and began to put the gum in his mouth.

"I tell you you could do that?" said Adamson.

"What?"

Adamson half grinned. "Just kidding you, man."

"I knew that." Stefanos relaxed his shoulders. "Say, I'm no Ford expert, but I remember when Lincoln-Mercury was putting out some really strange models. Didn't there used to be a Cartier-edition Lincoln, way back?"

"Yeah, had the Landau roof with the opera window cutout. New York Cartier gauges on the dash, too."

"And there was this other model they had, two-tone job, came out in the late seventies—"

"The Mark Five Bill Blass." Adamson smiled. "All the brothers who *thought* they were stylin' had to have that one."

"Well, I'll let you get back to it."

"Yeah, I better."

Stefanos looked Adamson over. "You know, you don't mind my sayin' so, the shape you're in, you could put the fear of God into Mike Tyson. You ever do any kickboxing, anything like that?"

Adamson adjusted his glasses. "Never *had* to."

"Right. Thanks a million, hear?"

Adamson nodded and got back under the hood of the Mark.

AT FIVE-THIRTY in the evening, Stefanos sat behind the wheel of his Dodge in the parking lot of the Prince George's Plaza metro station, waiting for the tall man in the Acura to drop Erika Mitchell off. A couple of minutes later, the car arrived. Stefanos wrote down the Virginia plate numbers as he watched the man and Erika in silhouette through the Acura's back window.

The Acura pulled out of the lot. Stefanos put the Dodge in gear and followed.

The driver of the Acura took East–West Highway to Riggs to New Hampshire, cutting off on Kennedy. Stefanos stayed back a quarter mile. The Acura drifted off Kennedy and went up First Place, pulling over to the curb in front of a row house there. Stefanos parked his Dodge a half block south.

Two young men came from the row house and walked to the Acura as the driver let down his window. One of the young men handed something to the driver. Darkness had fallen now, and Stefanos could not see what had transpired.

The young men stood around talking to the driver, and then the driver pulled the car off the curb and rolled north. Stefanos followed.

As he followed, Stefanos considered what he had just seen. A young black man who did not appear to have worked that day was driving a thirty-thousand-dollar car. He briefly met with two other young black men, who passed him something through his window.

If the young driver had been white and living in Potomac or Ward 3, Stefanos might have come to a different conclusion, or no conclusion at all. After all, you could drive by Churchill High School or St. Alban's in the middle of the day and see a parking lot filled with Acuras and BMWs.

But this wasn't Ward 3, and Stefanos had to make the leap: Erika Mitchell had a history of going with young men who flirted with the drug trade. Now she was hooked up with the driver of the Acura, most likely also a drug dealer.

Stefanos pushed a tape of the Getaway People, a mix of old-school funk and Beck-style hiptronics, into the deck. "Does My Colour Scare You?" came forward, and he turned it up.

The Acura cut up Blair Road and went north along the west side of the railroad tracks. It turned left on Rittenhouse. Stefanos waited, hung a left onto a residential street of modest, proudly maintained homes, watched the glow of the Acura's taillights flare as the driver braked. The Acura swung right into a driveway.

Stefanos drove slowly down the block, checking the addresses. He neared the spot where the Acura had turned, and he cut the Dodge to the curb. He got out of the car and walked down the sidewalk.

The driver of the Acura was stepping out of his car as Stefanos approached the house, a small, clapboard, single-family home. The Acura was parked in front of a detached, locked-down garage.

Stefanos kept walking. He was reading the address and making a mental note of it when he bumped into a man.

"Fuck you think you doin'?" said the young man, low slung with a stoved-in nose. He made a sweeping motion with his hands.

"Sorry," said Stefanos. "I wasn't watching—"

"Gotdamn right you sorry. You about the sorriest mother-fucker I seen all day."

Stefanos walked around the man and kept on, glancing back over his shoulder. The young man was standing there studying him, giving him the requisite hard look. The driver of the Acura stood by his car. He had heard the exchange and was studying Stefanos now, too.

Stefanos quickened his step. He made a right on 2nd, another right on Sheridan, and circled the block. He got into his Coronet, U-turned it, and gave it gas.

He stopped at Blair Liquors up the road. He bought a can of Budweiser and a pint of Old Crow. He sat in the car and had a deep drink from the bottle. He drank some more. He opened the can of beer and lit a cigarette. He was breathing normally now, and he headed for home.

TWENTY-TWO

O<small>N</small> **SATURDAY** morning, Dimitri Karras drove his faded navy blue BMW down into Maryland's St. Mary's County, following Bernie Walters's pickup all the way. They stopped for coffee, then stopped again for ammunition and bait, and made one last stop at a drive-through liquor store, where Karras watched the clerk pass a case of beer through the window of Walters's truck. Pulling out of the lot, Karras saw a puff of smoke come from the driver's side of the F-150 as Walters lit a cigarette.

They drove down Route 5 and then 242, through the towns of Clements and Dynard and onto back roads skirting the western shore of Clements Bay, an offshoot of the lower Potomac. A hard dirt road led them through woods to a clearing opening to two hundred feet of brackish creek. Walters parked the truck next to his pop-up trailer, and Karras pulled in beside him. Walters had a beer in his hand as Karras met him by the truck.

"Care for one?" said Walters, holding up the can.

"No, thanks, I'm good." Karras zipped up his coat.

"A little cold," said Walters, who wore only a down vest over a denim shirt, blue jeans, and his Orioles cap. He shaded his eyes from the sun and studied the clear sky. "But not bad."

Karras looked around the property. "Nice, Bern."

"Yeah, it's pretty fine. When the weather breaks and these trees fill out, you're really alone back here. Which is how I like it. I don't even have a phone line."

"You're gonna stay down here all week without a phone?"

"What do I need it for? And if I do need to make a call, I'll just drive up the road to town."

"What are you going to eat?"

"I've got a generator, but I cook with propane and I rarely use the electricity." Walters nodded at the Jiffy John set back from the trailer. "I put that in for my guests. Me, I just pee in the grass and shit in the woods."

"That's mighty natural, pardner. But you won't think I'm a pussy if I use the toilet, will ya?"

"Do anything you like, Dimitri. I won't think a thing."

Walters killed his beer and tossed the empty into a box filled with empties that was lying in the bed of his truck. He grabbed a fresh beer from the cab.

"Feel like takin' a walk in the woods?" said Walters.

"Sure. Maybe we could do that thing we talked about."

"Okay. Shotgun or handgun? I got both."

"Handgun."

"Be right back," said Walters, heading for the trailer.

BERNIE WALTERS emerged from the trailer with a day pack slung over his shoulder. He got the box of rounds he had purchased from out of the pickup and put that and some of the empty beer cans, plus one unopened can, into the pack.

They walked into the woods. Walters pointed to a deer blind

he had built in the branches of a tall oak as they crossed a dry creek bed. Karras followed him up a rise and into a clearing where an ancient, rusted tractor sat in tall brown grass. There was a row of upended logs along the far side of the tree line.

"We'll set up the cans over there," said Walters.

"You shoot out here yourself?" said Karras as they crossed the clearing.

"With my pistols, yeah."

"What about your shotguns?"

"I used to hunt deer with 'em."

"What did you do with the deer after you killed it?"

"Well, I used to clean it and take it home. Lynne would freeze the meat, and we'd eat venison stew all winter. Vance, he hated it. But I haven't killed a deer in a couple of seasons. Mostly I just sit up in that blind I showed you. Sitting up there, listening to the woods...it's peaceful. Like being in God's natural church." Walters's eyes shot over to Karras. "You ought to try it sometime."

Walters set the cans up on the logs. He and Karras walked back thirty yards, and Walters reached into the pack.

"Here's the Colt," said Walters. He handed Karras a .45 automatic in a leather holster, along with the box of shells.

"Go ahead," said Walters. "Release the magazine and load it."

The magazine slid out into Karras's palm. He got down on one knee and thumbed the rounds into the empty magazine. It took some time; his dexterity was hampered by the cold.

"This thing full?" he said.

"One more," said Walters, watching closely. "Give it a little pressure now and feel the tension on that spring. That's it. Now replace the magazine."

Karras stood. "Just aim and fire, right?"

"Pull back on the receiver and put one in the chamber. Check your safety. There you go."

Karras bent his knees deeply, steadying the butt of the gun with his left hand.

"You don't need to crouch down like that, Starsky. This ain't no TV show. But use both hands like you're doing. And if you're going to shoot more than one round, remember to space for the recoil. Otherwise, with that gun kicking, you're just gonna be firing wild. That's it, that's my lesson. Go ahead."

Karras fired out the clip, slowly and deliberately. The shots silenced the bird and animal sounds that had been there moments before. A steady tone sounded in Karras's ears, and both hands were numb with vibration.

Walters squinted and wiped beer from his chin. "You hit exactly one."

"I need more practice."

"Go ahead," said Walters, dropping the empty can to the ground and reaching into his pack for a fresh one. "I got nothin' but time."

Karras loaded the magazine more quickly than he had on his first attempt.

Walters watched him and said, "Why you want to learn to shoot all of the sudden?"

"You never know when you'll need it, right?"

Walters regarded him closely. "You ever kill a man, Dimitri?"

"No," lied Karras. A round slipped from his hand, and he stooped to pick it up.

"I have," said Walters, feeling the start of a daytime drunk. "Course, you know that, seein' as how I'm one of those Vietnam veteran, killin'-machine soldiers you've heard so much about."

Karras palmed the magazine into the butt of the automatic. "Think you could ever kill again?"

"No," said Walters. "I'll never kill again."

Karras turned to face him. "Not even if you came face-to-face with the men who killed your son?"

"No," said Walters, "not even then. I do hate those men, Dimitri, I'm not gonna lie to you. But I've forgiven them. Only the Lord can decide their fates."

Karras turned back to the targets. He closed one eye, extended his gun arm, and aimed. "Well, you're a better man than I am, I guess."

Karras squeezed off a round. He fired again and again, spacing the shots. He lowered the gun when it was empty.

"You got two that time," said Bernie.

"I'm improving."

"Course, you wouldn't be firing at a little old beer can for real. I mean, you'd be aiming for a bigger target. We're talking about a man here, aren't we?"

"Yes," said Karras.

"Always aim for the body," said Walters. "Never the head. You're not that good. Most men aren't, no matter what they think."

"Right."

"Lead that body just a little if it's moving."

"Okay."

"And keep firing your weapon until you've accomplished what you set out to do."

Karras nodded. "Thanks, Bernie."

"You about done?"

"I'd like to try it a few more times, if you don't mind."

"Fine with me." Walters looked sadly into his beer can and made a swirling motion with his hand. "After that, maybe we'll catch a little lunch."

They drove up to Leonardtown in the pickup and had crab-salad sandwiches and chowder at a local dive. Walters drank beer, and Karras drank ginger ale. They returned to the property in the afternoon.

Walters and Karras went down to the dock with fishing rods, folding chairs, bait, and beer. A plastic owl had been nailed to the top of one of the pilings, but it had scared away no birds. Gull shit was splattered on the owl and nearly covered the planks of the dock. Walters and Karras put the chairs out facing the water and baited their hooks with bloodworms. Karras cast his line out into the creek as Walters cracked a beer.

"I'll have one of those now," said Karras.

"Now you're talkin'," said Walters.

Karras drank down a healthy swallow. "We just jerking off here?"

"Probably. You might snag a few perch. But it's mostly therapy."

Karras nodded at the water. "This part of the bay?"

"They call it a creek."

"It's wide as some rivers I've seen."

"I know. And it's a good fifteen feet deep out there in the middle. But they still call it a creek."

Karras felt a chill and zipped his jacket to the neck. He looked at Walters. "You're not cold?"

"Hell, no. I sleep out here on this dock some nights, Dimitri. I'm talking about this time of year, too."

"You shittin' me?"

"Nah. It's been a mild winter, anyway; most nights have stayed in the forties the times I been down. I get out here in a sleeping bag, lay on my back, and look up at the stars.... I sleep like a baby, man. I don't come down here to lay up in some stuffy trailer."

"What're you, part bear?"

"I just like it here, that's all."

Walters used his Zippo to light a cigarette. They kept their lines out in the water, and after a while Karras noticed the bow of a wooden boat peeking out of the water in the middle of the creek.

"See that?" said Karras, pointing to the area marked by a small red buoy.

"Yep," said Walters. "When you see that bow, it means the tide's going out. You're gonna see more of it the rest of the afternoon."

"Who sunk that boat out there?"

Walters smiled. "Vance."

"You must have been pissed off."

"Not really. It was an old piece-of-shit rowboat that came with the property. Never was seaworthy, anyway. Vance liked to go out in the boat by himself. He'd float out there and think. He always was, what do you call that, introverted."

"You mean introspective?"

"Sure, Professor. Whatever. Anyway, that day he was taking in water. Vance was like, ten years old, and he wasn't much of a swimmer. I sat out here on this dock and watched him sink that boat. He never even looked at me, sitting here. He was afraid I'd think he was a sissy or something if he asked for my help. I guess I waited too long to go out there, because when that boat finally went under, it went under fast. And then Vance was just floundering out there in the water. He was wearing blue jeans and sneakers, and the weight was taking him down."

Walters pinched the bridge of his nose. Tears gathered in his closed eyes, and Karras put a hand on his shoulder.

"Vance screamed, 'Daddy!'" said Walters, his voice cracking. "I can remember the sound he made, the fear in it, even now."

"It's okay, Bernie."

"Lord," said Walters in a quiet way. "I am drunk."

"It's okay, man."

Walters wiped his eyes and swallowed hard. "Well, anyway. I jumped off this dock and got out there. He had gone down a couple of times, but he was all right and I got him back in. I hugged him tight when we were on dry land again. It felt strange because I never did hug him all that much as a child. Strange, but good. Yeah, that was a good day. The two of us had something together that day."

"Why'd you leave the boat out there?"

"We just decided to leave it so we could read the tides. I marked it with that buoy to protect the other boats running back on this creek. Now snapping turtles and water moccasins live around that boat. You can see their heads coming up there all the time."

"That's some story," said Karras.

"Yes, it is."

Karras and Walters sat there quietly for another hour, listening to the water lap at the pilings as barn swallows dove and drifted through the sunlight. Karras checked his watch and stood from his chair.

"I better be taking off. I've got that party tonight back in town."

"Go ahead, buddy. Oh, and that handgun?"

"The Colt?"

"Take it with you."

"You serious?"

"I have my shotguns. They're beautiful pieces of work, and I enjoy owning them. But I have no use for a handgun anymore."

"All right. And, Bernie...thanks for the day."

"My pleasure. I enjoyed the company, pal. Now get goin', so you don't miss your city bash."

"Okay. Stay warm."

Karras left Walters on the dock. Karras worried about his being down here, drunk and alone, for an entire week. But he figured that Bernie was in his element. Bernie would be okay.

MARCUS CLAY had moved from Mount Pleasant to the Crestwood area of D.C. when a chain had come to town and bought out Real Right Records, his four-store operation, back in 1986. Clay had taken the windfall and moved his family uptown to this quietly affluent neighborhood situated between 16th Street and Rock Creek Park. It was a long way from his childhood apartment off 13th and Upshur. Only his closest friends knew just how far he'd come.

Karras parked on Blagden Terrace, a few houses down from Clay's modest split-level. He walked to the house and was met by Clay at the front door.

"Hey, buddy," said Clay. "Knew it was you. Heard the muffler rattlin' on that three twenty-five of yours."

"I wouldn't have missed it. How long we been knowing each other?"

"Damn near forty years."

"Happy birthday, man. And it is a good day. Gotta understand, though, it's a little bittersweet for me, seeing you turn fifty years old. It's weird to see a friend age right before your eyes—"

"Uh-huh. Well, you can just wipe away those sympathy tears. 'Cause you're right behind me, man. So don't be talkin' about that fifty stuff like it's just me."

Karras laughed. They hugged and patted each other's backs.

"Come on in," said Clay.

Karras entered the party. "We People Who Are Darker than Blue," from *Curtis*, was on the stereo. Karras might have predicted it—Clay was the ultimate Mayfield freak.

Elaine Clay came over and embraced him. "Hey, Dimitri."

"Hey, beautiful."

Marcus Jr. walked by and double-bucked Karras's hand. M.J. was already tall and strong like his old man, with his mother's intelligent eyes.

Karras grabbed a beer. He talked with Clarence Tate and his daughter, Denice, now at Howard Law. Tate's face glowed unashamedly with pride for Denice. Karras hugged them both and drifted. The music had gone from Mayfield to *Innervisions*-era Wonder, and now to Michael Henderson's *Solid*. Karras saw a woman he'd known from the late seventies, and she asked him to dance. They slow-dragged to Henderson's "Be My Girl." *Motor-Booty Affair* got played after that, and they stayed on the floor. He noticed George Dozier, a retired cop and friend of Marcus's, dancing beside him with his wife. Karras broke a sweat, and after the dance took off his sweater, revealing an old Hawaiian shirt underneath. He ran into Al Adamson, tough as ever, who pointed at Karras's shirt and laughed. Karras went and got another beer. In the kitchen he talked with Kevin Murphy and his quiet wife, Wanda, both of them gone gray. Murphy's shirt was pinned up where his arm was missing; Karras patted him on the shoulder before walking away. Then someone dimmed the lights, and the party partnered up and slow-danced to "That's the Way of the World." Karras stood alone, quietly sipping his beer, the EWF tune reminding him of hope, and how it had once been in this city that was his home. But he wasn't sad. He was with his friends. He hadn't felt this good in a long while.

Clay, dancing with Elaine, his chin resting on her shoulder, winked at Karras from across the room. Karras raised his beer and smiled.

TWENTY-THREE

ON THE opposite shoreline, the sun fell behind the forest of pine, and dusk settled on the creek. Bernie Walters had another beer, watching the clouds reflected on the water. The creek was calm and smooth this time of day. Looking at the creek like this, with the clouds painted on its flat surface, it was like he was looking down on the sky. *If you looked at it long enough,* thought Walters, *you'd come to believe that you could jump off the dock and never hit water. If you jumped you would just fall out, into the sky.*

"Jeez," said Walters, looking at the beer can in his hand, "I better slow down." He set the beer on the dock, rested his hands on his belly, and leaned his head back against the chair.

He woke in darkness. The clouds had cleared, revealing a ceiling of bright stars and a bright half-moon in the black sky. The air was cool but not bitter. It would be another mild winter night. He'd sleep right out here on the dock; it would be nice.

Walters reached into the cooler for a beer and lit a cigarette. It was too late to think about cooking supper. Walters decided he would just drink.

He drank another beer, and then he was out of beer and got up from his chair. The dock seemed to move beneath his feet. He peed off the side of the dock and tottered up to his pickup, parked beside the trailer. He grabbed a six-pack from the bed and a fresh pack of smokes off the dash of his truck, and his sleeping bag from the back of the cab. He stumbled and fell to one knee on the way back down to the dock. He gathered the things he had dropped and squinted, looking toward the water. The dock was clearly defined in the moonlight. Soon he was on the dock and back in his chair.

He cracked a beer and lit a cigarette. Looking out across the water he thought of his wife and son, and he began to cry. He wiped tears off his cheeks and beer from his chin. The tobacco burned down to his fingers, and he flipped the butt into the creek. He sat in the stillness of the night, listening to the quiet run of water beneath the dock and around its pilings. He killed his beer and decided to call it a night.

Walters spread his sleeping bag between his chair, his cooler, and his fishing rods and the edge of the dock. He was too drunk to move everything back now. He would be all right.

He removed his Orioles cap, set it on the dock, got into the bag, and zipped it to his neck. He lay on his back, folded his arms across his chest, and looked at the stars, the last wisps of clouds, the moon. His eyes grew heavy and he fell to sleep.

He dreamed that he was falling.

He opened his eyes, and he was falling. The black water rushed up to meet him.

The cold water shocked him. He was numb at once, and his head went under as he tried to free his arms from the bag. He freed one arm and kicked furiously at the bag. Now his head was out of the water, and he used his free hand to try and unzip the bag, but his hand was like a club. He kicked at the bag, moving himself away from the dock. The bag and his clothes were heavy and he was going down again and he kicked.

"Aaaah!" yelled Walters. "God!"

He kicked, and the bag was down around his waist. He went under and came up and kicked and now his legs were free. But his legs were moving very slowly. His clothing weighed him down, and he couldn't seem to move his legs. He treaded water and almost at once he was tired. He saw that he was far from the dock and the pilings around it. His arms ached. He tried to float, but his clothing and boots dragged him down. He let himself drop beneath the water so that he could rest. He fought and broke the surface of the water with a gasp. He could no longer feel his feet. His arms barely moved. He looked at the shoreline and knew he could not make it to the dock.

Daddy!

Walters turned his head. He was near the sunken rowboat. He could see the tip of the bow.

He used his shoulders and will to cut the water and move toward the boat. He went under and came up. He choked in air and moved toward the boat again. He shut his eyes against the water that was rising and then he closed his mouth and he was down.

He felt something solid and grabbed it. He pulled himself to the solid thing and hugged it.

I have reached the boat, thought Walters. *I'll float myself up now and I'll be at the boat and above the water and I'll hold onto the bow while I get my breath.*

He tried to push away from the boat, but he was held fast. His down vest or his shirt, *something* was snagged on the boat. He panicked and writhed violently, watching the bubbles from a cough of exhale explode around him. Something slid across his neck, and he shook his head in panic and was bitten in the face.

In his panic, he let out the rest of his breath.

He had no air in his lungs. He was dizzy and his chest burned and he could no longer move his arms or legs.

In the gray water he saw shapes. The silhouettes of a woman and a little boy dog-paddling toward him.

I love you, Vance. I was always proud of you, son.

Bernie Walters relaxed. He opened his mouth and breathed. The creek flowed into his open mouth and flooded his lungs.

It didn't hurt. It was peaceful. His chest didn't burn and he was no longer cold or anything else.

The darkness came like a kiss.

TWENTY-FOUR

FRANK FARROW lit a Kool. He leaned forward, dropping the match into a kidney-shaped ashtray set on a cable-spool table in front of the living-room couch.

Roman Otis stood in front of a rectangular mirror, running a little gel through his long hair, softly singing the Isleys' "For the Love of You." He couldn't quite hit the highs like brother Ronald, but he had it in spirit. That was one nice love song there, too.

Otis smiled, admiring his gold tooth. He patted his hair, turning his head so the gel caught the light. You had to be careful not to put too much of that gel in your hair. He'd seen some brothers in the old days overdose it, goin' for that Rick James look, came out lookin' like glue and shit.

"Hey, Frank," said Otis. "You just dye your hair again, man?"

"Some stuff I picked up at the drugstore down in Edward-town," said Farrow.

"Finally got that shoe polish out, huh?"

"Yeah."

Otis pursed his lips. "Looks good, too."

Farrow glanced at Gus Lavonicus, sitting at an old desk, trying to write a letter to his wife. He had the push end of a pen in his mouth, and his lips were moving as he struggled to compose the words. His legs were spread wide, as he couldn't hope to fit them under the desk, and he was fanning them back and forth. When you got right down to it, thought Farrow, the guy was nothing more than a giant child. Farrow should not have agreed to let Otis bring him along. But he'd never say no to Roman — the two of them went that deep.

"How's that letter to my sister comin', Gus?" said Otis.

"I'm trying to find the right words."

"Tell her she's prettier than a flower," said Otis, "some shit like that."

Farrow sipped red wine. He dragged on his Kool. "That what you'd tell her, Roman?"

"If that was my woman? I'd just go ahead and tell her that I planned to split that thing like an ax to an oak."

"You always did know the right thing to say to women," said Farrow.

"Goddamn right I did."

"I can't say that to Cissy," said Lavonicus in his monotone.

"No," said Otis. "I don't recommend that you do."

Booker Kendricks, Otis's third cousin, came from the kitchen with two bottles of beer in his hand. He was a small, spidery man with rheumy eyes and rotten teeth, a multiple sex offender with violent attachments who'd finally gone down on a sodomy rape beef. Even Otis knew that his cousin belonged in prison for life. But the system had coughed Booker Kendricks back out onto the street.

"Here you go, Roman," said Kendricks, putting a bottle in front of Otis. He snapped his fingers. "Aw, shit, did I forget you, Gus?"

"I don't drink beer anyway," said Lavonicus.

"Yeah, you must be in training for that athletic comeback you're gonna make someday."

Lavonicus watched Kendricks as he turned on the living room's television set. Despite the fact that Kendricks was a relative by marriage, Lavonicus didn't care to spend much time around him. Sometimes he got the feeling that Kendricks was putting him on. He didn't like that.

"Here we go," said Kendricks, sitting in an overstuffed armchair. "Got the Bulls and the Knicks."

Otis had a seat on the couch next to Farrow. "You all right, man?"

"Itching to do something," said Farrow. "That's all."

Kendricks watched Larry Johnson sink a jumper, then wink at the bench as he jogged down the court. "Look at L. J., man. The man thinks he's *all* that."

"Johnson can play," said Lavonicus, who had turned the chair away from the desk to watch the screen.

"Johnson can pa-lay," said Kendricks, mimicking Lavonicus, then slapping his own knee in laughter. "Aw, shit, Gus. Say, man, tell me what it was like in that post-ABA career you had. Weren't you on the squad of one of those teams that used to play against the Harlem Globetrotters?"

"The New York Nationals," said Lavonicus softly. "I only did that one season." They'd thrown him off the team after he coldcocked one of the Globetrotters who had called him a name. The fans had laughed like crazy; they thought the knockout punch had been in the script.

"Yeah, I remember the green uniforms y'all had. How'd it feel to be ridiculed, having balls passed between your legs, gettin' the pill bounced off your head and shit, night after night?"

Lavonicus felt his ears grow hot. He imagined they were red

now, the way they got when he let guys like Kendricks get to him like this.

"It was a job," said Lavonicus, and he turned his chair back to the desk.

Farrow stabbed out his cigarette.

Otis leaned back on the couch, closed his eyes, and picked up the Isleys' tune where he had left it in his head. He imagined that he was back in California. Frank had called him, and he'd come, but he didn't much care for the East Coast. His work, it demanded that he move around. Sometimes it seemed like one big circle. Do a job, grab some money, spend the money, do a job...try to stay ahead of the law. Well, what else was he gonna do? He knew the way it would end, too, but it didn't do much good to think on it. This was the life he had made for himself. He had accepted that a long time ago.

"Look at Rodman," said Kendricks, pointing at the screen. "That is one genuine nigger right there."

They had all stopped listening to Kendricks. Farrow picked up his beer and went to the front window of the house. He looked out into the absolute darkness.

They were in a small brick rambler in the woods of southern Maryland. Off 301 somewhere and down a couple of two-lane blacktops, near a place called Nanjemoy, that's all Farrow knew. They'd stayed here before the May's job, but Booker Kendricks had been in Lorton then, and they'd been alone. This Kendricks could really get on his nerves. But Kendricks would be all right if anything went down. Farrow knew his history, and his type.

Farrow imagined they could do a job in D.C., and finish their business, in the space of a week or so. Then they could all get on their way.

Headlights appeared down the long dirt road that cut

through the woods to the house. As they approached, Farrow could see that these were the lights of a late-model car.

"Here he comes," said Farrow.

Kendricks pulled a Rossi .22 from underneath the chair. He locked back the trigger without moving his eyes from the screen.

The headlights were killed out in the yard, and then there were footsteps and a knock on the door. Farrow looked through the peephole and unfastened the dead bolt. He pulled the door open and stepped back.

"T. W.," said Farrow.

"Frank," said Thomas Wilson, stepping inside. "Long time."

TWENTY-FIVE

Y**OU REMEMBER** Roman," said Frank Farrow.

"How's it goin', man?" said Thomas Wilson, nodding at Otis.

He saw that Otis was still dressing sharp. Still doin' that Nick Ashford thing with his hair, too.

"I'm makin' it," said Otis, smiling amiably, reaching over and shaking Wilson's hand.

Wilson did not let the handshake linger. You could mistake Otis's easy manner for weakness. He had seen a couple of men make that mistake up in Lewisburg. Roman Otis wasn't nothin' much more than Frank Farrow with a smile.

"Say hello to Gus Lavonicus," said Farrow.

"Gus," said Wilson. He saw an ugly white giant sitting at what looked like a child's desk. The giant waved awkwardly and turned his attention back to the sheet of paper before him.

"And this here's Booker Kendricks," said Farrow.

Wilson looked at the skinny, greasy-lookin' hustler with the yellow eyes, slouched in the chair. A pistol hung limply in his clawlike hand. Kendricks did not acknowledge Wilson. Wilson felt it was just as well.

"Beer?" said Farrow.

"Yeah, okay."

"Get T. W. a beer, Booker," said Otis.

"Damn, can't y'all see I'm watchin' this shit?" said Kendricks. "Starks is getting ready to light it up, too!"

"Get it," said Farrow.

Kendricks went to the kitchen as Wilson took a seat on the couch next to Otis. Farrow stayed on his feet. He leaned forward and rustled his pack of Kools in Wilson's face.

"Cigarette?" said Farrow.

"Nah," said Wilson. "Thanks."

"This used to be your brand in the joint, I remember right."

"I gave them up a long time ago."

Charles convinced me to throw them away for good.

Kendricks returned, placed an open bottle of beer on the cable-spool table in front of Wilson. Kendricks went back to the oversize chair and had a seat.

Wilson sipped his beer, fumbled it as he placed it back on the table.

"You seem a little uptight," said Farrow, catching Otis's eye.

"I'm tired is all it is," said Wilson. "Took me over an hour to get down here from D.C."

Farrow slowly paced the room. "How is it up in town? Any heat that you can make out?"

"None."

"Good. Me and Roman were thinking you could set us up again with some kind of thing. Something cleaner than the last time. Less risk."

"I'm working on it. Been out in the bars at night, listenin' to people talk. Trying to find out where the after-hours action is these days. I'm thinkin' a bag rip-off, or a high-stakes game. Somethin' y'all could take off quiet."

"I like the way you're thinking."

"Get you in and out of town real quick."

"That's our intent. We need a substantial payday this time. Roman and Gus here have run into a financial setback. Your cut will be the usual—ten percent. That okay with you, T. W.?"

Wilson nodded.

"Tomorrow we'll see Manuel and Jaime. You've called them, right?"

"Yes."

"What'd they have to say?"

They said you killed a minister in cold blood down on the Eastern Shore.

"They said to come on by," said Wilson. "They'll have a car for you on Monday."

"I need something with a little muscle. I've been driving this piece-of-shit truck—"

"They're on it," said Wilson.

"Damn, boy!" shouted Kendricks, jumping up from his chair and shutting off the set. "Can't nobody in this league fuck with the Bulls?"

"Hey, Booker," said Otis. "Keep your voice down, man."

Kendricks dismissed them all with a wave of his hand. "Y'all are just way too serious for a Saturday night. I'm gonna take a walk, catch some air."

Kendricks slipped the pistol into the pocket of his baggy slacks and put on a jacket. "See ya later, Tall Tree," he said, smiling at Lavonicus before leaving the house.

Lavonicus blinked his eyes hard, but he did not raise his head.

When the door closed, Otis said, "Hard to believe that man shares a drop of my blood."

Farrow said, "Where's he goin', anyway, in this cold?"

"I don't know," said Otis. "But if I owned one of these farms around here, right about now I'd be putting a lock on the barn door."

"Likes those kickin' mules, huh?" said Farrow.

"I don't even think they have to kick to get his fancy. All he needs is the right texture to get him started. You want to know the truth, I wouldn't even trust my cousin around a rare steak."

Wilson cleared his throat. "That about it? 'Cause I got to make the drive back into town."

"Wait a minute," said Farrow, turning to Lavonicus. "Gus, give us a couple of minutes alone here, will you?"

"Sure." Lavonicus stood and ducked an arched frame as he entered the hall to the back bedrooms.

"Gus don't know much about the details of our history," said Otis. "He don't *need* to know, is what I'm sayin'."

Farrow stopped pacing and looked down at Wilson. "You find out where that cop lives?"

"No," said Wilson. "Not yet."

"What about his sons?"

"His sons live with him. That much I got from the papers."

"Find his address," said Farrow. "I owe him a visit."

Wilson nodded and said, "That it?"

"One more thing," said Farrow. "Want to get this out on the table once and for all, and then bury it."

"Go ahead."

"Your pizza chef friend. I want to make sure you're not carrying a grudge over what happened."

"I'm not. I told you as much on the phone."

"Look at me, T. W., not at the floor."

Wilson locked eyes with Farrow.

"What happened in that pizza parlor was a necessity," said Farrow. "In a situation like that, when you pull the trigger one time you have to keep pulling it until nobody's left alive. Charles might have been the most stand-up guy who ever walked down the block, but the cops would've broken him, and he would've fingered us all to make a deal. Anybody would have. What we did to him was just business and self-preservation. Ours *and* yours. So I want you to tell me now that you don't have a problem with what went down."

Wilson's mouth twitched.

"Do you have a problem, T. W.?"

I'd kill you now if I was man enough. But I am not man enough. God help me, I'm as weak as they come.

"No," said Wilson. "I don't have a problem."

"Good," said Farrow. "I'll see you Monday at the garage."

"Right."

Wilson killed his beer. He stood from the couch and walked from the house.

"Man's still got that tired Arsenio fade," said Otis, pushing his own hair back behind his ears. "Needs to get himself to a shop where they're doin' that new thing."

Farrow listened to Wilson's Dodge pull away. "What do you think of him?"

"The man is troubled, that much is plain. But troubled don't mean dangerous."

"No, it doesn't. Wilson's weak and afraid. He always was someone you could push around."

"So we got nothin' to worry about, right?"

"He's paralyzed," said Farrow. "He'll never make a play."

THOMAS WILSON gripped the steering wheel tightly to stop the shake in his hands. Anger was making his hands shake, but there was something else, too: fear. The fear was stronger than the anger. And the knowledge of this made him ashamed.

Wilson turned left off the two-lane and drove north on 301.

How had he come to be with these kinds of men? Looking back on it, it was an obvious path that had brought him to where he was now.

His life had turned with his coke addiction. He understood completely what Dimitri Karras was riffing on at those meetings, though of course he could never admit to Dimitri or the rest of them that he was a member of that same NA club. By way of explaining the hole in his personal time line, he had only told them that he had gone away for a few years to find his calling. Gone away, hell. Put away was more like it.

It had started as a casual thing for Wilson, back in the late seventies. That's the way it always started with this shit; cocaine was the drug that always drove the car and never gave up the keys. By the time you knew it, it was too late.

Wilson had started dealing to support his habit. He was arrested and charged twice, but the judges were right, the jails were full, and he did no time.

After a while Wilson figured, if you're gonna be into it, why not step it up, make some bigger money, get into it for real? So he hooked up with a dealer who controlled the action down around the dwellings at 7th and M in Northwest, and he became this dealer's mule. Wilson began to make the regular Amtrak run from Union Station to Penn Station and back again. It was safer than being out on the corner, and it seemed to be risk free.

But Wilson had misjudged the stealth of his dealer's rivals, who'd gotten the time of his run from a nose-fiend on the street. The cops pulled Wilson and his black leather suitcase off the Metroliner at the 30th Street station in Philly, busted his dumb ass right there on the platform. With Wilson's priors and the quantity confiscated, he took the big fall. They sent him up to Lewisburg, the federal joint in PA.

In prison, Wilson got free of his coke jones but collected fateful relationships with many men: Frank Farrow, Roman Otis, Lee Toomey, Manuel Ruiz, and Jaime Gutierrez among them. On the last day of his bit, he promised Farrow and Otis he'd stay in touch.

When Wilson got out, he vowed to stay straight. But from his muling days he remembered how it felt to have money, real money, in his pocket all the time. His mother had died when he was in Lewisburg, and his uncle Lindo was good enough to hook him up with the hauling job. Lindo was all right to talk to during the day, but Lindo was old-time, and Lindo wasn't his boy. That distinction would always go to his lifelong friend, Charles Greene.

One night he and Charles had a couple of drinks and Charles got loose with his tongue. He began to tell Wilson about the pizza parlor where he had been working for some time. How the place was more or less a front for a large gaming operation, numbers and book and the like. How the man who co-owned the joint, Carl Lewin, was his own bagman. How Lewin made May's the last stop on his run, the same day, same time, every week.

Wilson thought of the money, then thought of his old acquaintances from Lewisburg, Farrow and Otis. Tough guys, professionals, who made it their specialty to take off other criminals. He had the idea that he could contact Farrow and set this thing up. Get Manuel and Jaime, who had gone into the chop business at a garage in Silver Spring, involved as well. He talked himself into it, and then he talked Charles into it, too. Convinced Charles that this was ill-gotten money anyway, it would just be going from one set of dirty hands to another. His employer would never, ever know. And no one would get hurt.

After the bloodbath in the kitchen, Wilson did not go to the law and confess his involvement. The atmosphere was lynch-mob heavy in town in the weeks following the murders, and Wilson was…well, Wilson was scared. Much as he had loved Charles, he couldn't bring Charles back. He didn't want to go to prison again, and if he did go, Farrow would find a way to reach him on the inside. No, there wasn't any kind of good that could come out of going to the law. That's what he thought at the time. And then he went to the meetings, thinking that hearing the stories of the others might ease his pain. There, he became friends with the victims' relatives, and their pain became his. He hadn't figured on that. It was like there was a nest of angry spiders now, all the time, crawling around in his head.

Now Farrow wanted him to set up the cop in the wheelchair, and maybe his sons.

Wilson approached the lights of the strip shopping centers along the highway side of La Plata. He cracked the window to let in some air. It felt kind of stuffy in the car, and there was a tightness in his chest.

He knew he was a coward. It was because of his cowardice that things had come this far.

Once you were in with Farrow and Otis, you were in with them for good. He could follow them or kill them or run. Those were his choices.

He prayed that when the time came, the Lord would let him be a man.

TWENTY-SIX

ON MONDAY morning, Nick Stefanos leaned out of the open window of his Dodge at the P. G. Plaza Metro station and snapped photographs of Erika Mitchell meeting her new boyfriend in the parking lot beside his idling Acura. Stefanos steadied the long lens of his Pentax as he shot. He caught Erika and her boyfriend embracing and he got one of them kissing and another of Erika getting into his car.

Stefanos dropped the roll of film at a shop on Georgia Avenue and smoked a cigarette in his car as he looked over the list Al Adamson had given him, checking the addresses against the detail map he kept in the Dodge. He pulled off the curb and drove over to Hyattsville, to a garage off Queens Chapel Road.

C. Lewis, the seasoned-leaning-to-elderly owner of the shop, had no knowledge of the red Torino, mentioning only that it was "one beautiful car." He added that there had been fewer than a hundred manufactured of that particular model, so locating it shouldn't prove to be all that difficult. Stefanos thanked him, and Lewis said, "Say hi to Al."

Stefanos drove back into Northwest, to a garage named

Strange Auto near 14th and Arkansas. Go-go music was pumping from the open bay as Stefanos approached.

The owner, Anthony Strange, informed Stefanos that "the only thing I'll touch here is Mustangs. Torino ain't nothin' but an overgrown Maverick, and I ain't *even* gonna tell you what I think of them." His mechanic, a very young man with a black knit cap pulled low on his forehead, laughed and turned up the Back Yard CD he had coming from the box.

Out on the sidewalk, Stefanos looked at the next name on his list. The place was just up over the District line. He wasn't far from there now.

THOMAS WILSON was standing in the back of the garage, talking to Manuel and Jaime, when the bell rang from the front of the bay.

"That would be them," said Wilson.

"Yes," said Manuel.

Jaime Gutierrez dropped his cigarette to the concrete and ground it under his boot as Manuel Ruiz went to the bay door. He hit a red button beside the door; the door lifted, and a Ford Ranger rolled into the garage. Manuel lowered the door as Frank Farrow parked the pickup beside a two-tone Falcon.

Farrow and Roman Otis stepped out of the pickup. Otis stretched his long frame and followed Farrow to where Wilson and Gutierrez stood. Manuel met the group, and Farrow shook his hand.

"Damn," said Otis, rolling his head so that his neck muscles relaxed. "Tall man like me can't take a long journey in a truck that size, for real. Got used to the size of that Mark you hooked me up with, Man-you-el."

"I am pleased that you like it."

"Goddamn right I like it. That's a beautiful car."

"What've you got for me?" said Farrow.

"Is over here," said Manuel, and they followed him as he led the way. Farrow looked at the red Mustang with the Formula tires with raised white lettering and the black scoop on the hood.

"A Mach One?"

"Yes," said Manuel. "Nineteen seventy-three, three fifty-one automatic. Original white interior. Beautiful."

"It's red."

"That's right."

"Does it run?"

"It is very straight."

Jaime nodded in agreement and lit another cigarette.

Farrow ran his finger along the waxed surface of the hood. "You have clean tags for it, amigo?"

"Yes."

"Put them on. And get rid of that Ranger any way you see fit. It's on the hot sheet by now."

"Okay, Frank," said Manuel. "You can sit in the offi while we put on the tags, if you wish."

"You said 'offi,' " said Otis, showing his gold tooth. "But you meant 'office,' right?"

Manuel smiled thinly.

"Come on with us, T.W.," said Farrow.

Wilson said, "Right."

The office was small, and many of the papers on its cluttered desk were smudged with grease. Otis had a seat on a wooden slat-back chair and put his feet up on the desk. Farrow sat on the edge of the desk and put fire to a Kool.

"So, T. W. Any progress on finding Detective Jonas?"

"Not yet."

Farrow looked at Otis. "Gimme that phone book over there, Roman. The D.C. edition."

Otis handed him the directory that was on the desk. Farrow flipped through the pages, found the one he was looking for, and folded the book open so that Wilson could see it.

"Here's Jonas, right here," said Farrow. "On Hamlin Street. Now give me that detail map over there, Roman."

Otis did it, and Farrow turned to the page representing Northeast.

"You said Jonas lived in Brookland, right, T. W.? Well, here's Hamlin Street, smack in the middle of the Brookland neighborhood, right here." Farrow dropped the detail map back on the desk. "Funny how easy it was to find Jonas. I walked into a Seven-Eleven this morning and got the information out of a book just like this in a minute flat. You know, he was in the phone book all the time."

"I didn't think to look in the directory, Frank," said Wilson, trying to put some levity in his voice. "I mean, who *would* have thought—"

"You didn't think. Or maybe you were just trying to avoid more trouble." Farrow stood and walked over to Wilson. Wilson seemed to shrink before him. "I know you don't like conflict, T. W. But when I ask you to do something, I expect it to be done."

"Listen, Frank—"

"Don't let it bother you, all right? Wouldn't want your nerves to get the better of you." Farrow removed his black-rimmed nonprescription glasses. "Now. How's it going on our upcoming prospects?"

"Working on that," said Wilson. "Been out in the clubs, listenin' to people talk. Gonna find something real good for the two of you, you'll see."

"You been clubbin', huh?" said Otis. "Must be gettin' a lot of pussy, too, with that up-to-the-minute look you got goin' on."

"Find something soon," said Farrow. "We don't want to be here any longer than we have to." Farrow checked his watch. "Come on, let's see how they're getting along out there."

"I'll just wait here," said Otis, "let my legs straighten out for a while."

Farrow and Wilson walked back out to the garage. Going around the corner, they nearly bumped into Manuel and Jaime and a man in a brown leather jacket they were talking to. The man's eyes widened slightly at the sight of Wilson.

"Hey," said the man in a friendly way.

"How you doin'?" said Wilson.

"Nick Stefanos," said the man, extending his hand. "Remember?"

Wilson remembered. It was that investigator, Dimitri's friend, the one from the meeting last Tuesday night.

NICK STEFANOS found the street called Selim in downtown Silver Spring and parked his ride outside Hanagan's Auto Body behind a late-model Chrysler product. He rang the bell beside the door of the unmarked bay located between Hanagan's and Rossi Automotive, and zipped up his leather as he waited. The door opened and a short, black-haired, Indian-featured Hispanic stood in the frame. The name "Manuel" was stitched across his uniform shirt.

"Yes?"

"Nick Stefanos. I'm an investigator with the District of Columbia." Stefanos flipped open the leather cover and let Manuel inspect his ID. "Do you have a minute? I have a couple of questions."

Manuel looked over his shoulder and back at Stefanos. He

knew Stefanos was not a cop, but the investigator tag had raised the red authority flag in his mind. This was Stefanos's intent. If this Manuel was like most people, he'd let Stefanos have his minute, if only to get rid of him for good.

"What is this?"

"A case I'm working on for the courts."

"A court case?"

Stefanos decided to cut right to it. This one's shell looked hard enough.

"It's not about you or your business," said Stefanos. "I'm not IRS and I'm not immigration. I'm just trying to locate a particular car."

"What kind of car?"

"A Ford." Stefanos blew into his hands. "Look, can I come in and warm up?"

Manuel looked him over. "Come on. But I have much work to do today, okay?"

"I'll be quick."

As they entered, Stefanos saw a mechanic in the back of the garage quickly pull a tarp over an early-seventies, muscled-up Mustang. Stefanos only saw the car for a couple of seconds, but the lines were unmistakable. Stefanos walked toward the mechanic, whose obvious, urgent action had sparked his curiosity. Manuel walked beside him.

"You're Manuel Ruiz, right?"

"Yes," said Manuel, clearly perturbed. "How do you know this?"

"Al Adamson. You know Al, don't you?"

"*Sí*. The Continental man."

Stefanos kept walking. The mechanic met them past an entranceway to a hall of some kind. All of them stepped around a corner.

"You must be Jaime Gutierrez," said Stefanos. He noticed the teardrop tattoos on the side of Jaime's bony face.

"Yes," said Jaime, glancing nervously at his partner.

"I won't keep you guys. I'm trying to locate an old Torino. A special-edition Ford called the Twister, red—"

Jaime spoke Spanish to Manuel, and then Manuel said, "We know of no such car."

"You guys specialize in Ford restorations, right?"

"We do not know this car," said Manuel. "I do know of a Torino man, though. On Route One in Laurel."

"Who is it?"

Manuel gave him the man's name and the location of his garage. Stefanos was writing it down when he heard the voices of two other men, and then the men, one white and one black, were right upon them as they turned the corner.

Stefanos recognized the black man. It was Thomas Wilson, one of the guys from Dimitri's group.

"Hey," said Stefanos.

"How you doin'?" said Wilson with a shaky smile.

"Nick Stefanos. Remember?"

"I forgot something in the office," said the white man, walking back around the corner.

Stefanos speed-scanned the man before he turned: medium height, solid build, flat eyes, thin lips, a Cassavetes type with dyed-black hair and Clark Kent glasses on his lined face.

"What you doin' here, man?" said Wilson in a friendly way.

"I'm working a case. How about you?"

Wilson spread his hands. "Gettin' my car checked out."

"Thought you drove a Dodge," said Stefanos, realizing then that it was Wilson's car he had parked behind out on Selim. "This is a Ford shop, isn't it?"

Wilson forced a grin. "Yeah, but my boys here...they make an exception when it comes to my short."

"Okay." Stefanos closed his notebook. "Well, I've gotta run. Thanks for your time, Manuel. Take it easy, Thomas."

"Yeah, man, take it light."

Stefanos shook Manuel's hand. He nodded to Jaime and Wilson and walked from the garage.

Driving back into D.C., he thought of the teardrop tattoos on Jaime's face: prison tats, or those from a gang. He thought of the odd, hard man who had rushed off. He thought of Thomas Wilson, a Dodge man, getting his car done in a Ford restoration shop. He wondered what Wilson was doing hanging around these men. And he had that crazy feeling again, the same feeling he'd had the night of the meeting: the feeling that something was not right.

TWENTY-SEVEN

AFTER THE man in the brown leather jacket had gone, Frank Farrow and Roman Otis emerged from the office and crossed the garage.

Farrow said to Thomas Wilson, "Who was that?"

"Ask Manuel," said Wilson with a clumsy shrug.

"You knew him," said Farrow. "I'm asking you."

"I met him at a party last week," said Wilson. "Seeing him here today was just one of those accidents."

"He was looking for a car," said Manuel.

Jaime dragged hard on his cigarette and stared down at his boots.

"He looked like some kind of cop," said Farrow.

"I don't think so," said Manuel. "He was only looking for a car."

Farrow regarded Manuel and said, "All right. How much to use the Mustang for the week?"

"Seven hundred," said Manuel.

"You've raised your rates."

"The car was bought from the *Old Car Trader*. It is all legal, down to the plates."

"Here." Farrow counted out seven hundred-dollar bills. "Have something ready for me that I can buy when I bring the Mustang back. I want it clean and fast."

"You will have it," said Manuel.

"'Bout ready, Frank?" said Otis.

"Yeah. Let's go."

"See you later, Man-you-el," said Otis. "Jamey."

"Stay in touch, T. W.," said Farrow.

Wilson said, "Right."

Farrow and Otis went to the Mach 1 and settled into its white buckets. Farrow cooked the ignition; the rumble echoed in the garage. He looked across the buckets and smiled at Otis. Otis took his .45 from his coat and slipped it beneath his seat. Farrow put the automatic in gear.

They drove south on Georgia Avenue. A cop car passed them on the right, its uniformed driver slowing down to have a look at the Mach 1.

"He likes it," said Farrow as the cop car accelerated and sped off.

"You drive a red car, it's gonna attract some attention."

"You heard Manuel. Everything checks out, and he wouldn't lie to me. Besides, I'll keep to the speed limit, Roman."

"I know that, Frank. Always did feel comfortable with you behind the wheel."

Otis found HUR on the FM dial. The DJ was starting into the Temptations' "A Song for You," a beautiful track from their late period. Otis did his best with all the vocal parts. He wasn't too solid on the highs, but he thought he sounded pretty good.

"Where we headed now, Frank?" said Otis when the song was done.

"Gonna see if Detective Jonas is home," said Farrow.

Otis studied the detail map he had lifted from the office. "You ain't thinkin' of doin' that cop today, right?"

"Just want to say hello to his sons if they're around."

"That's what you got in mind," said Otis, "you want to be makin' a left at the corner up ahead."

"MR. LYNCH," said Nick Stefanos. "If you could just give me a minute here—"

"Keep talkin'," said Lynch. "I can listen to you while I'm workin'."

Lynch had his head in the engine of a '71 Torino. The engine was a 351 Cleveland; the car was green with a white roof. Lynch turned a wrench with a thick, scaly hand.

"I'm trying to locate a red Torino," said Stefanos.

"I know, I know, you already—"

"A Twister, special edition. Red."

Lynch backed up and stood to his full five-feet-two. He was a pink-faced, froggish man with a hops belly and a comb-over of blond-gray hair.

"Why didn't you say so?" said Lynch. "For God's sake, you could have saved me all this talk."

"You know the car?"

"Ain't but one like it in the area. And yeah, I know it. I restored the sonofabitch myself."

Stefanos felt a tick in his blood. "You have the name and address of the person who owns it?"

"I have the name. Have an address and a phone number, too, but both of them are worthless. I'm tellin' you the truth 'cause I found out the hard way, see? This black bastard, he stiffed me for two grand. He's the reason I got that sign posted over there."

Lynch pointed to a "No Checks, Cash and Charges Only" notice posted by the register.

"What's this guy's name?"

"Forjay. Sean Forjay. Young buck with one of those big Afros they all used to wear." Lynch regarded Stefanos strangely. "Hey, what's wrong with you?"

"Nothing," said Stefanos, thinking of Forjay, the top-of-the-heap dealer down on Kennedy.

"Yeah," said Lynch, "Forjay's one of those niggers, you never want to see him again, just loan him some money. Hey, where you goin' so fast, buddy?"

Stefanos walked quickly through the open bay door. On the way to his car he lit a smoke.

"**WHO WAS** the man in the leather jacket?" said Manuel Ruiz.

"Friend of a friend," said Thomas Wilson. "An investigator for the public defender's office, downtown."

"He knows nothing about us?"

"No. He's only looking for a car. Thanks for covering me there."

"We need no more trouble with Frank."

"That's right. We all want to get out from under Farrow. We're together on that, right?"

Manuel glanced at Jaime. "That is right. I prayed that we would never see Frank again after what happened at the pizza parlor. He killed your friend, those other people...that child. Now he has killed a man of God. We are thieves but not murderers. And we have children of our own."

"Maybe he'll just go away," said Wilson.

"And maybe," said Manuel, "we can help him to go away."

Jaime patted his breast pocket for his pack of cigarettes. The pocket was empty, and he frowned.

"What'd you do, Manny?" said Wilson.

"The tags on that Mustang. I stole them myself last night, from a luxury car in Forest Heights. You can be sure that the owner was outraged. The tags are on the hot sheet, I am certain, as we speak."

"Red muscle car with hot tags," said Wilson. "Man could get pulled over real fast, drivin' one of those."

Manuel nodded at Jaime and said, "That is not all."

Wilson said, "What else?"

"Jaime is an expert brake man. He fixed the master cylinder on the Mustang so that the brake fluid would leak out. The brakes will fail on that car for sure. I would say in the next four or five days, they will fail altogether."

"What about the idiot lights?" said Wilson. "That'll tip Frank off."

"I fix the idiot light," said Jaime.

"Aren't you two afraid?" said Wilson.

"Yes," said Manuel, "we are afraid. The way men in war are afraid."

Wilson said nothing, staring at Manuel. Then he looked at his watch. "I better be goin'. Meeting my uncle Lindo down at his warehouse."

"You go," said Manuel.

"I'll keep you two up on things," said Wilson.

"Please," said Manuel.

They shook hands with Wilson and watched him walk from the garage.

"Will he give us up?" said Jaime.

"I don't think so," said Manuel. "He is stronger than he knows."

"What about the man in the leather jacket?"

"What Wilson said was true. He was only looking for a car."

"I hope we are right," said Jaime, "to try and cross Frank."

"He is a devil," said Manuel. "So we have to try."

Jaime reached into his pocket, remembered that he was out of cigarettes.

"I need to buy smokes," said Jaime.

"You have a fresh pack in the offi," said Manuel.

"You said 'offi,'" said Jaime with a tight smile. "But you meant 'office,' right?"

TWENTY-EIGHT

ROMAN OTIS turned up the volume on the radio. WHUR was playing the Floaters' "Float On," and the hypnotic instrumental intro was filling the car.

"Aw, shit, Frank," said Otis. "They're playin' the long version, too. If I lived in this town I'd have my radio dial locked on this station right here."

They were parked on Hamlin, a few houses down from the house of William Jonas. Farrow looked through the windshield at the bay window of the detective's split. He could see vague outlines moving behind the window. Well, that couldn't be Jonas; Jonas was a cripple confined to a chair.

Farrow tried to block out Roman's voice. He didn't care for music, especially when he was working, but Roman did, and he let him listen to it, and sing, to his content.

"Libra," said Otis, "and my name is Charles. Now, I like a woman that's quiet..."

As Otis mimicked the spoken verse, he noticed the dash of the car. Usually, when you were listening to the radio with the ignition off, a red light came on in the dash. Otis figured maybe this old model didn't have that feature. Or maybe it did and the light was broke. The truth was, Otis knew dog *shit* about the workings of cars.

Farrow turned the volume on the radio down a notch.

"How do you think Gus is gonna work out with us?" said Farrow, keeping his eyes on the house.

"I don't know. Gus is all heartsick over my sister, you want to know the truth."

"Will he pull his weight when the time comes?"

"Gus has a temper, that's a fact. My cousin Booker needs to get with that."

"But will Gus kill if he has to?"

"As far as unnecessary mayhem goes, uh-uh, I don't think he'd go for that."

Farrow squinted. "You think this is unnecessary, Roman?"

Otis thought carefully before he spoke. He was about as close to Frank as any man could be, but he didn't want to get on his wrong side, just the same. Long as he'd known him, Frank had been a violent man. No conscience, either, which could be a positive in their profession. That no-conscience thing was what often kept men like them alive. But the way he'd run over that kid after the pizza parlor kill, that had been extra cold, even for Frank. And killing that churchman out in the country? Otis could not see where that had been justified. Frank had always been ice. Lately, though, it seemed like he was enjoying the bloodletting a little too much.

"I wouldn't say it's unnecessary," said Otis. "Only thing I'm askin' is, let's be smart about it, right? I mean, we're sittin' out here in the broad daylight and shit. We were lucky to get out of this town the first time around, Frank. I just don't think we ought to be so fast about temptin' the gods of fate, man. You know what I'm sayin'?"

"It was you who said we could come back here for this. Remember?"

"I remember." Otis sighed. "I'm with you, man. You don't have to doubt that, hear?"

"That's all I wanted to know."

A tall young man with a leather book bag slung over his shoulder came from the Jonas house and walked toward a Toyota parked on the street.

"There's one of his sons," said Farrow. "Looks like the one from the photograph we sent to Jonas. Christopher is his name."

Christopher Jonas got into the Toyota, started it, and drove down Hamlin. Farrow ignitioned the Mustang.

"Here we go," said Farrow, pulling off the curb.

Otis kicked the volume up on the radio to where it had been.

"Cancer," said Otis. "And my name is Larry. And I like a woman that likes everythang and everybody . . ."

THEY FOLLOWED Christopher Jonas across town and southwest, over to Georgia and down New Hampshire for a long stretch, around one of D.C.'s many circles, past a hospital, to where students walked the sidewalks along dormitory-style brick buildings.

"George Washington University," said Otis, studying the detail map. "Boy must have a brain in his head."

The Toyota went into a garage. Farrow did not want to be trapped inside the structure, so he went around the block and found a spot on the street. The meter where they parked was without a head, as were most of the meters they'd seen since they'd been in town. They sat in the car, waiting. A cop car sat idling at a red light ahead. The light turned green, and as the cop car prepared to accelerate, another car ran the opposing red, blowing through the intersection. The cop car did not pursue the offender.

"That's not the first time I've seen that," said Otis.

"Yeah," said Farrow. "Man could get the crazy idea that there's no police presence in this town."

"Our kind of place," said Otis. "Right?"

Christopher Jonas emerged from the garage and crossed the street.

"Wait here," said Farrow.

He stepped out of the car and followed Christopher on foot. Otis reached over, turned the ignition key, and hit the power button on the radio. Otis decided to let the car run while he listened to music. Frank wouldn't like it if he put a drain on the battery.

Christopher Jonas went into an eat-house called D.J.'s. Farrow hung outside and looked through the plate glass window. He watched the Jonas kid greet a couple of his friends, two white kids and a Paki-looking girl, at a long table. Jonas kissed the girl and had a seat by her side.

Farrow went around the corner to a bank of pay phones and dropped thirty-five cents in one of the change slots. He punched in the number he read off a slip of notepaper he had pulled from his coat.

"Jonas residence," said a female voice on the other end of the line.

"Afternoon," said Farrow. "Would it be possible to have a word with Bill?"

ROMAN OTIS watched Farrow go around the front entrance of the carryout shop up ahead. He could see a sliver of Frank, lifting the receiver off a pay phone. He wondered what Frank was up to now.

Watching Farrow, he sang along softly to that Manhattans single "Kiss and Say Goodbye." This was one of those special classics that Otis did so well.

A campus cop car slowed down as it passed the Mustang, then accelerated and took a right at the next corner.

"'Understand me,'" sang Otis, "'won't you try-yi-yi; let's just kiss and say good-bye....'"

Otis was on the last verse when he looked in the rearview and saw the campus cop. The car had circled the block and was slowing to a stop and double-parking behind him. Otis took his shades from his breast pocket and put them on. Without leaning forward, he reached down and touched the butt of the .45 he had slipped beneath the bucket. He pushed it back an inch or so and let himself relax.

The cop got out of his car and walked to the driver's side of the Mustang. He made a motion for Otis to roll down the window. Otis reached across the bucket and did it. He looked up at the cop: white boy, wearin' his first mustache, couldn't have been more than twenty-two or so.

"Officer," said Otis with a wide smile.

"Afternoon. Something wrong?"

"No, sir, not a thing."

"I noticed the car was idling without a driver."

"Waitin' on my friend. Was trying to keep the heater running, cold as it is."

"It's not all that cold today."

"Is for me. I'm up here from Florida."

"Where's your friend?"

"Makin' a call on the corner there. He should be right along."

The cop shuffled his feet. He looked at the Korean place called D.J.'s on the corner and back at Otis.

"Excuse me a minute," said the cop. "I'll be right back."

Otis saw the cop go and get into the driver's seat of his car, the door open, one foot out planted on the street. He watched the cop lift the radio mic, speak into it as he read the plate numbers off the car.

"C'mon, Frank," said Otis, more annoyed than anything else. "You fuckin' around *too* much now."

DEE JONAS handed her husband their cordless phone.

"Jonas here."

"Bill?"

"Yes."

"How's it going?"

"Who is this?"

"An old friend. I'm back in town for a few days. Thought I'd say hello."

"Who is this?" repeated Jonas.

"You have a good-looking family, Bill. I'm looking at your son Chris right now, and he's a very handsome boy. Got a lot of friends, too. He's sweet on an Indian girl, Bill. You know that?"

Jonas looked over his shoulder. His wife was back in the kitchen. He lowered his voice and said, "I'm going to ask you again—"

"Chris is tall. He drives a Toyota and he carries a leather book bag."

"Coward."

"What's that?"

"You're good at keeping your distance. You sent me a photograph. Isn't that right?"

"That's right. I'm the man who put you in that chair."

"What kind of rock did you crawl out from under?" growled Jonas.

"All kinds of rocks. Reformatories, state prisons, federal joints...I've been under all sorts of rocks my whole life, Bill."

"Keep talking. Tell me more."

"You killed my brother Richard, and now I'm going to have to kill your son. That's all you need to know. Good-bye, Bill."

"Damnit!" yelled Jonas.

Bill Jonas heard a click on the other end of the line. Then he heard a dial tone and threw the phone onto the couch.

Dee Jonas had come from the kitchen. She was standing by its entrance, wringing her hands on a towel.

"What is it, Bill?" she said.

"It's nothing," said Jonas. "I lost my temper at a salesman, is all. Shoulda taken my number out of the book years ago."

Jonas wheeled himself to the bay window. He rubbed his knuckle against his teeth and felt his wife's hand on his shoulder. He looked down at his skinny, useless legs lying crookedly in the seat of the chair.

"Richard," said Jonas under his breath.

"What?" said Dee.

"Pack your bags. Pack bags for our sons, too. I want you all to go down to Tidewater, to your mother's place. It'll only be for a few days."

"Why, Bill?"

"Don't ask me why."

"You can't stay here by yourself."

"I can get from my chair to my walker. I can get in and out of the bathroom, and I can cook. So don't tell me I can't."

Dee lowered her voice. "But the boys aren't going to want to go."

"Tell them that aunt of yours wants to see them. The one been in that nursing home for ten years? Tell them she's dying and she wants to say good-bye."

"But Aunt Carla's not dying. She's gonna outlive us all."

"Tell them anything you want to, then," said Jonas, staring out the window at the street. "Whatever you tell them, I want y'all out of here by tonight."

FRANK FARROW racked the receiver. He walked around the corner of D.J.'s and saw the campus cop car parked behind the 'Stang. He crossed the street with his head down, staring at his feet. He heard a siren coming from somewhere behind him, and as he walked the siren grew louder.

As he approached the Mustang, he looked briefly at the cop, sitting behind the wheel of the car, one foot out on the street. The cop was young, nothing more than a boy. There was fear on the cop's face, and something close to panic. He couldn't even meet Farrow's eyes.

The siren grew louder.

"Goddamnit all," muttered Farrow.

He reached the Mach 1 and got behind the wheel.

"Put your seat belt on, Roman."

Otis nodded. The metal-to-metal seat belt connection was made with a soft click. Farrow pulled the shifter back to D and hit the gas.

The Mach 1 left rubber on the street, fishtailed on 22nd, and then straightened, clipping the door of a black Camry parked at the curb. They passed Christopher Jonas and his friends, who were walking out of the carryout on the corner and staring at the speeding car.

"We got Johnny Law at twelve o'clock high," said Otis. "That's a real one, too."

"I see him."

Farrow turned sharp left on G, pumped the brakes, and then

punched the gas to bring them out of the skid. The D.C. cop followed, the overhead lights spinning, the siren on full.

"Watch it, man," said Otis, as a female student ran across the street into their path. Then they were nearing the girl and almost on her.

Otis said, "Frank."

Otis leaned over and pushed the wheel in a counterclockwise direction. The Mustang swerved around the girl. For a second Otis saw her stretched-back, gray-as-death face.

"Where?" said Farrow.

"Left on Twentieth," said Otis.

Farrow cut it hard. They sideswiped a parked Amigo before getting back on course. The cop car made the turn fifty yards behind them.

"Right on K," said Otis.

"That the next street?"

"The next big one, yeah."

A car jumped the curb to avoid collision ahead. Farrow speed-threaded his way around another.

"All right, Roman, here we go."

"You got a red light up there, Frank."

"I see it."

"You plannin' on blowin' it off," said Otis, "you might want to think about landin' on your horn."

Farrow goosed the accelerator as Otis's fingernails dented the white bucket seat. Otis saw a flash of spinning green metal, heard horns as they dusted the stoplight. He turned his head and looked through the back window. The cop car had been slowed by the cross traffic. Farrow hooked a right onto K, kept it at sixty as he made the next three greens.

"Take New York Avenue straight out of town," said Otis.

"Then Fifty down to Three-o-one south. We get lucky enough, we might just make it out of here."

Farrow screwed a Kool between his lips and pushed the lighter into the dash.

"I had to pump the hell out of those brakes back there," said Farrow.

"We can check it out later. Just keep drivin'."

"We got made," said Farrow with a frown. "Why do you suppose that is?"

"Have to ask Man-you-el the next time we see him." Otis smiled. "Guess you was wrong about that po-lice presence, Frank."

Farrow pulled the lighter from the dash and lit his cigarette. The menthol felt good hitting his lungs.

CHRISTOPHER JONAS walked through the front door of the house on Hamlin, saw his father sitting in the living room with tears in his eyes. Christopher had only seen his father cry once, on the day his mother, Christopher's grandmother, had passed away.

"What's wrong?" said Christopher, dropping his day pack by the door.

"You all right, son?"

"Why wouldn't I be?"

"Come here."

Christopher went up the foyer steps to the living room and hugged his father. It was awkward, bending down like that, but he didn't break away. His father held him tight and didn't seem to want to let go. He finally did release him and Christopher stood.

"Everything okay, Dad?"

"Yes." William Jonas wiped tears from his face. "Go on back

to your mother's bedroom, now. Your brother's back there with her. She wants to talk to the both of you, hear?"

"Sure you don't want me to stay with you for a while?"

"Go on, boy. Do as I say."

Jonas watched his son, tall as a weed, disappear into the hall. He turned the chair and wheeled himself to the couch, where he found the phone and dialed the police. He considered the man's threats as he listened to the phone ring on the other end. He cut the connection before the call was answered and tossed the phone back on the couch.

TWENTY-NINE

THOMAS WILSON took Route 4 east of the Beltway, through the old town of Upper Marlboro and onto a long asphalt road that dipped down and ended at a small industrial park set back along a creek that drained into the Patuxant River. He drove his Intrepid past squat, one-story garages and storage facilities, and then past a large green Dumpster, turning into a very narrow alley set between two sets of warehouses. The alley ran for a hundred yards and opened to a deep parking area and another set of warehouses that bordered the wooded area fronting the creek. Wilson parked beside his uncle Lindo's flat-bed, wood-railed truck. He used his key and entered an unmarked warehouse set in the middle of the strip.

Lindo was heavy in the middle and wore red suspenders over a navy blue shirt. He had a neat gray mustache and kept his gray hair closely trimmed. Lindo looked up from the paperwork he was doing at his particleboard desk as Wilson entered. The room was bright with dozens of fluorescent lights mounted in its drop ceiling.

"Been waitin' on you," said Lindo. "You asked for two hours today, and I agreed. But what you took was more like three."

"I apologize, Uncle L. Somethin' came up."

"Well, we best get goin' before we get behind. Got to make the park run before we do our run in the District."

Lindo got free rent in the warehouse in exchange for once-a-week hauls for the industrial park's tenants. Wilson didn't know for sure why his uncle needed the warehouse—three thousand square feet of space, housing a bathroom and an old, beat-up desk—but he suspected that having it made Lindo feel like a businessman rather than just the junkman that he was.

"The tenants been complainin'?"

Lindo reached behind him and lowered the volume on his box. Lindo liked that old-time, street corner–harmony jive from when he was comin' up in the fifties and early sixties.

"Naw, the tenants are all right. That fellow owns that carpet warehouse, down past the alleyway? He came over earlier, asked when we was gonna haul those remnants of his. But I expect he was havin' a slow day and really only came up here for some company. He had a look at all this empty space and told me we ought to hold a card game here on Friday nights. Said we'd never get caught, as nary a soul comes into this industrial park weekend nights. Said we could do it right, too. Have a bar, music, a couple of good-lookin' women to dress it all up. A real after-hours thing. I didn't know if he was serious or not, so I had to tell him that I gave up gambling, liquor, and women over twenty years ago."

"You did?" said Wilson.

"Well, I gave up gambling, anyway."

"Excuse me, Uncle L.," said Wilson. "I better change into my work clothes so we can get it on."

Wilson walked back to the bathroom, where his coveralls were hung behind the door.

He chuckled under his breath, thinking of that fool rug man. Imagine, a high-stakes, after-hours card game, back in this industrial park, on a dead-ass Friday night. And then he thought, maybe it wasn't so foolish after all.

You planned it right, it could work.

DIMITRI KARRAS sat at the bar of the Spot, eating Darnell's special, a tomato-based cod stew with onions, garlic, oregano, and potatoes. Anna Wang sat beside him, smoking one of Mai's cigarettes. Mai stood behind the bar, her arms crossed, a smoke dangling between her chubby fingers.

"The special didn't go so well today," said Anna.

"It should have," said Karras, scooping up the juices with a heel of French bread.

"A little too esoteric for this place," said Anna, loud enough for Happy, seated two stools to her left, to hear. But Happy just brought his cigarette slowly to his lips and gave it a loving drag.

"The man can cook," said Karras. "He needs the right vehicle, is what it is."

Maria Juarez came from the kitchen, went behind the bar, grabbed a can of pineapple juice from the shelf, and shook the can. A welt had risen on her cheek, and her eyes were red from crying. She managed to smile at the group before returning to the kitchen.

"Fucking bastard," said Anna.

Karras saw James Posten give Maria a hug at the entrance to the kitchen, and then James came out and headed for the basement steps. He stopped to say a few words to Ramon, who cradled a full bus tray. Ramon set the bus tray down and followed James down to the basement.

"Where's Nick today?" said Karras.

"He gave me his shift again," said Mai. "Must be busy with one of those cases. I like when he's busy. I need the work."

"Yeah, but no time for sergeants," said Anna.

"Andy Griffith," said Karras.

"Huh?"

"You're too young."

"I have plenty of time for my Sergeant DeLaughter," said Mai coyly. "You have to make the time, and honey, the night time is the right time." She wiggled her eyebrows at Anna.

A drunk on the end of the bar began to sing loudly to the song coming from the house stereo.

"'Gypsies, tramps, and thieves,'" sang the drunk, "'we'd hear it from the people of the town, they'd call us...'"

Karras winced.

Mai laughed and said, "What, Dimitri? You don't like my music?"

"Put it this way," said Karras. "If I was Phil and I walked in right now, I'd have to let you go."

"Just for playing this song?"

"If there was any justice," said Karras, "it would be a firing offense."

NICK STEFANOS picked up the developed photographs he had taken of Erika Mitchell and her boyfriend and drove south on Blair Road. Night had fallen, and the streets were slick with a brief shower of cold rain.

Stefanos pulled into the Blair Liquors lot and went to the outdoor pay phone. He phoned Ronald Weston, Randy Weston's brother. He described Erika Mitchell's new boyfriend to Weston, asked him a question, and got a quick response.

"One more thing," said Stefanos. "Did Erika have a key to your brother's crib?"

"Sure, man. She was hangin' at that joint, goin' in and out all the time while he was workin.'"

Stefanos thanked Weston and next dialed Jerry Sun at Hunan Delite. He asked him a question and got another quick response. Stefanos thanked Sun, cut the line, and dropped another set of coins in the slot.

"Elaine," said Stefanos. "Glad I caught you in. I'm running out of change here."

"You know I never get out of here before seven or eight. What's up?"

"I'm close to breaking the Weston case."

"Talk about it, Nick."

"Got a question for you first. You run those plate numbers I gave you the other day?"

"I have it right here."

Elaine read the name of the ice green Acura's owner to Stefanos. He wasn't happy, but there was the satisfaction of having done a job and done it well.

"You still there?"

"Yeah."

"Tell me what's going on."

"Tomorrow. I'm going to let you buy me lunch. Say, one o'clock? I'll meet you at Scholl's."

"I'll be there. Look, Nick, have everything ready for me then. No more secrets, okay? The trial starts in a couple of days."

"Right. See you at Scholl's."

Stefanos got back in his car. He swung the Dodge out of the

lot, went a couple of blocks, turned off Blair onto Rittenhouse, and parked halfway down the street.

He pulled a full-size black Maglite from his glove box and stepped out of the car. He was breaking his own rule about working outside at night. This wasn't necessary; he was nearly sure he had the answers now. He told himself this as he walked down the sidewalk toward Sean Forjay's house.

The green Acura was not in the driveway. There was a light on in the house, but the light meant nothing. Stefanos looked around quickly and stepped past the empty gravel driveway to the locked-down garage. Along the top of the garage doors was a series of small rectangular windows. Stefanos got a log from a nearby stack of wood and set the log on its end. He balanced himself atop the log, pushed the rubber button on the shaft of the metal flashlight, and engaged the bulb. He pointed the light through one of the rectangular windows. He knew what he'd find.

The red Torino was parked in the garage.

Stefanos was grabbed from behind and thrown to the ground.

He rolled and came up standing, the flashlight still in his hand. He had landed wrong on his neck, and for a moment he fought dizziness. He squinted to make out the young man standing before him in a crouch. It was the low-slung young man he had bumped into, the one with the stoved-in nose.

"Hold up a minute, man," said Stefanos.

The young man smiled. He charged Stefanos, his head down. Stefanos swung the Maglite up, connecting it to the young man's jaw. He heard a crack and breaking glass, saw the young man leave his feet, his eyes fluttering up in the last flash of light.

Stefanos turned and ran, the head of the Maglite gone, its

cracked shaft still in his grip. His feet grazed the sidewalk as he booked. He thought of the days he had run from the cops as a child and beaten them, thought of the first time he had won a fight, and he laughed.

He reached his car. He was still laughing as he turned onto Blair Road and gave the Dodge gas.

NICK STEFANOS poured three fingers of Grand-Dad into a rocks glass and took it and a cold beer out to his living room, where he had lit a fire. He stood before the fireplace, listening to a Circus Lupus LP called *Super Genius.* The cut was "Breaking Point"; the rhythm section kicked, and the guitars made it rock. Stefanos drank deeply of the bourbon and set the glass on the mantel. He looked down at his fingers playing air guitar below his waist and he smiled.

Alicia Weisman arrived a little while later. He kissed her on the lips as she removed her coat. She went to walk away, and he drew her back to him and kissed her again.

"What's up with you?" she said, not unhappily.

"Nothing. Can we just stay in tonight?"

"Damn straight. Let me get a drink."

"Bring another beer for me, too. Okay?"

Stefanos built the fire up and got down to his T-shirt. Alicia played *Soda Pop * Rip Off,* by Slant 6, and Stefanos played *13-Point Program to Destroy America,* by Nation of Ulysses. He called it "the greatest punk-rock record of all time."

She laughed at his hyperbole as she looked into his unsteady eyes. "You're not gonna get too drunk tonight, are you, Nick?"

"Not if you don't let me."

She pulled her black shirt over her head and tossed it aside.

"That's a start," said Stefanos. He kissed her, running his

hand down her bare arm. "Your skin is soft. You smell good, too. I ever tell you that?" He smiled.

"Why so happy?" she said.

"I can't explain it. Adrenaline. I had a good day today. What happened today wouldn't be good to someone else, but it was for me. And now there's you."

They embraced. The room was warm, and they stripped naked. Stefanos put a Stan Getz on the platter. He came back and held her, and they joked and talked. They made it on the couch and they woke in the morning in each other's arms.

THIRTY

NICK STEFANOS handed a stack of photographs to Terrence Mitchell. Stefanos sat in the morning light that streamed through the front window of Mitchell's house and looked at the passing traffic out on Chillum Road. He looked at a squirrel running up the trunk of a dogwood tree. He didn't want to look at Mitchell.

When Mitchell was done he straightened the stack as he would a deck of cards, straightened it again as he struggled with what he had just seen. His shoulders sagged, and he leaned back into the couch.

"Who is that with Erika?" asked Mitchell.

"A drug dealer by the name of Sean Forjay," said Stefanos. "Your daughter's seeing him regularly."

Mitchell looked away. "Are they tight?"

"After you drop her off at Fort Totten, he picks her up at the P. G. Plaza station every morning and returns her there early in the evening."

"So Erika has no job."

"I don't know that, Mr. Mitchell."

"But she *has* been lying to me."

"I would say so, yes."

"This world," muttered Mitchell. He stood, went to the window, and stared out into his front yard, the fence that surrounded it, its barbed-wire cap. With his back to Stefanos he said, "You can't stop it from reaching you. You can try, but it doesn't work."

"Mr. Mitchell—"

"Isn't that right."

"I suppose it is."

Mitchell touched his hand to the glass. "I know you think I'm some kind of stiff. But there was a time...Let me tell you, I knew how to have fun. The house parties we'd have in the basements, with those blue lights, dancing with the young ladies to the Motown sound. The concerts at the Howard, back in the early sixties? You could check out six bands for a buck-fifty, man. Hell, I saw James Brown and the Flames at the Howard when J. B. was the boss for real. Yeah, I knew how to have fun. And the city was alive.

"But the city changed. And then my wife left me, and it was just Erika and me. So I moved us out here...to this. A brown patch of grass and a pile of bricks under the power lines. I wanted to protect her, see? But I couldn't protect her, Stefanos. You can't stop it from reaching you. No, you can't."

"This is the world we've got," said Stefanos.

Mitchell continued to stare through the window for another minute and then he stood straight. "Go ahead and give me the rest of it. I know there's more."

"Okay. Here's what I think. Forjay is the top dog down around First and Kennedy. Randy Weston and Donnel Lawton were small-change dealers compared to him, but he still wanted them out. He also wanted Erika, who was tight with Weston, all to himself. He figured out a way to get everything he wanted at once."

"What puts Forjay at the crime scene?"

"A tricked-out red Torino was spotted leaving the crime scene just after gunshots were heard around the time of death. I found that Torino last night, parked in Forjay's garage."

"So Forjay framed up Weston."

"Yeah. He got ahold of the key to Weston's apartment. It would have been easy for him to plant the gun. An anonymous call tipped the police to the whereabouts of the murder weapon. They made the arrest."

Mitchell nodded slowly as he put it together. Stefanos didn't feel the need to go the rest of the way: that it was Erika who had the key to Weston's crib. That Erika, most likely, had made the anonymous call.

Mitchell said, "What's going to happen to my little girl?"

"I don't know," said Stefanos. "But I still need you to alibi Randy Weston."

Mitchell turned, his eyes rimmed red. "Randy Weston could not have killed Donnel Lawton. He was here in this living room when that boy was killed."

"You'll testify to that?"

"Yes." Mitchell looked down at Stefanos. "What you said to me the other day, about me bein' no better than those criminals out there... You were wrong."

"I know it. The truth is, I knew it then."

"You try to keep Erika out of this," said Mitchell.

"I'm going to meet with Weston's defense counsel this afternoon." Stefanos stood and shook Mitchell's hand. "I'll do the best I can."

"YOU'RE A cheap date," said Elaine Clay, watching Stefanos chew his food.

"Look at this," he said, excitedly pointing the knife at his plate. "Chopped steak, mashed potatoes and gravy, tossed salad, and biscuits. The whole thing was, what, four and change?"

"Uh-huh."

"How's yours?"

"A little bland, to tell you the truth."

"The food is good, but you have to spice it up yourself. They don't salt it on account of all the potential heart attacks in this place. They keep the A-1 and soy sauce behind the register. You have to ask for it when you pass through."

"You're the Scholl's expert, huh?"

"I've been coming here my whole life. Well, not *here*. My grandfather used to take me to the old Scholl's at Vermont and K."

Stefanos looked around the cafeteria, filled with old folks, working stiffs, and bus tourists, and a diligent multiethnic staff. Religious sayings and Christian icons hung on the walls. He nodded to an ancient geezer with a flowing gray beard, reading a newspaper with the aid of a magnifying glass.

"See that guy? He eats here the same time every day."

"That's great, Nick. Can we get back to the case?"

"You're just upset because there's no lawyers in this place."

"Yeah, I'm really feeling naked around all these common folk." Elaine had a bite of chicken à la king and laid down her fork. "So Terrence Mitchell is definitely going to testify."

"That's right. You going to get Sean Forjay charged with the murder?"

"It's not my job to get anybody charged with murder, you know that. I'll feed the information you dug up to the D.A.'s office as a courtesy. Other than that, when Weston gets acquitted, I'm out."

"The cops should have nailed this one to begin with."

"They made what they thought was an easy and clean arrest.

There's too many unsolved homicides out there for them to overcomplicate the ones that fall into their laps solved."

Stefanos swallowed a mouthful of mashed potatoes. "Sean Forjay's gonna walk, isn't he?"

"The car proves nothing. The murder weapon had no prints. There *are* no witnesses. From where I sit, I don't think they even have enough to charge him."

"Unless they put Erika Mitchell on the stand."

"They're not going to know a thing about Erika Mitchell. I need Terrence Mitchell's testimony. If he gets angry or fearful for his daughter and decides not to testify, Randy Weston goes to prison. I'm not going to jeopardize Weston's acquittal for some vague concept of justice."

"What's justice got to do with any of this?"

"Nothing. You need to get past all that. If you want justice—"

"I know, I know." Stefanos pushed his empty plate to the side and sat back in his chair. "Anyway, it's a job."

"You did a *good* job, Nick. Randy Weston is not a hard kid. You know what would have happened to him in prison? What he would have become? You saved his life."

"I hear you. Thanks."

"I owe you for this one."

"There is something you can do."

He asked Elaine to run a background check on Manuel Ruiz and Jaime Gutierrez. He gave her the address of their garage. The lease records would have their home addresses. Knowing this would prevent Elaine from confusing them with anyone else.

"Here's one more name while you're running those checks," said Stefanos. "A guy named Thomas Wilson."

Elaine hesitated for a moment. "What's going on? You taking side jobs again?"

"No."

"Okay, go ahead and play it like that if you want to. Anything else?"

"Well, yes. You could reimburse me for a flashlight."

"Why would I do that?" said Elaine.

"I broke it on the job," said Stefanos. "If it's all right with you, I'll just go ahead and send you the bill."

THIRTY-ONE

WILLIAM JONAS picked up his phone and punched a number into its grid. While he listened to the phone ring, he rubbed his finger on the checkered grip of the service revolver that was lying in his lap. He sat behind the bay window of his house, looking out onto Hamlin.

The call was answered, and the voice on the other end said, "Boyle." Jonas heard a young kid and a teenage kid arguing in the background.

"Danny, it's Bill Jonas."

"Hey, Bill. Sorry I haven't gotten back to you on the letter and envelope."

"That's why I'm calling. I've been contacted again by the man who sent the letter."

"Through the mail?"

"By phone. I'd like to see you, Dan. I need to see you *tonight*."

"Any idea where he was calling from?"

"He's in town. He followed my son. He *threatened* my son."

"All right," said Boyle. "Have you contacted anyone else yet?"

"You mean have I called the station?"

"Yeah."

"You're a cop. I'm calling you."

Jonas listened to dead air as Boyle put his hand over the mouthpiece. Then Boyle got back on the line. "Okay. I'll be right over. But I'm bringing a friend."

"Who?"

"A guy named Nick Stefanos."

"I met him last week at the meeting," said Jonas. "Private cop, right?"

"Don't hold that against him. I've been with him in situations before. He's good at what he does, and we're gonna need him. He's friends with Dimitri Karras, the father of—"

"I know who Karras is."

"Stefanos has a connection to all this."

"Bring him," said Jonas.

"Bill? If what you say is true, I'd get your family out of town for a few days."

"It's already done."

"Good. I'll see you soon."

William Jonas cut the connection. He wheeled himself back away from the window and sat calmly in the shadows of dusk.

"NICK?"

"Yeah."

"What, did I wake you up?"

"I was takin' a nap, Boyle. What's up?"

"I've got something you might be interested in."

"Oh, yeah? What's that?"

Boyle told him everything he knew.

"I don't want to hear it," said Stefanos when Boyle was done.

"It's true."

"I don't care if it's true. Call the cops."

"Bill Jonas called *me*."

"You shouldn't even think twice about it, Boyle. Call the cops. Call the ATF and the FBI and the SWAT team. Get all the alphabet guys in one room and *mobilize*, just like they do on TV. But stay out of it, man. And leave me out of it, too, hear?"

"Tell that to your buddy Karras."

"Don't play me, Boyle."

"I'll be over in a little while to pick you up."

Stefanos looked down at the hardwood floor. He pictured the group he'd met the week before. He thought of Karras and the bartender's wife, who'd broken down. The nice guy in the Orioles cap, and Wilson, the troubled friend of the pizza chef, who was somehow not who he seemed to be.

Stefanos pinched the bridge of his nose. "Gimme time to take a shower."

Boyle said, "Right."

STEFANOS SHOWERED and changed into a black shirt and jeans. He was taking his leather off the peg by the door when the phone rang. He slipped into his jacket and answered the phone.

"Nick, it's Elaine."

"Hey, what's up?"

"I had Joey A. do those background checks for you."

"That was fast."

"Like I said, I gave it to Joey A."

"Go ahead."

"All three of the guys you asked about have records. And they all served time together. Ruiz and Gutierrez went up on an interstate auto-theft beef. Thomas Wilson fell on a dope bust back in the early eighties."

Stefanos was not surprised. Thomas had mentioned "straights" at the meeting. It was a con's term for those not in the life. And Gutierrez had the prison plumage stamped right on his face.

"Nick?"

"Yeah."

"What's going on?"

"Nothing. I had a hunch about those guys, and I was curious, that's all. Where were they incarcerated?"

"Lewisburg."

"Okay. What's Wilson's street address?"

Elaine Clay gave it to him and said, "Anything else?"

"No, that's it. Thanks a million, hear?"

Stefanos hung the phone in its cradle. So Wilson was an ex-con and so were his friends. So what? It probably didn't mean a thing.

A horn sounded from out in the street. Stefanos left the apartment and walked to Boyle's car.

BOOKER KENDRICKS pulled his head out from under the hood of the red Mustang. He turned to Roman Otis, who was standing next to Gus Lavonicus in the yard.

"It's simple, cuz," said Kendricks. "Brakes ain't workin' so good 'cause you out of fluid. Need to put some dot three in this motherfucker right quick."

"You know I don't know nothin' about cars, Booker."

"Well, fluid's all it is."

Farrow came from the house, walked over to Otis, and lit a cigarette.

"T. W. called," said Farrow.

"He line us up with anything?" said Otis.

"He heard something about a big-money card game on Friday night. He's trying to firm up the details."

"That would work," said Otis.

"He fix it?" said Farrow, nodding at Kendricks, standing alongside the Mustang.

"Just needs a little fluid," said Otis. "I'll pick up some while we're out."

Farrow looked at the group. Otis was dressed sharp as always. Kendricks wore a shiny maroon shirt tucked into gray slacks. Lavonicus sported a Western shirt with imitation pearl buttons and lasso detailing embroidered across the chest. He wore a surplus coat over the shirt.

"Don't get into any trouble," said Farrow.

"Just gonna have a couple of cocktails," said Otis. "Goin' crazy sittin' around this joint."

Farrow walked back into the house.

Kendricks lowered the hood of the Mustang and wiped his hands on a rag. He gave Lavonicus the once-over and smiled. "Well, y'all look ready enough."

"Where we headed, man?" said Otis.

"Place off Three-o-one. Understand, they got bars down here for the brothers and bars for the white boys. There's a little bit of crossover but not much. We goin' to this white joint 'cause they got one of those machines you like."

"That's okay by me," said Otis.

Kendricks glanced at Lavonicus again. "Whoo-eee, pardner. Wait'll they get a look at you."

They walked to the Mark V, parked at the edge of the woods by a stand of tall pine. Otis got behind the wheel, ignitioned the Lincoln, hit the power switch on the stereo, and pushed the button marked "CD." Lavonicus folded himself into the seat beside him, and Kendricks settled into the backseat. The Commodores came from the rear deck speakers.

" 'Zoom,' " said Otis. "This here's got to be one of the most beautiful songs ever recorded."

"It sounds nice," said Lavonicus, awkwardly moving his head in time.

"People make fun of Mr. Lionel Richie. But I'd like someone to name a more perfect tune than this one right here."

Otis turned onto 301 and drove north. " 'I wish the world were truly happy,' " he sang, " 'living as one....' "

Kendricks directed Otis into the parking lot of a sports bar a couple of miles south of La Plata. They got the fish-eye from the guys at the main-room bar as they walked through to a paneled room in the back and had a seat at a four-top near the fire exit. At a nearby table, someone laughed at Lavonicus, then stopped laughing as Otis looked his way. Some guy was up onstage doing Garth Brooks, singing along to the karaoke. He had a beer in his hand and he sang off-key.

Otis and Kendricks ordered mixed drinks, and Lavonicus went with a Coke. Otis went off to examine the playlist and found one he knew: "I'm So Lonesome I Could Cry," by Hank Williams. Well, he knew the Al Green version, anyway. He decided he'd get up there and sing it like Reverend Al.

Otis took the stage, closed his eyes, and gave it his best shot. He tried to inject a little soul into the shitkicker arrangement, even threw in some of his hand interpretations, but nothing could make it fly. Lavonicus was the only one in the house who clapped when Otis was done. Otis thanked the audience and walked back to his seat.

He saw a couple of countrified black men seated at a deuce, and he nodded as he passed by, but the brothers did not nod back. Otis had a seat at his table.

"You sounded good, bro," said Lavonicus.

"Let's get the fuck on out of here," said Otis, swallowing the rest of his drink in one gulp. "Bunch of Charley Pride–lookin' motherfuckers in this place, anyway."

Otis missed Cali. He couldn't wait to get back home.

THIRTY-TWO

DAN BOYLE lit a Marlboro and shook the flame off the match. "You don't mind, do you?"

"No," said William Jonas. "It's all right."

Boyle exhaled. Smoke settled in the living-room light. Nick Stefanos stood by the bay window and leaned against the wall.

"You're certain it was him," said Boyle. "Maybe the photograph and the phone call were both some kind of twisted prank."

"'You killed my brother Richard,'" said Jonas. "That's what the man said to me on the phone. I've only killed one man in my career, Boyle. And the Richard thing, it never went out to the press. Only the killer would know that."

"What else?" said Boyle.

"It's like the man was mocking me, giving me details. Told me where he'd been incarcerated, all the way back to his reform school days. That he did time in state and federal prisons, too."

"Lewisburg," said Stefanos, putting it together now.

"That's the federal prison," said Boyle, "up in PA. Why'd you mention that?"

Stefanos didn't answer. He went to the glass table where Boyle had dropped his hardpack. He shook out a cigarette and lit it.

"He fed you something, Bill," said Boyle. "You're looking for a guy who served time in state and federal prisons, who has a brother named Richard. You feed that information into a computer, you're going to get a list of names. It's going to be a big list, but it's a start. But you know that already."

"That's right."

"So why'd you call *me?*"

Jonas glanced over at Stefanos and back to Boyle.

"You can speak freely," said Boyle.

"All right," said Jonas, lowering his eyes. "I'm not going to lie to you, Dan. There's been talk about you in the department for years. They say you're way off the edge. They say you put away suspects your own way when you see fit. That you and that old partner of yours, Johnson, did that Hispanic child molester a few years back, before Johnson retired. They say you carry throw-downs and drugs to leave at the crime scenes you fix. I've been a part of those conversations myself. Even got on my high horse about it a couple of times—until now."

"So there's been conversations," said Boyle steadily. "I'm gonna ask you again: What do you want from *me?*"

"This man and his partner put me in this chair for life. And now he's threatening my family."

"I'll get you protection."

"There is no protection. You can apprehend him, but you know guys like him have friends. My family would always be in danger, if not from his own hand then from someone he's sent."

"You can't just sit here and wait for him to come."

"I pray he comes," said Jonas.

Stefanos dragged on his smoke, trying not to look at the useless legs on Jonas.

Boyle had no such reservations; he nodded his chin at Jonas's chair. "You can't do it alone," he said. "You know it. So stop acting like you can."

"He'd be on my turf," said Jonas. "And he would lose."

"No. *You'd* lose."

"So what do you propose we do?"

Boyle sighed. "I'm going to move in with you for a few days. Wait this thing out."

Jonas nodded. "Thanks, Dan. Thanks for not making me ask."

"We need to go over this again. I want to know everything the man said when he called you up."

Jonas recounted the entire conversation.

When he was done, Boyle said, "How about Christopher? He notice anyone following him that day?"

"No. I don't want him to know that he was being followed, either. But I did ask if anything strange had happened that day, and he said no. He mentioned some car chase thing on the G.W. campus, but that was it. A cop car after some old red Mustang. Other than that, not a thing."

Boyle looked at Stefanos. "Any thoughts, Nick?"

"Huh?"

"You all right? You don't look so good, buddy."

"I'm fine." Stefanos butted his smoke. "Listen, I gotta take off."

"All right, go ahead. Let me talk with Bill here for a minute, and I'll meet you at the car."

Stefanos shook Jonas's hand. "Take care."

"Right."

Jonas waited for the door to close behind Stefanos. "He didn't add all that much to the conversation, did he?"

"He's a listener," said Boyle. "I'll pick his brains on the ride back."

"You gonna stay here tonight?"

"Yeah. Let me go home and talk to my wife, pack a suitcase with clothes." Boyle grinned. "Toss a couple of throw-down weapons and some drugs in the suitcase while I'm at it."

"I apologize for that," said Jonas. "The fact is, I'm gonna feel a whole lot better with you around. This sonofabitch comes around, we're gonna get him. Right?"

"Bet it," said Boyle.

STEFANOS HAD Boyle drop him at the Spot. Boyle tried to engage him in conversation, but Stefanos wouldn't bite.

"You got nothin' to say about all this?" said Boyle as he pulled over on 8th.

"I need to think," Stefanos answered.

Boyle let him go.

AT THE bar, Stefanos ordered a Bud and a shot of Grand-Dad. Mai put the D.C. directory next to the drinks, along with the house phone. Stefanos found Wilson's number next to the Underwood Street address Elaine had given him. He left a message for Wilson, had his beer and shot, smoked a couple of cigarettes, and told Mai to hit him again. Darnell came out and talked with Stefanos for a while, then went back to his dishes.

Stefanos dragged on his cigarette, thinking of Darnell. He'd done hard time in Lorton for a stupid mistake, but someone had seen fit to give him a second chance. Out of that chance, Darnell had become an exemplary man.

Stefanos's call came through while he was finishing his second round.

THOMAS WILSON bought a .38 Special from this guy he'd seen at the Hummingbird and the Jamaican Breeze and a couple of the other clubs out on the avenue. The dude was a skinny rock-fiend from the neighborhood, all angles and nerves. They did the transaction in Wilson's car. Wilson passed him three hundred-dollar bills for the strap and a box of shells. The bluing had rubbed down on the barrel, but the gun dry-fired fine and looked otherwise sound. The skinny cat, guy by the name of Raymond Allison, went away, his head jerking left and right as he quick-stepped down the street, and Wilson went in the opposite direction, to a dark bar named Sandy's, over near Princeton Place.

Wilson was already a little high from a double cognac, but he had another as he sat alone at the bar. "Dazz," an old Brick single, was playing on the stereo. He used to like this one, but he was distracted and wasn't paying much attention to the song.

He'd taken a few steps tonight. He'd *acted*. That was something for him. He'd called Farrow down at the house in southern Maryland, planted the card-game scheme in his mind. He'd bought a gun. All right, so he'd done a couple of things. Question was, he got Farrow and Otis into that warehouse, what would he do then?

A couple of guys down along the bar laughed loudly at something one of them had said, and when Wilson looked over, the smaller of the two stopped smiling and gave him a real hard look. Wilson's blood moved, but he turned away and looked into his drink. If anything started he knew he'd get punked out. Knowing this was hard for Wilson, for any man, to accept.

Wilson sipped his cognac. It felt funny, sitting here this early on a Tuesday night. Usually, about this time, he'd be in the meeting with the rest of the group, drinking coffee, talking, telling jokes. But they'd all decided to cancel, as Bernie was down in the country on vacation and it wouldn't be right to do the thing without Bern.

Wilson went to the pay phone back by the rest room. He phoned Bernie's house and left a message on his machine, telling Bernie he hoped he was resting up real good down on his "plantation." Country-lovin' fool didn't even have a phone down there on that property. Wilson would have liked to have heard Bernie's voice right about now.

A young woman approached him on her way to the rest room. Wilson patted his fade and said, "What's goin' on, girl? You look *fine*, too." The woman went right on by without a word.

Wilson phoned his place for messages. His uncle Lindo had called to talk about Dexter Manley, whom he'd seen on the Glenn Harris show on channel 8. And Dimitri's friend, that investigator named Stefanos, had called as well. What was up with that? Wilson dialed the number Stefanos had left on the machine. A woman answered and then Stefanos got on the line. Sounded like Stefanos was in a bar his own self.

"What can I do for you, man?" said Wilson.

"I know about you, Thomas," said Stefanos. "I know about Lewisburg and the men in the garage. Maybe we better have a talk."

Wilson didn't answer.

"Thomas?" said Stefanos. "I'll see you in a half hour."

"Where?" said Wilson.

"The Spot," said Stefanos. "Out on the street."

*　　　*　　　*

DIMITRI KARRAS and Stephanie Maroulis had dinner at the Thai Room on Connecticut and Nebraska, then went back to Stephanie's place and watched that cop show everyone liked on TV. Karras noticed that every time they ran out of ideas, the writers would send the main character into a bar so that he could fall off the wagon again for an episode or so. But he liked the show all right. It was something to pass the time.

"This is the kind of night married people have," said Karras. And Stephanie said, "What's wrong with that?"

They got undressed and folded their clothes neatly and made love quietly, and she fell to sleep with his fingers stroking her hair. This is also how it is for married people, thought Karras. And then he thought, It was just like this with Lisa. It's not so bad.

He woke up in the middle of the night and looked at the nightstand to check the time on the clock radio. He noticed that the photograph of Steve Maroulis was no longer there.

NICK STEFANOS crossed 8th Street and walked to the Dodge Intrepid idling at the curb. He opened the passenger door and climbed inside. He handed Thomas Wilson a can of beer and opened one for himself.

"Drive uptown," said Stefanos. "You can drop me at my place in Shepherd Park."

Wilson drove along the Southeast business district, around the Capitol and into Northwest. He went west on Pennsylvania Avenue and cut north on 14th Street. As he drove, he confessed. "That's it," said Wilson. "If I changed things to go in my favor, I didn't mean to. I've told it to you as straight as I could."

Stefanos nodded. He had drunk his beer quietly while Wilson talked, and he had interjected nothing.

Wilson shifted in his seat. "You got no comment?"

"You covered it."

"All right, then. How'd you get hip to me, man?"

"I marked you as a con the first time I met you. Did a background check and Lewisburg came up. That murderer—what's his name?"

"Farrow. Farrow and Otis."

"Farrow would be the man I saw at the garage."

"Yes."

"Farrow shot his mouth off to Bill Jonas when he was threatening his family. Told him that he was an alumnus of several institutions, including a federal facility. Lewisburg's a federal joint. Jonas's son Chris saw the same red Mustang I saw at Ruiz and Gutierrez's shop. It wasn't hard to connect the dots."

"I been waitin' for this for two and a half years," said Wilson. "Dreading it and welcoming it at the same time. Can you understand at all what I mean?"

Stefanos looked out the window, nodded toward a lit storefront at 14th and S. "That used to be my grandfather's place, right there. Nick's Grill. You'd never know how much pride went into that place from the way it looks now. Funny how you live in this town long enough, all these old buildings hold memories of some kind."

"Ain't you got nothin' more to say than that?"

"No," said Stefanos. "And don't look for any sympathy from me, either."

"Yeah, okay." Wilson's hand tightened on the wheel. "You wanna know somethin', man?"

"What?"

"Been many a night I wanted to kill myself. Just do it quick and check on out."

"Why didn't you?"

"When it came time, I *couldn't* do it. And there was another thing I couldn't do: Much as I wanted to, I couldn't tell my friends that I had set their loved ones up to die. In the end I couldn't do either one of those things. I was just plain paralyzed. I guess that makes me a coward, right?"

"Yes," said Stefanos. "You're a coward."

They drove through the U Street intersection and up into Columbia Heights and beyond. The light from the street lamps above crawled across their laps. Past Arkansas they climbed a hill and neared Colorado Avenue.

"Couple more streets and you'll be making a left," said Stefanos.

"What're you gonna do?" said Wilson. "You fixin' to turn me in?"

"I haven't told anyone a thing. You want to know the truth, that's not what you need. The law can't do any more to you than what's been done."

"What, then?"

"Left here." Stefanos killed his beer and dropped the can on the carpet. "I'm going to give you a little time to sort it out. We've got Bill Jonas under protection, but only for a few days. You need to make your peace with Dimitri and the others. Then we'll see."

"Dimitri will kill me, man. And then he'll want to kill them."

"Maybe so. You need to tell him just the same. Pull over behind that old Dodge." Stefanos handed Wilson his card as the Intrepid rolled to a stop. "Three days."

Stefanos stepped out of the car and crossed the dark street. Wilson watched him go.

THIRTY-THREE

"ALL RIGHT, James," said Dimitri Karras. "I need to call out some burgers."

"Go ahead, man."

"You wanna turn down that Luther first?"

"Yeah," said Darnell, not turning his head from the sink. "Can't think with that man bellowin' and shit."

"How much you need to think about to clean off a dish?" said James.

"Now you gonna take me for bad?" said Darnell. "Arabs and Jews be walkin' down the street holdin' hands the day I let a man wearin' makeup talk to me like that." Darnell laughed deeply.

"Aw, go ahead, Darnell."

James Posten twirled his spatula and sang as he went to the box, cut the volume on the Luther Vandross by a notch. He patted Maria Juarez on the ass as he went by, and Maria turned and did the same to him. But it was a halfhearted step back from their usual kitchen play. Maria's left arm was bruised from elbow to shoulder, and the pain was clear on her face.

"James?"

"Talk about it, Dimitri."

"I got a bacon-cheddar, rare. I got provolone, well. And I got a plain, extra rare."

"You want it bleedin', huh?"

"Knock the horns off it and walk it through a warm room."

Anna Wang entered the kitchen and pinched Karras on the arm as she passed.

"What's happenin', Anna?"

"Melvin's at the bar reciting the entire eighteen-minute Isaac Hayes version of 'By the Time I Get to Phoenix.' He's still on the intro. I needed a break."

Anna went to Maria and kissed her on the cheek. "Nice presentation on the salad today, *señora*."

"Thanks, Ann."

"That's *señorita* to you, girl," said James. "'Cause Maria looks young as one and pretty as one, too."

"Okay, James. Can I just add, the burgers are coming out perfect?"

"Go on, girl," said James, "get back to the dining room where you belong. We don't need your kind around here, or your compliments."

James smiled to himself as Anna left the kitchen. He turned to say something to Maria, but he saw her wince as she tried to pick up a bowl of lettuce and his smile turned to a frown.

NICK STEFANOS walked into the kitchen after the rush. They were all glad to see him back after missing so many shifts. Karras had the feeling Stefanos had been avoiding him, though, the entire afternoon.

"Hey, Dimitri."

"What?"

"Dan Boyle called. Remember his uncle he talked about, the cop who knew your father and my *papou?*"

"Yeah?"

"He's not doing so hot. They've got him in a nursing home, and Boyle says he's failing. Boyle's been talking to him about you and me, and he asked to see us. It would be a good thing to do. What do you think?"

"When?"

"Later this afternoon, after my shift."

Karras shrugged. "I can do that. I'll go home and shower and meet you back here in the bar."

"Sounds good. Hey, you seen James out there on the floor? I got a live ticket with some hots on it and I need him."

"He's out by the basement stairs, talking to Ramon. They been gabbin' about something for the last ten minutes. I'll tell him to come on back."

"Say, Nick..." said Karras as Stefanos left the kitchen.

Karras knew Stefanos had heard him. It was odd that he would just walk away.

ROBERTO JUAREZ came in around three o'clock and stood on the landing. He wore a white imitation-silk shirt under a thin leather jacket. He stared at Stefanos behind the bar without recognition or a smile. Stefanos went to the reach-through and told Maria that her husband had come to pick her up.

At the top of the basement stairs, Ramon went, "Tss," and Roberto Juarez turned his head. Ramon connected his thumb to his forefinger and put them to his lips, miming an imaginary toke. Juarez grinned stupidly. Ramon went up to the landing, and Juarez followed him out the door.

A couple of minutes later, James Posten emerged from the kitchen dressed in his fox-head stole and carrying his jeweled walking stick. Stefanos watched him go to the front door, open it, and go outside.

James Posten walked down 8th. He said hello to a pool player named Mattie, who stood outside Athena's, the neighborhood women's bar, smoking a cigarette. He passed the riot-gated athletic-shoe store and turned the corner into the alley.

Ramon and Juarez were back in the alley, hitting a joint. James stopped for a moment to prop his walking stick against the brick wall and then kept striding toward Juarez. Juarez held the joint up in offering, pursed his lips, and made kissing sounds at James. Juarez smiled contemptuously at James, and when James reached him he threw a deep right into Roberto Juarez's face. He aimed for the brick wall behind Juarez's head, and the punch landed squarely and collapsed his nose.

Juarez screamed. Blood splashed out into the alley.

Juarez tried to cover up, but James Posten combinated to the same spot. Juarez's nose had been pushed off to the side, and now it was just smashed cartilage and a loose flap of skin. Juarez went down to the alley floor moaning, tears streaming across his ugly face.

He reached out to Ramon, and Ramon laughed.

"Now you know what it feels like to get hit by a man," said James very quietly. "Don't even have a dream about takin' your hand to your wife or your little girl again."

James walked back to the head of the alley and picked up his walking stick. Ramon followed. They turned and headed down 8th Street, back toward the Spot.

"Where you learn that, Jame?" said Ramon.

"West Baltimore," said James.

Maria was waiting by the service bar with Darnell when James and Ramon came back in. Anna Wang was sitting at the bar next to Karras, who was eating his lunch. Happy sat alone, working on a Manhattan. Stefanos was behind the stick, one foot up on the beer cooler.

They watched James give Maria a kiss. Five minutes later Roberto Juarez entered the Spot and stood on the landing. Blood covered his white shirt and smeared his face. His eyes were glassy, and he was having trouble standing up.

Happy turned his head, looked Juarez over, then turned back to his drink.

"James just took away everything that guy ever had," said Stefanos.

"Someone ought to call an ambulance," said Anna Wang, reaching for one of Stefanos's cigarettes.

Karras nodded and cut into his chicken-fried steak.

Roberto Juarez reached a hand out to his wife. Maria's eyes narrowed as she buttoned her cheap coat and raised her chin.

"You do that?" said Darnell to James.

"Sure did," said James.

"Hard to believe a man wearin' eyeliner could put a hurtin' on another man like that." Darnell looked admiringly at James. "You sure you tellin' the truth?"

"*Got* to tell the truth," said James.

"An' shame the devil," said Maria Juarez.

She straightened her shoulders and raised her chin. They watched her cross the barroom floor.

DIMITRI KARRAS finished his lunch and drove his old BMW up into Northwest. He walked to his building at 15th and U. He took the elevator to the fifth floor, walked down the hall, and turned the corner to his apartment. Thomas Wilson stood outside of Karras's door.

"Dimitri."

"Thomas. What're you doing here? Aren't you working today?"

"I took the afternoon off. Needed to see you, man."

"You sick or somethin'? Your eyes don't look right."

"Need to talk to you, Dimitri. Need to tell you somethin' *now* and get it out quick. Don't stop me while I'm talking, 'cause I might not ever have the courage to tell it again."

Karras regarded Wilson curiously. Wilson's gaze was level and true.

"Say it," said Karras.

By the time he was done, Wilson was sobbing. Karras's shoulders had sagged and there were tears welled in his animal eyes. His lip was trembling, and his fists were balled and shaking at his side.

"Dimitri," said Thomas Wilson. "I am so sorry for what I've done."

Karras screamed. Wilson stood passively as Karras leaped toward him.

He's going to kill me now, thought Wilson. He was strangely relieved. It surprised him for a moment that he was not afraid.

Wilson saw a white blur in the dim hall light. He saw nothing, felt nothing after that.

THIRTY-FOUR

Boyle and Stefanos were at the bar drinking when Karras arrived, late in the afternoon, at the Spot. Stefanos was working on a beer, and Boyle was tipping a shot of Jack Daniel's to his lips. Karras put his hand on Stefanos's shoulder and nodded at Boyle. Stefanos turned his head; Karras's face was tight-jawed and pale.

"Anything wrong?" asked Stefanos.

"Not a thing," said Karras.

Boyle drank off the rest of his beer and stashed his Marlboro reds in the side pocket of his tweed while Stefanos went around the bar and grabbed a six-pack from the cooler. Mai made a couple of hashmarks on his tab. Stefanos, Karras, and Boyle exited and got into the Coronet 500 out on 8th.

The nursing home, a one-story, white-brick affair fronted by a flat, brownish lawn, was in the town of Greenbelt, in Prince George's County. They signed in at the desk under the scrutiny of a chubby receptionist, who was eating a late lunch from a sectioned foam tray. Boyle had two cans of beer tucked beneath his raincoat.

They walked down a carpeted hall, the smell of soiled diapers cutting the still air. They passed a room where a woman sat with her face down on a table. A man's gravelly voice came loudly from another of the rooms: "Nurse...nurse...nurse," over and over again. The nurses on shift, black immigrants from the Caribbean and Africa, stood together at the end of the hall, conversing, ignoring the man's plea. Television sets, the volume turned unnaturally high, blared from every direction in the home.

"In here," said Boyle, and they followed him through an open door.

A heavy, shapeless old man was lying in a railed bed, his head elevated by pillows. He stared through a large window, shafts of sunset streaming across his body. Next to his bed was a small table on wheels, on which sat a tray of cold, untouched, pureed food. The stench of urine drifted off the bed. The room had the unmistakable smell of death.

"Uncle Jimmy," said Boyle, and the man turned.

"Danny."

Jimmy Boyle smiled. His face was fleshy, his jawline nearly invisible. Ashen baggage hung beneath his faded brown eyes. A thick hearing aid had been surgically implanted in one of his ears. His dome was covered with brown spots, and the strands of hair that remained were like brittle thread, both yellow and gray in the light.

"This is Dimitri Karras," said Boyle. "And this is Nick Stefanos."

Jimmy Boyle looked directly into Karras's eyes as he shook his hand.

"Good to meet you," said Karras.

"And you."

Jimmy Boyle made a tired gesture with his fingers. "Come on, fellas, have a seat."

Stefanos pulled up the room's sole chair, and Karras had a seat on the edge of the bed.

"It's too crowded in here for me," said Dan Boyle.

"Go ahead," said his uncle. "Give us some time alone."

Boyle kissed his uncle on the top of his head. Before he left he said to Stefanos, "I'll be down in that sitting room by the reception desk."

"Close the door on your way out," said Karras. He couldn't stand to hear the voice of that man, still calling for the nurses.

When Dan Boyle was gone, Jimmy Boyle said, "Well. Always nice to have visitors. Thanks for coming out."

"My mother spoke of you often," said Karras.

"Your mother was a fine woman."

"Thanks. She said you were one of my father's closest friends."

"Going back to the Depression," said Boyle. "We were a gang who all grew up in Chinatown together. Sons of immigrants, all of us. Your father and a kid named Billy Nicodemus, who was killed on the beach at Anzio, in the war. Joe Recevo, an Italian boy. Perry Angelos. Perry's still around."

"What happened to Perry?"

"He got rich. Opened a few carryouts and bought the properties early on. He's got nine grandchildren or something, and he's been with the same girl, Helen, for over fifty years. Perry always was the smart one of the bunch." Boyle smiled weakly. "Didn't look for trouble like the rest of us. But he's a good egg."

"Do you have children of your own?" asked Stefanos, who noticed the absence of cards, candy, and photographs in the room.

"I never married," said Boyle. "Except for a spell when some pharmacist got me hooked on pep pills, I've always been fat. A helluva lot fatter than I am now. The ladies didn't much care for men built like me, but the fact is I had my special preferences myself. I always did crave the company of colored women, see? But back then, well, you'd never think to bring a colored girl home to meet your father. Funny, here I am getting sponge baths from dark-skinned gals every day. What I dreamed of my whole life, right? Trouble is, I can't get the equipment to come to attention anymore. But it's still pleasant. I do look forward to those baths, every day."

"Speaking of the nurses," said Karras, "why don't they respond to that guy yelling for them right now?"

"Ah," said Boyle with a dismissive wave of his hand. "There's nothing wrong with that guy. He's just afraid to be alone. How a man faces death is as important as how he lives his life. Do you know what I mean?"

"I think so," said Karras.

"Sure you do. You're your father's son. And your father feared nothing, to a fault. Hell, Pete's the man responsible for getting me my gold shield."

"I heard something about it from my mother," said Karras.

"There was this killer named Gearhart, a big dandy who worked for a loan shark named Burke. Pete tagged Gearhart as a killer and handed me the collar. I was made detective straight away."

"Burke," said Karras.

"You know the name," said Boyle.

"I know that someone named Burke killed my old man."

Boyle nodded. "Pete and Joey Recevo had both worked for Burke at one time, just after the war. Something bad happened between Pete, Joey, and Burke. Burke had your father's leg busted up pretty bad, and then Pete was out. Big Nick Stefanos gave him a job in his hash house, over on Fourteenth. In nineteen forty-nine, your father died in a gun battle in Burke's row house in lower Northwest. Joe died beside him. I always figured the whole thing had to do with Karras turning in Gearhart. And I felt plenty bad about that." Boyle looked at Stefanos. "But then Costa, the little guy who worked with your grandfather, set me straight."

"Costa?" said Stefanos. "When was that?"

"Right before he died from cancer, a few years back. I went over there to see him at his place. He wanted to get some things off his chest before he passed. He didn't know if it was right to tell you. I was the regular coffee-cop at Nick's Grill all those years, and he knew I was one of Pete's old friends."

It was warm in the room. Stefanos wanted a beer. He wanted to smoke a cigarette. He looked at Karras and for the first time noticed the skin scraped from the knuckles of Karras's right hand.

"What happened?" said Karras.

"Burke had been shaking down Nick for protection money all along. He sent some men he knew from Philly to talk to Nick, and they pushed him too far. Pete and Nick and Costa slaughtered those men in the back of the grill, late one night."

Karras and Stefanos said nothing.

Boyle cleared his throat. "Burke must have found out that they killed his associates. He couldn't let it lie. I figure he planned to take down Nick and burn his place to the ground. Joe Recevo knew it and tipped Pete. Joe and Pete stood together and turned Burke's row house into a battlefield. They stepped in and stopped it all right there."

"Dimitri's father saved my grandfather's life," said Stefanos.

Boyle nodded. "What they did was beyond the scope of the law. But the law isn't always the answer. What they did was *necessary*. And it's important that you know. That who they were is passed on to their own blood. If it's not passed on, then their lives meant nothing."

Stefanos glanced up. Karras was staring at him, and he looked away.

"I'm tired," said Jimmy Boyle.

"We'll leave you now," said Stefanos.

Karras squeezed the hand of his father's friend.

THEY FOUND Dan Boyle in the day room, sitting beside a bloodless, gray man in a wheelchair. Both of them were drinking beers.

"Come on," said Karras, putting his head in the doorway.

"Right," said Boyle.

The three of them left the building. Darkness had fallen. They walked across the parking lot to the car.

"I could use a drink," said Karras.

"Now you're talkin'," said Boyle. "Guess we'll head back to the Spot. Okay by you, Nick?"

Stefanos didn't answer. He was thinking of his grandfather, Nick Stefanos. He was thinking of Dimitri's father, Pete Karras, and Jimmy Boyle, the man facing death back in that bed. Knowing with certainty that nothing was accidental. That everything started long ago and led to something else and couldn't be stopped. Knowing now, too, that he and Dimitri Karras were linked for life.

STEFANOS, KARRAS, and Boyle entered the Spot. Karras and Boyle found two stools in the center of the bar. A small man wearing a beret drained his beer, put his coat on, and waved good-bye.

"Good night, sweet princess," said the man.

"See you, Charlie," said Mai.

Closing time at the Spot was anywhere from seven-thirty to eight o'clock—an unusual arrangement for a bar. But the

Spot's drinkers were working people and cops who got plowed early and made their way home, stopping at other joints along the way. The neighborhood juicers were hip to the house hours and went elsewhere late at night. That was how Phil Saylor wanted it to go.

"I got it, Mai," said Stefanos, walking around the bar.

"Thanks, Nicky." She reached behind her, undid pins, and shook out her hair. As she did this her breasts jiggled inside her marine T-shirt.

"Do that again," said Boyle.

"Do what, Danny?"

"Go on," said Stefanos, "get out of here. Say hello to Sergeant Slaughter."

"It's DeLaughter. And I will."

She kissed Stefanos on the cheek and bolted out the door. Stefanos set Karras up with a beer and put a Jack and a beer in front of Boyle. Boyle picked up the A section of the *Post*. He read intently, chuckling under his breath as Stefanos finished up with Mai's closing procedure.

"Here's one for you," said Boyle to Karras. "Ah, jeez. The press dug up some internal memos on the mayor's million-dollar security detail. This story talks about how the guys on the detail drive the mayor around town, drop him off at 'unscheduled stops,' and sit out on the street and wait. Sometimes they check on him, and he comes to the door 'partially clothed.' The mayor says he's just visiting 'associates and political supporters' and looking for 'some good conversation.' The taxpayers are footing the one-million-dollar bill for the mayor to whore around, and the schoolkids in this town can't get protection or books or roofs that don't leak. Yeah, and that general they got to run the schools, he's doin' a *real* good job. And you know what? If the mayor runs again he's gonna get reelected.

And if he gets reelected, the people who voted him back in won't see Home Rule again for a long while." Boyle lit a cigarette and talked through the smoke. "Funny city you guys live in, right?"

Neither Karras nor Stefanos replied.

Boyle folded the newspaper and tossed it aside. Stefanos pulled the green netting off the inside lip of the bar, rinsed it, and laid it out on the service area to dry. He put *Jacks & Kings*, an old Nighthawks tape, into the box. A guy named Hap had left it one evening in the bar.

Boyle got up, went to the phone, and called William Jonas. He told Jonas he'd be over to his house shortly. Then he went back to the bar and had a seat.

"My wife worries about me," said Boyle before killing his shot of Jack.

"I'll bet," said Karras.

Stefanos cracked three more beers. He served Karras and Boyle. He opened a bottle for himself, tipped it back to his lips, and drank hungrily.

"Hey, Nick," said Boyle, "hit me with another mash."

Stefanos poured Jack Daniel's into Boyle's shot glass.

"Christ," said Karras, "you guys like to drink."

"Think we might have a problem with it?" said Boyle.

Karras sipped his beer. He was no drinker, but it tasted good tonight.

"Turn this up," said Boyle. "I remember seeing these guys at the old Psychedelly. 'Bout time you played some good music in this joint. And they say white boys can't play the blues."

"Sorry to disappoint you, Boyle, but it's blacks and whites playing together on this one. Muddy Waters's backup band. Guitar Jr. and Pinetop Perkins on the ivories."

"Pinetop Perkins," said Boyle. "Who the hell is that?"

They drank some more. They listened to Boyle talk about the jungle out there and his daughter's third-world boyfriends and how Keith Van Horn was going to dominate in the NBA. Karras said little, smiling strangely at Stefanos until Stefanos had to look away. Then Boyle looked at his watch and told them he had to go.

"I'm baby-sitting tonight," said Boyle, winking at Stefanos as he slipped into his wrinkled raincoat. He left money on the bar, clapped Karras on the shoulder, and left the Spot.

Baby-sitting, thought Karras. Couldn't Boyle come up with anything better than that? Who in the hell would ever leave a baby with Boyle, anyway?

He relaxed. He was glad that Boyle was gone. Karras finished another beer.

Stefanos poured three fingers of Grand-Dad into a heavy, beveled shot glass and set it next to his bottle of Bud. The lights went out in the kitchen, and Darnell walked from the darkness. He adjusted his leather kufi on his head and buttoned his coat.

"Late for you to be getting out," said Stefanos.

"Was waitin' for your redneck friend to leave," said Darnell. "He asks me if I can dunk again, me and him are gonna have it out."

"Can you?"

"Funny." Darnell looked at the bourbon-and-beer setup in front of Stefanos. "Want me to hang around? You could drop me uptown."

"We're gonna be a while," said Stefanos.

"Let me get on out of here, then," said Darnell. "Dimitri. Nick."

Stefanos locked the front door behind Darnell and went back around the bar.

"Darnell tries to pull me out of here every night," said Stefanos.

"He doesn't have too much luck, I take it."

"Not too much. I guess I'm one of those guys who can't be saved." Stefanos put one foot up on the beer cooler and raised his glass. "*Yasou, re.*"

"*Yasou, patrioti.*"

Karras touched his bottle to Stefanos's glass and the two of them drank.

An hour or so went by. Slowly and quietly the edge came off, and they drifted toward the soft world. Cigarette smoke hung in the light falling from the Spot's conical lamps. Stefanos put on an old Otis Redding, and it was beautiful and sad. Karras sang "You Don't Miss Your Water" while Stefanos smoked a cigarette. Stefanos thought Karras's voice was pretty nice. Neither of them said a thing after that.

Stefanos finished his shot of bourbon and poured another, knowing that he was coming to that place where he would talk. After the nursing home, there was never any question that he would tell Karras about Wilson and the men who were in town. That time had come. He looked at Karras and Karras was smiling in that way again and Stefanos leaned his elbow on the bar.

"Dimitri."

"What?"

"Look here, man. There's something I've got to tell you."

Karras laughed and shook his head.

"What's so funny?" said Stefanos.

"This about Thomas Wilson?"

"Yes."

Karras smiled. "I've been wondering when you were gonna come to that."

THIRTY-FIVE

S O THOMAS spilled it," said Stefanos. "I'm a little surprised."

"So was I."

Stefanos raised his chin. "What'd you do?"

"I hit him," said Karras. "He let me hit him. I hit him in the face and I kept hitting him until I had nothing left. I left him there in the hall of my apartment building."

"What happened then?"

Karras studied his skinned knuckles. "I went into my place and I sat on my bed. I talked to myself and rubbed my face and got up and stared out the window. I washed my hands and paced around the apartment and then I went back out to the hall. I thought I might have killed him, but he was conscious. Sitting up, with blood on his lips and a gash on his cheek from where my ring had caught him. One of his eyes had begun to swell shut. He reached out his hand, and I took it and lifted him up.

"We went back into my apartment and I gave him a towel. I waited for him to get clean. He came out of the bathroom, and we sat in my living room and talked."

"About what?"

"About what we were going to do next."

"And?"

"Detective Jonas is Boyle's baby-sitting job, right?"

"That's right."

"The men who killed my son are in town because they want to hurt Bill Jonas. They're here to do another job, too, and they think that Thomas is setting it up."

"What are you going to do about it, Dimitri?"

"What I've been hoping to do for the last two and a half years. I'm going to kill those men."

Stefanos looked into his drink. "What about the law?"

"Like the man said. The law isn't always the answer."

Stefanos finished his bourbon and put another glass on the mahogany. He free-poured two shots and slid one glass over to Karras. He uncapped two more beers.

"You know what it is to kill a man, Dimitri?"

"Do *you*?" Karras had a sip of bourbon and held the glass up to the light. "I suppose you're going to tell me now."

"Crack wise if you want to. But I'm trying to talk you out of it because I know what it's like. You're talking about taking a life. You can't reverse it. And after you've done it, you're never the same."

"I do know what it means," said Karras. "But it's not going to stop me from killing those men."

"You must have a plan," said Stefanos.

"A plan?"

"How's it going to work?"

"Thomas Wilson is going to bring them to me."

"Don't count on it. Wilson's weak."

"He's strong enough."

"I don't think so."

"Think what you want. He asked me for another chance, and I'm going to give it to him. He'll do fine."

Stefanos rubbed his thumb along his lower lip. "You going to tell the waiter's father? How about Stephanie Maroulis?"

"I'm not going to tell either one of them a thing. Bernie's found his peace and so has Stephanie. This is for them, too, but they'll never know. And I'm trusting you to keep it from Bill Jonas—and Boyle. I don't want to have a thing to do with Boyle."

"You're not going to make it," said Stefanos. "These guys will kill you before you have a chance. You're going to die and get Wilson killed, too, and for what? I'm telling you, man, this idea of yours is bullshit. It's fucked."

"All right, you've said it. Now leave it alone. You've got nothing to do with it, hear?"

"We've got too much history between us for me to leave it alone."

"You heard Boyle's uncle. Your grandfather gave my old man a job when he was a washed-up cripple. My old man stopped those loan sharks from burning down your grandfather's grill. I'd say our slate is clean. We owe each other nothing."

"You're drunk," said Stefanos, looking into Karras's waxed eyes.

"Yeah, I'm drunk." Karras had a swig of beer, keeping his eyes on Stefanos.

"You better pray to God that you know what you're doing."

"God," said Karras with contempt. "Now you're going to tell me you believe in God."

"I'm like most men, I guess—that is, if they're honest enough to admit it. I believe some days and some days I'm not so sure. The truth is, I'm just trying to figure it all out."

"There's nothing to figure out. God was invented for children and old people who are frightened to die."

"The night I killed that man I thought the same thing. That there was no God. But look around you. There's too much good in the world, man—"

"Good? What about slavery? What about the Holocaust and Pol Pot? The Armenian slaughter. The young men who've been killed throughout history fighting wars in the name of God. The children who've died in this city in the last ten years. What kind of god would allow these things to happen?"

"I don't know."

Karras leaned forward. "What did my son do to God? Why did he take my little boy the way he did?"

"I don't know," said Stefanos softly.

"That's right, you don't know. But *I* know. The answer is, There is no God. Everything's just an accident. And when it's over there's nothing. No existence and no sensation. Nothing at all."

Stefanos shook a cigarette from his pack. He put it between his lips and struck a match. "I'm sorry for you, Dimitri."

"Sorry," said Karras. "I'm sorry, too. You know what I'm most sorry about? That I lied to my son about God. That's right. We were down at Hanes Point in the spring; I think Jimmy was four years old. We were walking around the speedway, and Jimmy said, 'Dad, how come you can't see God?' I said to him, 'People can't see God, Jimmy, they can only imagine him.' And Jimmy said, 'When you're dead can you see him?' And I said yes. Jimmy looked out at the channel and thought for a while, and then he made this flip of his hand and said, 'Aw, gimme a break!'"

Karras laughed sharply, thinking of his son. He pictured him in the sun at Hanes Point, the skip he put into his walk when he was happy, that flip of his hand, his dimpled smile. While Karras laughed, tears gathered in his eyes. The tears broke and rolled down his cheeks.

Stefanos handed him a bev nap and looked away. "Here you go, man."

Karras wiped at a thread of mucus that had dripped from his nose. He wiped the tears off his face.

"I was like you," said Karras, his voice desperate and strained. "I thought there might be a God. I *hoped* there was a God because I couldn't believe that death would ever separate me from Jimmy and Lisa. I mean, if you believe that death can do that, then nothing makes sense, right? But when I saw Jimmy in the morgue that day—"

"Dimitri."

"When I saw him in the morgue, *Nick*, lying there... his body was black all over from the bleeding he'd done inside, and his arms and legs were bent crazy and broken in pieces beneath the skin.... His face was so swollen, man. I knew then that there was no God. I'd known it all along, I guess, in my heart. I shouldn't have lied to my son."

"Dimitri, man. Don't."

Karras's mouth twitched up into a frightening smile. "He was wearing a rabbit's foot that day, Nick. I had given it to him, and I told him to clip it to his shorts. I told him it would bring him luck. Told him it would be lucky if he wore that rabbit's foot on his shorts..."

Stefanos smoked the rest of his cigarette while Karras cried. Karras cried freely for a while, and then he wiped his face and got off the bar stool. He tripped on the way to the bathroom and grabbed a chair for support.

Stefanos made a pot of coffee. He heard Karras vomiting back in the bathroom. He waited for some time and went back to the bathroom and found Karras washing his face over the sink. There was puke on the collar of his shirt, and his face was the color of putty.

"How do you take your coffee?" said Stefanos.

"I take it black."

The coffee was steaming in a mug when Karras returned. He drank it down and had another while Stefanos restocked the beer cooler and replaced the green netting along the lip of the bar.

Stefanos dimmed the conicals. The neon Schlitz logo burned over the center of the bar and bathed the room in blue.

"You about ready?" said Stefanos.

"Yeah," said Karras, who had gotten the color back in his face. "Let's go."

They walked to Stefanos's Dodge. Stefanos stumbled as he stepped off the curb. He reached into his pocket and handed his keys to Karras.

"Here you go, Dimitri. I'm too gassed."

Karras got behind the wheel, fastened his seat belt, and ignitioned the Coronet. He engaged the transmission and drove down 8th toward Pennsylvania. They had been in the bar for hours. The streets were empty and dark.

"You can't stop me," said Karras. "I want you to know that."

"I do know it," said Stefanos. "But I had to try."

THIRTY-SIX

MANUEL RUIZ was replacing the headliner inside a '64 Falcon on Thursday morning when he heard the phone ringing back in the office. He wiped his hands off on a shop rag and walked back to the office and picked up the phone. It was Farrow on the other end of the line. Manuel had been expecting the call.

Farrow's voice grew increasingly agitated as he related the story of the cop and the chase through the G. W. campus. Manuel denied that the Mustang's plates were dirty.

"Perhaps it was just that you and Roman look suspicious," suggested Manuel.

"Perhaps," said Farrow with annoyance. "But if it happens again—"

"It will not happen again," said Manuel. "Those plates are clean."

"Okay. But here's another thing. You gave me a car with bum brakes."

"The brakes, they do not work properly?" Manuel winced at the insincerity in his own voice.

"They're working better since we dumped fluid into them."

"My apologies, Frank. This was our mistake."

Jaime Gutierrez entered the office, looking for cigarettes. Manuel pointed at the phone and silently mouthed the word "Frank." Jaime nodded.

"Never mind," said Farrow. "You have my new car ready for me? The one I'm driving's getting red hot."

"Yes. It is very fast."

"I'm going to pick it up early Saturday morning. I would say two a.m."

"We will wait."

"Good. See you then."

Manuel cradled the receiver. Jaime found his cigarettes in the desk drawer and struck a match.

"He is coming to get his new car after midnight tomorrow night," said Manuel.

"You haf a car?"

"No. T. W. says we will not need it."

"What if T. W. is wrong?"

"Then God help us."

Jaime dragged deeply on his cigarette. "What else?"

"He made mention of a problem with his plates."

"But it was not enough of a problem."

"No," said Manuel.

"What about the brakes?"

"They put fluid in. So I suppose the brakes will not stop them either."

"The fluid, it will leak out again," said Jaime. "The brakes will fail."

Jaime tried to say this in a casual way. But he muttered a prayer under his breath, crossing himself quickly as he walked back out to the shop.

*   *   *

ROMAN OTIS stood behind the house at the edge of the woods in Nanjemoy, practicing his draw. He had his .45 holstered on the left side of his belt line so he could draw with his right hand. He found that his "Back to Oakland" ID bracelet occasionally caught on his belt as he drew the gun. Of course, he could just leave the bracelet or his belt behind for this particular job. But the bracelet was his lucky charm. And he felt it was important for a man to look like something when he left the house for work.

Frank Farrow came out the back door of the house and walked down a set of wooden stairs to where Otis stood.

"Hey, Frank," said Otis. "Tell me what you think of this here."

Otis raised his arms above his head and rotated his hands at the wrist. Gravity and the action made the ID bracelet slip down beneath the cuff of his shirt. Otis's right hand flashed down to the grip of the .45. He drew it and dry-fired into the woods.

"Why all that?" said Farrow.

"When I raise my hands and shake 'em," said Otis, "it'll be like my signal for you to let go."

"Okay, Roman," said Farrow, who had given up on trying to figure out the peculiarities of his partner. "Whatever you say."

They heard the cackle of Booker Kendricks coming from the front yard, and underneath it the booming monotone of Lavonicus.

"Booker just won't let up on Gus," said Otis.

"Your cousin's an amateur," said Farrow.

"He's fuckin' with the wrong man," said Otis.

"Well, after tomorrow night we'll never see him again."

"We all set?"

Farrow nodded. "The card game's at midnight at an industrial park in a place called Upper Marlboro. T. W. says it's all young brothers flush with drug money, playing pinstripe gang-ster like they seen in the videos. Gonna be a whole lot of dirty greenbacks there, Roman."

"And guns, I expect."

"There could be, yes. We'll just have to go in hard and fast. And this time we'll have an advantage."

"How's that?"

"T. W. got the key to the place. We're gonna go in a couple of hours early, before the players arrive, and check everything out. The layout, the exit route . . . everything. Make sure there's no surprises."

"How'd T. W. get the key?"

"Paid off a man who works in that space during the day."

"Another inside thing. Don't that boy ever learn?"

"He's scared. He just wants us out of town. It'll be all right."

"We *will* be leavin' town after the job. Right, Frank?"

"I figure we'll pick up the car from Manny, slide on over to Detective Jonas's house in the middle of the night, do a lit-tle mayhem there. Then we'll leave town." Farrow looked closely at Otis. "You don't have a problem with that, do you, Roman?"

"I'm with you," said Otis carefully. "You know that."

"What I wanted to hear."

"There is something else I wanted to talk to you about, though."

"Go ahead."

"Gus. He don't belong with us, man. The man's plain love-sick over my sister. I brought him with me from Cali 'cause I wanted company on the ride. He wouldn't do us no good—"

"Get him out of here."

"Thanks. I was thinkin' I'd drive him up to D.C. today. Put him on one of those cross-country buses they got."

Farrow said, "Fine."

He turned and walked back up the stairs.

Otis breathed out slowly. He hadn't been certain that Frank would let Gus book. The thing was, he didn't like the sound of this card game heist and he sure didn't want to make a widow of his sister. Young boys playin' gangster. Shoot, any kind of drama could go down there. And then there was Frank on his revenge trip. Taking stupid chances, playing with that cop over the phone, following his kin. Now he wanted to go to the man's house after the job and fuck with his family and shit. None of it felt right.

Well, at least Gus would get out clean. As for Otis, he'd stay with Frank, despite the funny feeling in his gut about their future. Ice-cold as he was, Frank had always watched out for him, even saved his life one time in Lewisburg. Once you made the decision to partner up with a man, whoever he was, it just wasn't right to walk away.

Roman Otis went around to the front of the house. Kendricks and Lavonicus were by the stand of tall pine near the Mark V, parked alongside the 'Stang.

"You don't have to tell me that you played for the Spirits," said Kendricks, "'cause I know. But I'm tellin' *you* that you don't know what the fuck you talkin' about. They used to call Marvin Barnes 'B. B.' on account of that nigger had one tiny-ass head. Had a head on him small as one of those BBs you load into an air pistol, man."

"I'm telling *you*," said Lavonicus.

"I'm telling *you*," said Kendricks, mimicking the monotone and laughing.

Lavonicus's ears turned pink. "Listen. B. B. stood for 'Bad Boy.' Marvin 'Bad Boy' Barnes, get it? I don't care what your friends say because I was there."

"Aw, go ahead," said Kendricks.

"Hey, Gus," said Otis. "Come in the house with me for a minute, will you?"

Lavonicus walked across the yard with Otis.

"What's up, Roman?"

"You're goin' home. How's that sound to you?"

Lavonicus gave Otis his clown's smile as he ducked his head under the door frame and entered the house.

GUS LAVONICUS packed a bag quickly and said good-bye to Farrow, who was standing in the kitchen, drinking a glass of red wine and smoking a Kool.

"Be back in a few hours, Frank," said Otis.

Farrow said, "Right."

Lavonicus and Otis left the house. Kendricks was still out in the yard. He smiled at Lavonicus as he came down the steps. Lavonicus and Otis walked toward the Bill Blass Mark V.

"Where you off to, Stretch? Takin' a trip or somethin'?"

"I'm goin' home," said Lavonicus.

"I'm goin' ho-ome," said Kendricks.

"I'm just droppin' him off in D.C.," said Otis.

"Goin' back to see your woman?" Kendricks cackled. "The darker the berry, the sweeter the juice, right, Gus?"

"See you later, Booker," said Otis.

"Hey, maybe I'll ride with y'all."

"I don't think that's a good idea," said Otis, but Kendricks got ahead of them and stepped along toward the car.

"So, you like the sisters, huh, Gus? You prefer 'em to your own kind, that's what it is?"

Lavonicus said nothing.

"How's a big man like you do it with a little thing like my

cousin Cissy, you don't mind my askin'? I mean, what you do, bounce her all around in your lap and shit? Or do you hit it from behind, man, hog-slap that thing...?"

They were nearing the stand of pine by the car.

"What'samatter, Gus, you done lost your tongue?" Kendricks looked over his shoulder and up at Lavonicus and laughed. "You got some red-ass ears on you, too."

Lavonicus grabbed Kendricks by the neck and slammed his face into the trunk of a pine. Blood erupted, and pieces of bark flew from the tree. Lavonicus released Kendricks. Kendricks's arms pinwheeled, and he fell back and lay still.

Lavonicus's mouth dropped open. "Did I kill him, Roman?"

Otis looked down and studied his cousin's face. "Naw, man, he gonna be all right. C'mon."

They got into the Mark V and started down the long drive that cut through the woods to the two-lane. After a bend in the drive, Otis snapped his fingers and cut the engine.

"Hold up, Gus. I forgot my driver's license at the house. Gonna walk back and pick it up."

"We could just back up the car."

"Need to stretch my legs before that long trip we got. Be right back."

Otis got out of the car and walked toward the house. When he got to the yard, he looked in the front window. He did not see Frank. He went to Kendricks and grabbed him by the ankles and dragged him into the woods. Kendricks was slight and easy to move. His head bounced on rocks and a tree stump, and his body swept a path in the dirt. Otis took him down a grade to a gully of brush and dried leaves.

Otis stood over Kendricks. His forehead was caved in and cracked open. Otis could see a part of his cousin's brain through all the blood.

Otis recited a brief and meaningless prayer. He had known Booker's mother, and she would have liked him to say a few words over her son.

"So long, cuz," said Otis. "You done gone and talked yourself to death. Now these animals out here gonna do you like you been doin' them."

He went back to the car.

Out on 301, Lavonicus fiddled with the radio dial.

"Want you to take care of my sister now, Gus, you hear?"

"I will."

"Ain't gonna lose that temper of yours with her, are you?"

"I'd never raise a hand to Cissy, Roman. You know that."

Lavonicus lit on a song and saw Otis smile.

"You like this one?" said Lavonicus.

" 'Love Won't Let Me Wait,' " said Otis, "by Major Harris. That's a bad motherfucker right there."

NICK STEFANOS locked the front door of the Spot from the inside and went back around the bar. He rotated a few cold beers out of the cooler, stocked a couple of cases of warm in the bottom, and put the cold bottles back on top. He took a bottle of Bud that he had buried in the ice chest and popped the cap.

"Thought you weren't going to drink tonight," said Alicia Weisman, who sat at the bar.

"I said that?"

"After how you felt this morning, remember?"

"Just gonna have one to take the edge off," said Stefanos with a tired wink. He tilted the bottle to his lips.

Alicia watched him. "Want to see some music? Nashville Pussy's playing at the Cat."

"The only pussy I want to see is right here in front of me."

"You silver-tongued devil."

"I make the language of seduction an art." The phone on the wall rang. "Excuse me."

Stefanos picked up the receiver. It was Boyle on the other end of the line.

"How's it going?"

"We're sittin' here watching that show set in the emergency room. The doctors got personal problems and I give a fuck."

"Anything?"

"Not a word. Bill feels better me bein' here and all, but if we don't hear anything by the weekend, I'm gone. He misses his family, and my old lady's complaining I'm not around. What's up with you?"

"Not much," said Stefanos.

"All right. Keep in touch."

Stefanos went back and stood in front of Alicia.

"So," she said. "What do you think? Do you want to go out?"

"Let's just go back to my crib, okay? I might be getting a call there."

"You working on something?"

"I just need to be near my phone."

Stefanos lifted his beer bottle and Alicia took it gently from his hands. She set it down on the bar.

"You don't need that," she said. "Right?"

He did need it. He loved her but, God, he needed it. It was stronger than her or anyone else.

"Right," he said, pushing the bottle away with the back of his hand.

She leaned over the bar and kissed him on the lips.

THOMAS WILSON ordered a cognac at the bar of an African club up on Georgia and Missouri, near the old Ibex. Wilson couldn't pronounce the name of the place, but he liked it all right. Once you listened to their music for a while, it got way under your skin, too. Those Africans talked real loud, standing around the bar. Sometimes you couldn't tell if they were arguing with each other or just being friends. But they pretty much left him alone.

Way he looked now, cut in the face and with a fucked-up eye, wasn't no one gonna try to talk to him, anyway.

Yeah, Dimitri had really worked him over. Afterward, even with the pain, it was funny how different he'd felt. Not good, exactly, or happy. More like clean.

Now that he'd done it, he wished Bernie had been there as well. He looked forward to seeing Bernie again. He wanted to tell him like he'd told Dimitri, and take it from Bernie like he'd taken it from Dimitri, if that's how it had to be. He wanted to feel clean with Bernie, and with Stephanie, too.

First he'd have to do this thing with Dimitri. Step up and be a man for Dimitri and Bernie and Stephanie. And for Charles. He could do that. He felt that he could.

Someone bumped him from behind. Wilson looked over his shoulder, not hard or anything like that, but in a curious way. The man who had bumped him started shouting something at him in a foreign tongue. Wilson ignored him, but the man kept shouting. One of the man's friends came over, and he could hear them laughing behind his back.

Wilson fired down his cognac. He got off his stool and left money on the bar. He was careful not to look at anyone as he walked from the club.

DIMITRI KARRAS drove north on Connecticut Avenue, downshifting at the start of a long grade. The old BMW had lost its juice; Jap cars and domestics passed him on either side. The Beamer's paint job had faded and its engine was weak, but he'd decided to hang onto it. Cars meant nothing to him anymore. The only time he'd get stoked by a ride was when he'd see a restored Karmann Ghia on the street. It reminded him of his old Ghia, that decade, those times. Yeah, the seventies had been a glorious ride.

Karras turned off Connecticut and parked along the curb.

He'd had a quiet day at work. Nick Stefanos had asked him a couple of questions and he'd answered him shortly or not at all. He didn't like to be unkind to Stefanos, but Stefanos was out. He was sorry he had talked so freely with him the night before. He shouldn't have gotten so drunk.

He got out of his car and took the sidewalk back to Connecticut. He walked to an apartment house on the corner, stood at the glass doors, waved to the woman at the desk, and was buzzed in.

After work, he'd met Thomas Wilson at his place. Thomas had told him the plan. It was a very simple plan and as good as any plan, he supposed. If he kept his nerve, and Thomas kept his nerve, it could work.

He took the elevator up to the sixth floor and walked down a carpeted hall. He knocked on a door and he heard muffled steps.

Stephanie Maroulis opened the door.

"Dimitri."

"It is me. Why so surprised?"

"It's not Tuesday," she said.

"I know it," said Karras.

They looked into each other's eyes.

"You're breaking our arrangement," she said. "You do this and everything changes."

"I'm ready for it to change," he said.

Stephanie stepped aside. He walked through the open door.

THIRTY-SEVEN

THIS WILL be the last day of my life.

It was the first thought that came to Thomas Wilson when he woke on Friday morning. He turned onto his side in the bed and shut his eyes. His stomach flipped, and he thought he could be sick.

Please don't let me be a coward, God. Please.

The phone rang, and Wilson reached across the bed and picked it up.

"Thomas, it's Nick Stefanos."

"Nick."

"I was with Dimitri on Wednesday night. I know you told him everything. I know what you guys are planning to do."

Wilson had promised Dimitri that from here on in he'd keep his mouth shut. He did want Stefanos's help. He welcomed it. But he wouldn't betray Dimitri, not again.

"There is no plan," said Wilson.

"Bullshit," said Stefanos. "You guys have got something happening and you think you can pull it off yourselves. I told

Dimitri and I'm telling you: You try this thing and you will die. You understand me, Thomas?"

"I gotta run," said Wilson. "My uncle's waitin' on me, man, and I got to get myself into work."

"You still have my card?"

"I got it."

"You call me, Thomas. You give me a call, hear?"

"I hear you, Nick."

"Thomas—"

Wilson killed the connection and sat up on the edge of his bed. He stood and dressed for work.

FRIDAY'S LUNCH, like every Friday lunch, was the most hectic two hours of the week at the Spot. Dimitri Karras, Maria Juarez, and James Posten had little time for idle conversation as they struggled to stay ahead of the orders flowing into the kitchen. Nick Stefanos and Anna Wang were in the weeds in the dining and bar area from noon to two. Ramon and Darnell had both broken full body sweat by the time the rush was through.

At two o'clock, Maria put her Tito Puente tape into the box. James grabbed his spatula, and he and Maria began to dance. Karras walked over to Darnell, who was wiping down his slick arms with a rag, his backside against the sink.

"How'd that catfish go today?" said Darnell.

"Went good, buddy. Looked good, too. In fact, I called eighty-six on it to Anna even though we had one order left. That one's for me."

"You earned it, Dimitri. Nice work today."

"Thanks." Karras drew a card from his wallet. "Here you go, man. This is the number for that friend I been telling you about. Marcus wants to hook up with you, show you how easy it can be to do this thing, if that's what you want to do. Got all sorts of options he wants to lay out for you, Darnell. Says he'd like to meet with you next week."

"That's cool. But I thought you were gonna come with me."

"Yeah, sure," said Karras, smiling sadly at Darnell. "If you still want me to."

"Damn right I want you to, Dimitri."

"Then I'll be there," said Karras, and he shook Darnell's hand.

Karras hugged Maria and James and thanked them for the good job they had done that day. He untied his apron, dropped it in the laundry hamper by the door, and left without another word. He sat at a deuce and ate the catfish special, avoiding conversation with Stefanos, and when he was done he told Anna and Ramon to have a good weekend, said good-bye to Stefanos, and left the bar.

Stefanos caught up with him out on 8th.

"Dimitri!"

Karras turned. Stefanos walked to him in his shirtsleeves and met him by the alley. He put a hand on Karras's arm.

"Where you off to, man?" said Stefanos.

Karras shrugged. "Goin' home."

"Don't just walk out of here without telling me, Dimitri."

"Telling you what?"

"When and where. I've got a right to know."

Karras looked around the street. He waited for a man to pass them on the sidewalk. When the man was out of earshot, Karras found Stefanos's eyes.

"Listen," said Karras. "I appreciate everything you've done for me, Nick. You hooking me up with this job, it put me back in the world. I'm almost at that place where I can see myself having some kind of normal life. But there's one thing left to do, and you can't be a part of that. You're out of it, Nick. It's not your affair. So forget it."

"I won't forget it," said Stefanos. "When is it going down?"

Karras looked down at the cracked concrete. "Tomorrow night."

"Look at me, man."

"It's set for tomorrow night."

"Where?"

"I'm not sure yet."

"You'll call me?"

"Okay, Nick." Karras nodded. "If that's what you want. Yes."

Karras and Stefanos shook hands. Stefanos buttoned his shirt to the neck and watched Karras walk to his faded navy blue BMW, parked along the curb.

"Liar," said Stefanos, who had seen the hesitation in Karras's eyes.

It wasn't going down tomorrow night. It was going down tonight.

THOMAS WILSON worked the day quietly with his uncle Lindo. He listened to Lindo talk about a woman he'd met at church and he listened to Lindo's Frankie Lymon tapes on the cheap cassette player in the dash of his shitbox truck. He listened and tried to answer when Lindo asked him questions, but other than those short responses he didn't say much.

Time crawled that day, but when quitting time came it seemed to have come too quick.

Wilson had gotten out of his coveralls in the warehouse bathroom and he went to the particle-board desk where his uncle sat, wearing spectacles and organizing the day's tickets. His uncle had swept the warehouse like he did at the end of every week, whether it needed it or not, and specks of dust swirled in the air. A dying fluorescent tube flickered in the drop ceiling above the desk, its light flashing on the warehouse floor.

"I can fix that for you before I go," said Wilson, looking up at the light.

"Got a box of replacement lamps coming in next week," said Lindo. He looked closely at his nephew. "You seem troubled today, Thomas. Somethin' you want to talk to me about?"

"No, sir." Wilson buried his hands in the pockets of his slacks. "Everything's fine."

"Go on, then, son. Have a good weekend. Rest up, 'cause come Monday we have a busy week."

"Okay, Uncle L. Thank you for everything, hear?"

Lindo glanced up at Wilson. "Go on, boy. Don't be so serious all the time. Go out and have yourself a little fun."

As he drove home, Wilson's guilt deepened over using his uncle's warehouse that night. His uncle took pride in that place, even if it wasn't much more than a cheap desk and some cinder-block walls. Wilson stopped in a surplus store in Lanham and bought a half dozen blue plastic tarps.

He passed the turnoff for his house and kept north on Georgia Avenue, turned left onto Quackenbos, made another left, and parked the Intrepid in an alley alongside a church. He stepped onto the grounds of Fort Stevens Park.

He and Charles had played here as children. He walked into a dry moat, then climbed a steep hill and jumped down alongside one of two cannons that remained in the park. A tattered American flag hung at half-mast nearby and made rippling shadows at his feet. He could picture Charles as a child, running with an imaginary rifle cradled in his arms, diving and rolling down those hills. He could hear Charlie's gleeful laugh.

Charles, thought Wilson, *I won't let you down.*

But a block from his house his stomach betrayed him, and Wilson pulled over to the side of the road, where he opened his car door and vomited his lunch onto the street.

DIMITRI KARRAS got up off the bed at around six o'clock. He had been lying there on his back for a couple of hours. He was oddly calm.

He found Bernie Walters's Colt .45 and a box of shells in the bottom of his dresser, wrapped in an old pillowcase. He ejected the magazine into his palm. He loaded seven rounds into the magazine, testing the tension of the spring on the last round. He pushed the magazine into the butt of the gun and slipped the .45 into its leather holster. He dropped the rig onto the bed and phoned Thomas Wilson.

They discussed the specifics of the plan. When they were done, Karras said, "Pick me up at eight."

Wilson said, "Right."

NICK STEFANOS phoned Dan Boyle at William Jonas's house and got Jonas first. He exchanged a few words with Jonas and asked to speak to Boyle.

"You going to be there all night?" asked Stefanos.

"Yeah," said Boyle. "Why, what's up?"

"I might need to speak with you."

"Something going on?"

"Sit tight," said Stefanos. "I'll let you know."

THOMAS WILSON sat at a small desk in the foyer of his house on Underwood. He broke the cylinder of his five-shot .38 Special and thumbed shells into its chambers. He spun the cylinder and wrist-snapped it shut. The snub-nosed revolver with the narrow checkered butt and the worn-down bluing felt small in his hand. He held the gun under the desk lamp and noticed that his hand was shaking. He concentrated and tried to make his hand stop shaking, but he could not.

He laid the gun down on the desk and pulled the phone toward him. He dialed Dimitri Karras.

"I don't know if I can do this," he said when Karras answered the call.

"You can," said Karras. "See you at eight."

Wilson listened to the dial tone. He dialed Bernie Walters's home number. Bernie's recorded voice came through the speaker and then there was a long beeping sound.

"Hey, Bern... Thomas here. I guess you got a couple more days of that Jeremiah Johnson thing you're doin' down there in God's country. I'm just callin' to say hello again. Was thinkin' maybe I'd drive down tomorrow morning and surprise you. Take you up on that offer you been makin' to me these last couple of years. Be a good chance for the two of us to talk, buddy. 'Cause we *need* to talk, see? Anyway... listen, if I don't happen to make it down there, man... I just wanted to tell you... I wanted to say that you been a good friend. I'm sorry for everything, but I'm fixin' to try and make it right. You been a good friend, Bern. You, uh..."

Wilson found himself stumbling on his words. He said good-bye to Bernie and cut the line.

"YOU ALL packed?" said Farrow.

"Ready," said Otis.

"I got a meet point from Wilson. Says we'd get lost if we tried to find it directly. Behind a closed gas station near the industrial park."

Otis nodded. "Here you go, Frank. This is you."

He handed Farrow one of the two .45s he had copped on Sepulveda, back in L.A. Farrow hefted the gun and checked the action.

"Where's your cousin?"

"Booker? He didn't come home last night and I ain't seen him all day."

Otis didn't want Frank getting angry over Gus's little accident. Once they got on the road and headed back west, Frank would never know.

"Just as well," said Farrow. "Leave some money on the table for him. That'll be good enough."

Otis pulled his hair back off his shoulders and banded it. He holstered his .45 into his waist rig and put on a ventless, checked wool sport jacket over his clean white shirt. He looked in the living-room mirror and smiled, admiring his gold tooth, the cut of his jacket, his hair. The look.

He left money on the table — a fifty-dollar bill on top of ten ones, so Frank wouldn't get suspicious. Wasn't any point in leaving too much for a corpse lying in the woods, even if the dead man was your kin.

"You ready?" said Farrow as he walked back into the room.

"Yeah," said Otis. "Let's go."

DIMITRI KARRAS was waiting on the corner of 15th and U as Thomas Wilson pulled the Intrepid to the curb at eight o'clock. Karras settled in the passenger bucket and fastened his seat belt. "You finalized it with Farrow and Otis?" said Karras.

Wilson nodded. He drove east.

They crossed the city. They rode the Beltway for fifteen miles and exited at Route 4. Wilson slowed as they drove through old Upper Marlboro.

"Run through it again," said Karras.

"I'm meeting them behind a Texaco that's been out of business a couple of years. We'll be passin' it in a mile or so. After I get you settled, I'll leave my car there and come in with them." Wilson swallowed. "Afterwards, we'll clean the warehouse, drive them back, and dump 'em behind the station. Get back into my car and split."

"It's simple. I like that."

"Yeah, it's simple. 'Cept the killin' part."

"You shouldn't have any problem with that. Just try to remember what they did to your friend."

Wilson's face was grim and strained in the glow of the dash lights. "Only God should do what we're plannin' to do tonight."

"You're scared," said Karras, "that's all. Don't cloud this up with talk about God."

"Yes, I'm scared. I don't want to die."

"Neither do I."

"You don't have to worry," said Wilson. "I'm gonna go through with this. But don't you tell me not to think of God or whether this is right or wrong. If I live through this, I plan to beg forgiveness every day for the wrong I've done. Knowing it's wrong is what separates me from Farrow and Otis." Wilson looked across the bucket. "What separates you?"

"Nothing. I hope to be just like them. I hope to kill them the way they killed my son."

Wilson spoke quietly. "You've lost your faith, I know. But if you make it tonight, believe me, you're gonna need to have something to help make you right. I was you, I'd look to God. Promise me you'll try."

"All right, Thomas," said Karras, staring straight ahead. "I promise that I'll try."

The road darkened as they went past the town. Wilson

pointed to a boarded-up gas station with a pay phone out front. Then there was more dark road and signage for an industrial park. Wilson turned right, took the asphalt road that went along rows of squat red-brick warehouses starkly lit by spots.

Wilson drove straight to the back of the deserted park. He made a tight turn at a green Dumpster and went through the long narrow alley to the wide parking lot that ended at another set of identical red-brick structures. He parked in the middle of the strip, cut the engine, and removed the tarps from the trunk.

"What're those for?" asked Karras.

"Gonna try to keep my uncle's place clean. We'll roll 'em up in these when we're done."

Karras waited while Wilson opened the warehouse door and hit the lights. The two of them stepped inside. Fluorescents flooded the space with an artificial glow. A single ceiling lamp flashed over a cheap desk.

Karras looked at the desk. "Doesn't this place have a phone?"

"My uncle uses a cell."

Wilson and Karras unfolded the blue plastic tarps and spread them out on the concrete floor. The warehouse was cold, and their labored breath was visible in the light.

"I better get goin'," said Wilson when they were done. "They'll be there pretty soon."

"Go ahead."

"Remember: You're the man who made me the key. You're looking for a payoff before they do the job. Don't complicate it more than that."

"I won't."

"Shoot Farrow quick."

"All I want is to look in his eyes."

"Don't waste no time, Dimitri. Shoot him quick, hear? I'll take care of Otis."

"All right." Karras shook Wilson's hand. "You all set?"

Wilson nodded. He turned and walked out the door. Karras heard the Intrepid drive away.

It was suddenly quiet. Karras stood on the blue tarp in the center of the warehouse and listened to the low, steady buzz of the fluorescent lights.

"YOU GOT the directions?" said Farrow.

"Got 'em," said Otis.

They walked across the yard to their cars.

"Smells like something died out here," said Farrow.

"Well, we are in the woods."

"Be glad to get back to civilization."

"I heard *that*," said Otis, dropping behind the wheel of his Mark V.

Otis put the car in drive. He hit the CD player, rotated the disks to *Slow Jams, Volume 2*.

"Oh, zoooom," sang Otis, "I'd like to fly away...."

Otis turned onto the two-lane. Farrow followed in the Mach 1.

THOMAS WILSON sat in the idling Intrepid behind the Texaco station. He turned off the heater. He could smell his own sweat coming through his clothes.

He looked at his watch. Farrow and Otis would be way up 301 by now. Another half hour, they'd be pulling into the lot.

He'd been all chest out when he was with Dimitri, talking about how he was going to "go through with this," saying it strong, like there wasn't any kind of doubt in his mind. But now that he was alone, the fear had slithered back in. Truth was, if he was to pull a gun right now, it would slip right out of his hands.

And then there were Farrow and Otis. They had that way of theirs that made him feel small and weak, even back in Lewisburg, when they pretended to be his friend. Otis sometimes referred to him as his boy. Errand boy was more like it. He never was one of them, and they had always let him know it, too.

The .38 dug into the small of his back. He shifted in the bucket.

He and Karras needed help. There wasn't any sense in denying it anymore. Maybe Karras was strong and crazy enough to pull it off on his end. But Wilson knew he couldn't do it. He'd be punked out like he'd always been punked out. He'd get the both of them killed.

Wilson was out of the car and walking around the side of the gas station. He was walking to the pay phone, telling himself that this was not another betrayal, that he wasn't being a coward, that he was trying to help his friend. He was talking to himself, sweating and shivering in the cold, when he dropped the coins and dialed, and he was still muttering something when the phone rang on the other end and the line went live.

"Hello."

"It's Thomas Wilson."

"Thomas—"

"Ain't got no time to bullshit, Nick. I need your help."

JONAS HANDED the phone to Dan Boyle. "It's Stefanos again. For you."

Boyle put the phone to his ear and listened intently. Jonas watched his face as Boyle nodded and spoke excitedly.

Boyle said, "See you then," and handed Jonas a dead phone.

"What's up?" said Jonas.

"I'm goin' out."

Boyle went back to the guest bedroom, grabbed a pair of gloves from his overnight bag and shoved them in the pockets of his khakis. He unzipped a canvas gym bag, drew his Python, and checked the load. He holstered the Python, reached into the bag, and withdrew his throw-down, a .380 double-action Beretta with a thirteen-shot magazine. He examined the magazine, slapped it back into the butt, and dropped the gun in the side pocket of his Harris tweed. He looked over his shoulder, then went back into the gym bag and extracted a Baggie holding confiscated snow-seals of powdered cocaine. He slipped the Baggie into the other pocket of his jacket and walked back out to the living room with the holstered Python in his hand.

"You gonna tell me what's goin' on?" said Jonas.

"When I get back. You got your piece?"

"It's in the drawer over there."

"Get it," said Boyle, lifting his wrinkled raincoat off a chair. "Until you hear from me, you keep it in your lap."

THE TWO-TONE Continental and the red Mach 1 pulled into the back lot of the Texaco station. The Mustang skidded on gravel as it came to a stop. Otis killed the engine on the Mark V, stepped out, and walked to the Intrepid. Wilson opened his door.

"T. W.," said Otis.

"Roman." His mouth spasmed as he tried to smile.

"Come on, man. We'll go in Farrow's short."

Farrow rolled his window down as they neared the car. "These brakes are shot again," said Farrow. "If you just push the pedal in, you get nothing. You got to pump the hell out of these things to bring it to a stop."

"Booker put the fluid in," said Otis. "I seen him do it."

"I'm tellin' you, Roman, they're fucked."

"Let me drive over to the joint, man, so I can see my own self."

"Suit yourself."

Farrow did not greet Wilson as he stepped out of the car. Wilson climbed into the backseat, and Farrow went around to the passenger side. Otis got under the wheel and put the car in gear.

"Where to, T. W.?"

"Pull out," said Wilson, "and make a right onto the road."

Otis tested the brakes both ways as they hit the asphalt. He pumped the pedal and managed to bring the Mustang to a stop.

"You're right, Frank. These brakes *are* fucked. Have to use the Mark when we do the job for real."

Farrow looked over his shoulder to the backseat. "What's wrong with your face, T. W.? How'd you get marked?"

"Got stole in the face in a bar," said Wilson.

"Let yourself get stole, huh?" said Otis. "Imagine that. You look a little tight, too."

"Got a minor problem, is all it is."

"What's that?"

"The inside man, the one who got me the key? He thought about it and now he wants an extra grand."

"He's already been paid," said Farrow.

"I told him as much," said Wilson, noticing a catch in his voice, wondering if they noticed it, too.

"And what happened?"

"Couldn't talk him out of it," said Wilson.

"I guess I need to talk to him myself," said Farrow.

"You're going to," said Wilson as they neared the industrial park sign. "He's waitin' on us at the warehouse right now."

THIRTY-EIGHT

C OME ON," said Boyle.

Nick Stefanos used his foot to tap on the high beams. The car ahead of them cleared out of the Beltway's left lane.

"That's right, buddy," said Stefanos. "Get out of the way."

"Can't you make this piece of shit move?"

Stefanos floored the accelerator. Boyle grabbed the armrest as the Coronet surged forward from a flood of gas. Stefanos swerved into the middle lane, passed an import on the right, got back into the left, and kept the pedal nailed to the floor.

"How long?" said Boyle.

"Fifteen minutes, I'd say."

Boyle reached into his pocket and brought out the .380. "Take this."

"I'm done with that," said Stefanos. "I told you once before."

Boyle dropped the Berreta back in his pocket. He shook a smoke out of his hardpack for himself and rustled the deck in the direction of Stefanos.

Stefanos put a cigarette between his lips and pushed in the lighter on the dash.

"Describe all the players to me," said Boyle. "I don't want to shoot the wrong guy."

The lighter popped out of the dash. Stefanos lit his smoke and handed the lighter to Boyle.

"**LOOKS LIKE** you done fucked up again, T. W.," said Otis. "You should've been more firm with that key man. Ain't you learned yet about these inside jobs?"

Otis turned into the industrial park and drove along the red-brick buildings.

"Man's taking a risk," said Thomas Wilson. "He just wants a little extra."

"I'll just have to explain it to him," said Farrow. "If he pushes it, he's gonna get hurt."

"Hope he takes it better than that other inside man T. W. had," said Otis.

"The pizza chef?" said Farrow.

Otis and Farrow exchanged a glance. Wilson saw the eye contact and thought he saw a brief smile crease Otis's face. They were fuckin' with him, he knew. Trying to keep him weak. Wilson's blood jumped at Otis's smile. But the feeling he had was not familiar. It was not a feeling of fear.

"You talkin' about Charles?" said Wilson.

"Whatever his name was," said Otis. "He didn't take it in a very masculine way when he saw what we had to do. The bartender, that light-steppin' waiter . . . shoot, man, you can believe that those two were afraid to die. But even that sissy waiter took it like a man compared to your pizza chef. You remember the way he begged us, Frank?"

Farrow nodded. "He cried like a girl."

"Screamed like one, too," said Otis.

Wilson felt tears come to his eyes.

Lord, give me strength to kill these men.

"Charles was a man," said Wilson, surprised at the force in his own voice.

Otis's eyes smiled in the rearview. "Listen to T. W., Frank. Gettin' all ma-cho on us now."

Wilson swallowed hard. "Make a left into that alley, where that Dumpster is."

Otis made the turn and drove slowly between the buildings. The brick walls were very close to the sides of the car.

"Damn, this is a tight squeeze," said Otis.

"Thought you liked tight things," said Farrow.

"You *know* I do," said Otis, smiling in the mirror, giving his gold tooth a lick.

The Mustang came out of the alley and then there was the wide-open lot and the strip of warehouses fronting the creek.

"Park in the middle," said Wilson, "by that door right there."

Otis pumped the brakes. The Mach 1 came to a stop.

DIMITRI KARRAS heard the rumble of a muscle car as it cleared the alley. He drew his .45, pulled back on the receiver, and jacked a round into the chamber. He slipped the automatic barrel-down into the holster, behind the belt line of his jeans and against the small of his back.

He reached behind him, drew the .45, and replaced it once again.

Karras heard car doors slam and voices as the men approached.

He thought of Bernie. He tried to recall Bernie's advice from that day in the woods. He couldn't remember what Bernie had said.

He was cold. He hadn't worn a coat so that he would not

fumble the gun. His teeth were chattering, and his hands had grown numb. He tried to raise spit and he could not.

He looked around the empty warehouse and backed up so that he was near the cheap desk. He heard the key turn in the lock and he backed up another step. The door swung open, and Karras stood still.

FARROW, OTIS, and Wilson stepped out of the Mustang. Wilson watched Otis twirl the car keys on his finger and drop them in the pocket of his slacks. Otis examined his ID bracelet in the light of the spot lamps hung on the exterior of the warehouse walls.

"What's the key man's name?" said Farrow.

"Dimitri," said Wilson. It was meaningless to lie about it now.

Farrow drew his .45 from his belt line and chambered a round. He looked at Otis and Otis did the same. They holstered their guns and walked toward the warehouse door.

Wilson looked over his shoulder to the alley before putting the key to the lock. He guessed it wasn't any use in stalling. Stefanos wasn't going to make it. Wilson had waited too long to call for his help. Just another fuckup in a lifetime full of them.

"Need help with that, T. W.?" said Otis.

Roman, always with that *thing* to his voice. Wilson turned the key roughly and opened the door. He went in first. Farrow and Otis followed.

FRANK FARROW saw a gray-haired man without a coat, standing by a desk in the back of the warehouse. A defective fluorescent light set above the desk flashed continuously across the man's face. The warehouse was bathed in fluorescence, and the insect sound of the lights filled the room.

Farrow, Otis, and Wilson moved forward. They walked onto a series of blue plastic tarps that had been spread out on the concrete floor. Farrow looked into the man's strange eyes as they approached him. There was something familiar about the eyes.

This is not a card game that's happening here tonight, thought Farrow. *This is something else.*

Wilson fanned off to the left of Otis. A looked passed between Farrow and Otis and they stopped walking.

"Who are you?" said Farrow to the gray-haired man.

"Dimitri Karras."

Farrow shifted his weight. "That supposed to mean something to me?"

"Jimmy Karras was my son."

Farrow spread his hands. "So?"

As Farrow's coat opened, Karras saw the butt of Farrow's gun holstered at his waistline.

No one spoke. Their breath was heavy and visible in the buzzing light.

"What is this?" said Otis, looking from Karras to Wilson, who stood facing him now on his left. "Y'all lookin' to take us off?"

"It's not a robbery, Roman." Farrow looked down at the tarp beneath his feet. "It's a slaughter."

"That's right," said Karras. "Like you slaughtered those people in the pizza parlor. Like you slaughtered my son."

Farrow nodded slowly. "That boy in the road. That's what this is about."

Karras drew the .45 from behind his back. Wilson drew the .38.

Farrow and Otis did not move their hands. Otis turned his head and saw the revolver in Wilson's hand. He'd shoot the white man with the blank eyes first. He knew that Wilson would never have the courage to use the gun.

Karras raised his gun and pointed it at Farrow's face. Bernie's voice entered his head.

Always aim for the body.

Karras lowered the barrel of the gun.

"Kill him, Dimitri," said Wilson.

Karras watched Farrow move a step to the right.

Lead that body a little if it's moving.

"Your son," said Farrow very quietly. "That was an accident."

"It's all an accident," said Karras.

"Kill him!" screamed Wilson.

Otis looked over at Wilson and laughed. The revolver was shaking wildly in Wilson's hand.

Farrow looked into Karras's eyes, the light winking on his face. Now he knew what had seemed familiar to him. It was as if Farrow were looking at his own eyes in the mirror. There was nothing in the man's eyes, nothing at all.

Karras stared back.

And keep firing your weapon until you've accomplished what you set out to do.

"I guess they got us, Roman," said Farrow.

"Yeah," said Otis. "Guess we oughtta just go ahead and surrender."

Otis raised his arms over his head. He rotated his right hand at the wrist as if he was waving good-bye. The ID bracelet dropped beneath the cuff of his shirt.

His right hand flashed down to his waist.

Wilson squeezed the trigger of the .38.

The slug blew through Otis's armpit and punched out of his back. The force of it spun him around. He drew his .45 and fired. Wilson felt his cheekbone rip away. He fell back screaming, still firing his weapon, as he took a second bullet in the groin.

Karras fired his gun. The .45 jumped in his hand and he fired again and the weapon bucked. He saw the blur that was Farrow through the ejecting shells and the gunsmoke that had exploded into the room.

Wilson was falling. He fired and saw blood erupt from Otis's neck as he drifted back. Wilson's last shot blew lights from the ceiling as he hit the concrete.

Karras saw flame spit from Farrow's gun. The roar of the gun was deafening, and Karras kept firing and felt something graze his scalp and it burned. The Colt's receiver slid open as the final shot was expended, and Karras tumbled over the desk as rounds blew through particleboard and bits of pressed wood bit sharply at his face.

He dropped his gun and covered up. A bell sound vibrated in his ears. Through the sound, he heard the door open at the front of the warehouse.

Karras stood and waved smoke from his face. The smell of cordite was heavy in the room. His feet crunched copper casings as he went to Thomas Wilson. He kicked the gun from Otis's hand and kept on walking for Wilson.

He knelt over Wilson. The left side of Wilson's face was ruined, a stew of blood and bone. There was blood in his lap and on his thighs and blood had pooled beneath him.

"I'm going to get help," said Karras. "You're going to live, Thomas, you hear me?"

Wilson blinked his eyes and squeezed Karras's hand.

"You came in a car," said Karras. His eyes felt wild and jittery, and he squinted to make them small. He didn't want Thomas to be afraid.

Wilson's eyes shifted in the direction of Otis.

"I'll be back," said Karras. "You're gonna be okay. You did good, Thomas, hear?" His words sounded hollow coming from his mouth.

Karras went to Otis. His white shirt was soaked red and it flapped beneath the left arm. He had taken another bullet in the throat. He was dying. A wheezing noise came from his open mouth.

Karras searched Otis's pockets and found the keys. Karras stood and sprinted for the warehouse door.

FRANK FARROW pulled his fingers away from his stomach, where he had been pressing them at the point of pain. There was a black hole ripped in his shirt, and blood leaked freely from the hole.

Farrow started for the Mustang and realized Roman had the keys. He stumbled toward the alley. He'd get to the main road, hijack a car up there.

He made it to the alley. He heard his name called and turned. The gray-haired man had come from the warehouse. He had yelled his name and now he was walking toward the Mach 1.

Farrow ran into the alley as the Mustang's ignition cut the night.

KARRAS FASTENED his seat belt. He put the transmission in reverse to back out of the spot. The car went back and he pushed down on the brake pedal, but the car did not stop, and he slammed the trans into drive to make it stop. The Mustang caught rubber as he blew across the lot and streered it into the alley.

Farrow was running down the alley, bent forward and holding his stomach, up ahead. There was no protection in the alley, and he was running to get through to the other side.

Karras accelerated. He reached Farrow quickly, and Farrow

turned and leaped up onto the hood of the car. Farrow was on the hood and he began to slide down the hood, and Karras could see that he was confused and afraid. Farrow grabbed the inlay of the scoop as he slipped down the hood of the car and Karras gave the Mustang gas. He pinned the accelerator and the car lifted as the speedometer climbed and Farrow's face through the windshield was all fear. His legs slipped down over the grille and his hands were white, gripping the scoop on the hood.

Past Farrow, Karras saw the Dumpster at the end of the alley, and he pressed down on the brake so he could swing wide of it, but the car did not slow and now they were heading straight for the Dumpster as the alley walls bled off at their sides.

Karras screamed over the screams of Farrow and they hit the Dumpster doing fifty. Karras saw a one-legged torso spin away from his field of vision and everything compressed at once. He met a wash of blood at the windshield and then he was showered in glass and black sleep.

STEFANOS AND Boyle heard the sonic collision of metal on metal as they entered the industrial park. Stefanos drove quickly, straight into the park, as Wilson had directed. They found the red Mustang, its front end totaled and smoking against the green Dumpster. They saw the body of Farrow, facedown and bled out on the asphalt nearby. One of Farrow's legs had been amputated at the thigh.

Stefanos skidded to a stop. He and Boyle got out of the Dodge. Stefanos jogged to the Mustang and went around to the driver's side. He opened the door and cradled Karras in his arms. Karras's forehead was cut and bleeding, and it had darkened and begun to swell. Stefanos brushed glass off his face.

"He dead?" said Boyle.

"He's breathing," said Stefanos.

"Gimme a minute to clean up."

"Hurry up, man. We've got to get him to a hospital."

The Mustang blocked the alley. Boyle stepped around it.

"Check on Wilson," yelled Stefanos.

Boyle walked down the alley. As he walked, he fitted his gloves onto his hands.

THOMAS WILSON had a dream.

He and Charles were running and playing in Fort Stevens Park. Charles was seven or eight years old, and when Thomas looked down at his own skinny forearms and legs, he realized that he was the same age.

They were playing army, and it was a bright spring day. The park's flag was popping in the breeze, and Charles was laughing and making shooting sounds with the invisible rifle cradled in his arms.

A white boy and a white man were silhouetted against the sun and standing on the top of the steep hill that semicircled the park. The man waved at Thomas Wilson.

"Come on, Charlie," said Wilson. "Let's go talk to that man!"

"All right!"

Wilson and Charles scurried up the hill to see what was on the man's mind. When they got there, Wilson looked up at the man, who now blocked the sun. The man's hand was on his boy's shoulder, and the boy's head was resting comfortably against his father's hip.

"What's up, mister?" said Thomas Wilson.

"Been waiting on you to get here, partner," said the man, pushing his Orioles cap back on his head.

Thomas Wilson looked around the park with wonder. "Sure is a beautiful day."

Bernie Walters smiled.

BOYLE STOOD over the corpse of Thomas Wilson. He opened the Baggie and unfolded the snow-seals of a couple of grams of cocaine and sprinkled powder on Wilson's face and chest. He dropped the snow-seals onto Wilson and left the .38 in Wilson's hand.

The one Stefanos had described as Otis was still alive. Bastard was making crazy sounds. Gasping for breath but also trying to sing or something. That's what it sounded like to Boyle, anyway. Boyle pulled the .380 from his jacket pocket and walked across the warehouse floor.

Roman Otis had always wondered how he would face death. He was dying now, there wasn't any doubt about that. He decided to think of good things, let it happen while he was off somewhere else. Die peaceful the way he'd always hoped he would.

He couldn't breathe too good. And it was hard to take his mind off the pain.

He'd had that Commodores song on his mind all day, couldn't get it out of his head. He tried to sing a little bit of that. He closed his eyes and imagined palm trees, riding along Little Santa Monica in his Bill Blass Continental, that girl he'd left behind at El Rancho, his favorite bar, down on Sunset.

He opened his eyes. A big white man stood over him, easing a round into an automatic he held in a gloved hand. Looked like some kind of cop.

Otis raised some spit. He tried to spit at the cop, but he was weak and, lying on his back like he was, the spit shot straight up about a foot or so and came right back down on his face.

With the luck he'd had today, would be just like him to go and spit in his own face. Otis laughed. It made a gurgling kind of sound that didn't sound much like a laugh, but that's what it was, just the same.

The cop took a step back, aimed the gun, and raised his palm to avoid the blow-back.

Watch yourself, Hoss, thought Otis. *Don't want to get any on that fucked-up raincoat you wearin'.*

STEFANOS HEARD a shot. Ten minutes later Boyle returned to the Dodge. He got into the passenger seat and looked over his shoulder. Karras was facing the seat, sprawled across the back bench on his side.

"Wilson?" said Stefanos.

"Wilson didn't make it," said Boyle, and Stefanos shut his eyes. "You clean off that Mustang?"

"I wiped it the best I could. What about you?"

"They get to this crime scene, they're gonna be nothin' but confused."

"Dimitri needs to get that forehead stitched."

"We'll take him into D.C.," said Boyle. "And pull over at a pay phone when we get on the road. I gotta phone Bill Jonas."

"What for?"

"He needs to call his family," said Boyle as Stefanos ignitioned the Dodge. "Tell 'em it's okay to come back home."

WASHINGTON, D.C.
JULY 1998

THIRTY-NINE

O N A warm, sunny morning, Dan Boyle and William Jonas sat in the living room of Jonas's house on Hamlin Street, drinking coffee and reading the Sunday edition of the *Washington Post*. In the past few months it had become a ritual for Boyle to stop by for some conversation on his way back from mass. Jonas's sons didn't care much for Detective Boyle, but the boys kept their displeasure to themselves. It was obvious that some kind of bond had developed between their father and the white cop.

Boyle read the "Crime and Justice" column of the Metro section aloud to Jonas.

" 'A Northeast man was found with multiple stab wounds in the stairwell of a housing unit in Marshall Heights. Police are withholding the name of the victim until relatives can be notified. A police spokesman says there are no suspects at this time.' "

"Guy loses his life and he gets three sentences of copy," said Jonas. "If that was a white man in Potomac got stabbed, it'd be front-page news. The *Post* might as well call that section the

'Violent Negro Death Roundup.' For all the value that newspaper places on African American life—"

"Yeah," said Boyle, scratching his head, wondering what Bill was so hacked off about. "I know what you mean."

"Keep reading."

Boyle continued. "Randy Weston, of Northwest, was fatally wounded last night in what several witnesses have described as a brazen homicide outside a Southeast nightclub. Police are holding Sean Forjay, also of Northwest, in connection with the shooting." Boyle looked up and smiled. "Sean. Think he's Irish?"

Jonas didn't answer.

Boyle handed the A section to Jonas and pointed a thick finger at a story below the fold on the front page. "You read this?"

Jonas looked at the story. The headline read, "After Three Years, Pizza Parlor Murders Remain Unsolved."

"I read it," said Jonas.

"The surviving family members of the victims declined to comment for the article."

"They talked about Wilson in there, how he was part of that support group."

"I know it," said Boyle. "Mentioned his bizarre death in a drug-related shoot-out."

"Shame he has to be remembered like that to his uncle Lindo, the one that had that hauling business."

"There wasn't any time to make it look any other way. Wilson died knowing he'd done good, I expect. But once you're dead, you're dead. I don't think he's listening to what anyone's saying about him now."

"You believe that?"

"Yeah."

"But you went to church this morning."

Boyle finished his coffee and stood. "Call me superstitious."

He shook Jonas's hand and told him he'd see him next week. He left the house.

William Jonas wheeled himself over to the bay window. Christopher was out front, mowing the lawn. Jonas watched Boyle greet his son with his idea of a black man's handshake. Then Boyle mimed a jump shot and punched Christopher on the shoulder. As Boyle walked toward his car, Christopher looked up at the window, where he knew his father would be, and rolled his eyes.

"Crazy bastard," said Jonas.

Someday, maybe, he'd tell his family that Boyle had saved their lives.

NICK STEFANOS pushed his plate to the side and reached into his pocket for a cigarette.

"More coffee, Nick?" said Darnell.

"Thanks."

Darnell poured from a pot. "How was your breakfast?"

"Beautiful. You know I like a good half-smoke with my eggs. And those grits had just the right texture."

"It's not gonna make you forget the Florida Avenue Grill."

"Not yet. But you're getting there, buddy."

Stefanos lit his smoke. Darnell looked around the small lunch counter he had purchased from a Korean up on Georgia Avenue, near the District line.

"Anyway," said Darnell, "it's mine."

"Dimitri and Marcus did you right, finding this place."

"Yeah, and that Clarence Tate ran some real accurate numbers. They got a nice business, those three. Doin' a good thing, too." Darnell leaned on the Formica counter. "With Dimitri and me gone, and you leavin' the Spot last month, wonder how it's gonna work out down there on Eighth."

"Phil will find some replacements."

"You miss it?"

"Elaine Clay keeps me busy with work. The Spot wasn't a good place for a guy like me, Darnell."

"I heard *that*. How you doin' with it, anyway?"

"So far so good."

"You *look* good, man."

"I'm trying." Stefanos got off his stool and reached for his wallet. He left three on five and slipped into his sport jacket.

"Where you off to, all dressed like that?"

"Church," said Stefanos. "Gonna say a prayer for a kid named Randy Weston."

"Say hey to Alicia when you see her," said Darnell.

"Gonna see her tonight," said Stefanos. "I'll tell her you said hello."

DIMITRI KARRAS and Stephanie Maroulis walked across the manicured grounds of the Gate of Heaven cemetery in Aspen Hill to the Walters family headstones. Stephanie said a silent prayer over the graves of Bernie, Lynne, and Vance Walters. They visited Karras's mother, Eleni, and brushed debris off the nearby marker for Jimmy's grave. Then they stopped at the grave of Steve Maroulis, where Stephanie's adjoining plot had been purchased three years earlier. Stephanie did her cross, and they walked to Karras's BMW, parked in the shade. Karras drove back into D.C.

Thomas Wilson was buried alongside Charles Greene at Fort Lincoln cemetery in Northeast. Stephanie held Karras's hand as he stared down at Wilson's grave.

"You okay?" she said.

Karras touched the knot of his tie. "Yes, I'm fine."

DIMITRI KARRAS lit a candle and did his *stavro* in the narthex of St. Sophia's Greek Orthodox Cathedral. Then he and Stephanie went upstairs to the balcony and listened to the remainder of the service. They enjoyed the choir and took in the atmosphere of the church. Stephanie's eyes were closed as she prayed for Dimitri and those who were gone.

Karras looked down to the nave, where the sons, grandsons, and great-grandsons of Greek immigrants and their families stood side by side in the pews. He noticed the graying hair of a man who stood alone, wearing a lightweight fifties sport jacket.

Karras smiled and whispered, "Nick."

THEY WAITED on the stone steps of the cathedral as parishioners streamed from the front doors. Bells chimed, and a warm breeze came off Massachusetts Avenue. Men were lighting cigarettes, greeting each other with firm handshakes, and children were chasing one another and laughing. Karras saw Nick Stefanos emerge from the church.

"*Yasou*, Niko!" said Karras.

"Dimitri!" Stefanos came to meet them. He kissed Stephanie on the cheek and squeezed her arm. He looked at Karras and smiled. "What're you doing here, man?"

"I should be asking you the same thing."

"Like I told you before: I'm just trying to figure it all out." Stefanos squinted up at the bright, cloudless sky. "Nice day. You guys feel like taking a ride?"

"Where to?" said Karras.

"I was thinking of Hanes Point."

"You go ahead, Dimitri," said Stephanie. "I've got things to do this afternoon."

Karras handed her his car keys and gave her a kiss. "See you later. Thanks."

They watched her descend the stone steps and turn the corner toward Garfield Street.

"You're a lucky man," said Stefanos.

"I know it."

"Come on. My ride's parked out back."

WE'RE GETTING married," said Karras as they drove along the Potomac, the wind rushing through the open windows of the Dodge.

"Congratulations, man."

"I love her, Nick."

"As you should."

Karras looked out the window. "She wants to have a baby. I want the same thing. This baby's not meant to replace Jimmy. No one will ever replace him in my heart. But I was a good father, Nick, and I didn't get to finish. And I feel like, if Stephanie and I have a child, then our meeting the way we did will have meant something. That everything that happened to everyone else will have meant something, too. Does that make sense?"

"Yes, Dimitri. It makes sense."

Stefanos parked the Dodge in the first set of spaces at Hanes Point. He and Karras got out of the car and walked across the grass to the concrete path that ringed the outer edge of the park. They leaned on the rail and looked out across the Washington Channel, the sun winking off its waters.

Karras loosened his tie at the neck. "It's beautiful, man."

"Yes, it is." Stefanos looked over at his friend. "So what were you doing in church?"

"I made a promise to a friend that I'd give it a try."

"And?"

"I kept the promise." Karras ran his thumb along the thin scar that creased his forehead, thinking of his son. He smiled at the memory, looking into the channel's brown waters.

"You still think you lied to Jimmy about God?" asked Stefanos.

"I don't know anymore. There are days when I'm certain that there is no God. And then I'll have a day, every now and again, when I think it might be possible. That makes me like most men, I guess. Which is where I've been trying to get back to all along." Karras frowned. "The question is, after what I did in the warehouse — after what you've done yourself — does God even care to save men like us?"

"I don't know," said Stefanos. "We'll find out soon enough, I guess."

Stefanos smoked a cigarette while the two of them looked across the channel.

"They used to call this 'the speedway,'" said Stefanos. "You remember that?"

"I know everything about this place," said Karras, pointing to the middle of the channel. "My mother told me that my father learned to swim out there on a day just like this, when he was a kid back in the Depression."

"And my grandfather would bring me fishing down here when I was a little boy."

"Lotta history."

"Yes."

Karras nodded to the restaurants behind the marina on the opposite shore. "Feel like grabbing a beer or something?"

"I don't think so," said Stefanos. "How about we just take a walk instead."

Stefanos pushed away from the railing and headed down the concrete path, Karras at his side. They walked unhurriedly along the speedway, as those who had come before them had done so many times.

ACKNOWLEDGMENTS

I'd like to express my appreciation to the staffs of the District of Columbia and Montgomery County library systems, who provided assistance in the research for this novel. Thanks to Sloan Harris and Alicia Gordon for their friendship and guidance; my longtime editor, Michael Pietsch, for his friendship, instincts, and smarts; and everyone down the line at Little, Brown for their general kindness. My wife, Emily, and my children, Nick, Pete, and Rosa, continue to be unselfish in sharing me with my work, and for that, and for everything else, I can only say, I love you very much. Finally, a special nod to Joe Aronstamn, who lives it every day.

Reading Group Guide

SHAME
THE
DEVIL

A Novel by

GEORGE
PELECANOS

George Pelecanos responds to questions from his readers

I love the title Shame the Devil. *How did you come up with that?*

There are two things. A lot of the book takes place in the kitchen of a bar. And it's based on a kitchen that I actually worked in, in Washington, D.C. There was a woman that worked there with me who, when you said something that she really agreed with, would say, "Tell the truth and shame the devil." And the other thing is, it's the title of a song by Robin Trower that I really liked.

Many would call Shame the Devil *a "hard-boiled crime novel." What would you call it?*

If you have to put a tag on it, I would say that it is a hard-boiled crime novel. It differs from some of my earlier books, which tend to end in an apocalypse, in that this book begins with an apocalypse and examines the aftereffects of violence on the families of the victims. And it tries to find answers with regard to attaining some degree of spirituality in a violent world.

I'm curious about what inspired you to bring back Nick Stefanos as a major character in Shame the Devil, *the last of the D.C. quartet.* King Suckerman *and* The Sweet Forever *were mostly about Dimitri and Marcus, but Marcus became a minor character in* Devil. *Was this planned or did it come about accidentally?*

Nick Stefanos sort of showed up as a toddler at the end of *The Big Blowdown*, and that's when it became clear to me that he would haunt the subsequent books. He is, after all, my alter ego, and he's an observer, just like me. I thought it would also add some resonance for the reader to get a look at his innocence, having knowledge of his fate even as he himself does not. Stefanos comes back, by the way, in my book *Soul Circus*.

Why did you decide to bring all of the characters together in this novel?

I wanted some sort of resolution for these people. And though it might not be a popular choice with some of my hard-core readers, I wanted to pick Nick Stefanos up out of that gutter he was lying in at the end of his books. Even with a character like Marcus Clay, I wanted the reader to see that good things can happen to strong people who keep on the path.

Nick has evolved through several jobs to now be the proud owner of a P.I. license. Is this it, or can we expect more twists and turns in his future?

I think I'm going to let Nick rest for a while. He's in a pretty good place. It's good for him that I don't put my hands on him for a little while anyway.

What are the key elements that make a mystery/crime novel "click"? What do they have to have, and what should they not be missing?

For me it always goes to characters. I'm not interested in the puzzle aspect of mysteries so much as I am the characters themselves and what makes them do the things they do. I don't think you necessarily have to like the characters or the protagonist of a book, but I do think you have to care about them. And so to me, that's the most important element.

I hear you are a big movie fan. What are a few of your favorites?

I think as a child in the '60s (I was just a little kid) there were three films that influenced what I do as a writer now. Those movies were *The Magnificent Seven, The Dirty Dozen*, and *The Wild Bunch*. And, in retrospect, it's because they're about a sort of honor and inglorious redemption. Then in the '70s I got into blaxploitation, kung fu, anything you could see at a drive-in. Although these films were cheaply made and not particularly well-written, there was a purity and honesty in their desire to tell a straight story and to make working-class audiences of all races happy by presenting a protagonist who won, and did so with an attitude. Right now I've been enjoying movies from the studio system once again. Pictures like *Three Kings, The Insider, The Straight Story*, and *The Limey* were all studio films that I thought were great.

How does writing a screenplay differ from writing a novel?

The obvious answer is that in a screenplay it's dialogue and action. You have to throw out the internal monologues. So, naturally, writing a screenplay is less creative than writing a novel. The other difference is that it's a totally different business than the book publishing business. By that I mean you have a whole lot more bosses, and there's lots more money involved. So as a writer working in the movie business, you have to be prepared for that. You have to listen to more people and understand going into it that it's not going to be an easy experience. I write screenplays for two reasons. I love movies and it was a dream of mine to write movies when I was a kid. And the other reason is—and this is very important—I want to send my kids to college. So screenplays are for my family; the novels are for me.

You've been executive producer on two films. What exactly does an executive producer do?

In the independent world, which is the world that I worked in, you do a little bit of everything. You raise the money. You get involved in the casting. You hire the talent. You put out any fires that occur on the set. You sell the film to distributors, and then you chase the money all over the world. So when you executive produce an independent film, you're talking about a two-year process, at least.

Questions and topics for discussion

1. Nick Stefanos struggled to stay on the straight and narrow during the course of *A Firing Offense*, *Nick's Trip*, and *Down by the River Where the Dead Men Go*. Do you think that by the end of *Shame the Devil* he is a changed man, or is he the same Nick as in the previous books?

2. *Shame the Devil* overlaps Pelecanos's Nick Stefanos novels and his Pete Karras novels, and offers resolution to events from both series. Did you feel like it focused more on one bloodline than the other, or did it spread its focus evenly between the two?

3. Family is an important bond in *Shame the Devil*, one that has a different meaning for each of the characters. How do you think the Farrow brothers' idea of family differs from Nick's? Or Nick's from Dimitri's? How does the bond of family bring Bill Jonas together with the rest of the survivors?

4. "Because he didn't believe in God, any kind of God, anymore" (p. 78). This is said about Dimitri at the end of one of the support group meetings, and it is a sentiment he returns to whenever he thinks about his son. How do Dimitri's feelings about God change by the end of *Shame the Devil*?

5. God and religion are recurring themes throughout *Shame the Devil*. The title of the book comes from James Posten's

motto "Tell the truth and shame the devil." How do you think that telling the truth changes the characters' lives? Do you think that their experiences with telling the truth change their ideas about faith?

6. Dimitri and Stephanie find comfort in each others' arms while trying to overcome the loss of loved ones. What role does grief play in their relationship? How do their dead loved ones bring them together—or work against them?

7. Do you think Frank Farrow is a psychopath, or a hardened criminal? Why do you think he murdered Reverend Bob? What do you think motivates him?

8. What role do cars (and their makes and models) play in *Shame the Devil*?

9. When Thomas Wilson confesses his role in the robbery to Nick, he says, "I been waitin' for this for two and a half years. Dreading it and welcoming it at the same time. Can you understand at all what I mean?" (p. 302). While Thomas did not play a physical role in the crime, he was the one who tipped off the Farrow brothers about the opportunity to rob May's, and he did not report them after it became a much bigger crime. Do you think that what he did was just as bad? He believes that Dimitri will want to kill him when he confesses—does he deserve that level of punishment for what he did? How does complicity weigh on the conscience?

10. Do you think that, in the end, each individual involved in the robbery at May's has gotten what he deserved? Have the karmic scales been rebalanced?

ABOUT THE AUTHOR

George Pelecanos is the author of several highly praised and bestselling novels, including, most recently, *The Way Home* and *The Cut*. He is also an independent-film producer, an essayist, and the recipient of numerous writing awards. He was a producer and Emmy-nominated writer for *The Wire* and currently writes for the acclaimed HBO series *Treme*.

. . . AND HIS LATEST NOVEL

In August 2011 Reagan Arthur Books will publish *The Cut*. Following is a brief excerpt from the novel's opening pages.

ONE

THEY WERE in a second-story office with a bank of windows overlooking D Street at 5th, in a corner row house close to the federal courts. Tom Petersen, big and blond, sat behind his desk, wearing an untucked paisley shirt, jeans, and boots. Spero Lucas, in Carhartt, was in a hard chair set before the desk. Petersen was a criminal defense attorney, private practice. Lucas, one of his investigators.

A black Moleskine notebook the size of a pocket Bible was open in Lucas's hand. He was scribbling something in the book.

"It's all in the documents I'm going to give you," said Petersen with growing impatience. "You don't need to take notes."

"I'd rather," said Lucas.

"I can't tell if you're listening."

"I'm listening. Where'd they boost the Denali?"

"They took it up in Manor Park, on Peabody Street. Near the community garden, across from the radio towers."

"Behind the police station?"

"Right in back of Four-D."

"Pretty bold," said Lucas. "How many boys?"

"Two. Unfortunately, my client, David Hawkins, was the one behind the wheel."

"You just have him?"

"The other one, Duron Gaskins, he's been assigned a PD."

"Duron," said Lucas.

Petersen shrugged. "Like the paint."

"How'd David get so lucky to score a stud like you?"

"I'm representing his father on another matter," said Petersen.

"So this is like a favor."

"A four-hundred-dollar-an-hour favor."

Lucas's back had begun to stiffen. He shifted his weight in his chair. "Give me some details."

Petersen pushed a manila file across the desk. "Here."

"*Talk* to me."

"What do you want to know?"

"How'd they do it, for starters?"

"Steal the vehicle? That was easy. The boys were walking down the street, supposed to be in school, but hey. It's early in the morning, cold as hell. You remember that snap we had back in February? This woman comes out of her apartment, starts her SUV up, and then leaves it running and goes back into the apartment."

"She forget somethin?"

"She was heating up the Denali before she went to work."

"Insurance companies don't like that."

"She left the driver's door unlocked, too. So naturally, being teenage boys, they got in and took the SUV for a spin."

"*I* would have," said Lucas.

"You *did*, I recall."

"What happened next?"

"From Peabody, David went south on Ninth to Missouri, then drove east. He caught North Capitol along Rock Creek Cemetery and took that cutoff street west, the stretch that goes by the Soldiers' Home."

"That would be Allison," said Lucas, starting to see it, like he was looking down at a detail map. He had a cop's knowledge of D.C. because he was out in it, street level, most of his waking hours. When he didn't have to drive his Cherokee, Lucas rode his bicycle around town. At night he often walked.

"Here's where they got in trouble. David, keep in mind he's fifteen, no significant driving experience far as I know, he loses control of the SUV. Sideswipes a lady in a Buick, which knocks her out of her lane and into a couple of parked cars."

"By now they'd be on Rock Creek Church Road."

"Yeah, there," said Petersen. "The woman in the Buick? Claims she's got neck injuries."

"That's not good."

"I'm gonna work something out with her attorney."

"This kid's father must be flush."

"He is."

"This where the police come in?"

"Happens to be a patrol car, coupla uniforms idling nose out at Second and Varnum see this collision."

"And the chase is on."

"Took the police officer a half minute to put his coffee down and flip on the siren and light bar. By that time, David knew he'd been burned, and he jumps the sidewalk and cuts right onto Upshur Street."

"Driving on the Sidewalk, that's a good one."

"Fleeing and Eluding, Leaving the Scene of an Accident, Auto Theft..."

"Kid's got a rack of problems."

"He fishtails when he hits Upshur. Comes out of that and pins it. You know Upshur going west there—"

"It's long and straight. Downhill."

Petersen leaned forward, getting into it. "This boy is screaming down Upshur, Spero. Blowing four-ways, Wale or whatever coming loud out the windows."

"Nah," said Lucas, chuckling.

"What?"

"Now you're making shit up. You don't know what they were listening to."

"True. They're coming down Upshur, the patrol car, pretty far back but gaining ground, in pursuit. Eventually our boys hit that commercial strip getting down toward Georgia Avenue, at Ninth."

"I know the spot," said Lucas. He was drawing a rough map, very quickly, in his notebook.

"And there's another cop car," said Petersen, "parked right there on the street. The driver is waiting on his partner, who's getting a pack of smokes in a little market they got in that strip."

"What market?" said Lucas.

"I don't know the name of it. Spanish joint, eight hundred block, north side of Upshur. Beer and wine, pork rinds, like that. It's in the file, along with the address. What happens next is, David sees this police car, and I guess he panics, and here's where he makes the last mistake. He cuts a sharp right into an alley, right before Ninth."

"And?"

"A car is parked in the alley, blocking their way. The boys get out of the vehicle and run; David Hawkins is apprehended on the street. The other boy, Duron, is caught a little while later, attempting to hide in the bathroom of an El Salvadoran restaurant around the corner."

"Who arrested David?"

"The officer waiting in the patrol car. A Clarence Jackson. By then the car in pursuit had arrived on the scene."

"How'd Officer Jackson know that David was one of the boys in the car?"

"In his report, Jackson stated that he observed two boys exit an SUV that they had driven into the alley. Jackson got to David first. The arriving officers arrested Duron in the restaurant."

"Where was Officer Jackson parked when he saw this?"

"It's in the file."

Lucas sat still for a long minute, looking at nothing. He closed his notebook and got up out of his seat. He stood five-foot-eleven, weighed one eighty-five, had a flat stomach and a good chest and shoulders. His hair was black and he wore it short. His eyes were green, flecked with gold, and frequently unreadable. He was twenty-nine years old.

Petersen watched Lucas stretch. "Sorry. That seat's unforgiving."

"It's these wood floors. The chair sits funny on 'em cause the planks are warped."

"This house goes back to the nineteenth century."

"Your point is what?"

"Ghosts of greatness walk these rooms. I start messing with the floors, I might make them angry."

A young GW law student entered Petersen's office and dropped a large block of papers on his desk. She was dark haired, fully curved, and effortlessly attractive. Tom Petersen's interns looked more or less like younger versions of his knock-out wife.

"The Parker briefs," said the woman, whose name was Constance Kelly.

"Thank you," said Petersen. He watched Lucas admire her as she walked away.

Petersen stood and went to the eastern window of his office. Below, on the street, lawyers pulled wheeled briefcases toward the courthouse, uniformed and plainclothes police bullshitted with one another, mothers spoke patiently and angrily with their sons, civil servants took cigarette breaks, and folks of all shapes and colors went in and out of the Potbelly shop on the first floor.

"Life's rich pageant," said Petersen.

"That's a rock record from back in your day, right?"

"Inspector Clouseau, originally."

"You got me on that one."

"I have twenty years on you. At times the perspective is obvious. Other times, no." Petersen looked him over with the respect that men who have not served give to those who have. "You've seen a lot, haven't you?"

"It's been interesting, so far." Lucas slipped his notebook into his jacket and picked up the David Hawkins file off Petersen's desk.

"Bring me something back I can use," said Petersen.

Lucas nodded. "I'll get out there."

Look for these other novels by George Pelecanos

Right As Rain

"With the appearance of this book, the hard-boiled mystery writer that Washington, D.C., lacked seems to have emerged from the shadows." —Nina King, *Washington Post Book World*

"What Pelecanos displays here, in great abundance and to entertaining effect, is a Tarantino touch."
—Janet Maslin, *New York Times*

Hell to Pay

Winner of the *Los Angeles Times* Book Prize

"Go ahead, call them crime novels. They are, no doubt about it, page-turning, two-fisted, hard-edged crime novels. But Pelecanos's books are also more.... Call them what you will, they're outstanding." —Adam Woog, *Seattle Times*

"A pleasure to read. . . . Unafraid, spirited, and profoundly entertaining." —Craig Nova, *Washington Post Book World*

Soul Circus

Winner of the *Los Angeles Times* Book Prize

"As polished and as exquisitely honed as the guns that wreak havoc in the neighborhoods where Pelecanos's novels are set."
—Carol Memmott, *USA Today*

"Powerfully affecting. . . . Pelecanos has the first-rate writer's ability to entertain you and break your heart on the same page."
—Malcolm Jones, *Newsweek*

Back Bay Books • Available wherever paperbacks are sold

Look for these other novels by George Pelecanos

A Firing Offense

"A contemporary classic...Pelecanos is a fresh, new, utterly hardboiled voice. A *Firing Offense* is full of virtuoso scenes of imaginative sex and substance abuse, suspenseful action, and brooding meditation on a newly lost generation."
— Pat Dowell, *Washington Post Book World*

Nick's Trip

"This particular entry in the series is as tough as they get: an urban nightmare of greed, betrayal, and kick-ass revenge."
— Bill Ott, *American Libraries*

Down by the River Where the Dead Men Go

"Nick and his incomparably seamy milieu, in their third outing, get an A."
— Kirkus Reviews

Back Bay Books • Available wherever paperbacks are sold